...riveting story based on facts

about a young woman who's clairvoyant

but runs from her Gift—right

into the arms of voodoo.

DEDICATION

This book is dedicated to the loving memory of "Nana," my mother/grandmother, and Blanche Juanita, my mother. My husband and family, I love you dearly.

ACKNOWLEDGEMENTS

I am most grateful and thankful to my Lord and Savior, Jesus Christ. I have truly "come this far by faith, leaning on the Lord." I give Him the praises and the glory for blessing me with the gift to write, leading me down the right paths, and letting the right doors open.

Many people have been a part of my endeavor and have supported me in many ways. I would like to express my thanks to each and every one of you for believing in and being there for me.

To my husband Ernest, thank you so much for your love, understanding, support, and belief in my gift to write. Your uplifting words of encouragement and diligence helped me to push on. Thanks for not giving up on me. Thanks to my sister and brother-in-law, Brenda and Carl Auzenne who were there to load my first software on my computer, set up programs and answer questions, no matter how crazy they sounded. Many thanks to my sister Anita Hawkins for her genuine support and belief in me. Love and gratitude to my three younger sons, Demetre, Brandon, and Steven who stayed out of Mommie's way and didn't bring liquids into the computer room. Thanks to my daughter Rochele who in her quiet way always believed in me. Thanks to my son Terrill for saying "I believe in you" and leaving me alone. To Mosie Lee Black, our senior family representative, I thank you for your encouragement and additional information. My late Aunt Marie Lawson, I thank for being there in my time of need. Thanks to my sister/girl Delores Martindale, one of my oldest and dearest friends, who kept encouraging me to get my book on the market. Thanks for all of your help and support. To my long time good friends and graphic artists, from our WaMu days, Cheryl (Slaybaugh) Green and Sharon Earl, much thanks for your encouragement, input, reading, and offers to help bring my work forward. You're the best. To my big sister/dear friend Blanche Gant who totally believed in my work and thinks my first writing of more than 1000 pages should be printed—thank you for your advice and encouragement. My sister-girl/dear friend who has more faith in me than I thought, Gloria Warren. Thank you so much for your prayers, support, and laughter when I really needed it. My adopted soul sister, Gay Kennedy-Horton, a sweet and loving friend who told me she "adored' my work, then tried to become my grammar teacher—thanks for reading my manuscript, providing encouraging notes and comments, and demanding more to read ASAP. Thanks to my girl, Melenese Richardson, who believed in me, loaned me books, and researched for me. To Julie Ann Oiye, a special librarian who helped me with research, believed in my work, encouraged me, told me I had a mainstream book—thank you for my night of "A Thousand and One Stars."

To Ruth Gains, a good friend, thank you so much for your support and belief in my work. To long time friends Larry and Bernice Williams, I thank you both from the bottom of my heart for all of your support. To Mari Mitchell, thanks for your support and research. To Phyllis Hatfield, my first editor: With your help I was able to see the real writer in me. Thanks for all of your suggestions, patience, and encouragement. A warm thanks to Claudia Scippio, for helping me find an editor.

To Drena Payne, another editor, I am thankful for you, your suggestions, help, and encouragement. Thanks to Voyce Jackson and her support. I am thankful to my play-mother, Dorothy Glass for much encouragement and support. To Joyce Morris (deceased), a special thanks. She thought I had a wonderful family legacy to leave behind one day. A special thanks to my good friend Jean Bryant for her support. A special thank you to my friend Donna Goggin for her enthusiasm and support.

Much thanks and gratitude to the Rev. Larry Harris for his support and wisdom. To my final editor Georgia S. McDade,

Ph.D., a godsend. I could not have gone forward without your enthusiasm and belief in my endeavor. A resounding thank you!

A very special thanks to Elliott Wolf and Kristen Morris at my publishing house. They welcomed me, took me under their wings, guided me with care, kindness and a quiet professionalism, and helped bring my book forward. You are the best!

An abundant thank you to my dear friends and supporters, Gloria and Ardie Warden, Darlene and William Watson, Charlotte Watson-Sherman, Janice Clayton, Ethel Hood, Dorothy Williams, Elaine and Jack Cornell, Sumi and Timothy Enebrad, Blanche and Floyd Gant, Rich and Cheryl Roodman, Terry Pile, Kris Tiernan, Donna and Sean Sheedy, Class of 1966, Carole Anderson, staff at VMC, Don and Pearl Jacobson, Mike Kelly, Gary and Betty Kohlwes, Fannie and John Sauls, Vicki and Michael Jesse, Jack and Diane Latterman, and my church family.

A copious appreciation to my play-sons Derrick Harris and Jovon Younger and my play-daughter Azizi Sheffield. May God bestow many blessings upon each of you.

To Nana, whom I called mama, now in Heaven. Thank you for raising and loving me. Thank you for telling me all those wonderful and inspiring stories as I sat at your feet or while combing your hair. Thank you for instilling in me my faith, hope, and perseverance. For without you I couldn't have come this far. It is the Gift from you to me that God has granted. I can feel you smiling down on me.

TABLE OF CONTENTS

PROLOGUE: A SPECIAL GIFT

Susie had always known from a tiny tot that she was different, special. For a while she liked being that way, the center of attention. But as time passed and she grew older, she didn't want to be saddled with the heavy burden of this *present* that had been bestowed on her. She decided she didn't want it for the rest of her life. She wanted to live a normal life the way her siblings would. She knew she couldn't, not with the voice in her ears, always waiting, speaking to her when she least expected it, along with images of strangers in distress floating around in her mind. Then there was the matter of the strange brightness that crept into her eyes, a brightness over which she had no control, a brightness which caused people to have violent reactions, and she was sure, near-death experiences.

Why, this special thing she had was bad enough to cause her to tremble and want to hide in a dark corner until it left her alone. Often she wanted to reach out to her mother for help, but she knew that her mother would not side with her.

So through the years Susie fought to forget what her purpose was in this world. And as time elapsed into weeks, months, years, she thought she had won. Then one day her world fell apart, and many storms roared into her life.

She found herself twisted in turmoil, the pain almost unbearable, the sorrow devastating. She felt her life slipping away the way a rose loses its beauty. Her only resource was prayer and faith. Prayer and Faith.

When she finally heard the voice again, she knew she just might have a second chance to live....

BOOK I

BEGINNINGS

There are many beginnings
for many people.
Some ordinary,
others extraordinary.

Carolyn V. Parnell

1

The blue jays paused in the sparkling sunlight, their pretty singing suddenly quieted. The yellow hammers which had been swinging from tree to tree did likewise. With stilled bodies and alert eyes, they focused toward the tiny little house in front of them.

Rubye Mae had risen earlier than usual, feeling quite happy. She stretched as best she could and patted her dropped stomach. After preparing breakfast, an unusual task for her, she prepared to work in the fields. But as she walked through the door, a huge pain stopped her.

She sent ten-year-old J. T. for the midwife and whispered to eight-year-old Ella Mae to boil water. The two youngest boys, Taylor, Jr. and Augustus were curled like baby cubs; asleep, snoring.

On April 15, 1913, Christina Morton forced her way into the world to claim her piece of it. At three pounds she was the smallest baby Rubye Mae had ever bore. Her worried eyes looked to the midwife, Sarah Ann, for assurance that her baby would live.

Sarah Ann, well-known to the white doctors in Perry County who called on her to help them in desperate times when their modern medicine failed, smiled and said, "Chile, don't you worry.

Yo' baby gon' live. You jest had it too close to the last one. You oughta know you gots to give yo' body time to heal foe havin' another chile, Rubye Mae, but this little, teeny-weeny thang sho gon' make it," she promised Rubye Mae. "Jest you give her some extra milk of yo's. None of that cow's mess," she winked.

Rubye Mae smiled, feeling better. Sarah Ann went about her tasks, never telling Rubye Mae it had taken several firm slaps on her narrow behind before Christina whimpered. She looked awful, with skin wrinkled and cracked like a road map, but she had no doubt that the baby would live.

Sarah Ann had finished with the baby's needs and was about to give her to Rubye Mae when she felt a sudden strangeness. Feeling ill at ease, she looked down at the infant and became stilled by the glowing light emanating from the child's eyes. She shuddered as a chill, colder than ice water, passed through her. *Oh, My Lawd, 'Ole folks' eyes'!* she thought.

She trembled within as she fought the urge to lay the child down. She realized that she couldn't move. Nothing about her could move as the child sent messages to her that caused her to want to cry out, to stop showing her things she couldn't comprehend, or even wanted to. Then it was gone.

She was so thankful she wanted to shout. Instead, she thought back to the time she'd seen 'ole folks' eyes'. It had been more than twenty years ago. She had never forgotten the strange, glowing light and the feeling of being naked, her soul being revealed. "They Gawd's chosen people," her grandmother and mother had revealed in hushed tones. Anyone who witnessed the Gift lived a long, satisfying life. And those who defied it met with disaster.

She held the special child close to her heart for a moment, shook Rubye Mae to wake her, then placed the baby in Rubye Mae's waiting arms for several moments. Afterwards, she laid her in a shoe box filled with clean rags, placed it in the chifforobe drawer to prevent Rubye Mae from suffocating her. Finally, Sarah Ann put a sugar rag in the baby's mouth to provide extra nourishment.

She turned to Rubye Mae who was dozing again. "Rubye Mae, I'm jest gon' get yo' navel string from you, so you jest relax and let me do the work, you hear?"

Rubye Mae grunted. Sarah Ann massaged Rubye Mae's stomach for a few minutes; then the afterbirth eased out. She examined it, counting the remaining knots on it.

"Rubye Mae, Rubye Mae," she said, slightly shaking her.

"Ummmmm."

"I see you ain't near 'bout through, gal. You still got a bunch moe chil'ren to bear."

Rubye Mae became more alert. "What you be sayin', Miss Sarah Ann?"

"I said, 'cordin' to this here aftah birth, you gon' have 'bout six moe chil'ren, gal."

"You right sho, Miss Sarah Ann?"

"Ain't nevah been wrong befoe, you knows that. So I guess I'll be seein' you, say 'bout every two years for a time to come." She smiled as she put the afterbirth in a tin container to be buried in the woods later.

After washing her hands, she said to Rubye Mae, "Now if you don't mind, I'll jest take this here can with me when I leave, so I can git rid of it proper like."

"Fine, Miss Sarah Ann," Rubye Mae mumbled, dismissing the nasty matter.

"Mind if I git me a taste of chewin' tobacco and rest a spell?"

"Nome. Help yo'self."

Sarah Ann removed a spotless handkerchief, a penknife from her pocket and unwrapped a square piece of chewing tobacco. Holding it between her thumb and forefinger, she cut a small piece off one corner with the small knife, and slipped it into the side of her mouth. She held it there briefly while she made herself comfortable in the rocking chair, next to Rubye Mae's bed.

She leaned back in the chair, rocked slightly, then slowly began to chew the tobacco, relishing it as if it were the best-tasting candy she had ever eaten in her life. This was a signal as well as a ritual; her job was finished.

Rubye Mae smelled the aroma which caused her mouth to water. She opened her eyes and gazed enviously at Sarah Ann, wanting her own piece. But she knew she couldn't resume her habit while the baby was so new. Tobacco caused babies to get the crud when she was nursing. Still, that didn't make her want it any the less. Settling for the smell, she licked her lips, and closed her eyes.

Finally deciding to answer Sarah Ann who had all but forgotten about her, she said, "Well, I 'spose you can be right, but we jest have to wait and see."

"Humm?" Sarah Ann answered.

"Bout them babies you said I'm gon' have. You know, the cord and all," she said softly, knowing she was interrupting Sarah Ann's quiet time.

Shucks. I had done forgot all 'bout that. Cain't a person git some rest aftah deliverin' a baby? "Oh, yeah. You gon' have them alright, jest you wait."

"Yes, Mam," Rubye Mae responded. Not believing the midwife, she pulled the sheet up to her chin and turned toward the wall.

"Humph," Sarah Ann thought as she watched Rubye Mae fall asleep. *Go on and wait. You sho gon' see six moe, unless you keep yo' legs closed. Jest you mark my words. But this one is differen' from all the rest of yo' chil'ren. Yes, Mam. You got a special chile here. Lawd, how I wish I could tell you. Humph, humph, humph.*

Shrugging her shoulders, Sarah Ann resumed rocking, enjoying her tobacco. Shortly, she slipped the sugar rag from the sleeping baby's mouth and called the baby's father, Taylor, to see his offspring.

Two days following Christina's birth, Rubye Mae returned to the fields with Taylor and left J.T. to look after Susie. Taylor had changed her name from the unlikeable "Christina" to the pretty "Susie." Every step Rubye Mae took toward the field caused her to become furious at their landowner.

"Mister Ardonson don't care 'bout nothin' 'xcept his damn crops and how much profit he can git," she fumed. She paused and stamped her feet, causing dust to fly at her eyes. Mindlessly she brushed away the grime and thought how much she disliked sharecropping. Why should she have to work like a slave on land that had once belonged to her family after the Civil War? So it was with acrimony that she left her baby and returned to being a "field-hand."

"You know Taylor, I'm tir'd of workin' in these fields," Rubye Mae said one day. "Where is it gettin' us but ole foe our time?" She stormed angrily, pushing the plow continuously ahead with her straight and proud back.

Taylor paused to glance at her and knocked the sweat from his handsome brow. "Rubye Mae, you gots to stop thankin' thangs gon' git bettah when you know they ain't."

"Why you say that?" she asked as she came back in his direction with the plow. "You done gon' and gave up gettin' away from this? What happen'd to all yo' plans, Taylor?" she asked quietly.

"That was jest a dream, Rubye Mae. But this is real, and we gots to live with it 'til we can do bettah," he said, his facial expression dismissing any further discussion.

"You sho don't sound like the man I mar-red moe then eleven years ago," she murmured under her breath, then jerked on the plow, almost turning it sideways. She missed seeing the tears in his sad eyes.

"What did you say, woman?" he asked gruffly.

"Ain't said nothin'," she answered as she threw hot, angry eyes at his back. "And neither did you, buster."

When Taylor had proposed to her twelve years ago, he had been full of dreams, promises and humor. They would work arduously and save their money, buy a piece of land and build a house. He didn't want to live on the white man's property and depend on whites as their ancestors had. He longed to break the chains and become his own man.

Rubye Mae stopped plowing as he passed her going the other direction. As her eyes bore into his back, she noticed that he was bent slightly forward already, and he was only thirty-four years old. His curly head of hair was plenty white. Worst, the look of hope was gone from him. *Defeated*, she thought.

She closed her eyes, lifted her head in prayer, and pronounced to the Heavens, "Dear Lawd, hear my plea, please help us. Our souls is so weary. I don't know how much moe my po' husban' can take. Amen." In those brief moments, the scalding sun had parched her thin lips. She passed her rough hand across them, brushed them with her tongue, then pushed the plow ahead.

That evening, when Rubye Mae and Taylor arrived home, the children sensed their unhappy mood. They quickly escaped to the crowded room the four of them shared.

Two-year-old Augustus cried quietly when his father hadn't stopped to grab and toss him around in the air as he usually did before he went to wash the field dirt from himself.

Rubye Mae yelled, "Git back in here, J.T.; I need yo' help."

"Yes, Mam," he said, appearing almost before she finished speaking.

"How was the chil'ren today?" she demanded as she pumped water into a bucket, her golden brown skin straining against the handle.

"They was good, Mama. We did everythang you tole us to."

"I have to see 'bout that. How's the baby?"

"She sleep. She was good. I gave her the bottles and sugar-rag like you said."

"Alright then. You go on and fetch me some wood so I can git through with this supper. Yo' daddy's hungry," she conveyed in lighter tones.

J.T. ran out the door, glad his mother's anger wasn't directed at him. Rubye Mae finished pumping the water, poured some into a kettle, dropped it on the stove, and used the last of the cut wood to start a fire.

"Wish'd I could make my husban' hot and ready as this stove gits. I know thangs is hard and his dreams done been squash'd, but that don't mean we gots to stay here and take this slavery mess. We ought to be able to have somethin' of our own like them white folks do. But then, most of them don't desire to give us a chance to have nothin' of our own. Thank we ain't even human most times. Lawdy, Lawdy."

"Did you say somethin', Mama?" J.T. asked as he put the wood in the box, next to the wall.

"I said, it took you long enuf to git back."

"Yes, Mam."

"Now, chile, you go back and see 'bout Susie while I finish supper. You did good today."

"Yes, Mam," he smiled after he left the room.

Later, when all the children were asleep, Taylor patted Rubye Mae on the shoulder and pointed toward the cradle.

"How ole is Susie now?"

"She ole enuf," Rubye Mae said, moving away from him.

"How ole, Rubye Mae?"

"Goin' on two months."

"Yo' woman thang over yet?"

Rubye Mae frowned as if suddenly smelling something obnoxious. She closed her eyes. She didn't answer him.

"You ain't too keen on talkin' to me tonight; is you?"

"What did you say, Taylor?" she asked, looking strangely at him.

"Woman, I said is you still seein' yo' menstrual?" he asked, frowning.

Serves you right, she thought. "Taylor, you know I hate that word. It sound like a pig bleedin' or somethin'."

"Rubye Mae..."

"Naw, Taylor, I ain't on no moe."

He grinned and patted her backside.

"Come on over here then."

She was still angry at him, and as much as she wanted to say no, she knew she couldn't. It was her duty as a wife to always oblige her husband's needs, no matter how much she wanted to chew him up and spit him out.

Rubye Mae was dozing when she heard Susie's whimper. She rubbed her eyes, eased from the bed, walked to the cradle in the darkened room. She picked the baby up and tip-toed into the kitchen. She rocked Susie several moments before checking her diaper. She rose to rinse her hands and breast with the lukewarm water from the kettle. Sitting down, she placed her milk-filled breast in the baby's mouth, rocked and sang softly to her until she sensed Susie was asleep.

Rubye Mae burped her and started back to the bedroom, but Susie wasn't having any of that. She became fussy.

"So you gon' be like yo' daddy and mess with me, too."

Susie whimpered as if she understood her mother's words. Holding her close, she whispered, "Baby, Mama didn't mean that. You one of the best thangs that's happen'd to me."

She walked to the window and pulled back the crisp, starched curtains. "Look baby, it's a full moon. A moon to look at and send yo' dreams to, and maybe someday they'll come true.

"Oh hell, I don't know what I'm ramblin' on for, standin' here, talkin' to you like you some grown up," Rubye Mae commented as she gazed into Susie's wide-opened eyes.

"You jest ain't gon' go to sleep; is you?"

As if answering her mother, a bright light appeared in Susie's eyes. Rubye Mae frowned, looked at the moon again, wondering if it was causing Susie's eyes to look so strange. She glanced at them again. The brightness alarmed her so badly and so suddenly she would have given away to a dead faint, but the groping light held her hostage as it penetrated her soul, touching its every fiber. Her bowels threatened to fail her. Her heart raced at more than one hundred beats a minute. The unknown hands of brilliant light probed her as nothing on earth could have. She was frightened to the point of losing her sanity. Despite seeing the strange objects, blurry visions, and other unexplainable things, she never felt any pain.

Moments later, she bucked as if someone had put ice down her back. The light disappeared. She felt her body trembling. She looked down at her baby. Susie yawned, closed her eyes, and fell asleep.

Rubye Mae stood rooted to the floor for what seemed hours, but it was only seconds as her mind and body tried to bring itself back to reality.

Finally, she was able to move to her room and place Susie in her cradle. Then she returned to the kitchen and sat stiffly in the rocking chair, reflecting.

Lawd, that light was the worst thang I ever saw in my life. My pretty baby layin' thaih with them strange eyes, yellow lights flickin' in them, jumpin' out at me like somethin' from anothah world, makin' me feel naked, showin' my soul. The light was holdin' me prisner while showin' all them thangs from the past and the future that I ain't 'spose to witness. Then it made me want to cry, and I couldn', run, and I couldn'.

2

Weeks later, Rubye Mae was still reeling by what she had witnessed and discovered about her baby. Although she knew the Lord had made her child this way, she realized it was very difficult to deal with Susie's unusual Gift.

And she didn't dare tell Taylor. He had too many notions in his head. He had been remote and distant of late. She knew something was wrong because she could feel the tension that seemed to manifest daily.

As they sat outside without words between them, she threw a quick look at Taylor. He was watching the children play a game of Mary Mac and fanning the horseflies away. Tears sprang to her eyes.

She glanced toward the children, then back at him. Briefly, she thought she might have been in the wrong place. But the laughter of her children told her otherwise. Feeling disconcerted, she stood to go inside, then paused as she covered her brow to block the glaring sun. She saw two images coming their way. She squinted and smiled.

She turned to Taylor, "It looks like Betty and Willie Lee comin," she said excitedly.

"Yeah. It's them. I can tell by the way Willie Lee jumps when he walks," Taylor offered and grinned.

Rubye Mae's smiled broadened. The four of them had been friends since they were in gunny-sack diapers. They had attended school and church together, worked the fields, planned their futures, and even married the same year, a month apart.

When Betty and Willie Lee had moved to Mississippi several years before, she had found time to pen a few letters to Rubye Mae. It had been more than six months since she had heard from Betty. Seeing them now caused her absolute pleasure.

They greeted each other with much affection and settled down to talk, catching up on each other's lives.

A short while later, Rubye Mae excused herself and Betty. She took Betty's hand and led her into the kitchen, and sat at the table.

"I got to talk to you, Betty," Rubye Mae said in a low tone. "It's 'bout Taylor and me."

For the next twenty minutes, Betty's face went through as many changes as one does while in the dentist's chair. She could not believe what she was hearing about her dearest friends. It hurt her badly to discover that they, of all people, were going through such pain.

"Every time I want to talk, he don't," Rubye Mae stopped and placed her hands over her eyes. "I'm so weary, Betty."

"Honey, don't you know why? Them dreams is what keeps them goin'. He prob'ly done lost them. When that happens, they stop talkin'. No hope left in them."

"I know that. And I feel pretty down myself, but I got to keep pushin'. Don't you git weary sometimes?"

"I gits weary too. But if I do, I know Willie Lee feels worse then me, 'cause he's the man and his weight is heavier."

"You mean y'all talk 'bout it?" Rubye Mae removed her hands from her eyes and laid them on the table.

Betty squeezed her friend's hand. "Rubye Mae, since when did men folk talk 'bout they problems, chile? I jest read his thoughts and see his 'xpressions on his worr'd brow is all.

"I want to hug and tell him it will be alright, but he gots his pride and all, so I leaves him be."

"I guess you right. But I needs to talk to my man. Not jest when he wants to roll 'round in the hay." Rubye Mae pulled at a loose strand of hair and played with it.

"Rubye Mae, I ain't nevah heard you talk like this befoe. It must be the blues aftah the baby. You'll git over it."

"It ain't the blues, and I ain't gon' git over it, Betty. I know my husband, and he's changin'. Somethin' ain't right no moe. We ain't close. I'm scared, Betty."

"Oh, Rubye Mae, don't go upsettin' yo'self this way. You know Taylor loves you. 'Member when he used to give you lightnin' bugs and say how the light from them was like his love for you?"

"He was only twelve, Betty."

"But he loved you then, and he still do, Rubye Mae. Thangs will be alright. Now come on and let me see that pretty baby I done heard so much 'bout."

They strolled into Rubye Mae's room and over where Susie lay sleeping.

"Why, ain't she pretty? She sho don't look like the po' thang you said she was when she was born," Betty praised as she peeked down at the infant. She was plump with no traces of wrinkles.

"She got them eyes," Rubye Mae said, her own growing larger. "When I first found out, it scared me so bad, if I coulda, I woulda mess'd in my drawers. I ain't got over it yet."

Betty whispered, "I heard 'bout babies born with them 'ole folks' eyes'. I even saw them one time, long ago."

"And you nevah tole me?" Rubye Mae moved closer.

"I was too scared then. And latah on, I didn't want y'all thankin' I was crazy like ole Mister Frank was. Always claimin' to see thangs othahs couldn'. Ghosts and the likes."

"But I was yo' best friend. You coulda tole me."

"But yo' Mama did. She tole you and me 'bout 'ole folks' eyes', and how scary they is. She tole us they special people, too. How they can heal and predict the future."

"You right, she sho did," Rubye Mae smiled. "And how they

can talk to voices nobody else can hear. Now I gots me a chile like that. Betty, I'm scared."

"I know. I would be too. You got to tell Taylor."

"Not on yo' life! Let him find out for his self," Rubye Mae frowned.

Deciding not to upset her friend, Betty turned back to gaze down at Susie.

"I'll git us some lemonade," Rubye Mae spoke in calmer tones, and slipped from the room.

"Come here, you pretty little precious baby," Betty cooed. She lifted Susie from her cradle and smiled at her. "So you one of them special people Gawd done seen fit to give us po' folks," she said softly.

Susie opened her eyes and gazed at her, a glowing light from her eyes shadowing Betty's entire being. Betty's mouth dropped open as the blinding, yellow light penetrated her soul, shaking her. One moment Betty felt like lead, the next, buoyantly in some other world filled with objects that scared her to the pit of her soul as the baby's eyes revealed things beyond her comprehension.

The brilliance faded from Susie's eyes. Betty dropped to the floor, holding Susie tightly in her arms. Not realizing it, Betty started to cry.

"Oh Lawd, she got 'ole folks' eyes' jest like Rubye Mae said. Betty was reliving some twenty years before. She was helpless, terrified.

Rubye Mae returned, sat the glasses on the table. She lifted Susie from Betty's arms and placed her in the cradle.

"You saw, didn't you?"

Betty answered by bobbing her head up and down. Her eyes were still wide, her mouth slack.

"Here gal, drank some of this," Rubye Mae offered, handing her the cool glass of lemonade.

Betty sipped the cold liquid and patted her chest before finally speaking. "It don't mattah how many times you see them eyes with that strange yellow light lookin' into yo' soul. It still scare you half to death. Rubye Mae, what you gon' do, chile?"

"Ain't nothin' I can do, Betty. Gawd done did what He want'd, and I have to 'xcept it. My chile is gon' be a healer and fortune-teller one day, and that's that. I jest hope I can be thaih for her." Rubye Mae sipped her drink, praying for strength.

"Lawd, Rubye Mae," Betty uttered, her eyes glassy and feeling three times their normal size, "You gots to prepare yo'self to tell yo' chile 'bout herself. It's gon' be hard. Harder for her then you."

Rubye Mae hugged herself, suddenly chilled by the hot breeze coming through the window. "That's 'bout the last thang I want to thank on right now, Betty. I know the time gon' come soon enuf, and when it do, I jest pray I can be thaih for Susie."

"You know I'll always be here too, if you need me."

"I know that Betty, but I'm gon' have to talk to Mu 'bout this since she done seen them moe then me. She even said we had a bootleg doctor in our family who work'd with a white doctor. He tole fortunes and thangs for the people they went to see. 'Course Mu said some people laugh'd at him, but he didn't pay people no mind. Jest went on 'bout his business."

"You sayin' this kinda thang can be pass'd on, Rubye Mae?"

"Naw...I ain't sayin' that. But it's kinda strange my chile that way, too."

"Did all he say come true?" Betty asked curiously.

"From what I been tole, yeah."

"Let's go back outdoors," Betty suggested, striding toward the door.

"Don't you dare tell Willie Lee 'bout this 'til Taylor finds out for his self, you hear?"

"Do a tree talk? Well, I'm a tree 'til Taylor finds out like we did," Betty laughed and hugged Rubye Mae.

3

It was a fine, spring day in late April. The robins, the redbirds and blue jays happily greeted their young and shared earthworms with them. The bumblebees buzzed around, lighting on the succulent flowers, relishing the sweet liquid.

Even as four-year-old Susie watched this wonderful scene of Mother Nature take place from her living room window, her eyes strayed down the long road, as they had for months; searching for her father.

She had been disappointed when her father hadn't appeared for her birthday, but she hadn't given up. She was certain he would return. It didn't matter what her mother believed. She knew he loved them all.

"Susie, why don't you come down from here," Rubye Mae urged as she stopped behind her chair and patted her curly, brown head.

"Cain't I stay a while longer, Mama?"

"Why, baby?" she asked in a strained voice.

"Daddy's comin' home, Mama."

Rubye Mae pulled Susie into her arms. "Susie, I done tole you many times befoe, yo' daddy ain't comin' back."

Susie's astute eyes examined her mother's face. "Mama, I know Daddy's comin' back. I saw him, Mama. I sho saw him."

"What do you mean, saw him? When, chile?"

"When I was sleep. He said he comin' home, Mama. With big presents."

Rubye Mae gave her a hard stare.

"He did, Mama," she insisted; her eyes strayed down the road again, full of hope.

Not wanting to upset her, Rubye Mae sat quietly for a few more minutes, pondering over the past few years. It had been hard living without Taylor. She remembered so clearly that dreadful night he had decided to leave his family.

"It's so cold out thaih, I don't thank my feet gon' ever be the same again," Taylor had predicted as he rushed into the house from the four below freezing December weather.

"It ain't been this bad in moe then two years," she had said as she placed their dinner on the table. They had sat down to a wonderful dinner of fried chicken, greens, and field corn which delighted two-year-old Susie. During their meal, Taylor made no conversation and kept his eyes downcast. Every effort she made to capture his attention failed. In their room, the tension thickened.

"You didn't talk durin' supper, Taylor. I want to know what's on yo' mind?" She pulled her sewing box from the drawer, sat and threaded a needle.

"Rubye Mae." The tone of his voice sent a warning signal. Suddenly she felt sick to her stomach, chills throughout her body.

"I'm leavin' Rubye Mae," he whispered abruptly.

His words were like a slap to her heart. Hot blood raced to her head. She felt dizzy. She didn't feel the needle that pricked her finger, drawing blood.

"What did you say?" she managed to ask.

He stopped pacing the floor and gazed at her. "I gots to leave. I jest cain't stay here and be yo' husban' no moe."

"Why you leavin' Taylor? What 'bout yo' five chil'ren?"

"I need my freedom. I cain't 'xplain it. I jest got to leave. The chil'ren will be taken care of. Maybe I'll be back."

"Is it anothah woman?" she asked.

"Naw, Rubye Mae, it ain't," he said softly. "It's jest me."

"I won't let you come back if you leave."

"Will you tell the chil'ren, Rubye Mae?"

"You the one leavin', you tell them," she said angrily. She dropped the sewing box, not seeing the blood on her hand, she stood before him. "You go in thaih and break they hearts, tell them you leavin'," she hissed as tears threatened to blind her.

Taylor left the room. Soon afterwards, the children ran in, crying, wanting to know why their father was leaving them. Finally, she was able to calm them and send them back to their room.

When Taylor returned to their room, he told her that he knew about Susie's Gift. He spoke as if he hadn't just ripped apart all their hearts. She hadn't answered him. She had left the room and stood outside inhaling the cold biting air, hoping to awaken from her nightmare.

She never saw Taylor leave. The following morning Susie had assured her that her father would return. Even though time passed swiftly, many months had elapsed before she adjusted to his not being there with her and the children.

Now, she no longer hated him for leaving them. She realized that he must have had his reasons. Maybe he couldn't stay with them and become a failure in their eyes. She knew he cared because he had left his brother to see after them.

Rubye Mae also realized that it had been the new baby on the way and the constant worry about the children that had sustained and kept her going. Whatever the reasons, she had made it this far.

Now that she was over the bitter pain, and the hurt, did she love him? Yes. That would always be. But could she trust him? Truly forgive him?

As if reading her mind, Susie looked at her and said, "Everythang will be alright, Mama. Aftah Daddy comes back home."

"If you say so, baby," Rubye Mae answered in unsteady tones.

She shooed Susie outside and watched as she ran down the two steps into the yard to play with Augustus, her favorite brother. Rubye Mae watched them play for a few minutes. She shook her head in reflection. "Lawd, that chile is somethin'. And them eyes, they jest pierce right through me sometimes. Now and then I git scared of my own chile. And when she tell me thangs, I don't want to, but I have to lis-sen to her."

Willie Mae, the newest addition to the family, gave out a scream. Grateful for the distraction, Ruybe Mae went to see about her.

That night, Susie dreamt. The same vision again.

She was screaming and zig zagging through the tall, old trees, trying to get away from the big, red beast chasing her. Even in the foggy mist, she could see his hanging fangs and glassy eyes. Several times she had felt its hot breath close to her face, and almost fell to the ground in horror.

She was gasping when she finally saw a dim light glowing in the haze. She ran on unsteady legs until she reached the A-shaped, gray house. As she raced up the steps, the door opened, let her in, then closed behind her just as the wild animal dashed onto the porch, knocking its head against the door.

Susie looked wildly around her. "Mama, help. Please help me!" she cried.

Her father appeared before her and fell on his knees. "Daddy is here now. Ain't nothin' gon' harm you, baby gal. Nothin'," he promised, embracing her.

"Daddy! Oh daddy. I'm so scared of that beast. Don't let him git me. Daddy, why did you leave us? We need you. Mama needs you."

"Aaaah, Susie. Daddy cain't 'xplain why he left y'all. But I do know that it was the worst thang I coulda done. I'm comin' back real soon. I'm gon' make everythang alright, baby." Then he vanished.

Susie reached out to him, only finding empty space.

Her screams pierced the entire house.

"Baby, wake up. Mama's here. You havin' a bad dream," Rubye Mae said, drawing a shaking Susie close to her breast.

Tears formed in Rubye Mae's eyes as she looked at her exceptional child. She had spoken to her mother about Susie. Mu had assured her that everything would be fine in time.

After Susie went through the denial, pain, sorrow and suffering that most like her did before accepting their powers.

She held Susie tightly and assured her she would protect her until her father returned. Susie smiled, closed her eyes, and slept. Rubye Mae glanced at her other children who were fast asleep. She shook her head and smiled as she left the room. A tornado could have blown the house away, and they wouldn't have known it.

Susie stood on a stool, gazing into the mirror. Watching those strange eyes change from mysterious to blank.

She leaned forward, pulling them upwards, sideways, downward. They were in her face, but did they belong to her?

"Why you lookin' at me like that? Like you lookin' inside me?" she asked, backing away, suddenly afraid of her eyes as they changed, resembling an owl's. She thought about what she had overheard her mother say to Miss Betty one day, not long ago.

"My chile powers is growin' so fast I don't know what to do. Sometimes I'm scared. I jest hope she ain't. I know I gots to talk to her, befoe long."

Even though she had been curious to stay and hear her mother out, she knew eavesdropping was forbidden.

She realized she had special powers. She had known since she was four, when her father had returned with huge presents, wrapped in bright paper and ribbons. Just like in her dreams. Everybody cried for days. It had been the happiest time of her life. She knew her mother was happy too, after she had gotten over being angry and hurt.

Susie slipped from the stool, closed her eyes, sat down again. She pulled her socks up on her small legs, a smile appearing on her face. Maybe she could ask her daddy about her powers. She frowned. She didn't want to scare him away.

She wondered if her powers were strong enough to make it rain, or make the flowers grow, or see down into the ground?

"I sho wish Mama would talk to me. I'm almost nine years ole.

I been waitin' for almost five years now. 'Course, I know she busy with the house and babies that keeps comin', but I need to talk to her, real bad."

She closed her eyes, squeezing them tightly, shaking her head. She was getting tired of having those dreams.

"Susie. Git in here and help me, chile," Rubye Mae called from the bedroom. She jumped. "I'm comin', Mama."

The crowing of the roosters aroused her each morning, pulling Susie into a brand new day. Glad to see the dawn and its glorious red and orange colors sitting in the splendid darkness of the sky, she dashed from the bed. After her toilette, she pulled on her clothes, fed the chickens, roosters and other animals. Then she gathered kindling, picked fresh eggs and was ready for school long before her siblings.

Susie walked three miles to school. There, she entered another world. One where she absorbed all the information from her teacher. She begged for books, returning them in record time, causing her teacher, Mrs. Rivers to scrounge around for more.

Mrs. Rivers truly admired and loved Susie. She realized Susie was unique. She would have done all she could to encourage her to expand her knowledge, if she had thought it appropriate.

The students soon started to tease Susie, saying she was too smart for school. Susie would only smile and ignore them. Her brothers and sisters weren't allowed to badger her because she didn't like to do all the things they did. They knew she was different from them, yet she was part of them, and they loved her as she was. They liked the idea of having a sister with those strange, dark, beautiful eyes that could change and make them light as the brightest sun.

November was in its last days when they arrived home from school. Rubye Mae stood waiting for them at the door, smiling broadly, her eyes slanted into pin-lines.

"Y'all hurry up. We movin'. Gettin' away from here at last." She hugged Susie and Augustus to her and pulled them into the house.

"Where we movin' to, Mama?" Susie asked.

"To a big city call'd Bur'men'ham." She didn't tell them Mr. Ardonson had lost most of his money during the war and had asked them to leave. He hadn't opted to thank them for their hard work, just to leave as soon as possible.

Taylor had found a job in the mines in Birmingham. Two days later, they moved into a three bedroom house with a large parlor and a huge kitchen. Excited, they ran from room to room, relishing all the space, fresh paint, and bold, colorful paper walls. Every now and then they would stop and peek out the window at the spacious yard with tall pine and oak trees.

Susie was excited because she wouldn't have to sleep in a room with her brothers anymore. The rooms were big enough to fit two beds. J.T. would have one to himself; the other would be shared by the youngest boys. Ella Mae, now eighteen, would have her own bed, and Susie would share a bed with her younger sister, Willie Mae.

It was better than living in a two bedroom house and having to sleep on a pallet on the floor. Especially in the winter when Jack Frost came knocking at your door, crawled under it, and played with you all night long while you tried to find heat from somewhere in the floor, then woke up in the morning to find your blood almost frozen!

That night, Susie sat with her cheeks in hands, gazing out the window, at the big dipper, thinking. *Well, here I am, past nine years ole, livin' in a new house, in a big city, and still don't know who I am.* "Hey you, Mister Big Dipper, can you tell me who I am? What I'm 'spose to be? Why I'm differen'? Well, I tell you, I don't thank I like it one little bit."

"Susie. Come away from that window and go to bed, gal," Ella Mae yawned and patted her pillow.

Susie walked to her bed and crawled under the warm home-made quilts, next to a sleeping Willie Mae.

"Susie, honey. You ain't so differen' that folks gon' go 'round starin' at you like you got a big, black mole all over yo' face. You differen' moe in the head and eyes, but they pretty eyes. I'm sho Mama will talk to you once we git settled down here."

"You was listenin' to me?"

"I only heard the last part, Susie, and it ain't no big deal to hear you talk to yo'self. You been doin' it for years and we ain't said nothin', didn't have to. We know you ain't crazy."

Susie was surprised at her sister's words, yet warmed by her love and thoughtfulness. This was the first time Ella Mae had talked to her about being unusual. She hadn't been conscious of doing that.

"Ella Mae?"

"Yeah, Susie."

"Do you thank I'll be able to have a regular life? Have chil'ren and git mar-red if I talk to myself and have these powers?"

"Yeah, Susie." She yawned and stretched. "You gon' be jest fine. It's late. Now go to sleep."

"Good night, Ella Mae," she said, feeling much better about being close to normal. She pulled the quilt up to her chin. "Dear Lawd, please let my Mama talk to me soon. Thank you."

4

Susie was just shy of eleven years old when Rubye Mae eventually sat her down, and explained to her the precious Gift she had been born with.

"Baby gal, this is hard for me to tell you, but I gots to try. I plan'd on tellin' you sooner, but...Well, now is jest as good as any, I reckon."

Susie sat anxiously, waiting to hear the words that would assure her that she wasn't a freak.

"When you was born, Gawd 'cided you should have a special Gift. A Gift He don't bestow on jest anybody. He saw fit to let you be born with what our peoples call 'ole folks' eyes'."

Susie's dark eyes changed to a light-golden brown, then back to its normal arresting tones.

She held Susie's hands. "Baby, you was the person born with the wisdom to see, read, and predict the future of peoples. To help peoples anyway you can. Save them from gettin' in troubl' or hurt."

She stopped and scrutinized Susie. Seeing the emotions playing around her face, she squeezed her hands tighter.

"I know it's a big 'sponsibility for you, but its yo's, chile. And, from what I been tole, if you try and run from it, Gawd whups you 'til you do it. Don't be 'fraid, chile. It's a bless'd and powerful Gift. All you have to do is follow yo' heart and lis-sen to His voice, and let Him be yo' guide."

Susie's heart raced like a frightened doe. She wasn't brave enough to tell her mother about the voices she was hearing nor ask if it were God talking to her. She couldn't question what made it a Gift.

"I know you have the Gift 'cause I saw it in yo' eyes when you was a baby. And some othah folks done saw it too. Even the mid-wife who deliver'd you, Miss Sarah Ann, saw it, but she didn't tell me 'bout it. When I first saw it, I was scared and didn't want to b'lieve it, but thaih ain't no denyin' what Gawd done did. I had to 'xcept it, and you gots to, too.

The dreams you been havin' all these years is part of it. They may be scary to you, but know this; they won't hurt you. They jest gettin' you ready for all you have to do. Then I'm tole you jest know when it's time. Peoples gon' be drawn to you, and some gon' hate you, but you cain't do nothin' 'bout that, so you let it slide off yo' back like rain water."

Susie's head was spinning. The little information her mother had given her made her afraid. She didn't want this Gift.

Rubye Mae, seeing Susie's struggle, asked, "Do you have anythang you want to ax me?"

"Yes...Mam. Mama, why...why did I git chose and the othahs didn't? Ella Mae and Augustus and them?"

"That's somethan' I cain't answer for you. Only Gawd can and He ain't gon' tell you."

"So thaih ain't nothin' I can do 'bout this Gift? It's mine always?"

"Naw, thaih ain't, Susie. It's yo's 'til you is call'd Home."

Susie pulled her hands away from her mother. "Well, I don't thank I want it."

Rubye Mae's mouth fell open, then she calmed herself. "Susie, I cain't b'lieve you said that. Honey, you cain't tell Gawd what you don't want, even if you don't want it. He gives to you what He see fit and you have to 'xcept it. Now, don't go 'round thankin' that way. It will only make thangs worser for you. You hear me, chile?"

"Yes, Mam."

"But, you can ax Gawd to help you and He will. And, Susie?"

"Yes, Mam."

"I'll be here too." She wanted to tell her how sorry she was for not being there for her before, but she couldn't. She felt too guilty.

"The voices. They keep comin', talkin', but I don't know what to do. It is Gawd, Mama?"

Rubye Mae's vein jumped in her forehead. "I'm 'fraid I cain't answer that for you. The only thang to do is talk back to them. It won't hurt you none, chile."

Susie was tempted to tell her about the dreams and visions she had been having until a few days before. She was glad those faces and hands had stopped talking and pulling at her, trying to tell her things she didn't want to hear or see. But she sensed they would return, and she wouldn't know what to do with them.

"Susie?"

She jumped in her seat, thinking it was the voice, then realized it was her mother.

"How often you hear the voice, Susie?"

"When I'm by myself at night."

"What it sound like?"

"It's kinda hard to 'xplain. It don't sound like no man or no lady. It sound like it faraway, like the wind whisperin'. Sometimes I git scared. And it make me thank I'm crazy to talk back to it."

"I know this is real hard on you and everythang. But as you git o-ler, everythang will git bettah for you, if you don't fight it. And, you ain't crazy. Crazy is Sugah Bell down the road. Ain't got the good sense Gawd done gave her. Ain't one eye-otta of sense in her big head," Rubye Mae voiced, trying to calm her, taking her in her arms until she relaxed.

"Alright then," Rubye Mae said after several quiet minutes. "Jest 'member I'm here if you need me." She released Susie and left the room.

That night the vision awaited her.

An old man with white hair, and a long beard stood at the foot of her bed, dressed in a white gown of cascading, rustling satin. His face was hidden by the shadow behind him, making him appear almost invisible. As he spoke, she became frightened and fought to free herself from the dream, but he held her toes with such powerful force, she thought he would certainly pull them off. She closed her eyes and turned from him, but he was under her eye lids.

"You must do as I say, Susie. Take your mother and brothers to the old road leading to Bessemer. Go two miles and you'll find the house. Go twenty-five feet into the yard, and have your brothers dig a hole there."

Not wanting to obey him, she tried battling him with her long arms. But his unseen power pinned her to the bed.

"Alright. I'll do it," she whimpered. The force released her. She thought of fighting herself out of the dream, but didn't as she could still feel its presence close to her. Finding her mother and brothers, she led them to a grand plantation house that had been deserted since the Civil War.

The full moon cast eerie shadows over it, causing the spider webs and the spiders to look as if they were coming through the dusty, window pane.

Susie cringed. She moved closer to her brothers who had located the spot next to a well and started digging. She and her mother watched. They dug and dug, but found nothing. Frowning, they turned to speak to Susie. At that instance, a swarm of yellow-jackets flew from the dark space, covering her mother and brothers. They bellowed and attempted to beat them off. The swarm stung every inch of their bodies, raising welts as big as a fist on their tortured skin.

Though they covered her from head to feet, their buzzing deafening. They didn't harm Susie as she flung her hands outward, screaming.

She was still shrieking when her mother ran into the room. Two weeks later, in another dream the old man returned.

He pulled on her foot again. She opened her eyes, and quickly covered them to keep the blinding, white light from hurting her eyes.

"Susie. Susie, I'm here to tell you that the dream you had about the yellow-jackets was a sign to you. A sign that you are chosen. Extraordinary. Things that hurt others cannot harm you. But, you must always remember to follow your destiny as God has chosen."

The pressure was gone from her toes. Her eyes opened. He had faded.

The months following, Susie's nights were spent wondering if the elderly man would return to her. Time elapsed, he didn't reappear, and Susie was finally able to sleep easily.

During the day, when she was often alone, she would sit in her bedroom window and look out at the sky, questioning why she had been chosen to receive this Gift.

Lately, unusual events assaulted her. She had begun to experience lightness of body and disassociation of her mind from her body. It had begun three weeks ago while she was performing her chores. Suddenly, her body was suspended in the air, floating like a balloon.

When she had been released from the power that held her, she had tried to run, but failed. Stilled by some kind of energy, leaving a void in her brain. She had felt nothing, and saw only blackness.

After what had seemed like hours to her, she felt her body released, and her mind returned. She ran home, tears flowing from her eyes.

She sat on the steps. She didn't know what to do or whom to tell. It seemed her mother wasn't there when she really needed her though she knew it wasn't her mother's fault. And her father had his own worries. She kept her fears to herself.

5

Susie and Ella Mae moseyed to the back of the house and sat down on a log near the creek. Ella Mae stretched her legs out and grinned. "She had a boy. His name is 'Boy' for now 'cause they cain't thank of no name for him. You shoulda been thaih. It was somethin', all that stuff come outta her with that baby."

"Ella Mae," Susie frowned and grabbed her abdomen.

"I'm sorry. I forgots you got a weak stomach."

Susie looked at her, leaned over, picked up a rock and threw it in the clear, flowing water. She watched it splash then said, "Tell me."

Ella Mae smiled. Then her face became stern as she mimicked the midwife's voice: "Well, Rubye Mae, it looks like you finally through with havin' yo' chil'ren. Yo' navel cord clean asa whistle." Ella Mae finished, laughed, and slapped her hand on the log in merriment.

"Yuk. How can it be clean when it come outta her?" Susie frowned distastefully, turning her nose up in the air as if smelling a foul odor.

"Susie, quit it. I mean, it's so smooth, cain't nothing come out of it to feed the baby with."

Susie jumped up from the log, pulled wood chips from the ground, placed them in a neat pile by the log, her wise eyes dancing in her pretty face.

Ella Mae watched her, wondering if her twelve year old sister could handle this grown up situation. But if Susie couldn't, Ella Mae felt the strong urge to let her know that she wouldn't have to help raise any more of their mother's children, after this baby. Susie had assisted enough in her past years to last her a life time.

Several minutes later, Susie sat down and whispered, "I'm glad she's through havin' them 'cause I'm tir'd of washin' them nasty diapers, and I know you is too."

Ella Mae, pretending to be shocked at Susie's words, "Gal, hush yo mouth." Then she leaned closer to Susie and whispered, "I'm right with you. 'Xcept this time, you the one gon' be doin' the work. Me. I'm plannin' on leavin' here and getting' mar-red as quick as I can."

Susie's hand swept over the logs, scattering them as she fell to her knees, next to the log, and set anxious eyes on her sister.

"Don't look at me like that. You won't be here too long, and you will have yo' education to help you do good. You won't need to git mar-red and have a man take care of you, unless you want to. But I want to git mar-red befoe I be a ole maid. I need to git away from these chil'ren befoe I don't want my own."

"But you ain't said nothin' to nobody, Ella Mae, not even Mama. Who you thankin' on marryin'?" Susie asked quietly, sitting next to her on the log.

"You know him. The pretty, tall man that sometimes comes here to visit daddy. We been talkin' and gittin' along for most on a year now."

"But Ella Mae, he ole. He ole enuf to be yo' daddy," Susie expressed, scowling at her sister. She didn't want to lose her best sister and friend.

"He's only thirty-one. Ten years oler then me. Stop frownin'. Them wrinkles gon' stick in yo' head."

Sensing Susie's pain, she offered, "You can come visit me."

Susie's solemn eyes lit up. She hugged her sister. "Thank

you, Ella Mae. But I don't know if Mama will let me with the new baby and all."

"Come on. Be happy for me. If I git away, maybe you can come and live with me so you can finish yo' schoolin' like you wants to. You lucky that Mama let you go this long, but I know she ain't gon' let you much longer."

They jumped straight up in the air when Mae Frances yelled, "Mama said, yall bettah git in here and help out!"

As they rushed toward the house, Susie covered her mouth and grinned. *I'm sho glad Mama cain't have no moe chil'ren. I don't understan' nothin' 'bout no ole birthin' cord, but that's fine by me. Pretty soon, I won't have to worry 'bout no moe dirty diapers to be wash'd in that big, black, potbelly pot, and no moe freezin' my bloomers off neither.*

Months later, Ella Mae married at the small church in Bessemer, Alabama, where she would be living. Susie watched the wagon move slowly down the dusty road, taking her sister away. Tears fought her, but in the end she won. She smiled and threw rice at them, praying her sister would remember her promise.

Weeks later, Susie wished Ella Mae was still at home, or that she had left with her. Two words. Mae Frances.

Mae Frances was born after the return of their father. Her mother's love child, she had overheard her mother's friend, Betty, say one day.

Mae Frances was devilish. Susie had observed over the years. Her sister had often brooded for their toys or dolls, after she destroyed hers. To keep them from getting a whipping, Susie and her siblings had tried to appease her by giving up their precious toys.

Through it all, Ella Mae had been there to intervene when Mae Frances had tried to perform. Now, Susie needed her. Even though she knew the tactics that Ella Mae had used—threatening

Mae Frances, causing her to believe that the haints would come for her if she didn't stop her, 'carrin' on'.

Susie stopped braiding her hair and said for the second time, "Mae Frances, please don't bother my doll. Wait 'til I git through plaitin' my hair, and we can play outside."

"But I want to see it, " Mae Frances insisted, grabbing the doll from the beside table.

Susie reached for and grasped the doll. "Mae Frances, please put my doll down. You know it's fragile', and I don't want it mess'd up. Daddy made it for me when I was a baby."

Mae Frances kept tugging at the doll. When Susie wouldn't let go, she yanked it hard, ripping a section of the doll's hair.

Susie cried, "Now see what you did?"

Mae Frances observed her other siblings in the room, started laughing and dancing around the room. Then she held the doll in the air, shaking it, the head wobbling.

"I'm gon' tell Mama on you," Susie cried. "You knowed bettah then to do this to my doll." Tears ran down her cheeks and onto her starched white collar.

"Who cares," the sassy nine year old said, sticking her tongue out. "Mama likes me bettah, anyhow."

Rufus, Augustus, Willie Mae, and Alice moved to the corner, not wanting to be in the way of whatever was going to happen.

"Mama don't like you no bettah then the rest of us. She's our Mama too! You ought to be shamed of yo'self for sayin' that. I don't care what you say, I'm tellin' on you. You mean, Mae Frances, real mean." Susie's tears flowed like a river on a stormy day.

"Cry baby. Look at you, thirteen years ole and cryin' like a baby. Take yo' ole stinky doll," she wrinkled her face and flung the doll to the floor.

"And you gon' be, too, when I gits through with you," Rubye Mae announced as she stormed through the door, having overheard her spoiled daughter's devious talk.

"Mama, I was jest playin', that's all." Her large eyes pleaded for mercy.

"Well, I'm gon' join in on the game, and I'm gon' be playin' with yo' hide 'till you cain't sit down for a week without bein' greased. You knowed bettah then to do what you jest did."

Mae Frances looked for an exit. Not finding one, she glanced down at the floor as if it would open and save her.

Turning to Susie, Rubye Mae ordered, "Go git me three, long, sap switches and plait them together, and brang them to me, quick like."

Susie ran outside to the side of the house, quickly twisted and broke three switches from the tree, snatched the leaves from the thick mass of skin—sucking bushes with shaky hands, then braided them as she ran back into the house, and handed them to her mother.

Rubye Mae had placed Mae Frances between her legs. Her backside faced forward, her head toward her mother's back. Rubye Mae held her firmly, by holding her waist with her knees.

She held the switches in the air. "Now, we gon' see who like who, moe. And we gon' see who like this game of yo's the best, me or you.

When I gits through with you, hei-fer you gon' know what to do from here on out. You understan'?"

"Ye..Yes..Mam, Mama." She barely moaned.

"WHAM...WHISH...WHAM...WHISH...WHAM...WHISSSS...the switches made as Rubye Mae put a fire under her.

When she finished, Mae Frances sat on the floor whimpering, knowing she better not holler. "Now, I want you to try something' like this again, or give anybody any moe troubl'. Nobody in this family treats each othah like dogs do. Nobody!" Rubye Mae narrowed her eyes at the others and left the room, switches in hand.

Susie rushed to her whimpering sister and pulled her into her arms as the others gathered around. "I'm sorry Mae Frances, but you shouldn' done that. Come on and let me help you to the bed. Augustus, git a wet rag for her face."

Soon after her whipping, Susie noticed a change in Mae Frances and smiled. *I guess that sap from them switches did moe wonders then words ever coulda, cause Mae Frances doin' her work like the rest of us, and mindin' when Mama ain't here,* she thought.

Suddenly, Susie's head started pounding. She felt as if she were going to black out. She retreated to her bedroom and sat on the floor in the corner and closed her eyes tightly.

She saw her mother wailing, wildly throwing her arms in the air. Screaming. Pulling at her hair and her clothes. Her eyes bulged as if they were coming out of her face. Saliva ran down her face. She fainted on the floor. And there, next to her was Mae Frances. Dead.

The shocking vision caused a scream in her throat. She quickly placed her hand over her mouth to keep it within. Panting, she trembled in a corner of the room and took several deep breaths to collect herself. Finally standing, she teetered to the table and splashed water from the basin on her tear spattered face, hoping its coolness would help.

She opened her eyes and once more clearly saw her dead sister. She crumbled to the floor.

6

The passing of time didn't quiet Susie's nerves or keep the clarity of the cruel vision of her sister's death at bay. During the day she kept busy, hoping that by bedtime she would be so exhausted she would fall asleep because her mind would be void, but the night only brought her more fear and apprehension with the recurrence of the vision. Thus, Susie began to lose weight and became withdrawn.

Finally, Rubye Mae, concerned and frightened, stepped in and demanded that Susie tell her what was wrong.

Shocked at hearing about Susie's vision and of Mae Frances' impending death, Rubye Mae fought the urge to scream and run to Taylor for support. Instead, she gently held and comforted Susie as best she could. Although she couldn't find the proper words at a time like this, she simply said, "Baby, what Gawd got plan'd, we cain't do nothin' 'bout. Jest know that He loves us all."

Later, Rubye Mae, feeling very despondent, went to Taylor and wept on his shoulders even though she didn't want to burden him, but she knew he needed to know about their child and her visions, and that he could possibly provide Susie with some of his wisdom and support.

Sometime later, Taylor took Susie for a long walk in the woods, one of her favorite enjoyments with her father. They sat on matching logs and listened to the lively sounds of the animals. He patted her on the back and smiled sadly.

"Baby, I know you prob'ly thank I done let you down. That I'm a weak man. Cain't take too much and all, but it ain't like that. Thaih's thangs yo' Mama jest don't tell me for fear I'm gon' leave her again. Even though I done tole her I would nevah do that no moe. For years now, she done kept thangs from me. She says I work hard, and she figured I don't need no moe problems when I gits home. Hog wash. Y'all my chil'ren.

"Now, I know it was my fault and all 'bout not comin' to you 'bout yo' Gift, but I figured I jest couldn' help you on that. And I couldn'.

"But this thang that eatin' you up inside is gon' be the end of you, if I don't try to do somethin' for you. Yo' Mama tole me the othah day 'bout that sight you saw in yo' head 'bout yo' sistah. Said it's been eatin' at you. You cain't sleep and all."

He paused and glanced at the small stream where they fished sometimes. He took her hand in his callused ones. "You know, I don't know much 'bout what goes on in the mind, but I know if you thank on it all the time, you can go crazy. I thank the best thang you can do is close yo' eyes, relax and see what happens. 'Stead of tryin' to fight the same thang over and over again. That is so, ain't it?"

She looked at her father, her eyes full of untold knowledge. He was right, to a certain degree. At least about not knowing what was going on inside her head. She wished she could talk to him. She loved him so much. But he was not a very strong man, and she didn't want to worry him.

He squeezed her hand slightly, reassuring her he could handle the situation.

"Yes, Suh. I do thank I'm gon' see it again. Or somethin' jest as bad. Daddy, is I'm sick in the head?"

"Baby, we done had moe then three hundred years of slavery and oppression on our peoples in this world, and with all the thangs our folks done went through back then and still goin' through now, ain't none of us in this family done broke down and lost our minds. Now, if you ax me, that's sayin' a lot. I don't thank you have nothin' to worry 'bout in that pretty head of yo's. Look up thaih, He said, pointing upwards. See them pretty blue skies and feel that hot sun burnin' down on us. Thaih's a Gawd up thaih doin' it, and jest like He doin' that, He knows what's goin' on in that head of yo's. Talk to Him and tell Him how you feel. Ax Him to make everythang alright for you. I guarantee you, tonight you will sleep and be bettah the next day, and the rest of them days to come."

Susie looked at her father for the first time and realized he had spoken more to her this day more than any other time in her life; and she was going on fourteen. She appreciated his thoughts, and the way he expressed himself. She felt safe. He wasn't soft after all, she reasoned, just lean with his words.

She smiled, showing pretty, long white teeth. "You sho can talk fine, Daddy. I feel bettah now." He released her hand and hugged her.

She felt different. A calmness surrounded her as she breathed in renewed strength. She began to realize that she could depend on him as well as her mother. He had been honest and there for her all the time. She adored him and knew that he loved her, and wanted her to be safe, happy and well.

"Thank you, Daddy. Thank you for everythang."

"Anytime I can help, jest let me know. Jest don't tell yo' Mama. She frets so much about me," he said and winked.

And it was true. Rubye Mae fussed over him as much as she did the children. It was almost as if she was afraid that something would happen to him if she let him worry too much or help raise the children.

When he asked her to stop worrying over him like he was a child, she would only say, "Taylor, I only have one husban', and I don't aim to see nothin' happen to you."

"What makes you thank somethang gon' happen to me, Rubye Mae?" he would ask while pulling her close to him.

"Man, you bettah stop. Watch yo'self, Taylor." She would say as if insulted and look to see if any of the children had seen him feel or kiss her. Satisfied, she would pull away from him, strut into the kitchen to cook, a slight smile playing at her pretty mouth.

They were closer than they had been before he left home. That's how they had been when they first married. When all the children were in bed, they would lie in each others arms and talk about the children and their hopes for their future.

They were thankful for Taylor's job in the mines and the house they lived in, and she didn't have to work in the fields anymore. She had hoped for more, her dream house. But it didn't seem probable. Times were too tough, especially for the colored people.

Sometimes they discussed leaving the South. That was just a wish. They realized it would be too difficult to move North with the number of children they had, especially with no family there to help them.

Neither of them spoke of the past, refusing to let it consume their happiness and love for each other.

It was because of that affection Taylor let Rubye Mae have her way, or let her think that she did. He found time to spend with all the children, talk with them about their future, his and Rubye Mae's childhood and their past aspirations.

Two days before Susie's fifteenth birthday, Willie Lee, an old friend, came to visit. Willie Lee sat in his brand new 1928 Ford, grinning and grinning, honking the horn, causing the chickens to flutter from their nesting place.

Taylor went to the door, saw the car, and called, "Rubye Mae, come on out here and see what Willie Lee done stole. I know he done took it 'cause he sho ain't got no money to buy nothin' this fine with."

"Hey, Taylor, ain't she somethin'?" Willie Lee remarked proudly, carrying his hand over the steering wheel.

"Man, you said it. This is a beauty. So where did you steal it from?"

"Now, you know I ain't done nothin' like that. You 'member, I tole you I was savin' for a car years ago. Jest didn't see nothin' I want'd, 'til now."

"It sho is fine, Willie Lee. Why ain't Betty with you?"

"I had to drop her off at her Mama's. She promised to help her bake bread."

"How she like the car?"

"She swears it's hers and she gon' take it soon as she learns how to drive."

"Well, I guess it's yo's then," Rubye Mae commented and smiled. "Y'all chil'ren stop peepin' out them windows and come on out here, and see Uncle Willie Lee's and Ant Betty's brand new car."

The children tumbled down the steps, then stopped several feet from the vehicle, their eyes revealing delight.

"Y'all wanna ride?"

They looked at Rubye Mae and Taylor.

"Y'all can ride. But make sho yo' hands is clean and stump yo' feets befoe you git in," Taylor ordered as he helped Rubye Mae and then stacked the children into the car until they were packed tighter than skin on a chicken.

Rubye Mae looked around and frowned. "Where's Susie and the baby?"

"She prob'ly don't want to come right now. We'll take a quick ride and come back and let her go." Taylor turned in the direction of the house and yelled, "Susie, we'll be straight back."

Susie stood, gazing in the mirror at herself, unaware of the events taking place outside her home. She searched her face, looking for signs of aging as was obvious of the fifteen-year-old girls at her church. They had lost their, baby fat; their bodies, including their faces, had become slimmer and more mature.

She peered at her eyes, mouth, neck, chest, then turned before the mirror, eyeing her small waist and narrow hips. She turned her backside toward the mirror, twisting her head sideways then shook herself. Nothing moved.

She pulled her long dress tightly around her and bounced again. Sighing, she dropped her dress and hunched her shoulders, deciding she appeared the same as any twelve year old.

But she was mistaken. There was indeed a change in her. Certainly all the boys had noticed her developing high breasts, narrow waist, and bottom that slightly swayed beneath the full dress when she walked. Rubye Mae had also noticed although she hadn't said anything, deciding that the time wasn't right.

Susie strolled through the house, searching for her family. Finding only the sleeping baby, she stood gazing at him, contemplating if he would have a better life than the rest of them. He was such a quiet little boy; he hardly cried, even when he was hungry or wet.

Sometimes she thought there was something wrong with him because he didn't act like the rest of the children she had helped to raise. But it didn't matter to her because she loved him. She leaned down and kissed him and walked back through the house, wondering where everyone was.

Then she heard a noise and looked outside. She smiled and ran to the door to see the new car their parents' best friends had purchased, momentarily forgetting all her cares.

She had been praying that Ella Mae would visit, and that same day, Ella Mae stopped by without her husband. Susie, elated, spoke to her about leaving home, and living with her.

"Susie, you ain't but fifteen. Mama ain't gon' let you go live with me and Otis Lee."

"But you promised me, Ella Mae. Least you could ax her."

Ella Mae pulled the dish from the sudsy water and rinsed it in the wooden tub of clear water, then handed it to Susie to dry and put away. "Alright then. I'll give it a try, but I ain't makin' no promises."

"Jest try. That's all I'm axin'."

Before Ella Mae entered the room where her mother was, she put courage on her face, strength in her legs, a lie on her tongue, and hoped the lie bump wouldn't appear on her tongue before she finished speaking.

Rubye Mae looked crossed-eyed at her as she sat down.

"Y'all through with the dishes?"

"No, Mam. Susie's doin' them. I need'd to talk to you 'bout somethin' importan'." She thought she could feel the lie bump starting to swell.

"I'm all ears."

"Mama, I'm 'xpectin'," she blurted.

Rubye Mae's eyes closed slightly. "Why, that's jest great, chile. When you due?"

"Six months. But the doctor said I'm kinda in the delicate way. That I need to rest with my feet up for a spell so I won't lose the baby."

"Humph. I ain't nevah heard tell no women in our family losin' no baby, but I guess the doctor knows what he's talkin' 'bout," Rubye Mae offered.

"Well, I don't want to take no chances. What I want'd to know is, if you would be in favor of lettin' Susie come in 'bout a month and help me out some, for a spell?"

Rubye Mae didn't speak for a few moments, then said, "I guess that can be 'ranged."

Ella Mae released the breath she had been holding. "Thank you, Mama. I won't forgit this." She sprang to her feet, kissed her on the cheek, and almost ran from the room.

Outside the door, she stopped and felt for the bump. Nothing. She smiled, then ran to the kitchen.

Rubye Mae laughed. "She's jest as pregnant as I is, and the Lawd knows I ain't." She shook her head and grunted. "But I'll do anythang to help Susie git her education. I jest wish'd she woulda come to me," she sighed, then looked up and smiled at Taylor as he walked into the room from his stroll.

It was difficult for Susie to leave home. All the children cried and begged her to stay. Mae Frances was the worst. But Ella Mae transported Susie to an entire new atmosphere, made real when she accompanied her down the hall of her cozy, little house, stopped before a door, and said: "Open it."

Susie looked at the closed door as if it would bite her, and then back at her sister.

"Go on, open it. It gon' be yo' room as long as you stay here."

"My ro.....ro...om?" she stammered.

"All yo's. Come on with me and look at it." She smiled.

Susie stood gazing at the iron bed, covered with a beautiful handmade quilt, made with some of the pieces from the material her mother used to quilt with. A chifforobe with a wall mirror hanging next to it stood in a corner of the room. The shining wood floor held handmade throw rugs made from flour sacks and straw. There were old magazines Ella Mae had gotten from a white lady in town, a picture of an elk on the wall, and a makeshift closet that had a pretty flowered sheet in front to be used as the closet door.

Susie didn't know what she was going to do with her own bed, let alone her very own room. It was still difficult to believe that her parents had let her leave home and come here so she could continue her schooling.

"Thank you, Ella Mae. This is all so pretty."

Ella Mae hugged her, and patted her on the back. "It's alright baby, you cry all you want."

Even though Susie was overjoyed, she wasn't going to cry, not in front of her sister. Since the incident years before, with Mae Frances, she had decided if she cried again, it would be alone.

"Yeah, all yo's. Now let me tell you what yo' chores gon' be. First, you don't have to git up 'til six o'clock.

Second, aftah I cook breakfast you clean the kitchen. And aftah lunch and dinner you do the same. Third. You 'sponsibl' for washin' yo' clothes and cleanin' yo' room.

Once a week we clean the whole house. Otis Lee will feed the chickens, pigs, cows and the rest of the animals. The rest of the time is all yo's."

Susie, too dumbfounded to speak, nodded her head in understanding.

Ella Mae smiled. "It's high-pass time for you to be with friends yo' own age, play a little bit with yo' doll, even if you is a bit ole now. That's alright too, 'cause you needs to have some fun. We gon' make sho you find some friends yo' own age."

"But what I'm gon' do with all my 'xtra time?" Susie asked.

"Baby, I jest tole you, have some fun."

"Oh," Susie replied.

"I know all this is new and it's gon' take some time to git use to, but you will. Now come on and help me fix supper."

She placed her arm through Susie's and they moved toward the kitchen. That night Susie started dreaming again. The dreams weren't frightening. Most mornings when she awakened, she thought of them and pushed them to a corner in her mind.

Ella Mae was shopping at a dry goods store while Susie stood admiring the pretty fabrics, wishing she could have several bolts to make dresses in all the spare time she had when a booming voice startled her.

She turned toward the voice. "How you be, pretty girl? I know you the one I been lookin' for all yo' pretty, young life."

She stared at the handsome, jet black, young man who seemed to have the prettiest gray eyes she had ever seen. "Who do you thank you talkin' to, with yo' fresh self? Git away from me!" she demanded and turned from him. She was shaking inside. She was used to being around boys, but this was different. He was gawking at her.

"Whoooo thaih," he said, moving in front of her. "The name is Robert Lewis, and I do say I'm pleeeeese' to meet you." He exaggerated and bowed. But, his eyes remained on her flushed face.

Blazing anger played in her eyes at his disrespect and fancy talk. Her words were like ice water being poured over his head when she spoke through gritted teeth, "I ain't no horse, so don't whoooo me. And if you don't git away from me, I'll..." She was interrupted by a pretty, bright skinned young girl.

"Please excuse my brother. He don't mean any harm. He jest cain't resist botherin' the pretty girls with all his hot air," she explained, yanking his arm, hard.

Susie noticed her speech was like her brother's, a thicker, stronger accent. They were from the North. "Well, he ought to learn some manners befoe it's too late," she responded with a half smile.

"My name is Blanche Juanita Davis, and you met my stupid ole brother," she gestured toward Robert Lewis who now had a silly grin on his face.

Susie smiled and held out her hand to Blanche, "I'm Susie Morton, pleased to meet you."

She looked at Robert Lewis and back at Blanche and said, "A little bit moe you woulda had a snagger'd-tooth brother."

They all looked at each other and burst out laughing. From that moment on, the three of them were inseparable, except on weekends, when Susie returned home to help her family.

Susie's weekend visits were always delightful. She enjoyed helping her mother and seeing her younger brothers and sisters. Spending time with her father was one of her great joys.

Rubye Mae was proud of Susie. She noticed the positive changes in her. She was pleased about her progress, her development and attitude. It had been a wise decision to let her special child leave home. Certainly she was more confident than before. Her haunted look had faded. Susie was budding like a sweet rose. She was going to carry the trait of the Johnson's, her side of the family: nice backside, high breasts, and small waist.

"You doin' alright at Ella Mae's?" she quizzed.

"Yes, Mam, I'm doin' alright," Susie answered, continuing her work.

"So you made some friends, yo' sistah said. That's real good. A girl needs them. But 'member, not too many. That makes for too much jealousy."

"Yes, Mam." Susie said, not understanding her mother, but not willing to question her at the moment. She paused and smiled. "I hope you git to meet them, Mama."

"I know I will. And I know they alright, if they yo' friends."

"Thank you, Mama."

"Sit down."

She laid the dust rag down and sat in a straight chair.

"You start'd to have dreams again?"

"Yes, Mam."

"What kind? Scary?"

"No, Mam, they ain't scary, but they seem to be tryin' to tell me to do somethang, but I cain't make them out."

"Is you tryin' hard to?"

"No, Mam."

"Gal, you cain't run from this. I done tole you that."

Rubye Mae threw her arms in mid-air. "Now, you almost six-teen. It's time you start doin' what you was put here for. Don't fight it. Let it come natural. It's jest like breathin'.'."

"Yes, Mam."

"Anybody seen yo' eyes change yet?" She lowered her arms and moved closer to Susie, her voice calm.

"No, Mam, I don't thank so." She sounded frightened.

"Thaih ain't no denyin' yo' Gift. Some bound to see yo' eyes sooner or latah, and in the end, it's good for them. Don't be 'shamed of Gawd."

"No, Mam, I'm not..." she hesitated.

"But what?"

"I'm scared, Mama."

"I know you is, but you gots to know thaih ain't nothin' to be scared of Susie," she reassured her, understanding her fears, yet helpless to assist her.

She stood up, patted and rubbed Susie's shoulders. "Don't be 'fraid of what Gawd gave you. Ax Him to help you. Show you how to use yo' powers. I don't mean to scare you, but if you don't start to use them, anythang can happen to you, and will keep on, 'til you do it. Do you understan' me, chile?"

"I thank so, Mama."

Switching subjects, she said in a stern voice, "You seein' boys yet?"

"No, Mam," she frowned.

"See that you don't. You got plenty time for them, latah. And while I'm on the subject, I know Augustus comes to see y'all, and goes cross that river bank to that coal minin' town. I know 'bout that place and them men. See that you and yo' girl friends don't cross it. Ain't nothin' thaih but bad news."

"I won't, Mama."

"I don't want to brang yo' Daddy into this."

"No, Mam," Susie responded. But she knew her father well

enough to know that if she courted an older man, he wouldn't frown on her.

"Alright then. I'll let you git back to yo' chores. And keep up the good work in school," she praised before leaving the room, a smug smile on her face.

Susie stood motionless for a moment, then shook her head. How in the world did she figure she would fool Rubye Mae Morton?

You ought to know you can't fool your mother. The voice had finally returned. This time, she wasn't frightened.

"Yeah. I guess I should know that by now," she answered and resumed oiling the table.

7

"Susie, you ain't gon' b'lieve this, but I'm sho enuf 'xpectin' again," Ella Mae blurted out.

Susie's kitchen hair stood on end for a moment as realization hit her smack in the face. All those fish she had been dreaming about was to let her know her sister was the one pregnant. "Ella Mae, that's real good to hear. I'm happy for y'all."

"Then why that strange look in yo' eyes?"

"I jest...Well, I jest hope this time you won't lose it like the last time."

Susie had heard her mother, Miss Betty, and her grandmother speak of dreaming about certain things and how it had come to pass, but she had never been superstitious.

Dreaming of fish was a sign that someone close to you was or would become pregnant. Muddy water and paper money foretold someone would pass away. Silver coins were a sign of good luck and dreaming of babies meant growing in grace. *Well, looks like I got to b'lieve it for myself, but I sho don't have to like it,* Susie reasoned.

A faraway look appeared in Ella Mae's eyes. She touched Susie's shoulder, invading her thoughts. "Lawd, I sho hope this one comes to term. But I ain't takin' no chances and lyin' neither."

"You thank that's why you lose the first one?"

"Maybe if I hadn't said I was 'xpectin' when I wasn't, the Good Lawd woulda seen fit for the baby to be born. Gawd don't take too good to lyin'. Thaih you go with that funny look in yo' eyes again, Susie."

"I don't thank Gawd would punish you like that." *I wonder if He gon' punish me though?*

"Well, all I can say is the Good Lawd give us everythang we got. I jest hope he's givin' out to me this time," Ella Mae said hopefully and patted her stomach.

Now ain't that the truth. He sho gave us everthang we want'd and then some we don't want. Like this Gift thang.

Susie moved slowly through the woods, bobbing her head and humming a tune while she picked herbs, berries, and roots which would be used to make bitter teas, hot tonics, and salves for illnesses ranging from the common cough to pneumonia and other ailments.

She remembered the time Willie Mae had a horrible chest cold and cough when she was very small. Worried, they called on the jack-leg doctor several times, but his efforts had failed. It was then that her dad's mother, Ma, had made a compress from bitter herbs and cow manure.

Ma had walked in the house, her bow legs causing her to sway sideways. "What y'all gon' do, wait 'til the chile sees Gawd foe y'all calls me?"

"No, Mam. We was jest 'bout to send for you," Rubye Mae said, frowning from the foul odor of the compress.

"Where is the po' chile?" Ma asked, not at all bothered by the odious smell.

"She's in here, Ma," Taylor offered, pointing toward the door, trying to keep from turning his nose up.

"Well, y'all sho don't have to act like y'all ain't nevah smelt nothin' like this befoe. I knows y'all pass wind that smell jest as bad or worser." She threw her head in the air and marched into the room, leaving them trying to decide if they wanted to laugh, cry, or run from the house.

Later on, when Willie Mae had recovered, she whispered, "That thang smelled so bad you'll git well jest to git it off you."

Susie smiled at the memory of the story and let it slip away. She paused from her task and breathed in the poignant air, hoping for rain. It had been months since the ground had drank the flowing showers, but the mosquitoes didn't mind at all as they thrived on the muggy heat, and sweet, human blood like Susie's.

She inhaled the scent of the berries and gingerroot before placing them in an empty syrup can and swatting a mosquito.

Feeling suddenly lightheaded, she leaned against a nearby tree that looked as if it was about to crumble from old age. Her body involuntarily twitched. She had the sensation of a presence nearby. Becoming alarmed, she pivoted her head from side to side, trying to find the will to run, but her body was busy attempting to control the trembling.

Abruptly, her body was lifted from the ground and into a sleeping position by a strong, yet gentle force. She fought to keep her eyes open, but lost the battle as her lids were forced closed. She felt drowsy, as if she were drugged.

Later, Susie found herself propped against the same old tree, her legs tucked beneath her. Disoriented and frightened, she glanced about her as if searching for someone.

She grimaced then wrinkled her nose as she inhaled a sweet, fruity scent, reminding her briefly of Christmas.

She stood on shaky legs and looked around again, but saw nothing. *I know somethin' is here 'cause I can feel it right next to me. What is happenin' to me?*

She became cold, then sweaty. Lastly, she shivered as fine goose bumps appeared on every available space on her body. Just as quickly as the episode occurred, it passed.

Taking no chances, Susie plucked her cans from the ground with the intent to run home. She smelled the strange fragrances once more and ran as fast as her small feet would take her, but in essence, she wasn't moving at all. She observed her feet and wondered why they wouldn't move. A hand touched her shoulder. Instinctly, she knew it was not human. She squealed. Sweat as large as pearls appeared on her pinched face. The presence was stronger, almost as if it wanted to be a part of her.

Susie.

She wanted to run.

Susie. Why do you run away from your Gift? There is nothing for you to fear. You are not cursed.

Her mouth trembled. She shook her head. "Naw. Go away," she whispered at the voice, a different voice.

Her eyes became like smothered coals; her body quivered like the broken earth during an earthquake. Her mind became a mass of blackness as her hands were gently forced over her eyes.

Horrified, she lost consciousness.

Minutes later, she awakened, sprawled face down on the warm earth. She sat up and looked around, dazed. She tried to stand, but was too weak. She sought to remember what had happened and wondered how long she had been there. She touched her face, examined her hands, legs, and feet, then stood on jittery limbs.

"Whoever you is, please leave me alone. I ain't did nothin' to you." All she could hear was the sound of the returning birds and a rabbit running through the woods.

She looked down at her feet. She moved one slowly in front of the other. Then she grabbed her buckets without stopping and ran until she reached Ella Mae's where she stopped at the foot of the steps.

The old voice returned. *I am part of you, and I will always be here to help you. You must never be afraid to use your Gift, your legacy.*

"But I don't want to have a Gift to do anythang moe then anyone else. I jest want to be normal."

But you are normal, with a special Gift. You were picked to teach, heal, predict, and help others in need. The visions you've been seeing were signs to you, but you didn't know it until they came true. You have to stop fighting and accept what God gave you.

She trembled and flopped down on the bottom step. She realized that she was being warned. Susie longed for her mother to hold and comfort her as she had many times before, but she knew that her mother also would agree with the voice.

She held her face in her hands. Vivid, unrecognizable images appeared before her.

"Naw!" she screamed and jumped from the step, fleeing into the house, the herbs all but forgotten. She paused when she heard her sister's voice.

"Y'all, I don't know how we gon' make it much longer with all the banks mostly closed down. Whoever woulda thought 1929 would be such a terribl' and sad year," Ella Mae offered.

"You know, it's a shame when a man cain't depend on the banks. I jest don't understan' how the white man go and let somethin' like this happen. Now, the po' farmers like me been hit so hard, we's got to depend on somebody else to help feed our family," Otis Lee complained, tapping his jar of ice water on the table.

"Don't I know it," Ella Mae moaned. "I cain't b'lieve this happen'd. Thangs is so bad. Shucks, we do good to find any collard greens growin' this year with the one or two seeds we managed to scrape up. I'm gettin' mighty scared."

Susie had sat in a chair nearby while they spoke, greeting them silently so as not to interfere in their conversation. While they talked, her mind spun.

"It's a shame when a man have to feed his family from a soup wagon," Otis Lee grimaced and looked hopelessly at Ella Mae.

Susie glanced at her brother-in-law. He was tall with kind brown eyes that either shined or looked dull, depending on the occasion. Then she gazed at her sister, who was light skinned with dark brown hair and eyes which were usually flirtatious.

"Well, it's a good thang we got Mister Jamison to come to our rescue," Susie offered.

"Yeah, he a good white man, helpin' all the people that work at the coal mine, and them that don't, while we fightin' this depression," Otis Lee said.

"But he late with the food this month," Ella Mae said, eyeing the empty plate, wishing it held hoe-cake bread, crisp bacon, fluffy eggs, and finger licking syrup.

"Don't y'all worry. The wagon will be here by tomorrow mornin'," Susie said with such conviction both jerked their heads and stared at her.

"Baby girl, is you alright?" Ella Mae asked.

"Yeah. I'm alright. He's comin'."

"You sho talkin' funny, Susie. You right sho you ain't feelin' sick?" Otis Lee inquired.

"I'm sho Otis Lee," she said and smiled.

As she turned toward her sister. A brilliant light appeared in her eyes, almost blinding Ella Mae.

"Oooh Lawd, them eyes!" Ella Mae exclaimed as she stumbled over the chair and backed up to the kitchen door leading outside, but she couldn't move any further as Susie's yellow, intense eyes captivated her whole existence.

Her heart raced. She forgot all time as a force pummeled her. She began shaking. Something was washing over her: light, hot, soothing liquid. Then she was seeing unmentionable things. Her eyes became enlarged, and she lost conscious. She slipped gently to the floor.

Otis Lee ran to her. Ella Mae? Ella Mae? Wake up!

Susie stooped next to her and touched her hand. Ella Mae opened her eyes and grabbed Susie's arm.

"Lawd, Susie, I done forgot 'bout yo' eyes changin' like that. You 'bout scared this baby outta me."

"I'm sorry, Ella Mae. I cain't control it. Let me help you back to the table. You'll be okay."

"Whoooooo. Wait a minute," said Otis Lee. "Y'all wanna tell me 'bout these eyes?"

Both of them had forgotten about Otis Lee, who was gawking at them as if they were rambling fools.

"I nevah bother'd to tell you 'cause...well, you didn't need to know, that's all," Ella Mae answered.

"I'm Gift'd," said Susie.

"You what?" His eyes bulged from his face.

"You heard her. She Gift'd. She can see, hear voices, and tell you thangs."

Otis Lee's face changed from fear to disbelief. Then he scratched his head. "Y'all ain't tryin' to pull the wool over my eyes, is y'all?"

They didn't answer.

"So you is Gift'd, and yo' sistah nevah thought it importan' enuf to tell her own husban'?"

"You don't thank I'm crazy, Otis Lee?" Susie asked.

"I woulda eventually tole you, Otis Lee," Ella Mae said.

He ignored Ella Mae. "Naw, chile. So yo' whole family done seen yo' eyes, Susie?"

"Everybody 'xcept Mae Frances. This don't happen all the time. I don't know when it gon' happen, 'til it's here. Then I cain't do nothin' 'bout it."

"And it be tole that the ones that see her eyes live a long time. I sho hope that's the truth," said Ella Mae.

He still refused to acknowledge Ella Mae. "So you say the wagon's comin' in the mornin', Susie?" he asked, looking directly into her eyes.

"Yes, Suh."

"Did you hear what she said, Ella Mae?"

"You know I did, Otis Lee," Ella Mae pouted.

"You sho don't sound like you b'lieve Susie."

"I do b'lieve her. I do. Now, can we talk 'bout somethin' else?" she shivered. "This kinda stuff gives me the willies aftah a while."

Susie excused herself and went to wash dishes, relieved to get away from them, glad they hadn't seen how upset she was. She was still reeling from the experience of her voice speaking without her knowledge or control, and feeling a slight pressure behind her eyes before they changed.

She slipped to the cool linoleum floor and hugged her trembling body. She knew she was changing. She felt like a freak. The visions, her voice and eye transformation were all happening interchangeably.

"Lawd, Jesus, is I losin' my mind?" she whispered.

Susie. You will not lose your mind. Your power is growing and you must prepare yourself for its use. The voice responded.

"What if I don't start usin' it?" she asked, but she already knew the answer. The voice had told her before.

"Well, you don't have to talk to me. I'm glad you ain't," she cried. When the voice didn't answer her, hot tears flowed down her cheeks.

Ella Mae entered the kitchen. "Susie, you cryin' and talkin' to yo'self?"

"Naw, Ella Mae. I jest got some soap in my eyes. They burnin' somethin' awful." She stood and turned her back to wash the dishes, trying to dismiss further conversation.

But Ella Mae wasn't taking any hints.

"Susie, I don't know much 'bout this Gift you got and all. I do know you differen' then you used to be. I cain't 'xplain it. You scared me tonight, but I'll git over it. I jest want you to know if you ever need me to talk to, I'll be here; or if you want to, I can send for Mama." She patted Susie's back.

"Thank you, Ella Mae. Right now I got to finish these dishes."

"Alright, Susie. If it bothers you, I won't push it."

The sky was casting its first glimpse of daybreak as the sunrise peeked through the clouds, bringing forth its beauty of rust and orange hues. Susie had lain awake all night to keep from dreaming.

She heard a distant clip clap, sat up abruptly and listened closer. It was the wagon. She hightailed out of bed and ran to Ella Mae and Otis Lee's room.

They were having a church picnic outside, under the tall maple trees. The minister, Rev. Petteway, had asked people to bring the food they had from their home and make this a day of thanksgiving. Everyone from miles away was invited, even those who couldn't afford to bring anything.

It was their way of helping each other during this rough time.

After everyone had eaten, they were welcome to take any remaining food with them, especially those who had children to feed.

There were several long tables filled with food of every kind: chitterlings, fried chicken, ham, turkey, bar-b-que ribs, collard greens, cabbage, beets, rutabaga, squash, salads, and assorted cakes and pies.

Susie and her friends, Robert Lewis, Blanche Juanita, and Betty Jean, all sat on a fallen tree in the back of the church eating and teasing each other.

"Look at yo' plate, Robert Lewis," said Blanche. "You sho you gon' eat all that food?"

"Hungry as I is, I'm gon' eat yo's and mine if you don't watch it," he said."

Susie and Betty Jean laughed at the two of them. "Y'all is always actin' up, no mattah what is goin' on. But this time, Robert Lewis, I thank she's right. Yo' plate is full enuf for three men twice as big as you," Susie offered.

"Y'all jest stickin' together against me. And look at you, Susie…"

His voice trailed off as someone from nowhere appeared and passed her hands through Susie's thick, curly hair and quickly fled. But the others, along with Susie, turned in time to glimpse the tail of a red dress flying through the woods and disappear behind a group of trees.

"What happen'd, Susie?" Blanche asked as she moved closer to her.

"I don't know, but somebody ran her hands through my hair before she took off through thaih," Susie said, pointing in the woods behind them.

"You want me and some of the othahs to go and see if we can find her?" offered Robert Lewis.

"Naw. It's alright. It was prob'ly somebody that know'd I don't like nobody messin' in my head and 'cided to pull a prank on me."

They sat talking and eating for several more minutes then Susie stood and said, "I got to go. My head feels real funny." She handed her unfinished plate to Blanche Juanita and went to find Ella Mae.

When they reached home, Susie said, "Ella Mae, my head is itchin' somethin' awful." Then she recounted what had happened.

"Susie, why didn't you tell me back thaih? We coulda tried to find the person and maybe found out what she did to yo' head. You know, it was prob'ly Johnnie Lee. She's always aftah you 'bout somethin' or nothah."

"Right now I jest want my head to stop itchin'. I thank I'll go wash it."

"Wait. Let me look at it first. Sit down here while I go git a comb and look through it."

She sat on the floor, between Ella Mae's legs. "Lawd, Susie. Yo' head is gettin' some kinda funny bumps in it with black specks," she said, frowning as she parted Susie's hair.

"Here, let me see a mirror," Susie demanded, yanking the large one from the wall. She parted her hair with the comb.

"Ella Mae, you right. I gots to do somethin'. I thank she put somethin' in my head, and my hair is goin' to fall out. I'm goin' to boil some water and put some..." she paused and looked at her sister for help.

Ella Mae hunched her shoulders at a loss. "Shoot, Susie. I don't know what to do, but tell you to wash it in vinegar, and find somebody tomorrow who might be able to help you."

Susie fought back tears as she realized she had ignored another sign.

"Susie? Susie, what is it? You lookin' funny again."

"It ain't nothin', Ella Mae. Nothin' at all."

Susie and Betty were strolling – on their way to Betty Jean's home. Susie had met Betty Jean Moore soon after meeting Robert Lewis and Blanche Juanita. Betty's family had moved from Pittsburgh to be with their relatives in Hueytown, a small town near Bessemer, to help their family wade through the Depression.

Betty Jean was a unique, pretty girl, coffee colored with a drop of milk added. Her eyes were light brown and sparkled when she wanted to do something naughty.

"Susie, is you gon' tell me why you been wearin' that scarf on yo' head for weeks now?" Betty Jean asked as they walked toward the forbidden bank where she lived.

Susie paused and looked at Betty Jean. "Cause my hair, it's all comin' out by the combful," she said and gingerly patted the scarf on her head.

Betty Jean's eyes grew large. "You joshin' me?"

"Naw, Betty. Look at this mess," Susie said as she pulled the scarf away.

"Oh, Lawd," Betty Jean gasped. "What happen'd to all yo' pretty, curly hair?" she exclaimed, as she gazed at short, dry, dull hair with bald spots here and there as large as silver dollars. "Yo' head looks like a polka-dot dress with nappy hair on it."

Susie quickly replaced the scarf then looked down at the ground.

"Who did it, Susie?" Betty Jean asked.

"It don't mattah, Betty. It's over. I jest want my hair to grow back. I'm usin' some brown stuff Mama mix'd up for me, and it seems to be helpin.'"

"Oh, naaaaw. Now I 'member. At the church thang we had. The person who...Oooh, Susie, I'm sorry. Why didn't you tell me? I woulda went aftah her and stump'd her butt into the ground."

"You woulda, but that's you. And anyhow, she's gon'. Left school the next week. Let's git goin'.'"

Seeing that Susie didn't want to discuss the issue any longer, she dropped it.

Then Betty Jean said in an uplifting voice, "Theodore's gon' to be glad to finally meet you aftah all that writin' y'all did while he was down in the mines. He's a changed man. Always grinnin' like some fool with no sense."

Susie tugged her arm, "Betty, I don't thank I can go with you today." She said and kept walking.

"Why on earth, not?" Betty Jean asked as she ran to keep up with Susie.

"I don't want to meet yo' brother like this," she said, pointing to her head. "If this thang came off my head, I would go straight through the ground and nevah come out again."

"Alright then. But when you change yo' mind, brang Blanche Juanita since y'all the ones been writin' him the love letters."

Susie hit playfully at her. "They ain't no love letters, jest friendship. I don't love no boys but my brothers."

"Try tellin' my brother that. I don't know how y'all got into doin' it in the first place."

"Blanche Juanita and me saw some posters on the trees months back 'bout writin' to single pen-pals down in the coal mines. She got 'xcited and want'd me to write with her, so I did. Yo' brother start'd writin' to me and that's that."

"Well, I guess it is," Betty Jean smiled and winked at Susie.

Susie didn't make an attempt to meet Theodore again, and Betty Jean didn't try to encourage her. Susie was grateful, and set her mind on growing her hair back and finishing school.

Although Susie realized she should have been focusing on her Gift, she chose to push it further away. Not mindful of all the warnings her mother had spoken of, or all the other signs.

8

"Baby gal, we's so proud of you," Taylor gushed with pride and affection, hugging Susie tightly.

"Thank you, Daddy," she patted her new hair style, delighted her hair had grown back in time for her graduation, even though it wasn't as curly as it had been.

Susie turned to her mother who had told her at least five times how proud she was of her. Susie said, "Mama, I cain't thank y'all enuf for standin' b'hind me and lettin' me finish school."

Rubye Mae smiled broadly. Her eyes turned into quarter moons as she beamed at her daughter. Susie had just finished the highest education level of anyone in her family, the eleventh grade, which meant she could teach school.

A mischievous glint appeared in her mother's eyes. "I know you and Ella Mae plott'd to git you away." She smiled and squeezed Susie's hands. "Yo' daddy and me figured you want'd it so bad, we couldn' take that away from you. I always want'd to go on to school, and so did yo' daddy. But 'cause we had to work in the fields, much like some of yo' brothers and sistahs, we lost the chance and the desire for learnin'."

"Yo' Mama's right, chile. I always thought I could be a pilot 'til

I was eight years ole. Then one day my daddy sit me down and 'xplain'd to me that color'd boys couldn' be that, no mattah how much education I got. I was still the wrong color.

"I had to quit school in the six grade. But I still had it in me that I could go back and one day be that pilot.

'Course I found out as I got oler what my daddy meant, and the kind of world we was born in, and that it weren't gon' change no time soon. So when the othah chil'ren didn't want to go on, we didn't make them.

"But you did. Now you got the chance to do bettah, no field hand for you. And we's proud of you, Susie. Real proud."

She hadn't heard her father talk so lengthy since the day they had walked in the woods when he talked to her about her losing her mind. "Well, I'm grateful to both of y'all for everythang. I'm lucky to have y'all for my parents," Susie said, then hugged them affectionately.

Hours later, alone in her room, Susie lay across the bed listening to the sounds of the house, enjoying the late hour. She smiled as she thought of Theodore. She had been pleasantly surprised when Betty Jean had introduced her to Theodore. She had noticed him earlier, at the church where the ceremony was held, but she didn't know who he was. After introducing them, Betty Jean departed, leaving her embarrassed and speechless.

But, he had put her at ease with his gentle smile and beautiful, dark eyes. Although he was years older than she, it didn't seem to matter. He was good looking and a dashing dresser. She liked the way he talked. She wanted to see more of him, she decided.

She knew her mother would probably object because of his age, but her daddy would allow them to court because he wasn't as strict and trusted her decisions.

In any case, it didn't matter. Even though she was only seventeen, she was finished with school and, therefore, considered grown, she decided. Her mother didn't need to know right now.

Susie wondered what it would feel like to be kissed by him,

and blushed, covering her face with her hands. Then she giggled. The thought of having a boyfriend excited her, yet frightened her as well.

Two weeks later, Susie, Blanche, and Augustus decided to cross the forbidden riverbank. Susie had second thoughts and almost turned around several times, but in the end, decided it couldn't harm anyone.

The bank was originally a huge hill whose bottom had been tunneled out by nature over the years, leaving a big enough area for a wide stream to flow under. The bank separated the single coal miners from most families living in the surrounding rural areas. It was considered taboo and forbidden by Rubye Mae and other mothers with young girls to cross the riverbank.

"I changed my mind. Y'all go on without me," Susie suddenly blurted out.

"You ain't gon' do that, Susie. You promised you would go," Blanche whispered as if someone was listening.

"Aaahhhh, come on, Sis. Thaih ain't nothin' to be 'fraid of while I'm here."

"I don't thank...I don't know...I jest got this funny feelin'."

"Susie, please don't talk like that," Augustus pleaded, looking at Blanche Juanita.

"Why you say that, Susie? You sound funny, like them crazy folks who talk 'bout snakes and thangs," Blanche Juanita said, frowning.

Susie and Augustus looked at each other. Her family and close friends knew she felt things others didn't. But she hadn't told her close friends because she didn't want to explain and have them think she wasn't normal.

"Naw, she's alright," Augustus offered. "Sometimes she says thangs like that jest to tease me." He took Susie's hand and squeezed it, assuring her everything would be fine.

"Well, let's hurry up then," Susie said and started to walk fast.

Five minutes later, they stood outside, at the foot of the steps of Theodore's door, while Augustus went inside to let him know they were there.

Susie and Blanche Juanita looked at each. The palms of Susie's hands were suddenly wet. She closed her eyes and breathed slowly, trying to calm herself. She reached into her dress pocket, pulled out her gloves and smoothed them onto her wet hands.

Blanche Juanita, quite calm, winked at her.

Augustus returned with Theodore who stopped close to Susie. He smiled at her, causing a tremble to shoot down her spine.

"This here is my sistah, Susie," Augustus said.

"We met at her graduation party," Theodore said to Augustus, his eyes still on Susie. "So good to see you again, Susie," he said in his clear baritone voice. Then he turned away while Augustus introduced him to Blanche Juanita.

"Pleased, Miss Blanche," he bowed and shook her hand, then turned back to Susie.

"So you already met Susie," Blanche Juanita said, disappointment filling her voice.

Susie nodded her head and looked down at the ground for a moment. *Git control of yo' self, Susie. He ain't gon' bite you.* She looked into his handsome face, finding him even better looking in the May sunshine.

"She kinda shy 'round boys. She ain't nevah court'd befoe," Augustus said.

"Augustus," Susie said, surprised. "I can talk for myself. You left befoe he got thaih, Blanche."

"I want to thank both of you for writin' to me. It help'd my time go faster down thaih."

"The pleasure was mine, I'm sho," Blanche said, her eyes fluttering like a baby bird's wings when it's learning to fly, causing her to look comical.

Theodore laughed and offered them a seat on the porch and some lemonade.

"Lemonade would be jest fine," Augustus said. "I'll come with you."

"Why you gots to act like some hen aftah the rooster?" Susie asked Blanche Juanita when they were alone.

"Susie, you know you want'd to talk to him, but you jest don't know what to say. It'll all come natural for you aftah awhile."

"Well, I sho don't aim to be fallin' all over myself."

"That's you. He's got everythang a man should have and more. Hummmmmm," Blanche Juanita chanted, licking her lips and rolling her eyes.

"You actin' like a hussy, girl. You ought to be shamed," Susie said, frowning.

"It jest might do you good to act that way sometimes, Susie. You gots to learn to let life take you away from this hard life sometimes and have some fun," Blanche Juanita winked.

"You talk like a woman who's been 'round for years and did it all. You ain't but a year or two oler then me."

"But, wiser 'bout boys, Susie. Here they come. Treat him good, Susie, he taken to you."

9

That fall, Susie was hired as an elementary school teacher at a newly built school for colored children in Bessemer, Alabama.

Meanwhile, Susie and Theodore's relationship moved very swiftly. For the first time in her life she realized what it meant and felt like to be admired by a fancy young man and to admire one in return.

Now, she understood how her sister had felt when she said she wanted to get married. She also understood the smiles that used to pass between her sister and Otis Lee.

One day, Ella Mae looked at her and teased, "Gal, you sho done changed. Look at you, all smiles and struttin' 'round like some proud queen and all. You bettah watch yo'self or Mama gon' want to know what's goin' on with you."

Susie's face fell. "You ain't tole her nothin', Ella Mae?"

"Naw. But she soon gon' find out."

"Well, I'll be eighteen soon, I'll tell her and Daddy then.

"You won't see eighteen 'til next year. You gots the rest of this year to hide from them."

"I don't won't to talk 'bout it, Ella Mae. Next month I'm goin' to be teachin' and makin' my own money. So in a way, I'm already grown."

"Well, you might feel that way, but if Mama 'cides you need a 'minder, you jest anothah chile to her."

Susie stuck her tongue out and said, "I'm goin' outside and wait for Theodore. We're goin' for a drive to Birmingham and take in a movie. Bye."

Susie sat on the back porch, picking greens and thinking of Theodore. He had taken her places she never knew existed and made her realize there was another life besides working and working and going to church.

She loved watching him play baseball and sitting in the juke joint listening to his four piece band. When he blew his saxophone, she felt all warm and cuddly inside, almost the way she felt when he kissed her. *Shoot, I might jest marry him one day,* she thought.

Apprehension suddenly filled her as she thought of her parents. She wanted so badly to tell them about him, but feared her mother would resist him because he was older than she or say he wasn't good enough because he lived across the riverbank. But she had no doubt her daddy would like him just because she did.

She decided it was time to stop deceiving her parents. Even though she would be grown soon, if they didn't accept him, she would stop seeing him until she turned eighteen. But she hoped it wouldn't come to that. "I'll jest have to face them and tell them. First thang tomorrow," she whispered to the pump as the water gushed into the pot.

Something was dreadfully wrong; she could feel it. She had risen early, finished her chores. Now she was on her knees, peeking out the front room window, gazing at the still morning, waiting.

Susie nibbled at her fingernails, trying not to think of the feeling of doom. She closed her eyes to suppress the haunting feelings and tried to focus on pleasant times. She smiled as she thought about her young niece, Mosie, and sat down on the sofa.

The family had been ecstatic when Ella Mae had given birth to a pretty, little girl. She had been a good baby and was now a chatty toddler who climbed on everything and loved following Susie around, and sitting in her lap while she told her stories.

She heard a sound and turned back to the window.

Something was coming toward the house at an alarmingly fast pace. She squinted her eyes, then realized it was her parents wagon.

Naw! Something screamed inside her. Susie gripped the back of the sofa and leaned closer to the window, her heart racing as the wagon came closer. Not realizing it, she jumped from the sofa and ran toward the front door, but before she reached it, Rubye Mae was banging it hard.

She took one look at her mother and enfolded her in her arms. She knew exactly what had happened to her father. "Ooooh, Mama. Mama, please tell me it ain't true! Please, Mama," she begged as she held onto her mother.

Rivers of tears flowed down Rubye Mae's cheeks as she stared at Susie. She shook her head and clenched her trembling mouth, closed her red eyes then looked at Susie again.

The last hope died with that look. "Mama!" Susie yelled. "Mama, Naw!"

"I know baby. I know. It still don't seem like it happen'd, but it did cause he ain't here with me, talkin' to me. Susie, yo' po' daddy done left me this time for gooood!"

Rubye Mae's voice trembled with pain and grief.

They sat sobbing in each other's arms until Ella Mae and Otis Lee ran into the room. Before they could speak, Susie looked at her sister, "He's gon', Ella Mae. Daddy's left us for good this time. He's dead," She moaned in a dull voice.

"Oh, Lawd,...Naaaaaaaw," she yelled and fainted in her husbands arms.

Mosie bounced into the room, observed her family's anguish, and started crying; then she ran to Susie and climbed into her lap for comfort.

"You know, Gawd giveth and He taketh it away," the preacher said, as he looked out at the grieving family and friends of Taylor Lee Morton the week following his passing.

All their faces were pained. They sat stiffly, their quivering lips indicating their sorrow.

The preacher was concerned about his dear friend, Rubye Mae, who was devastated. He actually feared for her life.

Rubye Mae had loved Taylor more than life itself. He had been her breath, her world. Each time he had seen her, she always fussed about Taylor doing too much, eating the wrong kind of food, or drinking with his friends, but all of it had been out of love, a love that had left her alone in this world, languishing for him each and every day.

He understood her pain and prayed that with time, she would bear the terrible loss and not follow Taylor. He hoped that Susie would be supportive during this dreadful period because she was the one her parents depended on the most even though they had never said so in words. Their actions had made it apparent.

The preacher diverted his attention to Susie, who sat fifth, as she had been born to Taylor. He saw disturbing emotions in her black-as-night eyes that made him flinch. Anger, coldness, withdrawal, fear: the scene made him shake inwardly and clinch several pages in his Bible.

"But, we as mere mortals should nevah question Him or His doin's," he continued. "He loves all us equally, and he promised us a home with Him if we take up the cross and follow Him. And our good brother Taylor did jest that, so I know he's up thaih right now, sittin' next to our Lawd and Savior, Jesus Christ. Yes, he is, brothers, sistahs, family, and dear friends."

Susie looked coldly at him, dismissing his words of comfort. Nothing he or anyone said would bring her father back or relieve her pain. God had taken her beloved father from her. She would never hear his voice or laughter nor feel his strong, comforting arms again.

Rev. Oxley saw Susie's eyes go blank and knew he had lost her. "Gawd want us to look to Him for comfort even though the

Good Book says we should rejoice when our loved ones leave this earth for a bettah place. He truly understan's our pain. He tried to catch and hold Susie's attention.

"Now, I know all y'all here is grievin' for Brother Taylor, and so am I. He was a good man, a good husband and father and a friend to anybody that had time for him. He was so kindheart'd, he didn't even like to go huntin'.

"But the Lawd done seen fit to call him home, and we got to bear with it 'til all the pain is lighter in our hearts and souls.

"All of us here are friends and Christians, and I know we all gone do the right thang for the Morton family. Be thaih for them when they need us.

"Death is hard on us, but it's somethin' all of us have to live with. So, brothers and sistahs, grieve and let nature take its course..."

Susie was relieved when he finally finished and grateful when they closed the casket. For a brief moment she wanted to yank her father out and make him stop pulling this horrible joke on them. She needed desperately to get away from everyone...her brothers and sisters, the wailing, everything. At the burial, she refrained from looking at her father being lowered into the cold earth.

When they arrived at her parents', Susie fought the urge to run from the place that had snatched her beloved father away. Instead, she put on a brave face and helped her mother into bed. Then she sat with her for hours before she fled to her sister's house.

The following months were desolate and stormy for Susie. She resigned from her teaching job and closed the world out. She became despondent and angry, remaining in her room for weeks, only coming out to make the necessary visits to see her mother. She ate only when coaxed or pushed by Ella Mae, who was also taking their father's passing hard, but was better equipped to handle her loss and pain.

Theodore, after a respectful period, dropped in to see Susie. Ella Mae, on her behalf, gave Theodore the news that Susie was not well and refused to see him. He was not deterred and returned many times before he finally stopped. Susie didn't care. She didn't care about anything.

Rubye Mae was in shock for months. All her children surrounded her; they cooked, washed, and cleaned the house, bought her pretty things, made dollies and quilts for her, everything they thought possible to help her. But she just shook her head and turned it toward the window and stared out for hours with no conversation.

When her friends saw that Rubye Mae wasn't going to talk, they came and just sat with her and kissed her when they left, many understanding her circumstances.

Two months later, Rubye Mae opened her mouth and screamed so loudly she could be heard miles down the road. Everyone that heard her was relieved because they knew she would survive.

But Susie was still consumed with bitterness, and remorse. *If only she hadn't talked to her father about her problems, or been there with him when he fell ill, maybe, she could have saved him.* The words kept rolling around in her head until she wanted to scream, but she didn't have the strength. So her days passed without her eating or attending to her hygiene. She only ate if Ella Mae threatened to have her sent to the crazy house. And the only person she would speak to was her niece. But Ella Mae didn't let Mosie stay near her too long.

One day Theodore stopped by and demanded that Susie see him or he would stay until she did. He hadn't seen her in four months, since her father's funeral. When she finally stood before him, he hoped the shock at seeing her didn't register on his face. She was a mere skeleton of herself, eyes protruding from her gaunt face with dark circles surrounding them. At first he wanted to run, then cry, and finally, just take her in his arms and hold her until all the pain and anguish left her. But he could do nothing. Instead, he gently but firmly insisted that he take her for a ride.

This became a habit for the next month: long rides in the country, taking in the fresh air, watching other people as they went about their daily lives.

Today he traveled a different route, towards Birmingham. Susie hadn't spoken since he picked her up. Nor had she said ten words since he had been taking her on the rides. He had spoken mostly when he felt the silence growing so thick, it threatened to consume both of them. Now he talked about Blanche Juanita and Robert Lewis, hoping to see a sparkle in her eyes again. When she did not respond he realized he was wasting his breath, he hushed.

He drove in silence for an hour before she beseeched quietly, "Why did he take my father from me? Why?" She started to wail loudly. Finally, some relief.

Theodore stopped the car and held her until she finished sobbing, then advised, "Susie you know Gawd does thangs that cain't be question'd. You know He loved yo' father and He loves you. It's alright to be mad, hurt and all them othah thangs, but don't blame Gawd. You know the teachin's of the Bible. It's alright to be mad, even at Gawd, for a spell. I know you hurtin', but it's also time you thank 'bout yo' po' Mama and what she goin' through too. She's suffer'd a great loss, and she still needs you.

"Susie, I know you ain't seen her in a long spell. At a time like this a mother wants all her chil'ren 'round her. Y'all all need each othah."

She realized that what Theodore was saying was so true. "I jest cain't go home right now, Theodore. Daddy's memories is still thaih, and I look for him every time I go. Please take me back home."

After the outburst in Theodore's car, Susie finally accepted the death of her father and was able to rationalize just how much her mother and siblings needed her, and each other.

Although Susie didn't feel equipped enough to return to work, she made the daily fifteen-mile trip to visit her mother and noticed the difference it seemed to make. Finally, she and her favorite brother, Augustus, were able to sit and visit.

Understanding and realizing the bitterness within her, Augustus suggested, "Susie, you gots to stop mopin' 'round and start livin' again. You know Daddy would want you to. He loved us and wouldn' want us cryin' for him everyday. Jest 'member, he's up thaih watchin' us, and he won't be happy if we down here all sad and mad cause he's in a bettah place then we is."

"I jest don't want him to be gon'. He was too young to..."

"To die. "I know that, but it won't brang him back. Daddy would want you to go on and teach and court, and git mar-red and have chil'ren. That would make him happy."

Susie smiled for the first time in more than six months. "He would want that, wouldn' he? He was such a good daddy. I loved takin' walks and goin' fishin' with him. I sho miss him."

"I know. Me, too, and the rest of the family miss him something awful, but we need to help git Mama through this."

"You right. I only been thankin' 'bout myself 'stead of her these last months." She picked up a fan and waved it in the air. "It's got to be much harder, much harder for Mama. Maybe I should move back with her for a while.

"Naw, Susie. You prob'ly bettah off where you is. Mama's got plenty chil'ren at home to keep her company. She jest need some of yo' backbone and love," Augustus advised.

10

Susie's father had been gone for a year before she was able to resume her position as a teacher and her relationship with Theodore. Yet something had changed about her. Before her father's death, she was the quiet, shy person who dressed in good taste and usually wore her hair in a bun or French roll. Now she seemed set on doing the things she knew weren't a part of her character.

When she suggested they go out almost every night for almost two weeks straight, Theodore only shrugged his shoulders and let her have her way. He hoped she would become the old Susie.

She was grateful for his patience and felt he really cared for her when he didn't question her. She realized how much she had missed him and longed to be as close to him as possible. When she looked in the mirror, she didn't see a different person, and she certainly didn't feel unusual, except having a hole in her heart, the spot where her father used to be.

Tonight, dressing for their date, she took pains with her long, reddish brown hair, weaving it in a new style, putting on snugger clothes and dabbing on sweet smelling perfume that she knew

Theodore loved. These actions were out of character for Susie, yet she never gave them a second thought.

They sat in his front room, holding hands. Theodore gazed into her eyes and let go of her hand. "Susie, I love you. I want'd to tell you for a long time."

"I...I nevah thought you felt that way," she said, thrilled at his confession.

"Then I must be bad about showin' my feelin's. You are a beautiful, endearin' and intelligent young woman. Any man would fight to have you as his own."

Susie blushed and turned away for a moment. *He sho know how to talk pretty,* she thought. "I like you too." She smiled, showing beautiful long, white teeth.

"Like me is all?" he teased.

"Moe then that." She couldn't bring herself to tell him how much she loved him. She felt suddenly dirty, loose.

"I would do anythang for you, anythang," he confessed before taking her in his arms and kissing her soft mouth, causing her to feel so much adoration she wanted to burst.

When Theodore let go of her, he was panting. "I thank I bettah take you home," he stood and pulled her to her feet.

"Yeah, I guess you bettah," she agreed, breathless. She felt weak and hot between her legs. It scared her, but it felt good.

At the door, she turned and looked into his gentle, lustful eyes and asked quietly, "Can I jest stay awhile longer? It feels so good here." She looked at the shadows playing on the walls from the reflections of the kerosene lamp causing the room to be cozy.

Theodore hesitated before saying, "I don't thank that's a good idea," then seeing the sadness appear in her eyes, decided against his better judgment and agreed. "Alright then, if you're sho. Let me git some moe wood on the fire."

When the flames were burning higher, he resumed his place next to Susie. She moved closer to him. He placed his arms around her shoulder. She smiled and laid her head on his shoulder and gazed at the red-orange fire.

"It feels so good here. I could stay forever." She snuggled closer, not realizing how much she was arousing him.

"I've miss'd you so much Susie," he whispered hoarsely, moving slightly away.

"I miss'd you too," she confessed boldly, realizing just how much and moved boldly into his lap.

Though surprised, he said nothing. She felt so good. "You know I want'd to ax you to marry me, but I plan'd to ax yo' father first...," his voice trailed off...Susie leaned into him, causing him to lose his concentration.

"I thank he woulda' liked you," she said and smiled.

"As much as you do?" he teased.

"Naw," Susie asserted and kissed his cheek.

Theodore longed to take her and make love to her right there. He held his hands from her as she continued. "You know Mama don't even know 'bout us. I have to tell her."

"Yeah." He gently removed her from his lap and took her hands in his. "I agree since I plan on mar-ryin' you."

"You serious 'bout gettin' mar-red?" she asked, suddenly wanting it more than anything in the world, feeling warm and mushy inside.

"I am. As soon as we talk to yo' mother, we'll set the date. Stay here a minute. I have to git somethin'," he said and left the room.

While he was gone, she closed her eyes and briefly thought of them naked. Her heart suddenly raced. Her eyes flew open, guilt and shame evident on her face. She didn't know why she suddenly had such a wanton thought. She had never seen or ever desired to see a man naked.

When Theodore returned, Susie's face matched the blazing fire.

"Are you alright?" he asked, sitting next to her.

"Yeah. I'm fine," she whispered.

"You sho, Susie?" he questioned, concerned.

"I'm jest fine," she assured him and smiled.

"Close yo' eyes and hold out yo' hand."

"Why?"

"It's a surprise."

She held out her hand, and he slipped a ring on her finger. Her eyes flew open! She stared at the ring. "Oooh my, this is jest beautiful! How did you...when did you git this?"

She glowed at him before looking again at the dazzling ring.

Its cluster of diamonds, shaped like a rose, set on a wide gold band, fit her slim finger perfectly.

Theodore touched her face to regain her attention and answered her question. "In Montgomery, a few months ago. I was hopin' you would say yeah."

"It's so pretty, Theodore...but I cain't wear it 'til we talk to Mama. You do understan'...?"

"'Course I understan', Susie. But I want'd to let you know how serious I am 'bout us. I truly love you and want you to be my wife and friend forever."

Happy tears filled her eyes. "I'll wear it 'til I leave," she whispered, moving toward him.

He met her halfway. "Come here, baby."

She melted into him as he kissed her eyes, lips, mouth. She held him close to her until that funny feeling washed over her, making her feel weak all over, then that craving, moving downward to her private area, again. Her mind warned her to move away, but her body wouldn't obey.

Theodore, aware of their passion rising, attempted to move from her, but she held him tighter.

All her mother's warnings and teachings fled as her body took total control of her mind. She allowed him to caress her, to touch her breast, and her body, and she yearned for more.

Theodore picked up her trembling body and carried her into his bedroom and gently laid her on the high bed.

He fell to his knees and tugged at her dress, touching her breasts, caressing her soft, hot body, losing himself in her sweetness. Somewhere in the distance of her mind she heard a voice say NO, but she ignored it as his touch sent fire through her, making her almost swoon.

"Susie, I, we.... Are you sho...I don't..." he moaned, caught up in passion.

It was storming inside and out. The clouds had turned so black, the only thing one could see, if brave enough to peek out their windows, was the lightning streaks, drawing erratic patterns across them.

Inside, the storm vaulting from Susie was just as frightening as she sat weeping hysterically over the loss of her virginity, the awful mistake she had made. She felt as if she had betrayed herself, her mother, and her dead father. Her parents would never forgive her for being so weak, for sinning. She felt dirty, used and ashamed. She was mad as hell at herself and Theodore for not stopping her.

She finally paused long enough to yell, "Why did you let me do this?" You know how I feel 'bout this...befoe mar-rage," she moaned and swung at him.

He caught her hand and held it. "Susie, I ax'd. I thought you want'd to. Please, baby. You know I wouldn' intentionally hurt you," he pleaded and tried to pull her close to him.

She drew back. "Don't you touch me," she hissed, her eyes blazing hot coals. "You ruin'd my life." Susie knew she was as much to blame as he was, but she couldn't afford to accept equal responsibility because she had failed herself and her family's moral standards. If she acknowledged her awful mistake, it would almost kill her.

"Yo' life's not ruin'd. I still want to marry you. We can git mar-red as soon as we take blood tests. I love you, Susie."

"Take me home," she demanded, looking for her clothes.

"I cain't. It's stormin' somethin' awful out thaih. We have to wait it out and hope the roads don't wash away. Come on and let me show you," he offered, not knowing what else to say.

Susie slapped him so hard, he reeled backwards, almost falling against an elk's head hanging on the wall. "I tole you, take me home, now!" she demanded. "I don't give a damns hell 'bout no storm."

He touched his wounded face and glanced at her in disbelief.

"I tole you I cain't go out thaih in this weather. We could drown or get wash'd away in a flash flood. He paused and massaged his stinging face.

"Susie, please try and understan' that I would nevah force myself on you or take advantage of you. I wouldn' touch you unless you gave me the word."

"Well, you shoulda know'd I didn't mean it. Now I won't be able to face my Mama and them 'cause of you." She yanked her dress from the bed and fled from the room.

Theodore gave her time to get dressed before he followed her into the living room. Without a word, she slipped through the front door and he behind her.

When Susie arrived at Ella Mae's she was surprised and frightened to see her mother and almost choked on her saliva when Rubye Mae spoke to her.

Briefly, she longed to run to her, fall into her lap, and tell her everything, but shame kept her away. She had sinned, committed one of the worst sins in the Bible. She knew the sin was written all over her guilty face. She lowered her eyes as her mother gazed intently at her.

"Where you been, Susie? It's so late we was gettin' scared somethin' had happen'd to you. Is you sick, chile?" Rubye Mae asked. Susie looked at Ella Mae and her mother. "I been drivin' 'round with a friend."

"You mean Theodore Moore?"

Susie's body became still as a board. "Yes, Mam."

"I know all 'bout him, Susie. I did befoe yo' daddy left this world, but I didn't want to come to you. I was waitin' for you to tell me. You don't have to sneak," she said softly, noticing the beautiful engagement ring on Susie's finger.

"I wasn't tryin' to sneak, Mama. And I was goin' to tell you, but I nevah got the chance. We jest start'd to see each othah again," she lied. Then remembering that she had been crying, she lowered her face again. But Rubye Mae had already surmised the situation.

"Where did y'all go when the storm came up?"

"To his sistah's house," she lied again. "She lives ten

miles from here." Worse than her shame, she was lying to her mother.

"His sistah?"

"Mama, I have a real bad headache. Will y'all 'xcuse me? I need to take a hot bath and lay down."

"Yeah, chile. Go on. We can talk latah."

Susie left, glad to escape her mother's wondering eye. She knew that if she remained in the room much longer, she would give herself away.

After scrubbing her skin almost raw and discarding the clothes she had worn in a bag to be burned, she crawled into bed, placing her hand under her chin. That's when she realized she still had the ring on. She pulled it off and threw it hard against the wall.

Rubye Mae knocked at her door and sat on Susie's bed. "I know you tir'd and sleepy, so I won't tarry. How serious is you 'bout this Theodore?"

"I ain't gon' see him no moe, Mama." Susie almost whispered.

"Y'all have a fight?"

"Nome."

Rubye Mae noticed that the ring was no longer on Susie's finger. "Baby, you ought to know you can talk to me if you need to. I'm here for you. I won't judge you."

"I know you is, Mama. Thank you." She fought hard to keep the rising tears back.

"I need to ax you this; then I'll leave. Them dreams and thangs. You ain't been havin' them for a spell, is you?"

Susie cringed inside, not wanting to talk about the Gift. No, Mam. I ain't had them for a long time now," she said, thinking how bad her mother's timing was.

"That's mighty strange that they would up and stop like that." A worried look appeared on her face. "You been runnin' from them, ain't you, chile?"

Susie didn't answer her mother right away, fighting the urge to scream and tell her she had more important things on her mind. Her life was ruined. Her stupid Gift had done her nothing but harm. Instead, she said in her calmest voice, "They jest stop comin, Mama."

"Jest like that!" Rubye Mae said, throwing her hands over her head and snapping her fingers. "Don't you thank it's been long enuf, Susie? You jest cain't up and 'cide you don't want somethin' that Gawd done seen fit to give to you.

"Gal, Gawd ain't nothin' to play with, so if you thank them dreams and voices is gon' to stay, then you a fool; And I ain't raised none of them, not to my knowin'.'"

Susie tried to answer her, but words failed her. She knew that if she spoke, she would probably say something she would be sorry for later. She closed her eyes and hid her face in her hands. She longed to have her mother hold her in her arms and comfort her as she had when she was a child.

But this Gift stuff was making her angry. She figured she had lost her only gift, her virginity. Her stomach tugged and twisted into knots, causing her to moan softly.

Rubye Mae stood next to her bed and touched her shoulder. "Is you sick, Susie?"

She started to wail as if she was a baby. Her body shaking like a discarded, lonely leaf in the wind.

Rubye Mae became frightened and held her close. "Chile, whatever it is, you can tell yo' Mama. I don't want to see you hurtin' like this. Is it Theodore?"

His name only caused Susie to cry harder. Rubye Mae decided to let her questions rest.

Finally, Susie asked Rubye Mae to leave her alone. Then she curled into a knot and cried until she fell into an exhausted slumber.

In subsequent weeks Susie felt as if she had just left the earth and stepped in the fiery floor of hell. Each day, Theodore knocked at Ella Mae's door, pleading to see her, and each time he was sent away. Susie hated him and herself for what had happened to her, and each passing day, her guilt grew more intense. She felt betrayed by him, rationalizing that she had depended on him to protect her, but he had tainted her instead. And who wanted damaged fruit? No one. Not even him, she reflected in her darkened room.

"Piss on him," she spat as she fell across her bed. Her eyes filled with anguished tears as she saw her future go up in flames.

When her next period failed to appear, she screamed, tormented. She became ill. Worse, she hadn't the courage to face her family.

One day, Rubye Mae stopped by and sat at her bedside. "Susie, you look like a ghost. I can almost see yo' bones through yo' face, you done fell off so much. If you don't git bettah soon, I'm gon' have to send Doc Hammond out here to see 'bout you."

"Mama, please don't do that. I jest have a bad cold.

I'll be bettah soon."

"Yeah. You been under the weather near two months, since that storm. You ain't hidin' nothin' from me, is you?"

"Mama, can we talk latah? I feel drowsy," she said and closed her eyes.

"Yeah, sho chile. I'll let you git some sleep," Rubye Mae slipped from the room. But Susie didn't sleep. She lay awake worrying. What was she going to do if she were pregnant?

How was she going to make it in the world with a bastard child? How could she survive the terrible shame she would bring on her family? She was glad at that moment her father wasn't alive to see how she had turned out. Then she cried because she had wished her father dead.

The next morning, Rubye Mae was waiting when Susie stepped into the kitchen. "Well, it sho good to see you out of bed, but I cain't say you look any bettah. You been cryin', chile?

"Mornin' Mama, Ella Mae," Susie said with a forced smile.

"No, Mam. I jest got some soap in my eyes. That stuff can burn somthin' awful."

"Mornin' Susie. Here, eat these biscuits, bacon, and eggs. They oughta do you some good," Ella Mae said, placing a full plate in front of her.

"Thank you." Susie looked at the plate and pushed the acid

down her throat. She suddenly felt as if her insides were coming out. It was then that she knew she was pregnant.

She forced some food down and glanced at her mother who was eyeing her closely. She dared her stomach to betray her.

"I'm gon' see how you feel befoe I leave here today and if you ain't doin' bettah, I'm sendin' for the doctor. I don't care how you carry on," Rubye Mae promised.

"I'm fine, Mama. I jest need to eat somethin'," Susie insisted.

"It's been a year now since you work'd. You plan on goin' back soon?"

Not with my stomach growin' everyday. Naw, my days of teachin' seems to be over. What she said was," No, Mam. I cain't right now. They don't have no openin'."

"Yo' brothers and sistahs ax'd aftah you. They been worrin', 'specially, Augustus. You his favorite sistah," Rubye Mae said, still gazing anxiously at Susie.

Susie quickly lowered her head and feigned a cough to cover her discomfort. "I'll stop by and see all of them soon, Mama." Then she blurted, "I quit Theodore."

Rubye Mae and Ella Mae stared at her for moment. "He jest ain't right for me," she said lamely.

"But I thought you said he was the nicest person, next to Daddy, you ever knowed, Susie," Ella Mae said.

"I don't want to talk 'bout it no moe," Susie said, raising her voice. Rubye Mae raised her eyebrows at Susie's tone of voice, then said, "It's alright, we understan', Susie."

But she knew they didn't understand anything. She didn't understand anything anymore. All she knew was her life had once again been turned upside down and she didn't know what she was going to do.

Later that night, Susie crept from her bed, packed a few belongings into her sister's hat box and a small suitcase, then stole way on foot, just before dawn broadened the horizon. She had decided to leave everyone she loved, to spare her family shame.

11

"You!" she spat. "You the one know what's goin' on here. Tell me where my chile is and what you done to her!" Rubye Mae demanded of Theodore.

He flinched and moved away from her, fearing she would strike him. "I'm sorry, Miss Rubye Mae, I don't know what you talkin' 'bout. I ain't seen Susie in nearly three months."

"My gal done up and left like a thief in the night, and you tell me you don't know why. Boy, I know you gots somethin' to do with it jest as sho as my name is what it is. She didn't jest up and go like that. I warned my chile 'bout this damn bank on Vestavia Hills. Y'all men don't have no morals."

Before he could respond, she reached up and grabbed his shirt collar. "Tell me where she is and what you done to her, or you'll be sorry. I'll have the law aftah you so fast you won't know who you is, boy," she threatened.

"Miss Rubye Mae...I don't know where she is. I didn't know she had left town."

"And I don't see why not, bein' y'all was together and was gon' git mar-red." She turned to Ella Mae and pointed her finger at her. "And you. I know you gots to know moe then you lettin' on."

Ella Mae's body squeezed into a long knot. "Mama, all I know is Susie said they broke up, like she tole us. I weren' 'spose to say nothin' to nobody 'bout her mar-ryin'." Rubye Mae gave her a I'll-whup-yo'-butt look. "I thought she was gon' tell you, Mama. She said she was." Ella Mae lowered her head.

"This is the first time you kept yo' mouth shut tighter then a baby can hold onto a tit, and it's the wrong time, gal."

She turned back to Theodore. "So you got her pregnant; did-n't you?"

Startled by her accusation, he stumbled backwards, catching his shirt sleeve on the door hinge while Rubye Mae continued to grasp his collar. He couldn't believe Susie would become preg-nant and take off without telling him.

"Answer me, man! If you can call yo'self one. Don't stand thaih with that stupid look on yo' face. That's the only reason my baby would leave here. 'Cause you done disgraced her and her family." She tightened her grip on his collar, causing him to gasp for breath. Then she yanked her hands from him as if he had a contagious disease.

"You low down, no good scoundrel. You tell me it ain't the truth," she spat venom at his feet.

Ella Mae rushed over to her. "Mama, you upsettin' yo'self, and he ain't doin' no talkin'. Can we jest try and find Susie?" she pleaded.

Ignoring Ella Mae, her eyes blazing like black, hot coals. "I don't care if you nevah talk again, I know you got my chile preg-nant, and I won't forgive you for it," she said before turning from him and slamming the door so hard behind her that the windows shook in their hinges.

When Susie had stolen away into the night, she had walked aim-lessly for miles, not knowing where to go. It was out of despera-tion that she decided to go to her mother's sister's home.

She boarded a Greyhound bus and rode for hours, then walked several miles before she arrived tired, ragged, and hun-gry at her Aunt Anna's.

After questioning her, Anna took her in. Susie had been relieved because she knew that her mother wouldn't think to look for her there because the two sisters didn't get along very well and seldom saw each other.

"Susie, Susie," Rubye Mae cried two days later as she pushed her way into her sister's house. "Honey, I'm so glad to see you," she said, grabbing and holding Susie tightly.

"Why did you run off like that, baby? You had me worr'd to death." She patted Susie's back.

"How did you know I was here, Mama?" Susie asked, trying to pull away, but Rubye Mae held fast to her hand.

"Honey, thaih ain't many places for you to run. I figured my sistah would take you in and let me know you done run away." She threw accusing eyes toward her only sister, Anna.

Anna had helped to raise Rubye Mae while their parents worked in the fields. Rubye Mae had never liked being told what to do as a child and resented it as an adult, but Anna was always there, telling her what to do, how to do it.

One day Rubye Mae finally told Anna to hush because she did not know any more than a skinny cat looking for a fat mouse in a vacant house filled with dead mice. Anna stopped speaking to her for months, but that was about all. She remained a busybody, still trying to run Rubye Mae's life.

"I don't know what y'all goin' on 'bout," Anna said in an innocent voice, staring up at Rubye Mae. "Susie ain't tole me nothin' and you come stormin' in my own house, iggin' me like I some snake you done kilt."

Ignoring her sister, Rubye Mae looked at Susie. "You ain't tole her?" Susie lowered her head, ashamed. Rubye Mae eyed Anna again.

"She only tole me she need'd to git a way for a spell," Anna defended, then threw an angry look at Susie before rushing from the room.

"We alone now; you can talk to me, Susie. Please tell me why you ran away. Is you pregnant, chile?"

"Oh, Mama. I'm so 'shamed, I don't know what to do," Susie cried and fell into her mother's arms.

"Now thaih, chile. It ain't the end of the world. I guess I knowed you was expectin' when I went to his house lookin' for you. She refused to call Theodore by his name. "I jest wish you had tole me, Susie."

"I want'd to Mama. Moe then anythang in the world, but I was too 'shamed," she sobbed, then pulled away, feeling like a thief who had gotten caught. And she had. Those stolen moments would be a reminder to her the rest of her life.

"Susie, we all do thangs we 'shamed of. But we's human bein's, and we make mistakes. I always taught you to nevah worry 'bout what folks thank of you. You ain't got to answer to them for nothin'. It's you that's importan'. We'll work out whatever thaih is to do. And you need to let the chile's father know 'bout this."

"Naw! I don't want nothin' to do with him. Nevah!" Susie's dark eyes glowed so brightly with anger Rubye Mae stepped away from her.

"Susie," she said calmly. "Don't git yo'self work'd up so, chile. It will work out. Yo' family will stick by you."

"It's jest as much my fault as it is his," she finally acknowledged, "but I don't want to have nothin' to do with him. I cain't stand the sight of him, Mama. He betray'd me when I need'd him."

"It's alright, Susie. Come, sit down, and let me git you somethin' to drank."

Susie refused to return home with her mother; instead, she agreed to leave Anna's to go and live with her uncle and aunt in Plantersville, Alabama, an isolated country town long forgotten by those who wanted a taste of the city life. Yet it was still a good place to fish and raise livestock and a family without anyone interfering with one's life.

Tom and Mattie Herd were glad to have Susie stay with them. She was like the daughter they couldn't have and had always been their favorite of all Ruybe Mae's children.

Susie knew they would never judge her. The following days dragged by like molasses pours in the winter time. Susie spent most of her duration gardening or making quilts, a tradition in her family. Her pregnancy was uneventful. She had no morning sickness and gained weight at a slow pace.

Her mother visited her as often as she could get the old horses moving up the road on the long thirty-mile jaunt. Each time she spent several days with Susie, hoping she could get her to change her mind and return home. Even though Susie dearly missed her family and close friends, she would not budge.

Sometimes, during the wee hours before morning, Susie would lie awake, remembering her friendship with Blanche Juanita, Robert Lewis, and Betty Jean. They used to be so carefree; laughing and teasing each other or simply just sitting quietly and enjoying each others company. The only thing that stopped her from seeing them was knowing they would pity her, and she couldn't bear that.

She became withdrawn, much like the little girl she used to be years ago when her father left and she sat looking out the window waiting for his return, knowing that her world would be right again, someday. But, this time she had no hope.

She sighed with relief when October eased in, watching as the green leaves turned various colors of browns, and yellowish gold. The sky changed from a clear light blue and fluffy white to shades of gray and muted blues. The pecan trees filled with sap and unripe nuts. As Susie observed the changes, she speculated about the transformation that was taking place within her, a new life, a life she would be responsible for. She wondered if she could be the baby's mother and father. And if she would be able to protect it from all the evil of the world.

On October 27, 1931, Susie bore down and gritted her teeth with the last pain before giving birth to a big, healthy baby girl whom she named after her best friend, Blanche Juanita.

The delivery had been difficult, but the midwife had been able to control the problems that arose. One look at the infant melted Susie's heart, and her hatred for Theodore disappeared. She smiled at her child, not noticing the strong resemblance she bore of her father. Holding her close, she whispered, "I love you, and I will take care of you and nevah let you git hurt by nobody."

BOOK II

STEPPING FORWARD
WITH PURPOSE

*Each step we take
is a risk.
But to never move
is certainly fear.
We must all take
the first step, for the
next might set us free.*

Carolyn V. Parnell

12

Like a foreigner in a distant land, Susie stood taking in her new surroundings, hoping this would be the place where she could commence a new existence for herself and her children. She missed them already even though she knew they were fine because they were with her mother. Soon, they would be with her, if her plans succeeded.

It was this or nothing else because her life had almost reached an impasse. She either had to continue living or give up and succumb to the earth's waiting arms. Ten long years had elapsed, and many an event had transpired, beating her spirit profoundly into the ground.

But to look at her outer appearance one would never know the inner struggles and turmoil she had endured. Each passing year had brought her closer to the realization that her disastrous life would have to improve if she were going to survive.

A year after giving birth to Blanche, she had gone home to visit her family. While there, her mother insisted she let Theodore see his child, so she allowed Rubye Mae to take Blanche to visit him. The following day she fled back to Plantersville, knowing she could never return home while her past remained there.

Then Susie met and fell in love with a man named Tommy, who lived about five miles down the road from them.

Tommy had been attending college out of town and had returned home for a while. Initially, she had been hesitant and non-trusting, but as time passed, she became fond of the handsome and intelligent young man. His love for life made her feel as if she wanted to live again.

They planned to marry and to leave the South as soon as he could find a job up North. Unfortunately, disaster had its tail ready to strike. One evening, shortly after their engagement, Susie had been attacked by a man that she later learned that Tommy knew. She also learned that he had been following her for months.

Susie's aunt informed her that the man hadn't gotten away. Tommy had found and beaten him so badly, she would never recognize him again. Later, the man had fled town, for which she had been grateful.

She found herself pregnant again, and her world crumbled. She knew the baby wasn't Tommy's because they hadn't been promiscuous. Her first thought had been to run as she had the first time, but she stayed and faced Tommy with the dreadful announcement, knowing he would surely leave her. But he hadn't, not until after the little girl was born and their lives began to sour.

Finally, Tommy admitted he wasn't strong enough to remain and deal with her attacker's child. She understood, but she hurt so badly she became physically ill, taking to her bed for several weeks.

Tommy left for New York, and her life became a living hell. She existed only for her children, breathing one day at a time, only because she had to. She became so despondent she contemplated suicide. Seeing her deterioration, her uncle brought Rubye Mae to stay with her for more than a year.

During most of that time, Susie closed herself to the world once again, refusing to see a doctor or be admitted into a mental hospital. When she was finally mentally capable of coping with her life again, she sent her mother home, and the remaining six years were spent taking care of her children and hiding from the world so she wouldn't be hurt anymore.

Now, thanks again to her mother, she stood here, in Selma, Alabama, watching colored and white people slowly move in various directions on the crowded, dirt street. The colored people were dressed in their Sunday best for their exciting Saturday venture into town, after having worked in the fields and white people homes all week. The white businessmen standing behind their stalls robbing every colored person they could of their hard earned money. She smiled and shook her head. Some people pushed wheel barrels containing harvested products; others led a mule and wagon loaded with cotton or raw peanuts.

Watching the activity, she temporarily forgot Selma was still suffering from the Depression, having survived because of its rich, black soil. Selma was known for its abundance of cotton as well as other marketable items which seemed to have saved it from defeat.

The sweet aroma of corn, peaches, watermelon, blackberries, tomatoes, okra, sugar cane, and much more induced homesickness.

"O-kra, o-kra, shu-ga cane, toe-may-toes and peas. Git it fresh from the sweet ground. Come on y'all," one red-faced, young man yelled.

"Walla-melons so sweet, make you hurt somebody if they want some of it," another vendor yelled and beckoned the now tarrying people.

Susie chuckled to herself, hoping she was going to like this busy, diminutive city. She didn't realize that the city held many secrets, including the deep roots of hatred that had been imbedded there for more than three hundred years. Her country life had been different. The white and colored got along fine.

Anyone passing through would have thought Selma was a peaceful, small town where colored and white lived in harmony. It might have been true for the whites, but the colored people didnot wear sunglasses. They realized their world was filled with demoralization and racism, even among themselves.

The poor and the middle class lived in two separate worlds, coming together only to do business at one of the corner stores, barbers shops, or bar-b-que joints that they were allowed to own. The poor were the worst off. They washed, ironed, cooked, cleaned, and raised white children six to seven days a week, all with a smile on their tired faces. Then they returned to their cramped one and two-room houses, some with no more than a mattress on the floor, a nightstand in the corner with a broken mirror over it, and a wood stove in the center of the room. Others could afford a high-bed and a few extras, but not much more. They had no luxuries or any of the best foods to eat unless the white people were good enough to share theirs with them.

When the week of slaving, as they called it, was over, they found comfort at the colored clubs, bootleggers' homes, corner café, or card and domino games run illegally at concealed homes. The fortunate ones slept most of the time, simply pulling their hats over their eyes. Others sat around drinking or grinning at jokes. For the less fortunate, the corn liquor consumed their minds, causing their troubles to spread through their tired bodies, prompting them to lose reality as their buried demons sprang forth to overtake their weakened souls.

Though most of them were faithful to their wives, some weren't. The unfaithful ones would become jealous if their friends danced too close to their mistresses or whispered in their ears.

"Hey you, git yo' nasty hands offah my woman," one filled with whiskey would say.

"She ain't yo' damn woman; she belongs to Carter 'round on Small Street. Why don't you brang yo' ole lady here, steada foolin' 'round with somebody else's? You dirty swine!"

That alone was enough to cause fistfights and knives to appear from hidden pockets, pocketbooks, or bosoms.

Then, someone in the bar or club would yell, "Oh Lawd, he's got a switchblade! Lawd, somebody stop him!" Or "Jesus, the crazy man's goin' to kill somebody! Please, Sonny, put that gun down. She ain't worth it. What 'bout yo' wife?"

Switchblades swung. The .22's or the .38's whistled deadly fire as the hidden demons seriously maimed or killed one of the broken souls.

Sundays presented the day of atonement. During church, the women who had witnessed the knifing or shooting would fall to their knees while the minister preached his rock-fire sermon. They would beg forgiveness in their loudest voice: "Oh Lawd, have mercy on my po' soul. I done went 'gainst Yo' will. I beg Yo' forgiveness, please, Lawd, Jesus." Some men would simply bow their heads and murmur softly to the Lord, seeking His forgiveness while other members in the pews screamed and shouted, fainted and confessed their belief in Jesus Christ. They repented, believing that they would stop being unfaithful and deceitful, that they would be strong enough to tell the other man or woman they were finished, and they carried that thought with them all week while they worked.

Then on Friday night...the circle began again.

But there was something much deeper and hushed in the sleepy city, the unspoken forbidden evil that simmered in the colored community that most didn't speak or want to think of: *Voodoo*. To utter the ugly word meant one believed in it, or knew someone who did. But whenever the need aroused, they used the words: spells, hexes, fixes.

And those poor souls who had come in contact with *Voodoo* and had lived to tell about it, believed; some of which were upright, trusted and believed in God as much as the next person. They knew one had nothing to do with the other.

They thanked God for making spiritual people and healers who could get the spells off if they sought them in time. Unfortunately, some arrived too late. There had been witnesses who saw snakes, frogs, and lizards inside of some ill-fated people.

Susie stopped in front of a grey boarding house on Griffin Avenue, in the colored section of Selma, and sat her two suitcases down.

"Hey, chile, come on in here. Let me take them heavy bags. Why you musta walk'd all the way from the bus station downtown," said a heavyset, light-skinned lady with red hair and freckles. She beamed as she reached for Susie's bags and started up the steps.

"Oh," she said, turning, "The name's Lou-Lou. Follow me, chile."

"Susie Morton," Susie answered.

"Well, come on in, Susie Morton, and I'll find you a real nice room upstairs where the sun don't cook you in the summer and Jack Frost won't freeze you in the winter. You too pretty for that." Lou-Lou winked at Susie as she stood on the wide porch and pulled at the screen door, holding it with her wide foot.

After Susie finished unpacking, Lou-Lou knocked at her door and entered with a tray filled with steaming food and iced-tea. "I brought this in 'cause I knows you hungry and thirsty, chile." She placed the tray on the table next to the bed and flopped her heavy frame in a straight chair.

Susie smiled at the sight of all the food: fried chicken, cabbage greens, corn bread, mashed potatoes. Her stomach growled in anticipation. "Thank you, Miss Lou-Lou. I guess I forgot to eat."

She took a sip of tea and sat down on the edge of the bed and pulled the tray forward. She didn't like eating strangers' food, but she thought this looked cleaned and smelled wonderful.

"Eat up, chile. Don't be shy. Now, let me fill you in on Selma. I know you from the country, and that ain't no insult, but Selma ain't that. We here is moe sophisticat'd. I knows you is impress'd by all the sights you done seen and that's good cause Selma can be that way."

She settled her heavy frame comfortably into the sagging chair. "Claims to be the biggest little city in the Bamas. And jest might be with all these rich white folks here. Now, they anothah story, but as long as you do what they say, most of them will leave you be."

She stopped to ensure she had Susie's attention then continued in a lower voice, "Now, some of our colored folks you gots to watch, too, 'cause they mix'd up or jest plain evil, but most of us is good folks. We slave hard in the white people's house, come home, go to church and mind our own business. Me, thanks to the Lawd, I'm lucky I got my own place to rent out, but that's anothah story, too."

"Then, thaih's the othahs." Her voice became almost inaudible. "The busybodies and the evil-mind'd ones. They too busy gettin' in yo' business, mine, and everybody's else's. And when they gits mad or wants yo' man bad enuf, look out. They run to the *voodoo man.*"

Susie almost choked on her food.

"Oh chile, I'm sorry. I shoulda knowed you ain't knowed nothin' 'bout this. But you needs to find out. Like I was sayin', they evil, but the first thang that goes wrong, they the ones quick to call on the name of the Lawd. Them kind you stay clear of," she warned as she twisted her wide bottom on the hard chair.

"Honey, they put them spells on you, and most times, cain't nobody save you on this earth. You best hope the Good Lawd ain't waitin' for you up thaih." She pointed her forefinger toward the ceiling. "'Cause He the only One can save you."

Susie laid her fork down, no longer hungry. She had heard the word mentioned only a few times in her life, but didn't know what it meant. "Spell? *Voodoo?* What do they do to you?"

"Honey, they gots all kinds of ways to git thangs in you. *Voodoo* is the word, but they use all kinds of evil thangs to cast spells and the such, thangs I jest cain't say, chile."

Susie placed her half-filled plate on the table. "Thank you for the dinner, Miss Lou-Lou. I thank I'll lay down for a while and rest now."

"Why, chile, I done gon' and run off at the mouth like a broke water pipe. I'm sorry, a bad habit of mine, I'm tole. But seein' you and how pretty you is, I thought it my duty to warn you."

"That's alright. I..."

"Chile, you didn't eat all yo' food," Lou-Lou interrupted.

"It's alright, I'm full," Susie said and smiled, even though she wasn't. The talk about *voodoo* had scared her, made her stomach queasy.

"Honey, I didn't mean to scare you, jest warn you," she repeated. Don't be too trustin' 'til you git to know these peoples here. Like the white, the colored gots their ways and can be real mean. But mostly we gots good colored people here."

She unraveled her shapely legs and walked to the door with the tray in her hands.

Susie followed her. "Thank you for everythang, Miss Lou-Lou."

"Don't give it anothah thought, chile. Rest good."

Susie yawned and laid down on the comfortable bed, glad to be alone. She liked Miss Lou-Lou, but she wasn't ready for any more trouble. And from the little she heard, *voodoo* spelled death, or something close to it.

She lay thinking about the information she had received. She wondered why she hadn't had any warnings or dreams about this place and its evils. But then how long had it been, she thought, since she had dreamt or heard voices? A few years? Many years? She couldn't remember and didn't want to. It seemed she was never warned about herself, only others. She had never accepted her Gift, so she hadn't grown in its grace and knowledge.

She thought back to the time when she had been living at her sister's and the experience she had. She had been lifted from the ground; voices had spoken to her; a presence had surrounded her. Finally, she had fled, been very afraid. Now, she wondered if she had accepted what had been happening to her, would her situation be any different now.

Clearing her head, she stood and pulled her clothes from her sweating body, and slipped into a cotton housedress.

As she cleared her clothes away from the bed, Susie thought about her children again, and tears filled her eyes. It was hard being away from them. She would find a way to have them with her soon, or leave Selma.

Soon, with the help of Miss Lou-Lou, Susie found a job as a cook at the Summerfield Road Café. Susie's only way to and from work was the Greyhound bus. She didn't like it, but it was acceptable until she could do better. She didn't mind the work, but she did object to her boss, a red-faced man who made it his business to touch her whenever he could. She bit her tongue to keep from telling him to quit for fear of losing her job, or something worse.

A month later, Susie quit her job and found a job nursing a three-year-old white girl and doing housework for the family. The Goldsteins were good and earnest people. Their little girl was very sweet and loved Susie from the moment she saw her.

Each night Susie returned home from work, took a bath, ate, then sat in the chair beside the window, gazing out at the low skies. She solely missed her girls, Blanche and Lola, who they called Sistah.

She desperately wanted them with her, never having been away from them before. But she couldn't send for them until she finished saving every penny she could, rented a house, and bought some secondhand furniture. Until then, she continued to write them several times a week.

Susie was racing up the steps to her room, her head down when she bumped into a tall, light-skinned, handsome man. After the apologies, they went their separate ways.

Several weeks later, Susie saw him again; they spoke and introduced themselves. His name was Nathan Norwood. He asked her out, but she kindly refused. A man was something she felt she didn't need in her life right now. They had only caused her distress and heartache in the past.

Finally, after many conversations with Miss Lou-Lou, Susie relented and accepted a date from Nathan. Dreading every moment, she dressed knowing the date wouldn't go well. She was extremely nervous; her mouth was dry, hands sweaty. She had no idea what she would talk to him about or how she could even stand being near him.

But Nathan was easy to talk to, and very much a gentleman. He drove to a small town outside of Selma and they dined in a small colored restaurant and discovered some prominent whites went there to dine on the scrumptious, New Orleans food. Much to her amazement, she was having a fine time. The music was mellow, the atmosphere warm.

After the first date, they went out every weekend, and their friendship, filled with lighthearted laughter, kindness, and a strong desire to be with each other turned into a courtship which swelled like a whirlwind in the hottest of summers.

They spent a lot of time going on long drives to Montgomery and Birmingham, picking up bar-b-que along the way, attending church, taking long walks in the country, fishing in the small country streams or in the Alabama River.

Susie and Nathan fell in love. Briefly, Susie thought of her former relationships, then quickly locked them in the past. This was her future, and she was going to do it her way.

Six months after meeting Nathan, November 12, 1940, Susie jumped the broom and became his wife. Soon afterwards, Susie sent for the children, and they settled into a two-bedroom adjoining house.

Each day, Susie rose with a smile on her face, knowing she had made the best decision of her life and looked forward to her future. She stood gazing out her bedroom window, her face one of purity and joy. The last ten years of her life washed away.

13

Months after her marriage, Susie awakened in a cold sweat. She rose and pulled on her housecoat, rushed from her bedroom into the kitchen, and put on a pot of coffee with unsteady hands. After all these years, her past had come back to haunt her. Just when she thought it was buried, the visions had returned.

Now, she realized she had merely deceived herself and cringed with fear. *Please go away and leave me alone. I don't want this...*

She poured a steaming cup of coffee and sat at the table, trying to calm her trembling soul, gripping the cup as if it would answer her plea to God, but she knew it wouldn't. She longed for Nathan's comfort, tears falling from her mystical eyes. She realized Nathan wouldn't be able to console her, not because he was weak, but because she had failed to tell him about her past. He would feel he had been cheated and that she had entrapped him. She also felt very strongly that he wouldn' understand.

An hour later, still rattled, Susie rose from the table and slipped back into bed and lay awake, reflecting on the vision. She had seen a child choking, a house burning in a raging fire, butt-naked people trying to pull clothes on as the fire consumed the house while they tried to escape. The worst part of the vision was the two girls. Her girls.

She shuddered and covered her mouth to keep the moan from escaping. She knew deep in her heart that she was being warned and this time she would not have the freedom of running away.

Dawn found her in the kitchen cooking breakfast.

The next several nights she remained awake to keep the vision away. However, a week later, it returned, and this onslaught of blurred visions lasted a month, causing her to lose sleep and become very jittery.

After each drenching episode she was so distraught she finally sought relief by reading the Bible, which helped at the moment. She understood what she needed to do, yet she wouldn't, so the visions continued, becoming clearer.

One night, startled from her sleep, she gazed at her sleeping husband and slipped from the bed. She could hear the roosters crowing and knew daybreak would soon arrive. She moved her anxious body to the washroom to clean her sweat-drenched face.

As Susie washed with cold water, she peered into the Mirror, and blinked at the strange pair of dismal eyes, staring into her grieving soul.

The washcloth slipped from her tense fingers. She slowly moved closer to the glass, placing both hands beneath her eyes for a moment, peering deeply into them, seeking answers. They became luminous reflections of yellow light, and her mind went blank.

Susie felt herself become lighter as her senses floated from her, leaving an empty shell of darkness behind. But her eyes, though unfocused, saw beyond and into the future, as objects, bodies, brilliant lights, skyrocketed past them as fast as light traveled, while her spiritual level escalated to an unknown, forbidden universe.

When the mirror released her, she staggered backwards, bumping against a nail on the door, but she felt no pain. Instead, she experienced a feeling of floating and light-headedness as her human mind resumed its normality. Her eyes were normal again, but she no longer felt the same. She was afraid.

Something had happened to her, but she didn't know what. She started to cry.

Susie.

Her trembling hands flew to the side of her head.

"Naw. Please don't," she moaned as her hair stood on end, and lacerations appeared on her face as large as golf balls, then quickly faded.

Why do you cringe so, Susie? Is it because you have failed to do what you were put here to do? Or, is it because you know you have to do it no matter how you try to run from it?

"I..." Susie searched for words. The voice sounded angry. She suddenly felt like a child being scolded for something she did wrong, and hugged herself to shield her body from the gripping pain in her stomach.

You don't have to answer me. I know you're scared, but you must not be afraid of yourself. The Gift is yours, and you can't give back what was given to you. You want to know why I left you. I did not leave you; you left you, the voice whispered, caressing her like a summer breeze blowing in the hottest of nights.

Susie's hands fell to her sides as she slipped speechlessly to the linoleum floor. The voice was somehow different, yet the same.

Susie. You're wise not to speak to Nathan about this.

He loves you, but he will not understand.

"The dreams. Why the dreams? The same one over and over. I cain't sleep," she uttered.

The vision is trying to tell you something. It is up to you to find out what it is. I can only tell you this: many things will happen to you until you acccept your blessing.

She became angry. "What do you mean many things gon' happen to me? Maybe you don't know, but enuf thangs already done happen'd to me. What else can thaih be!"

The voice didn't answer her.

She started crying. Nathan walked into the room.

"Susie, Susie. Whatever is the mattah with you? You sick?" he asked, then pulled her trembling body from the floor, and guided her into the living room.

"Ain't nothin'. Jest some female problems. I'll be alright in a while," she answered in a steady voice, pulling away from him.

"Susie, I know somethin' is wrong. I heard you tossin' in yo' sleep many a nights, and sometimes you screamed out. I want'd to comfort you, but you nevah ax'd me. "

"It's nothin', Nathan. Please go back to sleep. I'll sit in the front room for a while." She patted his leg and half smiled.

After he left, she sat by the window as if gazing outside, but her mind was soaring with anguished thoughts.

"Why did I have to be born with a Gift? Is it a curse or what?" she asked softly.

Susie. The voice is part of you. It can't leave you.

If you believe the way you were supposed to, you wouldn't be scared. And you ought to know you aren't cursed.

She ignored the voice, holding the palms of her hands up and examining them as if seeing them for the first time. Finally, she looked at the back of them as if looking for a hidden answer in the pores of her skin.

Not finding one, she made fists and placed them over her eyes, *wishing* she could turn back the hands of time, and hadn't been born this *way.*

Two nights later, she sat at the window again, gazing out at the shadowy evening. "Don't you understan'? My life's been hell. I ain't had no peace of mind 'til now. My life is finally content. I don't want to venture into nothin' else," she said to the voice.

You have to use your Gift. There just isn't any way you can get out of it, Susie. It has nothing to do with your being happy or interfering with your life.

She opened her mouth to speak, but couldn't as a vision materialized.

Several homes were ablaze. The angry, orange flames burst forth, causing explosions of windows and floors to cave in. People were rushing around, screaming, falling through the empty spaces. Trapped in the devil's blaze, children shouted for

*their mothers who ran from room to room trying to break through
the enclosed glass to reach them.*

*The flames caught at their legs as they ran; the inferno
chased and consumed them.*

Susie screamed and covered her eyes trying to hide from
the vision.

Nathan rushed to her side. "Susie, please tell me what is
goin' on, and don't tell me it's female troubl'."

She looked at him for a long moment before recognizing him.
"I don't want to do it," she mumbled.

"Do what?"

"The Gift," she moaned, forgetting the warning about telling
Nathan. "I don't want it, Nathan. Nevah did. I tried to tell Mama
and them, but they wouldn' lis-sen."

"What Gift? Susie, is you alright?"

"I thought it was gon'," she offered, looking beyond the room.
"It's been years since I heard voices and had them dreams. Now
they back and eatin' at me like a fever. But I don't want to. I cain't
fight it. It's too strong."

Nathan blinked several times. "Susie, you had bettah start
'xplainin' what the sam hill is goin' on here. I don't understan' nothin' you sayin', woman."

"I'm sorry, Nathan. I guess I d'ceived you. I shoulda tole you
I was born with the Gift to see into the future. To read palms, tell
fortunes. But I nevah want'd it. I tried iggin' it, hopin' it would go
away. Mostly 'cause I'm scared of it and don't want to be differ-
en' from othah people."

Nathan was silent for a long time, but Susie wasn't in any
hurry to speak.

"So, you was born with this and you cain't 'xcept it. I don't
understan' this, Susie." He shifted uneasy in his seat and moved
away from her.

"That's why I didn't tell you," she said.

"Well, it's a lot to put off on somebody. You shoulda tole me
befoe, Susie. Do you have them changin' of eyes?"

"Yeah, I do. And thaih's nothin' I can do 'bout it. Nathan,

I'm sorry I did this to you, but I thought it was gon' for good. I want'd it gon'. I want a life like everybody else I know," she said, longing for him to take her in his arms and say it didn't matter, that he would be there for her always. But he did none of those things.

She cried out inwardly. "Nathan, now that you done found out 'bout me, you don't have to stay mar-red to me," she suggested sadly, knowing she had to give him a way out for deceiving him.

He found a smile. "It woulda been bettah if you had tole me in the beginnin'. It's hard to take and it's gon' take some gettin' used to. If you a little strange, I guess it's alright. I love you, and I'll stand by you. I done heard of fortune tellers befoe, but nevah saw the eyes..."

Susie knew what he meant. He didn't want to see her eyes, but in a way, she wished he had.

Susie continued to have blurry visions for several more months. Then she had a lucid one.

Augustus was running down long narrow steps, his eyes bulging from his slim face. Behind him pounced a wild looking woman with red hair standing straight up on her head; clutching a butcher knife in her short fingers, she leaped down the steps after Augustus, who tripped over a fallen, dead tree. Just as he stood, she stabbed him in the back, over and over again until rivulets of dark red blood drained his body of all life. Screaming in her dreams, Susie awakened herself.

Unnerved, she jumped from her bed and ran into the living room and stood by the window, shaking. "Alright, tell me what is happenin'. Is my brother gon' die?"

So you are beginning to understand your visions.

"Tell me nothin' ain't gon' happen to my brother."

Not if you don't let it.

"I guess I bettah warn my brother, today."

"Mama, is you talkin' to yo'self?" Nine-year-old Lola, holding Blanche's hand, asked as they tip-toed into the room.

"I didn't know y'all was awake. Is y'all alright?" Susie said, turning from the window.

"Yes, Mam," Blanche answered as they each stood on either side of her.

"Who you talkin' to, Mama?" Lola asked again.

Susie gathered them in her arms, took a deep breath, and said, "Y'all sit down. I got somethin' to tell y'all."

When she finished telling her story about her Gift, she thought they would also shun her. Instead, Blanche asked in awe, "Can you tell our fortunes, Mama?"

"Make yo' eyes change, Mama." Lola begged.

Susie smiled. "Whoo, wait a minute, y'all. It jest don't happen like that. Y'all don't thank I'm strange in the head?"

"Nome," they said in unison and snuggled close to her, making her feel more loved than she had in a long time.

Soon after her visions, Susie went to see her brother, Augustus. "But Susie, you don't nevah talk 'bout havin' visions. Now, outta the blue, you gon' come to Bessemer and tell me my life ain't worth a plug nickel if I don't stay away from my woman!"

"I don't have to talk 'bout it, Augustus. If you go near her, you in for the fight of yo' life. I cain't make you stay away, but I'm pleadin' with you not to go."

"Well, I thank you for warnin' me, but I thank I'll be jest fine, little Susie."

She saw that he wasn't going to take her advice and tried one more tactic. "If you don't want Mama to lose a chile, then you bettah lis-sen and take heed."

Later that week, in Selma, Augustus stood smiling sheepishly at her door. "Hey Susie. How you doin'?" he asked as she admitted him.

She returned his smile. "Well, I see you here to tell me you lived anyway. Sit down."

"Susie, I ain't nevah been so scared in all my life when that crazy woman jump'd at me with a pot of boilin' water. I beg'd and finally got her to put it down. She did, then she pull'd a butcher knife on me! Tole me she was gon' cut my nuts off. I swear, I thought I was d-e-d, Susie, a dead man.

Then I 'member'd everythang you tole me and tried to git outta thaih fast, but she was too quick. I nevah knowed a woman with so much butt could move so fast.

"I don't know how I did it, but I got the drop on her and was outta that door and was runnin' for my car when the hot skillet came flyin' at my feet. That grease splattered all over my car, leavin' burnt marks, but I got outta thaih in one piece, thanks to you."

"You got to do moe then that, Augustus."

"I don't want to leave town."

"You will if you want to live. I tole you, she aims to kill you."

"What I'm gon' tell Mama?"

"You grown and ole enuf. You tell her the truth."

"Well, I guess I need to leave town anyway. The country ain't gettin' me nowhere, and Selma ain't that much neither. Maybe I'll jest mosey on up to De-trot, Michigan."

"You know anybody up thaih?"

"Yeah. I got a friend thaih. He's been tryin' to git me up thaih for years, and now's jest as good as any."

"As much as I hate to see you go, I rather have you up thaih safe and alive, then layin' in yo' grave here. Jest 'member to watch yo' roamin' ways, and you'll be alright. And write to me at least once a year," Susie added playfully as she walked him to the door.

"You know I will. I'm gon' miss you, baby sistah. I want you to take care of yo'self, and if anybody mistreat you, you let me know, I got somethin' for them," he said and hugged her.

"I sho will do that, Augustus. Bye now and take care."

She closed the door and went into the bedroom to find a handkerchief for her moist eyes. She missed her brother already.

Susie was placing the food on the table when Nathan arrived home from work. Since their discussion about her clairvoyance, their relationship had become strained, yet when she approached him about his distance, he denied it saying he loved her, making an excuse that he was just tired.

She had no doubt that he still loved her, but she also realized that he was somehow afraid, causing her to feel guilty and angry. Today, she had decided no matter what, they were going to have it out.

"Hi, babe, how you doin'?" Nathan asked as he kissed her check.

"Jest fine. How was yo' day?" Susie asked as she poured lemonade and walked to the door to call Blanche and Lola to supper.

"Not bad. The ole boss stay'd off my back, and I was able to git moe work done. Wish he would do that all the time stead of thankin' I'm gon' lay 'round and pretend I'm workin'," he said as he sat down.

The girls were cheerful around the dinner table, telling them about school and their friends. When they were finished and had cleared their plates, Susie shooed them out to do their homework.

Nathan attempted to follow the girls.

"Nathan, I need to talk to you."

"Baby, cain't it wait?"

"Naw. Please sit down," she sat and waited for him to return to the table. "Thaih's somethin' goin' wrong with us and I want to know what it is. Every since I talk'd to you 'bout my Gift, you ain't been the same."

"Susie, you gots to be imaginin' thangs. I love you."

"Then, I guess you love strangers too 'cause that's what's happenin', we becomin' like strangers, Nathan. I thank the problem is you 'fraid of me. You thank I can read yo' mind, but you don't have to be 'fraid of me. I'm the same person you mar-red, Nathan.

"When I tole you 'bout me, you took the news bettah then most woulda. I thought you was goin' to ax moe questions then you did. I know I woulda. But you closed yo mouth like a rat trap, and now you need to open it and talk 'bout us."

Nathan wrapped his large hands around the cool glass as if seeking comfort. He cleared his throat and looked at Susie. "You right, I do feel funny. Sometimes I wonder if you readin' my mind or if you can see inside of me. I try not to thank of you as bein' differen', but I know you is, and it's takin' some gettin' used to. But I do love you and want us to stay mar-red, Susie."

"You sho you do?"

"Yeah, Susie."

"You ain't got no questions?"

"Jest one. You will let me know if you have them visions or dreams 'bout me?"

"Sho I will. Now, I have to git this kitchen clean," she said and walked to the sink. As much as she loved him and wanted their marriage to work, she had a deep, sinking feeling that it would end.

Susie stared at the bubbles as the sink filled with hot water, her tears intermingling with the suds. She needed a man she could hold on to and draw strength from. A much stronger one than she knew Nathan to be. And although she longed for his understanding she realized he lacked the knowledge necessary to support her.

The water flowed over the edge of the sink and onto her feet, bringing her mind back. She automatically reached for a mop to clean up the mess.

Six months later, Nathan lost his job at Craig Field Air Force Base where he had been a bricklayer. When he informed Susie, she didn't worry, knowing that he would find another job soon.

Nathan looked for work over the next month, but jobs were hard to find. Susie worried because her four dollars a month income wasn't enough to take care of the rent, utilities, clothes, and food, but she didn't mumble a word to Nathan, deciding to be patient a while longer.

One evening, he walked into the room, reeking of corn liquor. Susie decided to ignore him although she was very angry. She had always hated the smell of whiskey, especially bootleg.

Nathan tried kissing her, and she pushed him away.

"What's the mattah, baby?" he slurred.

"You stank, Nathan. You been hangin' round with yo' friends playin' dominos when you 'spose to be lookin' for a job.

"You my wife. I gots rights."

"Right now yo' rights is to find work and brang home a paycheck. You too busy out thaih feelin' sorry for yo'self. And drankin' that stinky bootleg stuff ain't gon' change nothin'. You ain't got no rights to me 'til you straighten up."

"This ain't the way thangs 'spose to be. I'm doin' the best I can, and you act like I'm a dog 'stead of yo' husban'."

She frowned, turning her mouth down at him and walked away.

Two weeks later, Susie struggled from her sleep, choking from thick smoke, curling around their bed. Almost gagging, she rolled to her side and then her feet, frantically shaking Nathan.

"Nathan, wake up. The house is on fire. You git out while I git the chil'ren." She ran from the room, throwing on her housecoat.

She stood between their beds and pulled their hands at the same time. "Y'all git up, quick. The house is burnin' down. We have to git out, now. Come with me," she said and pulled them from the bed.

As they ran down the hall, coughing from the stench and flames that lapped at the ceiling and windows, Susie looked for Nathan, but didn't see him. She pushed the girls forward.

"Y'all git out and wait across the street 'til I git thaih." Then she turned and went back to search for Nathan.

Stopping at their bedroom door and gagging on the thick smoke, Susie fell to the floor and crawled to their bed. She felt around until she touched her husband's leg. She shook him hard, and when he didn't respond, she slapped him several times.

He started coughing. "Nathan, git on yo' knees and crawl. Now," she shouted. But he was overwhelmed by the smoke, she couldn't budge him. She knew if she didn't get him out, they both would burn up.

"Dear Lawd, give me strength," she pleaded, before grabbing Nathan by the shoulders and dragging him forward until they reached the front door, where she collapsed.

Someone saw them and ran up the steps and rescued both

of them just before the fire consumed the entire house, gushing out doors and exploding windows.

The fire destroyed everything except the fireplace, but Susie considered them lucky. Her sister-in-law, Pecola, welcomed them to her small one-bedroom house where they slept in the front room on the hide-a-way bed and the girls on a pallet.

Neighbors and caring people were generous enough to provide them with clothes to wear. Susie returned to work. Nathan lay around pitying himself and pretending to look for a job, often returning, wreaking of corn whiskey.

Time slipped by, and Nathan still hadn't found a job. Susie confronted him. "Nathan," she said, frowning at the smell of him, "I know it's been real hard on you and all since the fire, but we need to find our own house. The chil'ren and me are gettin' tir'd of stayin' here and livin' off yo' sistah."

"Okay. I'll find a job real soon. Jest don't fuss at me right now. I got a lot on my mind."

"Alright then. I'll wait two moe weeks, then I'm takin' the chil'ren and leavin'."

Two weeks later, Susie faced him with angry eyes.

"Nathan, I had it with yo' shit. All you do is nothin'. It's been months now. This fire jest seem to give you moe of a 'xcuse to do nothin', and I tole you if you didn't git a job, I would leave with the chil'ren. I meant it. So now I'm leavin."

"You 'bout the meanest woman I ever knowed. It's a shame when a woman go 'round threatenin' her husban' cause he's down on his luck."

"Well, I suggest you do somethin' to change yo' luck. You ain't the only one that's lost somethin', man. You don't know what it's like 'til you lose somebody you love. That material shit can be gotten again. But I guess you too busy feelin' sorry for yo'self to know that."

"Susie, shit. It takes time to do these thangs. You ain't bein' fair."

"You can talk to me when you 'cide you can be the man I marred. Bye."

14

Soon after leaving Nathan, Susie sat listening to the visiting minister preach at the church's summer revival. The evening was hot and humid. She sat, fanning at the hot air, various perfumes, and clean sweat the hot breeze carried across her face.

As the choir sang "Thou Shall Not Be Moved," Susie looked at her new friend, Uleena, who sat next to her swaying from side to side, caught up in the melody.

She had met Uleena right after the fire when she and other members from the church had brought bags of clothing and other necessities for her, Nathan, and the girls.

She had been drawn to Uleena. Whether out of loneliness or sheer desperation for a woman friend her own age, she didn't know. It had been a lifetime, it seemed, since she had close friends, and at times she wanted to go home and search for Blanche Juanita, Robert Lewis, and Betty Jean, but they were part of her past. Uleena's friendship was her future, and it was very refreshing and fulfilling.

They were the same age, and both had moved from the country several years before. Susie had been surprised their paths had never crossed. When they were together, they were so full of youthfulness and glee one would have thought they were young girls. They both told each other stories and laughed and looked at each other cross-eyed. But they were as opposite as two left shoes.

Uleena was shorter than Susie, with a big butt and blue gums when she smiled. Her hair was short and nappy, she had skinny legs, but she was full of life.

Susie yawned and covered her mouth with her gloved hand. She realized she had missed the prayer and the minister was now speaking. She was tired from all the moving, but she felt she needed to hear the word of the Lord.

"My sistahs and brothers, the Lawd sent me here this mornin' to deliver a message. A message we all must live by. My aah subject this mornin' is 'Keep the Faith'. Do y'all hear me out thaih?" He paused to get their responses.

"We sho do. We sho hear you, preacher."

"No mattah what happens to us on this earth, we must always 'member our Lawd and Savior done died on the cross for us. And if He kept the *faith,* then we, too, must do the same, chil'ren..."

Every person in the small brick building was mesmerized by Rev. Koffee as he walked, stomped, and moaned in the pulpit, screaming and stretching his short frame to the Heavens, to the Lord. Members shouted out the Lord's name and fainted; others jumped from their seats, waving their hands in the air, all caught up in the Holy Spirit.

"Y'all chil'ren out thaih! Do you hear?" The preacher shouted, patting his drenched face with a damp handkerchief.

"Yeah, I hear you..."

"Amen. The man knows what he's talkin' 'bout."

"Yall, ah, hump, hump, ah knooow, ah, what I'm ah, ummm, talkin' 'bout. Aaah, this evenin', yeah... Jesus said, if ah, you only b'lieve in me..."

Susie had completely forgotten about how tired she was as the minister's message touched her. She could feel the Holy Spirit around her.

Forty-five minutes later, Rev. Jerome Koffee sat down, drenched with sweat, having delivered a powerful sermon.

"What did you thank of the new preacher, Susie?" Uleena asked as they walked toward home.

"The Lawd sho call'd that man to preach. And he got the mouth to do it with. I ain't nevah heard a sermon like that.

He sho can make you feel like Gawd right next to you, holdin' yo' hands."

"Yeah. I nevah heard nobody preach like that," Uleena said. When she didn't hear a response, she turned to Susie. "Girl, where is yo' mind?"

"What? Oh. I was jest thankin' 'bout somethin'."

"Nathan. How he doin'?"

Susie frowned. "I guess he's doin' fine."

"So y'all ain't talk'd since you moved I see. You plan on lettin' him come back?"

"Depends," Susie said. "Now let's talk 'bout somethin' else."

When Susie arrived home, Mrs. Bosmun, her former neighbor, was waiting at her door. When Susie had rented the house, she had been surprised to find that her old neighbor was her new neighbor. She didn't mind the woman so much, even though she was nosey.

"Susie, did you hear that preacher? Chile, he was somethin' else. I tell you, my husban' can preach, but nothin' like that man."

"Yes, Mam. He sho can preach," Susie agreed.

"Did you meet him?"

"Nome. I was tired, and it was too crowd'd to wait in line to shake his hand."

"Did you git some food? I gots plenty here."

"No thank you, Miss Bosmun. I'm goin' to bed soon."

As she prepared for bed, she pondered for a minute, wondering why the woman had stopped by just to talk to her about Rev. Koffee. Shrugging it off, she started to climb into bed when she heard a knock at her door. Frowning, she went to answer it.

"Who's thaih?"

"It's me, Nathan. Susie, can I come in?"

"I'm gettin' ready for bed."

"Please. I need to talk to you."

"Well, hurry up and say it then, 'cause I have to go to work in the mornin'," she said as she let him in.

"I got my ole job back, and I want'd to know if you was still willin' to take me back," he asked as he stood twisting his hat in his hands.

"I ain't willin' at this time. If you still have yo' job in a month and 'cide you can go without drankin' 'til you stank, then I'll thank 'bout it and let you know then. Now good-night, Nathan," She said and walked him to the door.

A month later they reconciled, and the following months proved to be the best in Susie's marriage. They were happy and so were the children. Nathan taught her how to play dominos, the game she had originally hated. He played checkers and tic-tac-toe with the girls and told them wild tales about his childhood.

When Susie wasn't with him, she spent time with the children, teaching them how to sew, telling them stories, reading the Bible to them, talking to them about life. They were growing up fast, and sometimes she felt guilty she had missed out on so much with them during their younger years. She was very proud of them and often told them that.

One evening they were just finishing dinner when Susie went to answer a persistent knock at the door. It was Mrs. Bosmun and Rev. Koffee.

"Is it alright if we come in for a few minutes, Susie?" Mrs. Bosmun asked, showing pink gums and false teeth.

"We were jest finishin' dinner, Miss Bosmun," Susie said, slightly annoyed and surprised to see them. "But y'all come on in," she said, ushering them into the living room.

"I knowed you didn't git a chance to meet Rev'end Koffee here and I know how impress'd you was with his preachin'.

Since he was here visitin', I thought I would brang him by."

"That was nice of you, Miss Bosmun," Nathan said. "Sorry I didn't git the chance to hear you. Maybe next time."

Rev. Koffee grinned, his mouth spreading almost to his ears. "I'm gon' hold you to that."

"I did enjoy yo' sermon, Rev'end Koffee," Susie said, suddenly wishing they would leave. There was something about him that caused her to feel uneasy and suspicious. She was glad when they left.

"He seemed like a nice man," Nathan said.

"Yeah," Susie agreed as Nathan put his arm around her and winked.

"Why you sound like you didn't like him?"

"I didn't say that, but thaih's somethin' 'bout him that makes me feel...I don't know; I jest cain't put my finger on it."

Nathan stared at her for a moment. "If you say it, then I cain't deny that you wrong. But let's forgit 'bout him, alright?" He leaned down and kissed her lightly on the mouth. "I'll be waitin' for you when you finish helpin' the girls."

15

Susie stood watching Nathan's bus pull out of Selma, taking him to New York where he would to be sent overseas to fight the Germans. The army was asking all available men to sign up, and Nathan had felt it his duty to help his country.

While Susie was proud of him, she didn't want to risk losing him as she had all the other men in her life. When he told her his decision, she cringed inside, feeling a sense of doom, but kept it to herself, hoping she was mistaken.

Now, the man she loved was leaving her, and she thought of running onto the bus and begging him to stay with her so he would be safe. Burning tears scorched her cheeks as she stood looking at dust the bus left behind.

"Come on Susie, hon. Let's go home now," her sister-in-law urged, patting her back.

It was too quiet for Susie. She couldn't be still. She changed clothes and started scrubbing the floors, her tears mixing with the soapy water.

"Why in the world do I always find myself caught up in some kinda shit?" she asked the wet floor.

We all have bridges to cross, some more than others, the voice said.

"Well, I tell you, I'm tir'd of crossin' them. Maybe next time I won't."

You'll be alright. You're just angry and hurting.

"I sho don't need you buttin' in right now. And don't come tellin' me 'bout no visions. I ain't had none in a while, and I don't want to." She sat in the middle of the wet floor, moaning so loudly the children came and stood outside the door and cried with her. Even though the girls felt her pain, they knew not to interfere.

Instead they hugged each other for comfort and listened to her talk back to the empty space. Then they slipped back to their room, unnoticed.

You have a nice surprise in store, the voice said.

"I ain't in no mood for them neither," she said as she pulled herself to her feet and emptied the dirty water out the back door, put away the scrub brush and hung up the bucket. When the voice didn't respond, she shook her head sadly, and finally wiped at the drying tears. She found it strange that most times when the voice spoke to her, she was feeling down, or it was right before she had a vision.

Several days later, Susie was frying chicken when Blanche and Lola screamed, "Mama, Mama! Mama Rubye Mae's here."

Susie dropped the fork on the stove and ran into the front room. "Mama, it's good to see you. What a nice surprise." Susie hugged her mother, glad to feel her comforting arms.

"Baby, I had to come. I know you need'd yo' Mama with you for a spell, even if you is grown with yo' own chil'ren. Everybody needs they Mama sometimes. How you doin', chile?"

"I'm doin' bettah now that you're here, Mama," Susie said, trying to hide the pain in her eyes. She didn't want to tell her about the sinking feeling she had in the pit of her stomach or the nights she lay awake, waiting for bad news.

"Susie, I smell yo' chicken burnin'. You always did make the best fried chicken," Rubye Mae smacked her lips and pulled Susie behind her, hurrying toward the kitchen.

During dinner, Rubye Mae gave Susie a report on the family, and before long, she was smiling about the story of Augustus and his scrapes in Detroit.

"Alright. Now tell me how you doin', Mama, and what's been goin' on with you."

"Lots of thangs. I'm doin' jest fine as always. Swear I'll live to see a hundred."

"I know you will, Mama."

"Well, chile it's like this. With yo' brother Augustus in De-trot, the rest gettin' ready to follow and the girls thankin' on the same lines...

"Taylor, Jr., down in Mississippi, and Mae Frances got her a beau and thankin' on getting mar-red. I swear that whuppin' I gave her years ago saved that chile. Anyway, you know yo' brother, Boy...Lorenzo ain't no troubl'. He'll nevah be able to take care of his self, but he ain't enuf to keep me busy.

"So, I was thankin' on movin' on up thaih too. 'Epecially with Augustus naggin' me to come. Said he gon' buy a house for me and Boy."

Susie's face fell. "You thankin' on leavin' the South, Mama?"

"Yeah. I don't have no problems makin' new friends. I need to make new ones. All mine gettin' too old," she winked.

Susie couldn't help smiling. She loved her mother and hated to see her go, but she also wanted to see her happy. Her mother had changed a lot since losing her husband. She had grown stronger over the years. Now she was the strongest person Susie knew.

"And anothah thang," she lowered her voice, leaning toward Susie, "I needs to find me a boyfriend, and all the men here is too old, or cain't see me for all them young thangs twistin' they tails in front of them!"

"Mama. Shame on you," Susie said and slapped herself on the leg, shaking her head at her sassy mother.

"I came here to be with you for a while, Susie," Rubye Mae said, abruptly. "I know you hurtin' inside. Wonderin' where yo' man is and will he be safe. It's down right scary.

I'll stay here as long as you need me."

"Thank you, Mama. You're always here when I need you.

But you don't need to stay; I'm a grown woman, and I need to start dependin' moe on myself to git *me* over the rough roads. I'll cross this one too."

There you go, the voice said.

Susie almost answered it, but she didn't want to frighten her mother.

"I'm stayin'. I don't care what you say, tryin' to be tough. You was thaih for me when I need'd you all them years, helpin' to raise yo' sistahs and brothers, and then aftah yo' father pass'd. Family needs family."

"You right 'bout me goin' crazy with worry. Some nights I lay thaih wonderin' if he's dead, and I want to scream. It's hard not knowin' and harder when he's so far away. I'm glad you here, Mama."

"I jest wish I could do moe, baby."

Several weeks later, Susie sat reading several letters from Nathan, her face shining with happiness. Each letter assured her that he was fine, and stated how much he loved and missed her and the children. Soon she would look up and he would be standing outside the door, waiting to grab her into his arms, he assured her.

His letters kept her going. She was able to work faster at the Selma Candy Factory where she worked part time because the factory had cut back the employees' hours. She decided to do some seamstress work to keep busy and earn extra money.

Yet, as time passed, she still found herself in debt. Finally, she left the factory job and acquired a position at the Defense Plant where she was responsible for packing and stamping secret parts for the war, which enabled her to earn more money.

Uleena also worked there, and they were able to have lunch together. Uleena could make her laugh almost as much as her mother. She loved to talk and tell jokes, mostly about herself.

"Susie, you shoulda been at Mary's Café the othah night. Chile, Mary had to toss out ole Sam and his lady cause they was

gettin' too chummy. Tole them public places wasn't used as no
Mo-tel. But the two of them jest kept on kissin' while he push'd
them out that narrow door, payin' him no nevah mind. They was a
sight to see.

"Anyhow, when I left, they was still kissin' and carryin' on out-
side, and a crowd of people was watchin' them. For the life of me,
I don't see how ole Sam can hold on to them thick lips of hers.
But in this case I wish'd I had somebody kissin' mine."

"Uleena, I done tole you 'bout talkin' 'bout yo'self and othah
people. It ain't nice."

"But it makes you laugh, Susie. And you need to laugh moe
these days."

Susie shook her head. "It's time to go, the whistle jest blew.
I'll see you latah."

"Who in the world...what is all that bangin' noise on a Sad-day
mornin'? Where is that nosey Miss Bosmun? I know she heard all
this noise," Susie mumbled as she pulled on a housecoat and
rushed from her bedroom.

She flung the door open, saw two men dressed in Army uniforms, and tried to close it back.

"I'm sorry, Miss, we're looking for Mrs. Nathan Norwood," the
shorter man said.

"I'm her. What do y'all want?" Susie asked, turning to look
briefly behind her.

"Mrs. Norwood. We're sorry, but we're here to inform you that..."

The tall one interrupted, "Mrs. Norwood," he said in a foreign
accent, "We're here to deliver these papers to you."

He handed her the envelope covered with army stamps.

"What is this all 'bout?" Rubye Mae demanded as she came
to stand next to Susie. Susie dropped the envelope and slipped
to the floor before either one of them could catch her. The men
carried her limp body to the couch then quietly slipped away.

Rubye Mae picked up the envelope, laid it on the coffee table,
rushed to Susie's bedroom, grabbed the spirit ammonia from the

bedside table, raced back to the living room, and passed it under Susie's nose. The strong prudent order revived her.

"Naw. Naw," She moaned and tried to sit up.

"What is goin' on here, Susie? Them men had on army uniforms."

"You got to open it, Susie," Rubye Mae said, handing the envelope to her.

When Susie didn't take it, Rubye Mae opened it, shook the papers out, and tried to read them.

But Susie didn't need to hear; she already knew. "They kill'd my man. My husban' is dead. Oh Lawd Jesus, You took him from me, jest like my daddy," Susie wailed, sending chills through all their bodies before she fainted again.

The following days were like hell reaching its hands up and tormenting her as she drifted in a fog of shock and pain, refusing to speak to anyone. She felt empty, cold, and angry.

Days passed when she went into rages, lashing out at anyone who said the wrong things or made the wrong moves. Then she was numb again and went for weeks simply existing. Time was her enemy.

She sought comfort by sitting at her bedroom window, looking and seeing nothing.

When she could finally feel or think, she only hated, hated anyone that had a husband. She wanted no damn sympathy. She simply wanted Nathan. No one's kind words helped ease her pain nor the emptiness in her soul.

Rubye Mae saw Susie falling apart and felt helpless to do anything for her. Fearing Susie had lost her mind, she sent for Augustus.

Augustus beat the tears from his eyes when he saw Susie. "Little Sis, I'm so sorry this happen'd. I love you, and I'm here for you." But Susie didn't respond. Finally they took her to the hospital where she was treated for a month for severe shock and malnutrition.

16

Susie's reflection mirrored dead eyes, hollow cheeks and dry lips that resembled parchment paper. She gazed closer at her limp, lifeless hair and covered her eyes with her bony fingers before turning away.

Susie. You sure have lost it. You thank you have everybody fooled, but you don't. You have forgotten everyone but yourself. What about your poor children? What are they supposed to do while their mother is pretending she is doing better when she isn't? They see the same thing you see in the mirror. You keep on going this way, and you are going to hurt them too because they won't have a mother.

"I don't need yo' shit. I'm tryin' the best I can to live day by day. It's only been a few months since my husban' died. What do you want me to do? And my chil'ren is jest fine."

It's been six months. Your mother is doing the job you should be doing. She isn't their mother. They need you! You have to pick yourself up and carry the pain with you until it finally eases up. But you have to want to live.

"What damn life? I ain't got no life to live. If life's this close to hell, I sho don't wanna be here."

When the voice didn't respond, she turned around, opened her eyes, and saw Lola standing in the doorway. Startled, she tried to smile.

"Mama, is you alright?"

"Come on in, Sistah, honey. How you doin'? Where is Blanche?"

"I'm alright, Mama. Blanche is helpin' Mama Rubye Mae fix supper. She wants to know if you ready to eat."

She hesitated then said, "Yeah. I thank I will. Come on and let's go in the kitchen," she smiled, and hugged her child for the first time in months.

Spring arrived, bursting with sunshine and a warm breeze, filling the air with with the smell of sweet honeysuckle and the promise of a hot summer even though a hard rain had fallen that morning, leaving the ground smelling so good she could almost taste it. Susie breathed in the clean earth and suddenly felt some life stir within her. She took in the blossoms on the magnolia trees, as if seeing them for the first time.

The birds must have sensed her new attitude because they sang prettier than any she had ever heard. She smiled as she watched them fly after their mates and then bring worms back to their young. She turned her attention back to Blanche whose hair she was French-braiding.

Rubye Mae had observed Susie and decided it was time to let her fly on her own. "It's time for me to be gittin' on back home, Susie," Rubye Mae said. "I done wore out my welcome here," she smiled. "'Sides, Ella Mae prob'ly thank I done dump'd Boy off on her."

"I don't thank she does, Mama, but I know you need to git back. I'm grateful you stay'd this long." Susie said, wondering how she was going to get along without her mother.

As if answering her, Rubye Mae offered, "You done come a long ways. You look real good again, even got some color in them yellow cheeks and some meat on them thin hips. I thank I can trust you to keep takin' care of yo'self and the chil'ren."

Susie chuckled at her. "Miss Rubye Mae Morton. I don't know what to say or what me and the chil'ren woulda done without you. You been a Gawd send all these months."

"Yeah, yo' Mama gots to get on back and git ready for that big move up Nawth. But befoe I do, thaih's somethin' I wants to talk to you 'bout."

Susie quickly finished Blanche's hair and scooted her out of the room. Suddenly feeling uneasy, she turned to her mother.

"Susie chile, I know this is prob'ly the wrong time, but I need to git it off my chest since it been simmerin' in me for years. It's 'bout yo' Gift."

Susie frowned, and her face closed up.

"Susie, it ain't gon' do you no good to block it out. You twenty-nine years old and been runnin' for moe then twenty years. I know'd you warn'd yo' brother and saved his life, thank the Lawd, but you gots to do moe. You gots to do what you was put here for. So please thank on it, then pray on it. And don't blame Gawd for takin' Nathan; it was his time, chile."

Not wanting to upset her mother, Susie said, "Alright, I promise to do my best."

"Don't tell me that jest so I'll leave you alone. You oler and wiser now, so I know you ain't scared like you use to be. You know Gawd can and will put a whuppin' on you like nobody can if you don't obey Him."

Susie wanted to tell her mother to mind her own business. That she didn't need her mess about no silly Gift. If she were so special, why had the thief of death stolen her husband?

"Susie," Rubye Mae said, bringing her mind back, "You cain't run no moe. 'Sides, I see a change in you that you cain't see. Yo' eyes done changed again. They gots a mystery glow to them, waitin' for you to follow yo' spirit. Yeah, you gots all kinds of powers b'hind them eyes, lock'd up inside you. You gots to do it. You cain't fight and win, baby."

"You right 'bout that. I sho don't seem to win. My whole life is full of losin'. No mattah what I do or how hard I try, somethin' happens.

"I don't understan' how I'm 'spose to be Gift'd to see into other folks lives and help them when I cain't even help me. That's hogwash, Mama. Do you hear me? Pure hogwash. If I cain't help me and my po' chil'ren, how can I help strangers? Tell me, Mama."

"You know I cain't answer that," Rubye Mae said, surprised at Susie's outburst. "I know you hurtin' and mad inside. We all hurt bad one time or another in our life. I was that way too, but you cain't go 'round blamin' Gawd. You cain't lose faith."

Susie felt for a moment that her mother was inside of her, listening to her thoughts. "When I had faith, I still lost everythang."

"I can see I ain't gon' git through to you, Susie. You jest 'member what I said."

"Mama, I'm sorry. So many thangs done happen'd to me, sometimes I don't want to go on. From the time I was a little girl 'til now, I been losin' somebody importan' to me, and every time my heart jest breaks in two. I tried to do my best, and it don't seem good enuf."

"I know a lot done happen'd to you, but..."

"Mama, you may know, but you ain't felt it all. You don't know what it's like to have a person say he loves you, then takes advantage of you while yo' mind is weak, to have a baby out of wedlock and shame yo' family. To feel like you ain't worth nothin', that a man only gon' want you to use you. Then long comes a man who loves you for you and you plan on mar-ryin' him and movin' away to a bettah life. Then BAM! Jest like that, yo' life is pull'd from under you 'cause some sick man ravishes you. And you feel like dyin' or hidin' away from the people who love you 'cause you thank they don't love you no moe 'cause it's all yo' fault it happen'd.

"But you don't do nothin' but cry and beg Gawd to take you out of yo' misery while yo' belly swells with a chile you don't want.

"Mama, you don't know how much my whole body ached with pain and hatred for that rapist. How much I hated my chile befoe she was born. Then when I saw her, a innocent chile, part of me, I loved her moe then I loved me. But I still hated myself for lettin' it happen.

"And po' Tommy. He tried his best to stand by us. I could see the pain eatin' him up inside. His spirit was broken, Mama. And I blamed myself for that. But he nevah did. He jest kept comin' back for moe and moe pain, sayin' he still want'd to marry me. But I knowed he couldn' stand the sight of my chile, 'cause she was a constant reminder of my ravisher.

"But he woulda stay'd with me, and we woulda been two miserable people. I couldn' allow that, and I sent him away so he could regain his spirit. But when he left, he took part of me with him.

"It took me years to git over him, and I had promised myself I would nevah love another man, but I did. And what did it cause him and me? His life. Naw, this ain't no life. This is hell if I ever saw anything."

"Susie, you stop that kind of talk right now. You will not speak that way 'bout the life Gawd gave you. All His chil'ren suffer once in a while. You know you been taught how much He suffer'd, but He didn't deny His Father. I know the pain is awful, 'cause I can feel part of it, been part of it. I'm yo' mother, chile. When you hurt, I hurt too, but you got to find some way to live with it and not be bitter. It'll be alright, and you'll be able to stand it like the rest of us."

"But I ain't like the rest of y'all, Mama."

"That's why you got to let go of yo' evil thankin' and let the Lawd lead you stead of the devil, Chile!"

Susie hadn't thought of it in those terms. She never thought she was doing the devil's work. She cringed inside at those horrible words. "I'm sorry, Mama," she said and hugged her. "I have had so much bottled up inside for so long, I had to git it out. I'll do my best to git my life and the chil'ren back on the right track. I thank Gawd for you bein' you, and bein' my Mama."

"Anytime, Susie," Rubye Mae smiled and squeezed Susie to her, surpressing her tears.

Late that night, Susie stood gazing out her bedroom window at the darkened sky filled with thousands of brilliant stars. She still stung from her mother's words, yet she felt better. She wondered if Nathan was looking down at her and if he was smiling.

After the confrontation with her mother, she had walked to

the corner store and bought a pack of cigarettes. She didn't care what kind, she just wanted to calm her nerves. She plucked one from the pack and lit it. She inhaled the smoke and coughed several times. Wiping the tears from her eyes, she looked out into the quiet night again, searching for answers.

"Your mother is a wise woman. You should take heed from her."

"And you should leave me alone! I don't need to hear you and no hogwash mess right now. Please, jest let me have some peace tonight."

Susie, you got to try to pull yourself together and stop lying to yourself like you lied to your mother.

"I didn't lie to my mother."

You didn't tell her about the dreams you had before your husband died. You didn't tell her how you ignored the warning that he wouldn't be coming back home. That's the real reason you're so angry. You denied everything and you knew not to.

"I don't want to hear it. Leave me alone," Susie demanded, covering her ears as if by doing so she could stop herself from hearing the voice.

17

After Rubye Mae returned home, Susie functioned on automatic pilot for a while before she began to feel, think, and fully understand why, and what she was doing and what she needed to do. She must pull herself together and act as normal as possible for her children's sake if nothing else.

She decided to leave the defense plant and return to Selma Candy Factory as a wrapper where she was paid production wages, depending on how many sticks of candy she wrapped per day and boxed for shipment.

She spent many hours with Blanche and Lola, preparing special dinners, assisting them with their homework, teaching them the art of sewing, telling them stories her father used to tell her while they had waited for the fish to bite. Once in a while, she teased them about some silly issue and caused them much laughter.

The girls were elated that Susie spent time with them. They enjoyed having her to themselves although they missed their stepfather Nathan dearly and realized their mother did as well.

They comforted her during the times she spent telling them stories by taking the opportunity to comb her hair, rolling it with a pencil to curl it, soaking her feet in hot, sudsy water, and cutting her thick toenails.

Uleena offered to help. Susie hugged and thanked her, and then sent her away, explaining that she needed to spend time alone and with her girls. She hoped she did not hurt Uleena's feeling by sending her away.

Susie also rejected Mrs. Bosmun's attempt to cheer her up. She was not capable of functioning very well and chose to try to heal in private. Since she had suffered loss before, she knew she couldn't adapt to having people around her, even if they did mean well.

One day, Mrs. Bosmun showed up at her door with Rev. Koffee and Susie became so furious, she could barely breathe as she stood holding her door open.

"Susie," Mrs. Bosmun said, showing her pink gums. "I know you don't want to be bother'd, but I thank Rev. Koffee here will do you some good."

Susie looked at the woman, wanting to strangle her. Then she said, "You right, I don't want to be bother'd, but since y'all here, you might as well stay."

"Madam, we won't impose on you at this time; I'm sorry. Miss Bosmun jest thought you could stand to talk since it's close to a year since you lost yo' husband. We'll leave."

Susie didn't know why, but suddenly she wanted him to come in and talk to her. She found herself saying, "It's alright. I didn't mean to be rude. Come in."

They sat talking and drinking iced tea. Soon afterwards, Mrs. Bosmun excused herself and left, leaving Susie uncomfortable, but Rev. Koffee turned the subject to his childhood, catching her interest. She learned that he told stories as well as he preached, and soon she was caught up in his past.

An hour later he stood to leave. He had never asked about Nathan for which she was grateful.

"Thank you so much, Rev. Koffee. It's been a long time since I laugh'd so much."

"It does all us good sometimes, Madam. Jest let Miss Bosmun know if I can help you again. Good night, Madam."

Susie walked into her bedroom still smiling. She changed her clothes and turned the radio on for the first time since Nathan's passing. After praying, she slipped into bed and held his picture, now feeling completely empty, longing for him to be there.

She moaned, "Oh Nathan. I miss you so much. My world is so empty without you." She kissed his picture and placed it beneath her pillow and lit a cigarette, inhaling deeply. She coughed several times and lay back against her pillows, and started singing along with the song on the radio.

They call it stormy Monday, but Tuesday's jest as bad.

They call it stormy Monday, but Tuesday's jest as bad.

Wednesday's worst, Lawd, and Thursday's all so sad.

She hugged the pillow tighter, reeling from side to Side. Listening to the sad words brought back memories of Nathan. The song's last words drifted sadly from the radio.

You know I'm tryin' to find my baby. Won't someone please, brang him home to me...

Susie slipped from the bed to the floor, still holding the pillow to her breast. "Oh Lawd, please help me. Still my tremblin' soul. I want my husband so baaaadd. Nathaaann. Nathan, why did you leave me? Oh, Nathan, I loved you so much. I'm so lonely without you." She balled into a knot and cried until she was numb.

Two hours later, her entire body was temporarily suspended from the floor to the height of the bed. A warm glow penetrated her body, surrounded her, comforted her. She tried opening her eyes, but the light was too bright in the room. Her mind was made void as she was lowered into the bed.

She dreamt.

Susie drifted through a field of sweet roses, her body brushing against the thornless petals. Their softness caressed and enveloped her, making her drunk with its purity. She smiled radiantly as she floated in a flowing, yellow silk gown toward the heavens that showed neither day nor night; the sun and moon became one, casting forth love and light and mystery. She drift-

ed downward and stood at the entrance of a mansion, encased in the clouds. In the foyer stood a tall man whose face was hidden behind the blended glow of the sun and moon. But she knew he smiled at her because she could feel it in her soul. She received so much pleasure from that smile that she moved to touch him, but he vanished. When she moved forward again, her way was blocked; then the mansion disappeared, leaving her bewildered. Turning, she fled through the barren field where the roses had been. She became afraid and ran faster through the stark land, crying for help.

She awoke, screaming. She covered her mouth, looking around wildly, wondering how she had gotten in bed. She glanced around only to see Nathan's pillow lying on the floor. She picked it up and hugged it to her.

"Was it you I was dreamin' 'bout Nathan? Was it you tellin' me that I'm nevah gon' see you again 'xcept in Heaven? And how did I git back into this bed?" She cried.

"Mama, you alright?" Blanche asked as she slipped into the room, a worried look on her pretty, round face.

Susie looked up from her pillow. "Naw, baby. Yo' Mama ain't, but she sho gon' try to be for y'all. I'm sorry I woke y'all up."

Lola stood next to the bed. "Mama, we worry 'bout you. We don't want nothin' to happen to you like it did Daddy."

Susie dropped the pillow and hugged her children to her. "Y'all precious to me. I don't want y'all to worry. I'm gon' be here, the Good Lawd willin'. Now, y'all go back to bed and try to git some sleep. I'll make y'all some biscuits in the mornin' for breakfast."

"Yes, Mam," they said in unison and left the room with smiles on their faces.

"I have to pull myself together befoe I mess up my chil'ren. Lawd, please help me."

18

Rev. Miles JaRett was a devout Baptist minister as well as a catch-your-eye, grab-him-and-never-let-him-go man. He was a gentle man who had a great respect for women, and he owed it all to his deceased mother who had instilled in him that women were as important and equal as men and were to be treated with respect and honor.

Consequently, the women who chased him and thought they had caught him, were let down as gently as possible. He wasn't looking for a wife or girlfriend; he chose to remain free while traveling, visiting, and preaching at churches throughout the South.

All the available women had heard he would be preaching the revival this evening. They had fried and curled their hair to perfection, dressed in their best frocks, pushed into their high-heel shoes, sprayed on overwhelming perfume, and packed the church as if it was their last chance to find a husband and hear a divine sermon at the same time.

Susie, being the exception, sat watching him preach. She was mesmerized by his speech, demeanor, and charisma.

Her unblinking eyes followed his every move. She realized that he was the man she had seen in her dreams. She wanted to run, but felt the urge to stay, to be near this man. That frightened her so badly she felt her heart beating in her chest like African drums during a ritual.

Uleena leaned against her shoulders and whispered, "I see the preacher man affectin' you too. Girl, ain't he somethin' to b'hold?"

But Susie didn't hear her as she struggled with her emotions.

Uleena tapped her on the leg to get her attention. "Is you alright, Susie. You look kinda pale?"

"Yeah, I'm fine," she managed to say through dry lips.

After the sermon, she found herself standing in line, holding on to Uleena's arm so strongly that Uleena flinched and nudged her. "Susie, you tearin' my po' arm off. Is somethin' the mattah with you? You been actin' funny all evenin'."

Susie didn't speak.

"Susie, Susie," Uleena said urgently. "We gettin' ready to shake the preacher's hand. Let go of my arm. Is you alright?"

Susie looked at her and smiled. "Yeah. Why you ax me that?" She didn't release Uleena's arm.

Uleena couldn't answer. They were facing Rev. JaRett.

"You sho did preach a good sermon, Rev'end. You have to come back again soon and visit us," Uleena offered, batting her short eyelashes, extending her hand. *Umm, he's so fine.*

"Thank you, Sistah. I sho would like to come again."

Turning to Susie, his eyes took on a look of surprise and merriment.

"Sistah?"

"She's Sistah Norwood," Uleena offered.

Susie was glad she was holding Uleena's arm. Her legs felt artificial and her mouth drier than hot dirt on a summer day.

She loved the sound of his baritone voice, without a hint of a southern drawl. The warmth that flowed from his beautiful brown eyes penetrated her. She yearned to fall into his arms and stay there forever.

"The name is Norwood. Please to make yo' acquaintance," Susie whispered, then backed away as he extended his hand. She knew that if he touched her, she might embarrass all of them.

"These two chil'ren is Susie's, Blanche and Lola," Uleena volunteered.

He smiled and spoke to the girls, shook their hands, then looked at Susie again as she raced through the front door.

"Whatever is the mattah with you, Susie? You act like a haint is chasin' you or somethin'!" Uleena said when she caught up with her.

Susie wanted to tell Uleena that seeing Rev. Miles JaRett was like seeing a ghost, from her dreams, but he had turned out to be real. She felt like her heart and world were bursting.

"I'm fine, Uleena. I jest want to go home. Y'all chil'ren come on," Susie said and rushed down the street.

Days later, Uleena knocked at Susie's door. "I jest stop'd by to see if you was doin' alright. I ain't seen you at work."

"I took some time off. I had some thangs I need'd to git done," Susie offered, feeling badly that she hadn't confided in her friend.

"Well, I'm glad to know you alright. I thought maybe that good lookin' man had got to you like he did the rest of us. Shucks, girl, you should hear all the women talkin'," Uleena said, licking her thick lips. "Honey, they done gon' off they rockers, fannin' between they legs somethin' awful, hopin' he gon' give them a second look."

Susie smiled. *I sho know what they mean. That man is too good lookin' to be true, and I don't want to make no fool outta myself over him.* "He is a nice lookin' man, ain't no denyin' that. And he's prob'ly mar-red too."

"No, he ain't, chile. He's from Montgomery, and he's free as they come, not even a girlfriend. Now, ain't that strange? But who cares? I sho would go aftah him. Wouldn't you, Susie?"

"Naw. You know I don't chase aftah men."

"Well, honey. I sho would if I thought I could git this one."

Susie laughed and shook her head. "Then help yo'self if you thank you can git him." She wanted to kick herself because she yearned for him.

She was relieved when Uleena said, "You know that man ain't

gon' give me a second look, 'specially aftah he done saw you. Naw, you go aftah him, and I'll help you."

"I wouldn' need yo help if I went aftah the man, Uleena. And I ain't goin' aftah him."

"What if he chases aftah you?"

"Then we'll have to wait and see, won't we? Now, you come on and let me do somethin' to that nappy hair of yo's while you here. Who been doin' yo' hair since I stop'd?" Susie asked, pulling Uleena into the kitchen.

Following services on Sunday, Susie attempted to slip out of a side door, but she wasn't quick enough, Rev. JaRett stood in front of her. Her heart fell practically to the bottom of her flat feet. She squeezed herself to ensure that she was still breathing. She didn't like feeling this way about a strange man. Any man.

"Hello, Sistah Norwood. Could I have a word with you, please?"

Susie gazed at him for a moment, regained her breath, and turned to the girls, "Y'all chil'ren wait here." Then she moved several feet away from them and waited.

"I know you feel this is movin' way too fast...I've never ...I was just wonderin' if it would be alright if I stop'd by to see you?" Miles asked.

Her heart skipped several beats, then raced. "I don't Know, I'm kinda busy, and I work... I don't know you, Rev'end."

"Everybody else seems to. Weren't you even curious 'bout me as a minister? No. Don't answer that. You may hurt my feelings." He felt as if he were back in high school, attempting to get his first date.

Susie didn't respond, but her eyes questioned him.

"I know all 'bout you, Susie Norwood, from this small town." He spread his large hands outward in gesture, and revealed even, white teeth. "But I sho would like to git to know moe 'bout you except your name, address, and the number of children you have." He paused, hoping he hadn't gone too far. "If you don't mind."

"I guess it's alright. But I do have to..."

"Work in the morning," he smiled, his pearly, white teeth gleaming behind his wonderfully shaped mouth, as he finished her sentence. She smiled and backed away from him on unsteady legs. This man affected her too much.

"I'll stop by after church this evenin', 'round eight o'clock," he said as she left with the girls.

19

"You know, Susie, I noticed that Rev'end Koffee keeps droppin' by to see you when I'm here vistin'," Uleena commented as they sat in Susie's living room, listening to the radio. "Do he stop by every time he visit Rev'end and Miss Bosmun?"

"You know, I been wonderin' why he stops by here all the time myself. He start'd comin' by with Nathan...two years ago, but not often. Now it seems him and Miss Bosmun is always at my door."

"Well, if you ax me, I thank he's got a likin' for you, Susie."

Susie laughed. "Him? You gots to be puttin' me on. That man's at least ole enuf for my daddy. Would you want him?"

"Maybe. But I know when a man likes a woman, and that man is aftah you. Now, you gots Rev'end Miles and him," Uleena pouted. "You sho lucky."

"Uleena," Susie's voice became low, "I would advise you not to start spreadin' nothin' 'bout that man and me. That man don't mean nothin' to me, even if Rev'end JaRett and me hadn't been seein' each othah for months. And you cain't mean you would even thank 'bout seein' that man?"

"I ain't gon' spread no rumors, Susie. You my best friend. I jest don't understan' why two men is aftah you.

And he ain't so bad..." her voice faded.

"Only one man, Uleena. I'm courtin' Miles." She picked up her cold coffee and sipped it, frowning. She couldn't believe that Uleena would think about "Ole Koffee" and her together. And worse, that she would be interested in the man even if she didn't have Miles.

That evening, while Susie dressed for her date, she thought back to the evening Miles had come to visit her, six months ago. She had been nervous as two women in labor. But Miles had quickly put her at ease with his mannerisms. He had sat, drunk lemonade, and spoken very quietly to her. He had told her why he had chosen to leave New York and travel, ending up in Selma. Miles came from a large family, but his immediate one consisted of only him and his father. He had been born and raised in Montgomery, attended seminary college in New York. He loved traveling, movies, reading, swimming, fishing, and holding her hand.

Susie had been drawn to him because of his sensitivity, finding it unique for a man to be so tender with her and the children. He reminded her a little of her father.

The more she saw him, the more she desired to be near him. He made her want to rise everyday and live it to its fullest. Sometimes she felt guilty, but the voice would speak to her, and she would be comforted.

"Susie, open the door, girl. I gots somethin' to tell you," Uleena yelled urgently through the front screen door, frightening her from her reflections.

"Uleena, you always comin' here in a hurry," she said as she unlocked and opened the door. "Come on in and tell me what the huffin' is 'bout. You know Miles is comin' by tonight."

"Girl, I knows that," she said as she flopped on the sofa and crossed her thin, unshapely legs. She grabbed a church fan from the end table and waved it in the air. "I won't take long. I jest had to let you know I heard that Rev'end Koffee spreadin' news to his preacher friends that he gon' come aftah you. He don't care if you is goin' with Rev'end Miles."

Susie frowned and lit a cigarette. "Uleena, you know I don't care 'bout no hearsay shit. And, I don't want to hear nothin' Koffee is sayin'. I don't know why you come here with that mess."

"I want you to know 'cause Miles, Rev'end Miles might find out and that could mean troubl' for you."

"He knows me well enuf to know I ain't seein' nobody but him, and I don't thank he'll stoop to listenin' to hearsay, but thank you for carin'. Now, if you don't mind."

"Well, he ain't that bad lookin' and he can preach his butt off."

"Well then, you go aftah him, if you that desperate," Susie said as she walked to the door. "I got a man."

"You full of shit, Susie."

"And it's my shit, Uleena," Susie smiled as she opened the door wider. Uleena was pestering her, causing her to become angry.

Uleena walked slowly to the door. She wanted to stay and see Miles. She loved looking at him and envied Susie, but she wouldn't tell her that.

"Alright then, but don't say I didn't warn you."

"Thank you, Uleena. Now bye," Susie said as she ushered her friend out the door and ran to the bedroom to dress.

She was patting powder on her face when she thought of what Uleena had said about Koffee. She didn't want to believe the old preacher who had been so nice to her almost a year ago when she needed uplifting, would be spreading nasty rumors about him and her. A chill passed over her, and she shook it off.

Now, as she reflected, he might have had other intentions, though she hadn't noticed. He had been a complete gentleman, almost like a father, offering to do little jobs for her, here and there. She had thought it was because of his ministry and caring for people.

She frowned at her image and wondered if her life was going downhill again. Naw. I won't let it. I thank I'm fallin' in love with Miles, and I cain't lose him. He's become part of me.

Hot, unshed tears appeared in her mysterious eyes and for a moment she became frightened. Another chill passed through her. She gazed into the mirror and wiped the tears from her

blushed face. Then she sat, looking deep into the mirror, not seeing her image as her mind drifted.

She found herself humming:
I sit here wonderin', If this is meant to be.
Is thaih any hope, for me?
Or will it be the same
Ole thang, like befoe?
Naw, Naw, that could nevah be, 'Cause in my heart, I know
he's truly meant for me.
But will this last?
And what will he want
from me that I cain't return?
Will my dreams evah come true,
Or am I simply bein' anothah fool?
Jest anothah fool in love?
Anticipation, it's drivin' me wild.
Anticipation. Oh, I hope, jest for a little while.
Anticipation. It this meant to be?
I don't know, guess I'll wait,
Guess I'll have to wait, and see."

She stopped as suddenly as she had started. "Shit, Susie,
what in the world is got into you, makin' up some song like Billie
Holiday? Somebody would thank you gone off the deep end," she
chastised herself. She quickly walked into the living room where
she heard his special knock.

"Evenin', Miles. Come on in," she smiled as he entered and
kissed her on the cheek.

"Evenin', Susie. Was that you I heard singing'?" he asked as
he sat next to her on the sofa.

"Yeah, I guess I got kinda carry'd away."

"Sound'd like a nice song. Sad, but very nice."

"Thank you," she said, embarrassed.

"Hey now, don't feel shame 'round me. I love yo' voice, and I
love you, Susie," he said as he had, several times before and
kissed her lightly on the mouth. "Tell me 'bout yo' week, alright."

"Hold on," she said feeling silly. She went into the kitchen and brought out some pound cake and lemonade. Then they sat talking, giggling, holding hands and sitting close as two people in love can get.

Soon after their last date, Miles drove Susie and the children to Montgomery to a nice colored restaurant. It was their first time dining out together, and she was delighted.

Blanche and Lola were so excited they barely ate their food.

"Mama, this is so nice. Why don't they have places like this in Selma?" Blanche asked.

"They do, but they white, and we ain't allowed to go to them."

"Yeah. I don't know why the white people can have them and we cain't," Lola offered.

"That's jest the way thangs is, y'all. So let's jest enjoy all this nice food and the music so we can 'member it," Susie advised, smiling at them.

Miles smiled and laid his fork down. "You are two of the nicest girls I've ever met, do you know that? Yo' mother has done a fine job raisin' you all and you should be proud of her and yo'selves."

Blanche blushed, "Thank you, Rev. Miles."

Lola grinned and leaned forward, her eyes shinning.

"Thank you, Rev'end Miles. I'm glad you like Mama."

Susie's head jerked to the side, and she dropped her fork. She leaned forward. "Miss fast lady, watch yo' mouth. That's grown folks' business. Now eat yo' food like yo' sistah," she demanded lightly.

"Yes, Mam," Lola said softly, grinning inwardly. She sure hoped her mother and Rev. Miles would get married.

Blanche was also thinking the same thing. She wanted a father like the rest of her friends.

"Uleena," Susie reminded, "You and me been friends now for years. You jest like a sistah to me, so I figure I can talk to you 'bout a lot of thangs." They were in Susie's kitchen where she was pressing Uleena's hair.

Uleena nodded her head in agreement. "You know you can, Susie."

"Tell me, what do you thank of Miles?" she queried, peering closely at Uleena.

Surprised at the question, Uleena's heart skipped several beats and raced. She felt as if she were suffocating.

"Uleena?"

"What do I thank?" She paused to catch her breath. "I thank he's 'bout the finest man I ever set eyes on. Any woman would give anythang to have him." She hoped she sounded normal.

"Even you?" Susie asked, hiding a smile behind her arm.

"What kinda question is that to ax me? I'm yo' friend."

Susie released her laughter. "Oh shit, Uleena. I was jest teasin' you. That's why I ax'd you. Friends is 'spose to be honest with each othah. So he ain't yo' type, huh?"

Uleena made an attempt to stand. She felt the urge to run, afraid she would give herself away.

"Hold still so I can finish straighten' yo' hair befoe you sweat it back. I sho would tell you if I thought the man you was thankin' on marryin' was my type."

"Marryin? Y'all gon' git mar-red?" she asked, suddenly hoarse.

"Uleena, would you please sit up and be still befoe I burn you. You know you cain't move yo' head up and down while I got this hot comb in my hand, unless you want to go 'round with a brand of blisters on yo' neck. And to answer yo' question, yeah, I'm thankin' on gettin' mar'red. I love him. Why you actin' so surpris'd?"

"I'm sorry, Susie. I didn't mean to. I'm jest in a hurry. I got me a hot date tonight, and I need to git ready."

Taken aback, Susie almost dropped the hot comb on Uleena's neck. She held the smoking comb in the air and faced Uleena. "You got a what? When did all this happen, Uleena?"

Uleena squirmed for a second then smiled. "Yeah girl, I do. I met him at church two Sundays ago, on the way out the door. You was busy talkin' to the Rev-end."

Susie put the comb down and hugged Uleena. "Girl, I'm so happy for you. This is the best news comin' from you I heard in a long time. Why didn't you tell me?"

"Too busy girl. I'll tell you moe latah. Now, will you hurry up?"

"Alright. But tell me now," Susie said.

"Well, thaih ain't much to tell. He's tall and good lookin' with pretty teeth and bedroom eyes and talks real pretty too."

"Hum, sounds kinda like Miles."

"Yeah, he do look a bit like him, but he ain't no preacher." She wished Susie would hurry so she could leave.

"Well, hush my mouth. Let me put some curls in yo' head so you can git outta here. But you know I got to meet him. What's his name?"

"Henry Lee."

It was hours later that Susie realized Uleena hadn't congratulated her on her promising engagement, and that she had acted strangely after she mentioned marrying Miles. She scratched her head. "I wonder if she's lyin' 'bout her new friend? I don't know nobody at church named Henry Lee. But, why would she lie to me?" Susie said to herself. Puzzled, she decided to speak to Uleena soon about her new boyfriend.

20

Rev. JaRett was surrounded by five of his colleagues who were congratulating him on becoming the temporary Assistant Minister of New Hope Baptist Church.

Susie was standing in line, her eyes, searching for Uleena. "Y'all know where Uleena is?" she asked Blanche and Lola.

"Nome," Blanche answered.

"I saw her goin' toward's the ladies' room, Mama," Lola said.

"It's sho strange she didn't tell me. Oh well, she knows where to find us," Susie replied and turned to face the front of the church.

"Thaih she is, up in front of us," Susie pointed. *Somethin' funny is goin' on here, and I aim to find out what it is. Uleena been actin' too strange, come lately, and when I ax her what's wrong, she says nothin'. But nothin' is startin' to smell like somethin' is stinkin'. What in the devil is she up to?*

Her mind continued to race, gathering bits and pieces of memories. Then she saw Uleena extend her right hand toward Rev. JaRett.

A sudden brightness momentarily filled Susie's eyes, then she threw her hand into the air. "Rev'end JaRett," she said with such urgency that he withdrew his extended hand just before Uleena touched him. Uleena swung around and threw a look of hatred at Susie that would have killed her had it been able to touch her. She reached for Miles's hand again, but he was moving toward Susie.

When he reached Susie, she grabbed his arm and led him outside. After telling the girls to wait. She turned to Miles. Her eyes burned with yellow sparks. She blinked to shield them from the fiery August sun.

At that moment, Susie saw clearly, as if seeing a scary picture show, Uleena and Miss Bosmun. They were at Uleena's house, discussing Miles and voodoo. Uleena was fit to be tied. Her small eyes were red and bulging, as if she was straining to release some discomfort. Miss Bosmun looked hesitant, as if she didn't agree with Uleena.

She squeezed her eyes so tightly they hurt, blocking the alarming vision. She didn't know whether to run back into the church and confront Uleena or tell Miles. She was extremely hurt and appalled knowing that her best friend had betrayed her. She started to tremble.

"Susie," Miles spoke softly, touching her hand, guiding her under a shady tree. "Please tell me what's goin' on here, in thaih..."

She opened her eyes before he finished and looked at him. He blinked from the intensity of her eyes as they burned into him, causing him to feel naked, helpless, but not afraid. Then she blinked again, and he leaned slightly forward as if tired from running.

He shook his head and took both of her hands in his. "I know now. I always thought thaih was somethin' unique 'bout you. I have from the moment we met and I was so drawn to you. Yo' eyes have always been a mystery to me, quite differen' from any othah woman I've met..." his voice trailed off. A thoughtful expression on his handsome face, he scratched his head.

"Let me tell you 'bout what happen'd in thaih," she offered, dismissing his revelation. Me and the girls was in line when I miss'd Uleena. Then I saw her up thaih, gettin' ready to use her right hand, when she's left hand'd. She was goin' to use voodoo on you to git you to quit me and run aftah her."

"You jest answered my question. You got 'ole folks' eyes'.

You're clairvoyant, Susie. Aren't you somethin'? Thank the Lawd for you," he grinned, quite in awe.

"So you don't thank I'm a freak?" she asked, Uleena temporarily forgotten.

He picked her up and swung her around several times, before putting her down, causing the church members to stop for a moment and stare at them. "Susie, you have been blessed with the Gift to heal and lots more, a wonderful thang. And the reason I'm not afraid is 'cause I've witness'd it several times befoe. I'm overjoyed."

Blanche and Lola grinned and patted their patent leather shoes on the dusty ground.

"You mean you know 'bout this kinda thang?" Susie couldn't believe she had found someone at last who could probably help her to understand herself.

"Come on, dear woman. Let me take you and the children home. Then latah, we'll go for a drive so we can talk. Thaih's many a thang I need to know 'bout you that you've been holdin' back on me. And Susie," he said in quiet tones, as he escorted her by the elbow. "I promise you, she will nevah get me. I belong only to you."

She shook her head in agreement, hoping he was correct, remembering what Miss Lou-Lou, her old landlord, had told her.

Hours later, Miles stopped his car in front of a fine restaurant in Montgomery, Alabama. It was actually his place, closed for business as were all colored places on Sundays.

Susie told him about her knowledge of her Gift, about running from and denying it. She spoke of the dreams and visions. The things that scared her. But mostly she wanted to know why she had gone through so much when she had been born special.

Miles listened hard and patiently, then tried to answer her last question. "Susie, the only thang I can tell you is that we who b'lieve are all Gawd's children. But, those that He chooses to do His special business, must, or He punishes them jest like any parent would. But, He won't hurt you to spite you. He wants to make you understan' and obey His will."

Susie smiled and took his hand, placing it on her face and holding it there. She loved his large hands with the tiny hairs peeking from the pores. And she loved his smell, clean and crisp as hand-washed white clothes, hanging out on the summer line, blowing in the soft breeze.

"We'll get through this thang with Uleena. I'm sorry she's hurt you, that she's not the friend you thought she was."

"I jest cain't b'lieve it, Miles. I loved her like she was my own sistah. I don't know how I'm gon' tell her 'bout this, without stranglin' her."

"You'll find a way, Susie. Now, I thank we bettah git on back to Selma." He stood and pulled her to him, kissed her tenderly, and locked the doors to the restaurant.

"So that yellow bitch call'd out to him, and like the puppy dog he seems to be, he jest left me standin' thaih and ran to her like she was a bone he need'd to chew on," Uleena fumed as she paced Mrs. Bosmun's floor.

"So you didn't git to do it, huh?" Mrs. Bosmun smiled.

"Damn it. This ain't no laughin' mattah. You promis'd me it would work."

"I said if you shook his hand. It ain't my fault you didn't, so don't git mad at me. You the one want the man."

"You damn right I do," Uleena raved as she stamped her feet on the floor. I want him so bad I lied to her that day 'bout goin' out with a man that favor'd Miles. How do she git so lucky with the men?"

"If you was a man, you prob'ly would go aftah her. She a fine lookin' woman with a good brain, and she loves people. She do good by her chil'ren and mind her own business.

"She sho cain't help it if the Good Lawd gave her them Indian cheeks and them thin lips and keen nose," she grinned. "I sho wish I had her high titties." She shook her head slowly, rolling her large eyes toward Heaven, then gave a big sigh.

"I don't know why I come to you for help. You seem to be on her side. She got two men. Two'."

"Uleena, she ain't. I don't know why you keep tellin' that lie. The woman's only courtin' Rev'end JaRett. She cain't help if Rev. Koffee like her too."

"That's what I mean. The bitch can have her choice," Uleena's thick lips curved upwards, almost reaching her nose as she frowned. I got to thank of somethang else to take him away from her. You with me?"

Mrs. Bosmun held her hands up and backed away. "I don't thank I ought to have nothin' else to do with yo' voodoo, Uleena. That stuff ain't nothin' to play with. You could do somethin' wrong and end up killin' Susie. I don't want no part of it."

"Hell. I don't need none of y'all. I can git help from somebody that knows what they doin'."

"Why don't you try gettin' anothah man on yo' own?"

"You can go straight to hell, Miss Bosmun!" Uleena balled her fist up, threateningly, then ran out the door.

Soon afterwards, Miles pulled up to Susie's door. Mrs. Bosmun peeked out her window and ran into her bedroom and stayed there, quiet as the dawn before sunrise.

"You best be careful whenever Uleena is 'round you, Miles." Susie warned when he turned the motor off. "I got a feelin' she might try somethin' else."

"It's a shame people resort to that old African mess when they know bettah. Those evil witch doctors have been dead so long, I almost forgot they 'xist'd. But they can do anyone lots of harm. I'll watch my step."

"Love portions. I wonder why people call it that when they have to use the evil stuff to git a man or woman." Susie spoke more to herself than Miles. "Ain't no love in that mess," she shivered, turning to Miles. "I'm glad you talk'd to me 'bout this. My mother nevah did."

"And she wouldn't have. None of our parents would let us hear them talkin' 'bout that. It's a sign that we're uncivilized and evil. Non-Christian like. And everybody knows we's all good Christian folks and wouldn' hurt nobody," he joked, lightly.

"Hush yo' teasin'. This ain't funny."

"We have to find some humor in all bad things, sweetheart, but you watch yo'self too," he warned and touched her face gently. "Now I have to git goin'."

"Alright then. See you soon." She ran up the steps and into the house before Miles could walk her to the door.

To avoid Susie and be near Miles, Uleena moved her membership to New Hope where Miles was Assistant Pastor. She knew Susie well enough to know that she was not the kind of woman that needed to be near her man all the time. Too much pride and self-esteem. She hated Susie for her beliefs and strengths.

Susie was both pleased and sorrowful that Uleena had departed because it truly meant the ending of a friendship she had thought would last. She was hurt that her friend had betrayed her and vowed that she would have it out with Uleena one day. She promised herself that in the future she would be more careful choosing her friends.

Uleena made a trip to Mobile, Alabama, where she met and had one of the best known voodoo men around prepare a potion for her that would do exactly what she wanted. Then, like a snake, she waited for the right moment to strike.

That night, as she sat rubbing her rail-like legs with Vaseline, she grinned to herself knowingly. "Susie, you, yellow, high-falutin' bitch. Yo' time is comin, real soon."

When Uleena returned to Selma, she learned that Susie was visiting her uncle in the country and would be gone for two weeks. That Sunday Uleena placed her name on the sick list at church and asked for prayer, setting her plan in motion.

The following Sunday, she had one of the sisters deliver the message that no one had come to visit her and requested prayer at her bedside, by Rev. JaRett.

When Miles heard the request, he cringed inside and tried

desperately to get out of going. "Brother Jones," he said to one of the deacons, "Cain't you or one of the othah deacons stop by and see Sistah Woods. I had plans..."

"Pastor, I cain't do that. I'm leavin' for a convention tonight, and it's moe proper like for the preacher to see 'bout the sick. They 'xpects that."

"Well, Rev'end Jones should be back tomorrow. I'm sho Sistah Woods would like to see him since he's head minister."

"Nawww, suh. I heard she ax'd for you," the deaconess said pointedly. "And the Rev'end won't be back then."

He hated himself for agreeing to be here, standing on Uleena's porch, waiting for her to open the door. He had a sinking feeling that he was probably making the worst mistake of his life.

"Evenin', Rev'end Miles," she said in a voice that sounded like a frog trying to speak. I'm so glad you could make it. Come on in." She shut the door and stood close to him, inhaling his clean manly odor as he entered the house.

Her cheap perfume almost gagged him. She smelled like roses mixed with musk. He turned away and coughed before speaking. "Evenin' Sistah Woods. Sorry to hear you're ill."

"Thank you, Rev'end. Will you please follow me? I gots to lay down befoe I faint." She turned, flouncing her long, red dressing gown behind her. The odor of her perfume and her clothing reminded Miles of a woman of the night. He frowned, not moving.

She turned and croaked. "Please, Rev'end Miles. I gots to lay down." He covered his nose and reluctantly followed her. Uleena eased her heavy butt onto the bed and slipped her fluffy red slippers on the linoleum floor. She looked at the chair next to the bed. "Please sit down."

"I can only stay for a few minutes. I have an engagement at anothah church." He eased onto the straight back chair and sat forward as if posed to run. "Would you like prayer now?"

Ignoring him, she said, "Rev'end could you git me a glass of tea from the ice box? I feel so hot inside. The glasses is right over the sink. Brang two and the tea."

He stood quickly, relieved to get out of the room for a few

minutes. While in the kitchen he decided he would leave as soon as he took her the iced-tea. He didn't like the sick feeling he was getting in the pit of his stomach.

"Thank you, Rev'end Miles, she said when he placed the refreshments on the table next to the bed.

"Please pour some for us."

"No, thanks, Sistah Woods. I'm not thirsty." He remained standing.

She fanned herself with her short, thick hand.

"Please. It ain't polite to drank by yo'self in front of company. And I'm burnin' up inside." She pulled at her dressing robe.

He poured the brown liquid. As he handed Uleena the drink his eyes strayed to an ugly picture on the wall.

She waited until he had glass in hand. "Here's hopin' I have a quick recovery," she offered, pretended to sip her tea, and waited.

Miles drank the tea in one gulp and placed the glass on the table. "Sistah Woods, I must be goin'. Maybe I can drop by some othah..."

He didn't finish. Suddenly weak, he grabbed for and fell backwards into the straight chair and wiped at his hot brow with the back of his hand. "It's so hot in here," he slurred as if drunk and pulled at his suit coat.

Uleena smiled knowingly. She placed her untouched glass on the bedside table. "Yeah, it's so hot; I thank I bettah take this ole thang off. She flung the musk smelling gown to the floor and leaned forward on an elbow, exposing small breasts that hung like a milkless cow from her flimsy gown. "You need any help with that shirt, honey?" she grinned, showing her dark blue gums.

He didn't answer her as he struggled out of his coat and pulled at his tie, trying to catch his breath. He was losing all reasoning and felt the urgency to escape this evil woman.

His eyes were glazed, his body nimble; he stood and took several steps before reeling toward Uleena's bed.

She grinned, caught him, and pulled him on the bed. He tried to fight her roving hands as she pawed him, pulling at his clothes.

But he was helpless and lay in a stupor while she undressed him.

"Now, you jest relax and let Mama take care of you, my honey man," she whispered and kissed him fully on the lips. He didn't move.

She rubbed her thick hands over his bare chest, then kissed him again.

"Susie. Susie," he moaned as saliva gathered in the corners of his mouth and ran out.

"Come on, honey man. Let Mama show you how to love a real woman." She pulled at his pants and threw them on the floor, followed by his socks. Her eyes turned red as the devil's when she saw his manhood. She shivered and moaned and her serpent's tongue moved to touch his face.

She lay on him and began moving her body in rhythmic motion. "You the best lookin' man I have ever seen in my life. I love you, and nobody gon' have you. You all mine; you hear me, honey man?"

"Susie, Susie baby," he slurred but didn't move. "I feel sick."

Uleena's hands traveled up and down his body, but he didn't respond. He lost all sense of reality. He was somewhere between hell and hell. Totally defeated.

She whispered in his ear, "That yellow, high falutin heifer, bitch, ain't gon' have her way no moe. Not when I gits through with you."

She leaned over, reached into the nightstand drawer and took out the prepared rubber she had gotten from the *man* in Mobile, grinning Satan's grin as she slipped it over Miles' swollen manhood.

Miles reached for her, "Susie...Susie...Susie..., so sick," he moaned.

21

"What's goin' on here?" Miles demanded in a voice filled with ice-cold fear and panic as he awakened to find himself in a strange bed. He stared around him and gagged at the huge, hideous furniture in the bread-box of a room.

Then he yelled, "Where in the devil am I?"

Uleena ran from the kitchen where she had been cooking ham, eggs, grits and biscuits and stood in the doorway, smiling and looking like a buzzard who had captured its prey.

"How you feelin' this mornin'?"

"What in the hell is goin' on here? What, how did I get into this...this damn bed?" His nostrils flared, and his eyes bulged from his head as he fathomed what must have happened.

Uleena's smile disappeared, and she took a step back.

"Where are my clothes? Get them this minute!" He started to move from the bed but realized he was butt-naked. He felt nauseous and gagged, wishing this was only a bad dream he was coming out of.

"Why Rev'end Miles, whatever is all the fussin' 'bout? We had a nice time last..."

"Give me my damn clothes befoe I do..."

Before he could finished speaking, she ran from the room like a frightened cow and returned shortly with his neatly folded clothes.

"Put them on the bed and turn away from me!"

Quickly dressing, he walked and stood behind her. "Turn 'round," he ordered. He wanted so badly, for the first time in his life, to strike a woman. Uleena was shaking so badly, her stick legs moved like twigs in a windstorm as she faced him.

His handsome face was distorted in pain and disgust. "It seems you did what you've been tryin' to do all along. You must be 'bout the lowest woman on this earth to do what you've done to me and Susie. I've always respect'd women, but you don't belong in the same category.

"I'm sure you had me dressed with your voodoo, but if somethin' happens to Susie, I'm goin' to make you wish you..." He raised his hand to strike her, then lowered it.

"I wouldn't touch you if I was dyin' and you were the only creature on this earth who could save me."

He turned and fled home, fell on his knees, and cried like a baby, cursing himself for being so weak, wishing he could turn back the clock.

Meanwhile, Uleena slipped to the floor, howled like a wild animal and cursed the ground he and Susie walked on, vowing she would get even with them.

Days later, Susie sat on Miles' lap, wondering why he was acting so strangely, even though she sensed something had happened while she was away. For a moment, her stomach lurched. A sinking feeling. Cold fear washed over her.

She looked closely at Miles, trying to read his mood. "Do you have somethin' you want to tell me, Miles? She asked and held her breath.

"Well, I do feel a little under the weather," he managed to say, wanting to tell her everything, but the words wouldn't fill his dry mouth. He was ashamed and frightened that he would lose her.

He was too much of a coward to tell her that Uleena had gotten to him, had betrayed her. He had jeopardized them.

"Miles, what's botherin' you?" she moved from his lap and sat next to him.

He flinched inside. "Baby, I jest don't feel too good tonight. It has nothin' to do with you. I miss'd you, and I'm glad you're back, but I've got to get out of here. I'll come by early Saturday, and we can drive to Montgomery, if that's alright with you?"

"That's fine, but I thank maybe you outta see a doctor or somethin'. You actin' mighty strange, baby," she advised as she saw him to the door.

"I might do that. Goodnight, Susie."

"Goodnight, Miles."

He fled without kissing her goodbye.

Miles was no better on Saturday. "I'm sorry, I don't know what's wrong with me," Miles apologized as he pulled away from Susie, unsuccessful at kissing and caressing her. He stood and gazed out the window of the house he owned outside of Selma and sucked in a deep breath, feeling as dismal and chilled inside as the night he stared into.

"Miles, somethin' is wrong here." Susie said behind his back in a strained voice. "You been actin' funny for a week, and you startin' to lose weight. I tole you to go to a doctor."

He turned and pulled her back into his arms. "Always 'member I love you and want to spend my life with you. Will you do that, Susie?" He asked with such urgency that Susie became frightened.

She pushed him away and looked into his sad eyes. "I know you do. We talk'd 'bout that, but why do you sound like you goin' somewhere and won't be comin' back?"

"Oh, baby. It's nothin' like that. But I thank I'll have to leave for a few weeks. I'll let you know where I am and keep in touch." He needed to get away because he was hurting. His manhood was stinging so badly he wanted to scream out in pain. He was frightened for his life, and hers.

Miles fled to Montgomery, checked himself into the hospital, and had every test run on him that was possible. When all the results came back negative, he became more alarmed. He continued to lose weight, and his manhood was turning bright red. The staff at the hospital only seemed perplexed at his situation and gave him salve, saying he had a serious rash.

Finally, he went to his father and told him everything.

"Lawd, son," Rev. JaRett, Senior, uttered, "You have made the worst mistake a man can make, lettin' a bad woman git to you. I'm scared for you. What I can do is send you to a woman, a psychic lady, and I pray that she can help you. Lawd, I don't know why these thangs always seem to happen to the people who tryin' to be good. It's all in Gawd's hands, son. You want me with you?

"Thanks, but I'll go this alone. I jest hope I can git some help for Susie."

Susie slipped from her bed, holding her private area, experiencing burning pain. She ran into the dressing room, pulled down her panties and examined herself. She was red as a rooster's tail.

Alarmed, she made a doctor's appointment. Not even mildly concerned, the doctor told her she had a rash and gave her some salve to use. But over the next several days she became worse, developing a fever and a headache that pounded like a brick banging on her skull, no matter how many Stanback powders she took.

Mrs. Bosmun came to her aid, helping as such as she could by putting cool towels on her forehead and sitting with her while the children were in school.

Susie lay restless most of the day, but today she slept. And dreamt.

She floated across the Edmunds Pettus River Bridge. The sky was pitch black, but the full yellow moon brightened the night. Susie stood before a new, two story house that had a long narrow window on the side near the door entrance. Looking inside, she saw a woman who favored Uleena, but much older.

As if by magic, the window opened, and the woman handed Susie a tin snuff can and a black and white ointment jar filled with a gelatinous substance that resembled blackberry jam. Then the woman leaned forward and whispered in Susie's ear.

Susie turned and saw Uleena rise from the ground and stood grinning, her teeth larger than a wolf's.

"What you doin' here?" Susie asked.

Uleena didn't answer, just grinned wider before disappearing.

Susie walked quickly from the house. Crossing a bridge, she saw her sister, Ella Mae, standing before her.

"The lady in the big house tole me to put this on my face."

"You fool you," Ella Mae snapped, "That lady ain't doin'nothin' but messin' you up for Uleena." She grabbed the containers and flung them over her left shoulder, into the river.

Susie awakened from the vision hurting. She tolerated the pain. But the vision alarmed her.

The following day, Susie had a visitor. He informed her that Uleena's family lived just across the Alabama River, in Sardis. Susie was furious. Uleena had told her more lies than a screen door had holes.

But the information didn't help her find the answer to her problem. And she also had no answer why she hadn't heard from Miles who had been gone more than three weeks. As the days passed, Susie became worse.

An old family friend from the country, dropped in to see her, and was appalled at her condition. "Susie, whatever in the world is wrong with you? You look like somebody buried alive, gal."

"I don't know, Mister John. For weeks now, I been gettin' worse with this fever and pain. I went to every doctor I can thank of, and ain't none of them did me no good."

"You don't need no doctor. You need help." He sat down and held her hot, limp hand in his. "Let me tell you somethin' 'bout this preacher I know. For two years he walk'd 'round with a leg as big as a elephant. Then his body took on the swellin', 'til finally he couldn' preach no moe. Everybody gave up on him and wait'd for him to die.

"But the preacher was bullhead'd and weren' ready to lay down and die without a fight. He had somebody take him to a spiritual man. The man tole him his pulpit had been dress'd and he was near death but he could save him. He did, and that preacher walkin' 'round today, thankin' the Lawd for givin' him a mind to go to the holy man."

"What's that got to do with me?"

"You need that kind of help, and I aim to see you git it. I'll stop back by here in anothah hour and take you to git this spell off you."

"I don't thank that's it. I ain't been 'round nobody to git nothin' in me."

"You be ready when I come back, Susie," John said as he limped down the steps.

22

John helped Susie climb the steps to the Wizard's house. The Wizard was a spiritual man who had helped release many people from their voodoo curses. He was a tall, light-skinned man, sporting a thick brown beard on his thin face. He was dressed in unlaced army boots and wore a top hat; resembling a darker version of Abraham Lincoln.

Leaving John sitting in an overstuffed chair in the waiting room, the Wizard ushered Suzie into his study. The study was large, with bright floral printed wallpaper, chairs with cushions and a large, shiny mahogany desk. On the desk stood burning candles and a kerosene lamp that smelled of a vanilla cake, lightly seared; lending a mysterious quality to the room.

Against the wall, behind the desk, a long table held jars filled with assortments of two-for-a-penny candy and cookies, dill pickles, skins, peanuts and much more. Under any other circumstances, Susie would have been delighted to see a reminder of her childhood.

The Wizard helped Susie into a plump chair in front of his desk then eased into his large leather chair. No words were spoken as she sat watching him pull a piece of red flannel and seven cork stoppers from his drawer. He placed the items on the desk.

"Alright, Jack, do yo' trick," he said.

The seven cork stoppers started dancing around on the red flannel as if by magic. Mystified, Susie gazed intently as the objects jumped from the desk to the floor and back again.

"Alright, Jack, stop," he ordered, and the dancing ceased. He took the flannel and placed it over a round red bulb, then turned to Susie. "I know everythang 'bout you and yo' friend Uleena," he said. Then he described Uleena so well Susie thought for a moment she was standing before him.

After he finished explaining what had happened between Uleena and Miles, Susie shivered and fought back tears, covering her face for a moment to hide her pain and fear. She didn't want to be reminded of a friend that had used and betrayed her. Briefly she felt red-hate for the man who had promised to love her and never harm her.

"I'm sorry, Susie. But you must not blame him. None of this is his doin'." He paused and opened another drawer and pulled out a bottle of black liquid. "I want you to take this for three days, stop for two and start back and finish the rest of it. If you don't feel bettah, you come back to me. Young lady, you lucky to be alive." He stood, walked around the desk and held his hand out to assist her.

Susie didn't move. She longed to ask him how he knew so much, but she thought if she doubted him, then she doubted herself and her Gift. If God had given her a Gift to heal and see into the future, then why not others to stop people from doing evil, she reasoned. "Thank you," she whispered and extended her hand.

Back home, she sat at her living room window, gazing out at the sunset, then frowned as she saw images of the devil, Uleena, and Uleena's sister. She closed her eyes to erase the horred picture and hugged herself, rocking from side to side.

Then as clearly as she saw her hand before her eyes, she knew what the images meant. Uleena wasn't going to give up.

"Damn. Where is Miles with his cowardly behind?" She asked the silence of the darkening night.

Unaware that Susie had sought the Wizard's help, Miles contacted him, and made arrangement for him to visit her. He did not deem it necessary to inform Miles that he had already seen Susie.

Several days later, when the Wizard knocked at her door, Susie, in her weakened condition, was so surprised she had to hang on the doorknob to stand up.

He bowed and grinned as customary, shaking his head.

"Susie, Susie. I see you haven't been followin' my orders. Don't you know murder is a sin?"

She blinked at him as he led her to the sofa. She sat down gingerly. "I don't plan on killin' nobody, Rev'end Fields," she whispered, using his Christian name.

"You is, if you don't do like I tell you. You threw it out; didn't you?"

"Yes, Suh."

"Cain't you see you're killin' yo'self? You done lost a good deal of weight since I saw you, and you ain't that much bigger then a half pint no how. Them black rings under yo' red, watery eyes ain't for sport, I know. Lis-sen here. Wait, let me git you some water so you can take some of the medicine I brought."

He returned in less than a minute, sat next to her, gave her two tablespoons of the strong, dark liquid, causing her to frown with distaste as the burning fluid went down.

"I'm goin' to leave this with you, and this time you *will* take it or else. And drank plenty of water afterwards. You do understan'?"

Susie shook her head. "Yeah, I understan'. But what I don't is why you came here." She ignored the glass of water.

"Yo' Rev'end Miles sent me, thank the Lawd." He paused, handed her the glass of water then continued. "He found out he was fixed and wanted to make sho you got help. You'll be hearin' from him soon. And I'm gon' tell you again: don't blame him for this. He tried to fight it, but he couldn'. Thaih's some thangs in life that's too powerful for any of us. Voodoo is very strong stuff, if the evil stuff is put together the right way."

At that moment, Susie's eyes changed. The blazing yellow

lights flickered as if seeking answers from him while he sat mystified, unable to think or feel as her fiery eyes held him powerless.

When her eyes returned to normal, he fell back against the couch, shaking his head. "Lawdy, if you ain't got ole folks' eyes. You got the Gift jest like I figured. Gawd bless you. And He's sho gon' make sho you do it, too. Yes-suh-ree," he said and stood.

His tone changed to a secretive one. "In five days you will be feelin' almost like yo'self; but you must go to Uleena's house everyday with this dirt." He handed a brown paper bag to her. "It's got to be put in her house or you won't live. Aftah that, eat and drank as much as you can to git some of that weight back. And that burning under yo' clothes will go away." He tipped his hat and placed it back on his head as he left.

Susie stood in the doorway long after he had left, wondering how she was going to put the white looking dirt in Uleena's house. The thought of getting close to the woman made her cringe, but she knew she had to do it. Yet she hated the whole idea of the evil ritual. And as for Miles, she would handle him when she saw him, if she lived.

The following evening Uleena opened her door and saw Susie, a living ghost standing before her. Her small eyes bulged in her narrow face. Her large lower lip dropped open like a door with no hinge. She backed up and tried to close the door. *Why ain't she dead. Damn it to hell. I hate her.*

"Please, Uleena. I have to talk to you," Susie pleaded as she placed her foot inside the door, praying she wasn't showing her feelings: fear, anger, pain.

"I know it's been a long time, but I had to find out why you stop'd bein' my friend. I was so hurt when you jest took off and didn't say nothin' to me. Do you hate me, Uleena?"

Uleena gulped and swallowed, but didn't give an inch.

"I sho miss'd you, Uleena. We had so many laughs and fun together. You was my best friend," Susie uttered, desperate to gain entrance.

"Oh, alright. You can come in," Uleena said in a thin voice.

She thought Susie must be crazed to be at her door. *This could be a good time to finish her off,* she thought and smiled.

Susie found a chair near the door and sat on its edge.

"Thank you for lettin' me come in. Thaih's so much I need to know. Tell me what happen'd to us?"

"Oh, Susie, chile, I jest had to git outta thaih. Too many thangs was goin' on. And that man I tole you 'bout made a fool outta me. Tried to use me. I jest couldn' stay thaih, and I couldn' tell you. I was too shame."

You lyin' bitch. You know you tried to kill me, and when it did-n't work, you ran like a damn coward. "I know what you mean, but you coulda tole me. I was yo' best friend, Uleena. I woulda understood and stood by you." Susie paused to catch her breath, and calm her nerves.

"Why did you do it, Uleena?" She said, not being able to hold her tongue any longer.

Uleena's tiny eyes got smaller. "Do what?"

"Why did you claim to be my friend, then try to take my man from me? You know I loved you like you was my sistah."

"I didn't do that, Susie. I...I wouldn' do that to you aftah all you done for me."

If only you could go straight to hell for lyin.' "You sayin' you didn't try to use voodoo to git Miles?"

"Yeah. I swear I didn't. And if you want, I can come back and join the church again to prove it."

"Naw, you don't have to do that. But I been awful hurt, Uleena, and I miss'd you." *Now don't go too far, Susie, or she might want to be yo' pretend friend again.* But she needed to get the dirt under something, and she didn't want Uleena to be suspicious.

"I'm still yo' friend, Susie. I'm sorry for runnin' out on you and not tellin' you 'bout my problems." Uleena smiled the devil's smile, and Susie returned with an award-winning smile of her own.

Susie stood. I'm glad to know that. I feel bettah, but I have to be goin'." She pretended to look at her skirt. "Oh darn, I got a spot on my skirt. Can you git me a cold rag, Uleena?"

As soon as Uleena left the room, Susie took the dirt from her skirt pocket and threw it under the sofa where Uleena had sat, then moved next to the door.

When Uleena returned, Susie quickly took the wet cloth and dabbed at an imaginary spot and handed it back. "Thank you. Maybe I'll drop by tomorrow." Susie slipped out the door and waited for Uleena to follow.

"That would be fine, Susie. You take care. You look awful po.' You been sick?" She stopped and frowned, "What's that odor? Do you smell it?"

Susie sniffed the air. "Naw, I cain't smell nothin', but I been sick. My smellers ain't the best. Bye."

"Bye, Susie. You take care and try puttin' some weight on. You done got smaller then a minute."

"I sho will, Uleena," Susie said as she went down the steps. At the bottom, she heard Uleena sneeze. She smiled and walked down the street and was still smiling when she reached her front door. *You lowdown heifer. If you could, you would stomp and spit on my grave tomorrow.*

The next day, Susie was able to get the dirt in Uleena's house by pretending she wanted some collard greens from her garden. While Uleena was picking the greens, Susie threw the dirt under her bed.

The third day Uleena wasn't home, and Susie panicked momentarily as she tried to figure out how she was going to get the dirt in the house. Finally, she decided to sprinkle it from the front door to the bottom of the steps and hoped Uleena would track it into the house.

Five days later, Susie cooked and ate a huge meal of collard greens, fried chicken, yams, okra, potato salad and corn bread. Then she stood from the table, held her full stomach, and made a face that looked like a crossed-eyed dog; Blanche and Lola couldn't help laughing, glad their mother was almost herself once more. It pleased Susie to see smiles on their pretty faces.

Soon, the Wizard appeared at her door, grinning. This time, she smiled with pleasure.

"You doin' bettah, I see. But I brought you somethin'."

He offered her a brown paper bag. Susie looked into the bag and frowned at the roots and waited for an explanation.

"I want you to chew on them, then spit the liquid out like you would snuff. Do it three times a day 'til Sunday. Sunday's the day she gone try to git to you again. But I don't want you to hit her. If you do, I cain't help you no moe."

Susie stared at him with hooded eyes. He gave her a half smile. "Yeah, I know you got a temper when provoked."

Before Sunday service began, Susie was speaking to one of the deacons when Uleena appeared before her, almost out of breath.

"Excuse me. Susie, can I talk to you? I got somethin' I thank you gon' like. Here, try this." She tried to force a piece of chocolate candy into Susie's mouth.

Susie backed away, holding her hands up. "Naw, thanks Uleena. What are you doin' here?"

"Oh, jest vistin'. I want'd to be with you. Won't you taste this candy?" she begged, holding the candy up to Susie's mouth again.

Susie's hand went up to strike her; then she remembered the Wizard's warning. "Uleena," she admonished, her eyes blazing, "Don't try it again. I tole you I didn't want none. And you know I don't eat candy this early in the mornin'."

"I'm sorry, Susie." She said as she walked to the waste basket and tossed the candy inside.

Susie didn't hear her. She left her standing in the vestibule, fighting the powerful urge to keep from kicking her teeth out, especially when she saw Uleena discard the candy. She didn't sit in her usual pew.

Her eyes were closed when she heard his familiar voice. They flew open. She found him looking directly at her, sending her a message of apology. She turned from his pleading eyes, pretending to look for something in her pocketbook, but she couldn't ignore his voice.

"My subject today is, 'Beware of Friends for They Could Be Wearing Sheep Clothin'."

At that moment, Uleena slipped from the church, rushed

home, returned before she was missed, spotted Susie, and squeezed into a seat behind her.

Later, when members started shouting, ushers rushing here and there with spirit-of-ammonia, Uleena stood and carried her hand over Susie's head, in one sweep.

Susie turned, astounded to see Uleena. "What is it you doin'?" she asked angrily. "You know bettah then touch my head."

"Thaih was a ladybug in yo' head," she whispered.

"Even if thaih was, you couldn't see the front," Susie replied. Don't you ever touch my head again, Uleena," Susie glared at her then turned away.

"I'm sorry, Susie. I was only tryin' to help. Uleena sat down, removed her glove, balled it into a knot and placed it deep in her pocketbook. An I-got-you smile spread across her face.

When service ended, Uleena had vanished.

Her evil deed accomplished, Uleena had immediately left church, expecting Susie to die within minutes. Once home, she had disposed of the poison glove by burning it. Then she sat, waiting to hear of Susie's death.

After service, Susie looked for Uleena, deciding to give her a piece of her mind, but to no avail.

Outside, Miles, whom she had ignored after church, took her arm, excused her, and steered her away from the group of people gathering around them.

"Susie, I'm so sorry 'bout everythang. I just return'd late last night, too late to stop by. I know it's been moe than a month since I saw you, but so much was goin' on...I know I have some 'xplainin' to do, but not here." He looked at her with such honesty and sincerity she couldn't say no to him, no matter how angry and hurt she was.

"I sho hope you got a real good reason. So good the dead would b'lieve you." She pushed his hand aside and walked away, the girls trailing behind her with somber faces.

23

After taking the children home, Susie returned to church to help sell dinners for her usher board. She was preparing a plate when she had a dizzy spell. Swaying, she closed her eyes and held onto the table until the dizziness passed, and continued serving the meals.

Susie's mind wandered to Miles, and she became angry again. She hadn't bothered to tell him she wouldn't be home when he said he would stop by. Of course, this served him right, after all the hell he had put her through. *Layin' with that evil woman, then runnin' off like some coward and leavin' me here to suffer. Well, I know he ain't no coward, but I'm gon' let him have it good.*

Another wave of dizziness swept over her. She swayed, almost falling.

"Is you alright, Sistah?" a friendly, heavyset usher questioned, helping to steady her.

"I don't know, Sistah Heathy. This is the second time I felt this way. Maybe I'm comin' down with the flu or somethin'."

"Well, you jest come on over here and sit down while I git you a glass of water. It's hot in this kitchen anyhow, and you ain't been too long got over that sick spell of yo's." Before Mrs. Heathy returned, Susie slipped to the floor in a dead faint.

Half an hour later she opened her eyes and looked into Miles' worried ones. He sat next to her on the bed, holding her hands.

"You pass'd out, and I got thaih jest in time to brang you home. You feelin' any bettah, or do you want to go to the hospital?"

"Somebody else coulda brought me home."

He looked hurt. "Susie, please don't do this to me. I love you. I know I was a coward for goin' away and not contactin' you. But I was seriously ill and afraid that I had cost you yo' life. I was desperate and sought help from God, the hospital, my father, a spiritual woman, and then the Wizard, who I also sent to you. I didn't want to stay away; I had to."

She didn't respond. She hurt so much. She wanted so badly to forgive him. But could she?

"Susie, please try to understan'. At one point I was so bad off I want'd to commit murder; I actually want'd to kill that woman for what she did to you and me. The longer I stay'd away, the moe I 'cided she wasn't worth it.

"But it took a lot of prayin'. And each time I thought of you, I felt so guilty I knew I deserved to hurt 'cause I had betray'd you. I know thaih's nothin' I could say that would ease yo' pain and the feelin' of betrayal, but please let me remain a part of yo' life."

"It's too bad you didn't do all this talkin' befoe you took off and left me here to cope with the hurt and pain.

"Don't you know I went through hell, man? That woman tried to *murder me* by havin' sex with you."

She shook her head and stared at the wall before speaking again. "I jest don't understan' how you end'd up at her house and in her bed, and I guess I nevah will. And right now, I don't know if I want you in my life if it's goin' to cause me moe pain. Thaih's been so much of it already, too much for my chil'ren."

Miles stood up, tears filling his eyes. "Susie, I know what you went through, I almost died myself. The pain was almost unbearabl'. I couldn' begin to tell you much I hate myself for lettin' this happen. I'm real sorry, baby," he said and slumped in the chair next to her bed.

Her heart went out to him. He was such a good and sensitive man, and she loved him. Sitting on the side of the bed, she reached for his strong hands.

"I know you madder then hell at her. And I know you meant well and that you cared when you sent the Wizard, but that didn't make me feel any bettah when I was hurtin'.

Then when I saw you earlier today I want'd to hit you, hurt you the way I hurt'd."

He squeezed Susie's hands and held them to his sensitive mouth. "You have become my life. When you hurt, I hurt. Are you sayin' this is the end of us, Susie?"

"Yeah, I guess I am," she answered, shocking herself.

She wasn't so sure she wanted to quit him, but there was a vacant spot, way down in the pit of her soul that hadn't been there before.

He stood and released her hands. "Please don't make yo' mind up yet, Susie. Take some moe time to thank on us. Now, if you're alright, I'll be goin'."

"I'm fine, you can go," she answered, closing her eyes. She long to have him stay; however, she just could not handle it.

Miles looked at her with wishful eyes then slipped from the room.

Blue Monday morning. Susie sat up, stretched, and yawned before pulling her tired body from the high bed. After slipping into her house shoes and a thin housecoat, she walked into the kitchen to make coffee before going into the washroom.

On the way out she stumbled as a sudden pain stabbed at her brain, causing her to see stars and hear roaring in her ears. She turned and balanced next to the wall, and made her way back into the washroom where she splashed water on her face.

Feeling no better, she peered into the mirror and screamed a sound so piercing, it shook her entire body.

She slipped to the floor just as Blanche and Lola bolted into the room. They ran to her side and gasped when they saw her flaming, red scalp.

"Mama," Blanche screamed and started crying.

"Oh Mama, what happen'd to yo' po' head?" Lola moaned as she fell next to her mother, crying.

"I don't know," Susie moaned. "Y'all hush yo' cryin'. Go call Rev'end JaRett and tell him to git here, quick!"

They ran from the room. Susie crawled to the bed and pulled herself in, all the while moaning with pain.

It seemed as if Miles arrived in a matter of minutes and rushed into her bedroom. He took one look at her head and covered his mouth with his hand, turned, and ran to the phone. When he finished, he returned and took her into his arms.

"Blanche, Sistah, y'all girls go on to school. I'll stay here with yo' mother. I've call'd someone to come here to the house to help her."

They nodded and fled to their rooms, tears flowing.

Hours later, the Wizard walked into Susie's room. When he saw Susie, he gave his usual abrupt laugh and said, "I see you let her get to you, after all." He looked closely at Susie's head. Then he acknowledged Miles who was still holding her.

"It seems like every time I look 'round, this pretty lady gots troubl'. That Uleena just don't give up tryin' to kill her.

"I warn'd her about that evil woman, but she got to her anyway. I don't know," he said, shaking his head in disbelief. "I'm amazed she still livin'. This is bad, real bad stuff. "I know her scalp is on fire." And as if to prove his point, he held his hand over her head. "I can feel the heat comin' from it. Cain't use nothin' to cool it off, could kill her." He scratched his head.

"Sometimes this evil is too much for a spiritual man like me, but I keep prayin' to stay ahead of the devil. Lawd knows he's busy with Miss Susie." He reached into a brown paper bag and pulled out a jar filled with blue looking jelly. "I got to put this on her."

"Susie, can you hear me?"

She opened her glassy eyes. "Yeah."

"Susie, I have to put some of this on yo' head. It's gon' burn like all-git-out, but it'll cool you off and take some of the pain away."

He opened the jar and dipped his long fingers into the jelly substance that smelled like mint. It was warm to his touch as he rubbed it in the palm of his hands. "Susie, I want you to try and hold still while I rub this on you scalp. I'm gettin' ready to put it on.

"Hold her real tight, Rev'end Miles."

If Miles hadn't been holding her, Susie would have vaulted through the ceiling when the ointment touched her burning scalp. Her mouth opened, but the pain was so intense she couldn't scream. Instead, her body convulsed for several moments, and then she fell limp.

The Wizard pulled several more containers from his bag and handed them to Miles. "I want you to take this and wash her head in it twice a day, and each time, take the water and throw it out front, in the street, and say 'go', three times 'til all the stuff is gon'. And take these herbs and make some tea for her. They kind of bitter, so add some sugar and lemon and make her drank it all. She'll go the restroom a lot to git rid of the poison. She'll live, and her pretty hair will grow back."

"Alright." Miles was so visibly upset, his eyes flooded with tears. He felt Susie's pain. He was loaded down with guilt, almost to the point that he wished he had never met and fell in love with her.

The Wizard offered, "This ain't none of yo' fault, Rev-end. It's jest the evil stuff that some folks thank they can use and git what they want." He paused and turned to glance at Susie.

"I'm sorry to say, but the devil of a woman is gon' try somethin' again."

"What!" Miles yelled. "Somethin' or someone has to stop that vile woman."

"You will do somethin' 'bout her. Now lis-sen." He explained what the next attempt on Susie by Uleena would be and how they would stop it.

Four weeks later, Susie wrapped her healing head in a fancy scarf, pinned it on the side with a brooch and strutted into the colored retarded children's home fundraiser with Miles proudly by her side.

She was in the reception room speaking with several women when Uleena appeared, grinning as if they were still the best of friends. Susie glanced at her as if she were a fly on the screen door trying to get in her house, and continued speaking to the ladies in her circle. *If that witch comes and tries to butt in, I swear, I will beat her to an inch of her damn life. Please let me control myself and not act a fool.*

When they moved to the outside where a picnic area had been set-up, Susie asked one of the ladies serving food for a Coke-a-Cola. But before the woman could hand her one, Uleena offered her an opened one.

"Here, Susie. I jest got this one, but I don't want it."

Susie's eyes became beacons of fire as she glared at Uleena for a moment. She raised her hand to strike her, but Miles intervened. He took Susie's hand and led her away.

Uleena cursed under her breath, moved away from the crowd, and poured the soda under a shady table. Within minutes, the grass turned to the color of hay.

Uleena, having failed to kill Susie and take Miles as her own, left Selma, days later for New York.

When Susie heard the news, she thanked God and hoped she would never see Uleena again.

24

Susie opened the door and looked into Rev. Koffee's face. Surprised to see him, she ran her hands through her hair and waited.

"How you doin', Madam? I was jest passin' by and thought I would stop by to holler at you."

"You what...I'm doin' jest fine Rev. Koffee. But I'm busy right now, if you don't mind."

"Oh. I'm on my way home." He offered, twisting his brown derby hat in his hands.

Susie bade him goodbye and wondered why he was stopping by so often. Not finding an answer she shrugged her shoulders, dismissing the thought.

She sat brooding – about Miles. He was enough to keep her constantly occupied. She had hoped with Uleena out of their lives she and Miles would be able to put the past behind them and move on with their future. Though she had put all her effort and most of her energy toward mending their relationship, she found it was faltering. Yet she would not give up.

And Miles, who had always been so kind and generous to her

and the children had tried just as hard. She admired him for his diligence, his honesty, and his love for her.

Yet, as time elaspsed, she was astutely aware of Uleena and could not banish her from her mind. Each time Miles left her, Susie escaped to her room and cried. Finally, she pleaded, "Gawd, you know I have tried and tried to make it work, but I jest cain't take it no moe. The thought of them bein' together is so vivid to me. It still hurts too bad. I loved him so much. We coulda been so happy together."

Even though Susie had eventually decided to leave Miles, she hadn't the courage to voice it. Then she discovered that after six months Uleena had returned to Selma, a bitter taste entered and remained in her mouth. It was then that she decided to say good-bye to Miles the next time she saw him.

As Susie clocked out of work and walked through the door into the mild, May weather, she was so nervous, a slight chill passed over her. She needed to gather courage before she saw him. And she was sure she would before the evening was over. For now, she was grateful to be alone.

"Shit," she murmured as she turned a corner and spotted his car. *Does anythang ever go my way?"*

"Hi, babe. Get in. I've got a nice surprise I want to show you," Miles said as he leaned over and opened the door for her.

She peeked at him, squinted her eyes. "What is it?" she asked as she slipped onto the seat.

"A surprise."

"I hate surprises, and you know it."

"Not this one," he smiled, and her heart tugged, the armor slid away.

"Here, sit back, relax, and let me take you to it," he suggested, handing her an iced-cold cola.

She grunted but was grateful for the cold, strong liquid as it slipped down her throat. She wondered where he was taking her. Her pulse began to race.

"We'll be thaih shortly," he said as they headed northeast of Selma.

A while later, they stopped in front of a breath-taking, astonishing white house which stood on more than five acres of land. Two large Roman columns stood on each end of the massive house, and two smaller ones hugged each side of the steps that led to the porch which was more than ten feet wide. On the porch hung an imported hand-crafted swing, and next to it sat huge pots filled with glorious mixtures of fragrant flowers. The front entrance double-doors held the finest Italian glass which sparkled like the colors of the rainbow when the sun touched it.

Susie turned, bewildered, and gazed at the yard, finding it filled with pecan, pine, and magnolia trees.

She sniffed until she spotted the sweet luscious roses and honeysuckle bushes. Here was everything she loved, and wanted for her and her children.

"Come on, Susie."

"Who's house is this?" She didn't move.

"A friend's. Come on," he urged, taking her hand, pulling her through the wide doors.

"You didn't knock..."

The foyer was spacious, revealing a pale yellow and blue marble floor that shone like diamonds. She opened the double doors and gasped at the spacious parlor with wide Victorian windows that mirrored beautiful roses. She turned and looked at Miles who only smiled and led her to another door.

The living room held two sets of French furniture with matching drapes and sheers. The cool warm colors of peach, rose, and green reached out and pulled her into the enchanting area. She slipped her hand over the fine furniture, then glanced down to find she was standing on carpet so soft she couldn't feel her feet.

Miles smiled proudly, gently taking her hand, leading her to a grand kitchen with a large stove, ice-box and quaint eating area. The adjoining dining room held rosewood furniture surrounded by walls covered with pale pink wallpaper.

Next, he led her up winding steps to huge airy bedrooms.

The master bedroom made her gape with awe, its beauty beyond her imagination. The wallpaper was patterned with clusters of roses, deep pink and yellow. It was as if she were in a rose garden and could almost smell the enticing scents.

Suddenly, she needed to get away. It reminded her of the vision she had before meeting Miles, though she had never been in the house. It reminded her of the future she had always wanted but knew she couldn't have with Miles.

Miles, sensing her uncertainty, felt dismal. This was something he wanted to give her and the children. He had loved this place from the moment he planned the blueprints and watched the structure take shape. Even then he knew he was taking a risk.

But he wanted to give Susie something she had always wanted: her own beautiful home where she and her girls and he could live and be happy. He, however, would have preferred they move to Montgomery where his family and friends lived. Miles had decided that if Susie didn't want him, he would still give her the house.

Finally, Susie whispered, "Alright, Miles, tell me why you brought me here to look at this house?"

"Don't you like it?"

"Answer my question."

"Would you like to have it?"

"Miles, don't ax me no foolish question like that."

"It's not a foolish question. Please answer me."

"Why, sho I would. Anybody would."

"Then it's yo's."

"What?" she asked, taking a step backwards, shaking her head in denial.

"I had it built for you. You always said you want'd a dream house. You tole me how you want'd it to look. I did this.... I love you and the girls. I want us to be a family."

Susie turned away, not wanting him to see the tears, and her answer in her eyes.

My Gawd. How do I tell his po' man goodbye when he'd done all this for me and my chil'ren? Lawd, I don't want to hurt him, but I got to let him go.

"Are you alright, Susie?" Miles asked, standing behind her, lightly touching her shoulder. She could feel the tremble in his fingers.

She turned around and smiled. "Yeah. This is all happenin' so fast. What did you do, rob a bank or use yo' life savin's?"

"The cost doesn't mattah as long as you like it." He could tell that she loved the house, but he could feel a sudden coldness in the warm air.

Seeing his disappointment, she tried smiling again.

"I thank it's a great house, and I know the girls would love it. I prob'ly wouldn' be able to make them go back home aftah seein' it."

He smiled, encouraged. "Then we can brang them out latah today."

"Naw," she answered abruptly. Then in a soft tone she lied, "They have to go to the county to visit Uncle Tom. Maybe next week. As a mattah of fact, it's almost time for me to take them to the bus station."

When they were in the car, Miles turned to Susie and said, "What do you say we set a wedding date? Then we can go to Nouth Carolina and pick out the rest of the furniture, or you can change whatever you don't like."

Susie stiffened. Her mind raced. She rambled in her pocket-book and pulled out a cigarette and lit it. "I don't know, Miles, I ain't thought 'bout a weddin' date." She knew she was in shit-up-to-her-boots and didn't know how she was going to wade out of it. Her mind raced. *Tell him, fool. Don't keep the po' man hangin' like this."*

"Susie, you know I love you with all my heart. I know we have gone through some 'xtraordinary events in the last eight months, but I had hoped we could work it out and move forward with our lives. Thank of what we had befoe the trouble start'd. If you feel you need moe time, please let me know. I would nevah push you to marry me, even if it means my heart would be broken."

Tell him now, fool. "Miles, you're a good man and any woman is lucky to have you." She hesitated; her inner soul ached to its core. "But, I need jest a little moe time to thank 'bout us."

He turned and looked at her strangely. "Are you callin' us quits, Susie?"

Seeing the pain in his eyes, she turned coward. "I'll have to let you know 'bout everythang in a few days."

After her comment, Miles had driven so quickly, it seemed to her, that they reached her house in less than a minute. After seeing her to the door, he ran down the steps, jumped in the car, and took off angry and hurt.

"Susie, if you ain't the biggest coward. You had the opportunity to tell the po' man and git it over with and what did you do? Lead him on again. You should be shame," she whispered to herself as she prepared for bed.

Susie's days and nights were filled with memories of how they had met and fallen in love and how happy they had been. She thought at last she had met her soul mate and her best friend, and she realized she would never find another like him.

Yet, she spent the next days in torment trying to find the best way to tell Miles goodbye. She loved him, but she couldn't get the acid taste of Uleena out of her system. Consequently, she couldn't marry Miles, not even for the children's sake.

Ultimately, Susie faced him. She sat in his car. When he tried to touch her, she pulled away.

Her words spilled forth and stung him like a thousand wasps. "Miles, I'm truly sorry, but I cain't marry you. I tried all I know how to convince myself that it would work, but I would be deceivin' you and me. We would be miserabl'." She paused when he took a quick breath and closed his eyes. "You see, I jest cain't git this thang with you and Uleena out of my system. Til I do...I'm sorry." She fought back the searing water of anguish.

Miles looked at her. Tears filled his sensitive eyes. "I'm sorry too, Susie." His voice wavered. "I won't come back anymore, if that's the way you want it. But I want you to know that *somebody* had me where I couldn' sleep at night, and on my knees prayin' and cryin'. That same *somebody* is goin' to make you cry... If I could do this all over again, I would nevah hurt you or let anybody else do you harm. Goodbye, Susie," he said, tears streaming down his handsome face.

Susie opened the door, slipped from the car, and ran up the steps. His voice stopped her. "Always remember, I love you, and you should have been my wife." His words were like a goodbye kiss, spoken lightly, but having so much weight.

She slipped into the house and fell across the bed, hurting as if Miles had just died.

25

Susie laid down the skirt she was making for Lola and reflected on the past few months, fighting a foray of tears.

The past months had been filled with torture. Each passing day had served only to remind her of her loss of Miles and the crying spells that lead to horror for her and her family. She felt as if Miles had just driven from her life. She could still see his devastated face, his tear-filled eyes and hear his wavering voice. Those words, strange though they were, had played in her head daily. At the time she hadn't thought of them as odd; now she wondered what he had meant when he had said, "That *somebody* who had me where I couldn't sleep at night, and on my knees prayin' and cryin', that same *somebody* is goin' to make you cry..."

Susie cringed each time the message gamboled in her head. She felt as if there was something sinister about those charges and the promise they indicated. She wondered who that person could be and if she could prevent the situation from occurring. Then she asked herself why hadn't Miles said something to her before their last time together.

It was all too strange, too evil. But she needed to know what evil lurked around her. Deciding to squash her thoughts on the nerve attacking situation, she collected the skirt and continued sewing. But her thoughts rolled back to the moment when she had to tell the girls the devastating news of her breakup with Miles. And the events that followed.

Even though she had delayed for days, hoping she would be calmer when she had to speak to them, it had served no purpose. As she sat explaining to them, tears welled in her eyes. They had been overwhelmed by the awful news because they loved Miles as a father-to-be and had looked forward to her marrying him. She had tried to console them, but had failed miserably. The girls went to their rooms, wailing uncontrollably. It was much later that they were calm enough so that she could tell them that sometimes things just don't work out between two people.

Shortly thereafter, she had received a heart-wrenching letter from Miles, offering to give her the house he had built for her. She had felt as if she were going to crack into a thousand fragile pieces and would not be able to come together again. She found herself on the floor, praying.

Praying for peace, forgiveness, for guidance and strength, and anything else that she could think to ask her God for. Then she collected the Bible from her bedside table and read daily until her eyes burned and her brain became flooded.

Soon afterwards, she began to experience uncontrollable weeping spells everyday around two o'clock. Not wanting to confide in anyone, she prayed more, became more involved with the girls, started a vegetable garden, anything to keep her occupied. But she found to her dismay the spells still occurred. Weeks after the occurrences began, she felt the urgency to speak to someone because she believed she was headed for a nervous breakdown.

Finally, Susie spoke to Girt, a casual friend and a co-worker. Girt, who was fond of Susie, had noticed Susie leaving for the ladies' room at exactly the same time everyday. She became alarmed after learning the reasons and suggested to Susie that she take her to see a fortune-teller. Initially Susie refused, but desperate, she relinquished and agreed.

Later that evening she had sat smoking a cigarette and think-ing of her decision to go see this man that everyone, but her seemed to know about.

If I'm suppose to be a fortune teller, why cain't I figure out what's wrong with me, instead of goin' to see somebody, she pondered.

There are certain things you're not expected to know about you, Susie. And you haven't been doing anything about your pow-ers. You can't grow or help others.

"The long lost voice. I see you back." She spoke as if she had regular conversations with the voice. "I thought you said you was 'spose to stay with me and help me. But you been gon' so long, I forgot 'bout you."

You also forgot what you're supposed to be doing. It's been years, and you haven't even asked the Lord to help you strength-en your Gift. And you know you were supposed to be getting ready, but you didn't. But when things started to go your way, you forgot me and your Gift. But I never left you.

Now that you are at your last wits, you finally call on the Lord to help you. Susie, you know better than that.

"I always thank the Lawd for everythang, day and night. I pray for myself and othahs."

But you don't pray for wisdom as you are expected to. You said you were going to start taking your Gift seriously, but you didn't. Susie, you know not to play with the Lord.

"I do know that. I wasn't playin', at least I didn't thank I was. But you right; I thought I was doin' fine. And I stop'd havin' them dreams and thangs. I was glad. Now all I seem to do is cry all the time, like some fool."

You are no fool, Susie.

She didn't answer as she put out and lit another cigarette. What more could she say?

As promised, Girt took Susie to see Mr. Windmore, a spiritu-al healer. After Susie was settled in an overstuffed chair in Mr. Windmore's office, he smiled at her.

She didn't return his greeting. Instead, she glanced

around the small, snug study. His room was filled with the same kind of junk food as the Wizard's had been. *They all must like this stuff.*

"Naw, Susie. All of us don't like junk, but I love mine. Care for some?"

Susie jumped in her seat. "You readin' my mind!" she blamed, dumbfounded.

"It seems that way. Now, let's git down to why you're here. I know you been havin' cryin' spells for moe then a month now and you wonder'd if you was losin' yo' mind. You also sent the man away that loved you, and you feel guilty, and for a minute thaih, you thought that was the cause of yo' cryin'. But you know, deep down, it's somethin' else."

Susie, drawn to the short, round man and his wisdom, sat up straighter in the chair and leaned forward.

"The cryin' spells you been havin' every day, at two o'clock sharp." She noticed his speech was similar to Miles' then frowned, wondering where he came from.

"I hail from Louisiana. Don't thank when I'm speakin' to you; it distracts me."

She sat at the edge of the chair and looked directly into his keen eyes.

"The cryin' spells you been havin' have nothin' to do with yo' sanity. They are a sign that someone very close to you will expire. I know who it is, but I cain't tell you. I'm not 'spose to tell you. You will not be goin' with the family, and you will miss the opportunity to leave Selma and start a new life."

"If you cain't tell me, why am I sittin' here then?"

"I can tell you, but I have been warn'd not to. You'll see soon enuf," he said with a sad smile.

She was angry and stood to leave.

"Wait. Sit down. I have somethin' else to tell you." He leaned forward, both elbows on his desk, his large hands, clasped. "You have been runnin' all yo' life, Susie. You have been runnin' from a phenomenal force that is truly not goin' to let you git away with it. It is stronger than you, me, the World.

"You are a strong, wise, and intelligent young woman, but you are also scared and sometimes weak, weak in the spirit.

'Cause you are, and all of us have been, you have suffer'd unnecessarily. But one day you will do what is intend'd of you, and I don't have to tell you what that is."

Suddenly Susie was uncomfortable. This odd man was scaring her.

"Susie, it's okay to use yo' Gift. Yes, it makes you differen', but only in the spiritual sense. You'll find yo'self happier if you just open up to Gawd. He's got lots in store for you."

Susie stood abruptly and backed away from him. "I have to go." Then she turned and fled his office.

"I don't b'lieve him," she said to Girt as she grabbed her hand and led her from the overbearing man.

"You bettah 'cause he knows what he's talkin' 'bout, Susie. You can mark his words. They gon' happen 'cause he's the man the Lawd done surely call'd to heal and see the future."

Susie refused to discuss it, started talking about the upcoming revival at their church as they headed down the dusty road for Selma. Once again, she was denying her Gift.

Bang! Bang! Bang! It sounded as if someone was attempting to beat her door down. She ran from the back porch, to the front door.

Susie opened the door to the mailman. "What's all the bangin' for, Mr. Ike?" Then her heart skipped several beats as she noticed the telegram. Telegrams had always meant bad news to her and others she knew. Remembering her sister, Mae Frances, who lived in Washington, D.C. with her husband, who was expecting anytime, she decided it may be good news.

"Evenin', Miss Susie," Mr. Ike said in his flat tones. "I got a telegram for you."

"Evenin', Mr. Ike," she replied and waited for him to hand her the telegram.

As he started to hand it to her, he said, "Wait, I thank I got anothah one for you."

Susie dropped her hand and refused to take them. She shook her head and murmured, "Naw. Lawd, naw. I don't want to see them." She felt her insides tearing apart.

"But you gots to read them, Miss Susie."

She shook her head and closed her eyes in fear.

"You want me to read them?"

She trembled, "Yes, Suh, Mr. Ike, please do..."

One telegram was from her brother, J.T., who lived in Detroit, informing her of the death of their sister Mae Frances. And the other was from their sister Willie Mae, who lived in Washington, D.C.; it stated the same horrible news.

Hours later, one of the assistant ministers of her church found Susie wandering down the middle of the railroad tracks crying and moaning Mae Frances' name.

As soon as he assisted her into his car, the whistle from the train blew, and the locomotives whooshed passed them, rocking his car with its speed.

The minister cringed, thinking that if he hadn't gotten Susie off the railroad tracks, she would be dead because she had paid the train no attention.

Due to Susie's depression, she did not attend her sister's funeral. Instead, she remained in her room, in shock, refusing to speak to her children or anyone else.

Much later, when the shock wore off and reality sat in, Susie found it difficult to believe her young sister had died from childbirth. Mae Frances had given birth to a girl who had been named for her.

Susie was devastated over her sister's passing, but she knew it was killing her mother. She longed to be with her, but found it too difficult. Instead, she penned long letters expressing words of comfort and love because that's all she had to offer.

She took an extended leave of absence from work and sat idly around the house during the day. At night she read her Bible and prayed for forgiveness, asking God to help her become a better person, but she avoided asking for spiritual guidance in her Gift.

Months after Mae Frances passed, her husband wrote Susie, offering her a job as his secretary. She responded, thanking him, but refused his offer explaining that she couldn't leave Selma just yet.

Instantly, she knew that Mr. Windmore had been correct about everything. She shuddered violently as she remembered the vision all those years gone past when she had seen Mae Frances lying dead, on the floor. She felt faint. Gasping for air, she rushed to push the window up, flinging her head under it, breathing in the air so quickly, she hyperventilated.

After catching her breath, Susie turned from the window, numb. She felt nothing and didn't care. She lay across her bed, fully clothed and remained that way for days. She was left alone as she had been months earlier, simply because everyone thought she was still mourning the loss of her sister, which was true. However, she was also tormented because she realized the loss of more than twenty years of her life.

She had been given a special Gift and had refused to use it. Because of that refusal, she was similar to an infant, yet worse in the sense because a baby eventually learns to walk, talk, run, listen, and so on. She was worse because she knew better and hadn't bothered to learn how to go forth with her wonderful blessing. Now she felt as if she were never going to succeed at anything. She believed she was cursed. So she refused to speak to the voice she knew was waiting for her to take that step that would transcend her to higher and greater prosperities.

She retrieved Lola's skirt and tried to stitch it, but her vision was too blurred to see the needle. She laid the skirt down, walked into her room, fell to her knees and cried. She was so full of pain from all the awfull events that had happened and tried to dismiss them.

She realized that if she prayed and the voice returned, she would be lying to herself that she was cursed. And deep down, she knew she was gifted, special, but too stubborn to accept it.

26

Christmas season was at hand, yet Susie wasn't looking forward to the occasion. She found herself submerged in self-pity, and every attempt she made to pull herself up from the pits seemed only to make her feel worse. Blanche and Lola, who were usually happy and looking forward to all the holiday festivities, were caught up in their mother's mood. Susie realized the effect she had on them and attempted to appear enthusiastic for their sake, but when she was alone at night, she wept endlessly.

Five days before Christmas, there was a tap at her door. When Susie answered there stood her brother Augustus, grinning from ear to ear, his arms loaded with bags filled with gifts.

"Well, jest don't stand thaih with yo' mouth open. Let me in gal."

"Augustus? It cain't be you. Naw, it cain't be. How did you know where I stay'd?" Susie asked with such excitement and emotion in her voice, it almost made her brother cry.

"You know me. I lost yo' address and had to get it from Mama. You know I had to see my favorite sistah." He waited for her to let him in. "Is you gon' let me in, or not?"

Stepping out of his way, she smiled and said, "Come on in.

Come on in and let me see if it's you or somebody tryin' to play a trick on me." Her swollen eyes twinkled with mischief.

"Gal, you know it's me. You jest tryin' not to show no emotions, but you can cry if you wants to," he teased as he placed the bags next to the sofa.

"Augustus, you still a fool. Come here and give me a hug, man!" As she hugged him she thought, *Gawd done answer'd my prayers. Thank you Lawd.*

Tears of joy filled their eyes as they smiled at each other. "Let me call the girls in here. They won't b'lieve this. Blanche, Sistah. Y'all come in here for a minute."

When they saw their Uncle Augustus, they ran to him, and showered him with hugs and kisses. After the greetings, Susie shoed them out, then she and Augustus settled down and talked for hours. While carefully observing her, he talked of their mother, Rubye Mae. She was helping to raise Mae Frances' daughter which helped her accept the loss of her daughter. The rest of them except Willie Mae, were living in Detroit, Michigan, working for the Chrysler and Ford car foundries making more money than they thought possible.

Satisfied with the news about the family, Susie smiled and said, "Now, tell me why you here?"

"I'm here 'cause I want'd to surprise you. I miss you and so do the othahs. You the only one left here, and Mama been frettin' so 'bout you, so I said to myself, self, you bettah go and see yo' sistah and her chil'ren. So I gits in my ole car, and I drives days to git here." He smiled, picked up his coffee. "Aaaah, that's good," he smacked his lips together, then turned serious. "The 'Bamas ain't no place to live, Susie. I wish you would come away from here."

"I cain't go nowhere right now," she said and lit a cigarette, her hands slightly shaking.

"You sho lookin' good. Rev'end JaRett doin' somethan' to make you look that way?" he smiled mischievously, winking at her though he felt something was amiss.

She knew he was lying, trying to make her feel better. For a brief moment, a shadow passed over her face.

"We ain't together no moe, Augustus," she said and went on to explain what had happened between them.

When she finished, Augustus moved closer to her, put his arm around her, and gave her a brotherly hug. "I wish I had been here. Nobody woulda tried that mess, or they would be answerin' to me," he said in a threatening voice.

"It's alright. It's all over. And now that you here, everythang is jest fine. I still cain't b'lieve it's you, Augustus," she said and smiled at him as she patted his hand.

"Here," he said, handing her a beautifully wrapped gift, tied with her favorite color ribbon, yellow. "I bought you a special present 'cause you my special little sistah, and I love you. Go on, open it."

Smiling, she took the package and examined it. "So you jump'd in the car and drove down here as fast as you could, huh? Didn't take no time to stop on the way?" she teased.

He laughed, "Well, I did make a few stops."

"This is so pretty, I don't want to open it, and Christmas is right 'round the corner, you know."

"Yeah, I know, but it ain't for Christmas; it's for now."

"Well, if you insist." she beamed as she tore into the box. Surprised to see only newspaper after looking inside the package, she looked up at her brother and frowned.

"Go on, keep lookin'. I ain't tryin' to fool you."

She extracted newspaper and tissue paper from the box, until she pulled the last paper out, and saw a small box. She picked it up and examined it before lifting the lid.

Her eyes widened in surprise. Inside was one of the most beautiful cameo brooches, and beneath it, $25.00. She gazed at her brother for a moment before giving him a bear hug.

"Augustus, this is so...I jest love it. Thank you."

"Anythang to make my little sistah happy."

"And thank you for the money too. I sho do need it. You sho made mine and the chil'ren's Christmas, Augustus. You are a Gawd send." Her eyes twinkled with merriment.

"If you say so. If you say so, little one," he said and hugged her again, feeling much better because he had followed his intuition and come at this time. It pleased him to be of some assistance. After all, she had always given more than she had taken.

Several days before Christmas, they shopped for food and presents for the girls. Susie was ecstatic as she went from counter to counter in the department store, carefully inspecting the items.

Susie took so long in her selection, the white clerk finally asked her if she wanted to buy anything. That angered Susie because she knew that white folks always thought colored people were the biggest thieves in the world, and this person was no exception.

She also realized that if she wanted to buy anything from the store she would have to take the insults and watch herself or she could be thrown out or arrested and thrown in jail.

Soon she found two beautiful wool sweaters, and took the sweaters to the counter. The sales clerk looked at the price, laid the sweaters down. "Did y'all know how much these cost? Y'all got that much money?" she drawled, searching their faces, hers turning as red as a candy apple.

Before Susie could respond, Augustus intoned in a northern voice, "Mam, we know how much they are, without the tax. And she sure can a'ford them."

If the lady could have turned redder, she would have caught on fire. She made some unintelligent sound then said, "Y'all knows y'all cain't brang them back," she huffed.

Augustus paid for the items and they left, their heads held high, the nasty incident stored in their memory. They shopped until the stores closed refusing to let the incident dampen their spirits.

When they arrived home the girls were in bed which gave Susie a chance to wrap and hide their presents. Afterwards, she and Augustus sat and drank coffee.

The following days passed quickly as Susie, Augustus, and the girls prepared for the holiday. It was wonderful having her brother spend time with them. The day before Christmas they drove to Perry County to visit their Uncle Tom, and to cut a fresh Christmas Tree.

Tom was happy to see them and ecstatic over the gifts he

received from them, especially the chocolate cake Susie had baked. She invited him to go back and spend Christmas with them, but he declined the invitation, promising he would visit real soon.

On Christmas morning they attended sunrise service. The church was filled with wall-to-wall people, some Susie hadn't seen since the previous Christmas. Nonetheless, they were gathered for the next ninety minutes to give praise and thanks to their Lord and Savior, Jesus Christ.

The church roared with Christmas favorites, and anyone asleep on the street couldn't have slept for long as the glorious sounds rang beyond the closed doors and windows.

The minister's sermon about the birth of Christ raised everyone's spirits, soothed souls and hearts, making this day in their lives one of the best.

The aroma of the food and baked goods met them at the door and penetrated their senses, causing their mouths to water and their stomachs to growl.

Susie had spent Christmas Eve and all night preparing a feast which consisted of baked ham and yams, turkey and cornbread dressing, potato salad, collard greens and okra, string beans with red potatoes. Then before going to church, she had made cornbread, rolls, and creamed potatoes and gravy.

After eating a light breakfast, Blanche and Lola quickly cleaned the kitchen, anxious to open their gifts.

Giggling, the girls skipped into the living room and ran to the tree. Susie smiled at them, lit a cigarette, and glanced at Augustus who had been watching her very closely.

Susie curled her legs under her and sipped her coffee, thankful for her blessings. Tears formed in her eyes as she briefly thought of Miles and wondered what he was doing. Pushing the reflection aside, she thanked God for sending her brother to help make this day a very special one.

"Susie, is you alright?"

The girls looked up from beneath the tree when Suzie didn't reply.

"Mama, is you alright?" Lola asked anxiously.

She smiled and waved her hand in the air. "Don't y'all Worry. I'm jest fine."

They continued opening their gifts with, "Oooh, Sistah, look at this! Wow, Blanche, see this sweater. It's the best!"

"Thank you, Mama. Thank you, Uncle Augustus." And on they went, until all the packages were ripped opened and paper scattered everywhere.

Blanche and Lola hugged Susie and Augustus and excused themselves to their rooms, their gifts under each arm. Though Susie had tried her best to get caught up in their excitement, Augustus hadn't missed the sad, brief expressions that crept on her face and recognized she was hurting.

He watched as she gazed off into her own private world, unaware of her frown. "Ain't you gonna open yo's?" He managed to say pass the lump in his throat.

"Naw. I thank I'll jest lay here for a while and relax befoe we eat. If you want, you can go lay down, and I'll call you when it's time." She pasted a smile on her smooth face.

"Naw, I thank I'll stay here and keep you company, even if you go to sleep."

"Now, you know I don't nap." She rose from the sofa and slipped behind the beautifully decorated tree for a brief moment. She reappeared holding a small package wrapped in gold paper. She extended her hand.

"Here, I got a little somethin' for you. Merry Christmas."

He stood looking at her, surprised and pleased. "Susie, you shouldn' done that," he said, reaching for the gift with unsteady hands. He turned his back to her as a single tear forced its way down his face. He quickly wiped it away with the back of his hand and cleared his throat. He stared at the beautiful pearl handle razor. "You a mess, you know that," he turned, grinned and hugged her. "Thank you.

Susie handed him another package.

He took a step backwards, "Gal, what you tryin' to do, make

me cries?" he groaned in pleasure as he accepted the token of love from his sister.

"Naw. I'm jest tryin' to make you have a happy Christmas like you did us."

"Aaah, Susie," he said as he pulled out a brown leather strap that his brand new razor would be sharpened with. He grabbed her again and gave her a bear hug. "You know I ain't much good at words, but I loves you, and I thank you."

They pulled apart. Susie looked at him with love in her eyes. "Augustus, you will nevah know how much I thank you, and I love you too, baby brother."

He reached behind the tree and handed her more gifts.

"Naw, Augustus" she said refusing the expression of love. "You already done moe then enuf already."

"But if you don't open yo' presents, we ain't nevah gon' eat." "Okay," he said.

When Susie sat on the sofa, Augustus handed her the gifts. "Now you open them, and do it fast like. I'm gettin' real hungry now," he beamed, a twinkle in his eyes.

Susie looked at him, and like a little girl, she made a face at him and tore at the packages. The first one was a blue wool scarf that matched her two-year old winter coat; the second gift was cameo earrings from Blanche and Lola. She would hug and thank the girls later even though she knew her brother had helped to buy them.

When Augustus pulled a package from his breast pocket and handed it to her, she gave him a look as if to say, "Is you crazy, man, or is you rich?" She grinned, deviously. "You sho you didn't rob no banks on the way here?"

"Take it. 'Cause I ain't nevah gon' tell," he teased.

"But you already gave..."

"Would you jest don't fuss so, and take the thang and open it, gal," he said kindly.

"I wasn't goin' to say nothin'." She laughed as she ripped the paper, and pulled out a box. The girls gathered around her, having returned when they heard the delightful sounds from her. She removed the thin layer of tissue paper, and stared at the most exquisite watch she had ever seen.

"Oh, Mama," the girls squealed in unison.

The watch glittered with what seemed like thousand of diamonds as the reflection from the Christmas lights caused it to bring forth such colors that neither Susie nor the girls had ever seen.

"Augustus, this is jest beautiful. I nevah saw anythang so pretty befoe," she hugged and kissed him. "Thank you."

Augustus was so thrilled that he fought to hold back the tears. He brushed his hands over his head, his face. Then he said in a low voice to hide his sudden emotions, "Is it gettin' hot in here, or is it jest me?"

"I ain't hot. Is y'all girls?" Susie asked.

"No, Mam, I ain't," Blanche responded.

"I ain't, neither," Lola said, noticing her uncle's emotional display.

I cain't let them see me cry 'cause men's jest don't cry. That's only for the women and babies. He cleared his throat and smiled.

He didn't know that Susie had raised her children to be sensitive to everyones fellings. Men cried simply because they were human.

Promptly at 1:00 p.m., they sat down to dinner. After saying grace, they dug into the feast and filled their plates and stomachs to capacity. Blanche and Lola were so full they practically rolled from the table.

After dinner, Susie gave them a shoe box wrapped in bright Christmas paper, filled with various fruits, nuts, stick candy made in the Selma Candy Factory, and two silver dollars each. Later that afternoon they would visit their friends for several hours, something they seldom did. They smiled happily as they left the living room.

Later that evening, Susie and Augustus were lounging and dozing when someone knocked at the door.

Susie, tired from all the excitement, slowly pulled herself

from her comfortable spot on the sofa, stretched, and went to see who the unwelcome person was.

Her face dropped several inches at the sight of Rev. Koffee, his wide mouth spreading toward his ears.

Disheartened, she stepped back to allow him to enter.

"Good evenin' and Merry Christmas, Madam," he said cheerfully, handing her several packages, "These are for the girls."

Susie returned his greeting and thanked him for the presents, but she didn't want him there, especially not now.

But he seemed anxious to see who was visiting her, so she introduced him to Augustus. Astonishment showed on Koffee's face, but Augustus was able to hide his disbelief.

Susie offered Koffee a seat. "Can I offer you some refreshments?"

"Some dessert would hit the spot right 'bout now, Madam."

They sat in silence while he ate his sweet potato pie, each lost in their own thoughts.

"This 'bout the best potato pie I ever had. Maybe you oughta thank 'bout goin' into the bakin' business, Madam." he praised.

"You know, that's the same thang they used to tell her when we was little 'cause she was such a good cook. I tell you, cain't nobody cook like my sistah, not even our own Mama," Augustus said proudly.

"She sho got somethin' with this here pie." Rev. Koffee smacked his wide lips several times as proof of his belief. Besides home, her food was the only food he would eat. Simply because he trusted her.

After pushing the pie down, he sat for an hour talking about his classes at Selma University and his new church. When he began quizzing Augustus about himself, Susie gave her brother the eye, so when Koffee finished his inquiry, he knew nothing more than he had in the beginning. But Augustus knew a lot about him.

Beneath his calm manner, Augustus was completely appalled at this man who looked old enough to be their father and was shorter than a minute.

He couldn't believe this man was keeping company with his

sister. There was also something a bit too cocky about him. He didn't like the man.

"Where in the world did you find him?" Augustus charged after Koffee left.

"I met him years ago, before Nathan passed. I know you wonderin' how I got start'd with him," Susie said. "I didn't want you, y'all to know..." her voice trailed off, embarrassed.

"You sho said it. That man is all wrong for you, Susie. How did you hitch up with him? With some kind of spell or somethin'?"

"It's a long, ugly story, Augustus." She lit a cigarette and blew the smoke toward the ceiling.

"I got all night and then some."

"I...I was feelin' low aftah everythang happen'd with Miles. I stay'd at home, didn't go nowhere but to work and church for moe then a year or so. Then one day, Miss Bosmun, my neighbor, came over and beg'd me to go with him, Koffee, to this place he had in the country to harvest some crops.

"One mind tole me not to go, but I lis-sen'd to the othah one, even though at one time I had been uneasy 'round him.

But I toss'd that aside, too, 'cause he was a preacher and tryin' to help othahs." She paused and covered her face for a moment. She lit another cigarette.

"The damn man has to be usin' voodoo on you, Susie, or you a fool, and I know Mama ain't raised none of them."

"I didn't know you b'lieved in voodoo, Augustus," she said, dismissing his last statement, and not really confessing to hearing his statement about spells.

"Thaih's a lot of thangs we have to 'xcept in this life if we want to protect ourselves. Voodoo is a evil thang out thaih to worry 'bout. I had to find out the hard way."

"You did? What?" Susie asked, reaching for another cigarette and lighting it with shaking hands.

"Yeah. 'Bout two years ago, I was goin' with this good lookin' gal. We was havin' lots of fun, goin' out every weekend. Then she up and want'd to git hitch'd. But I tole her I wasn't ready for that. I back'd off and start'd to court somebody else.

"The new gal turn'd out to be the cousin of the girl I quit. I almost quit her but 'cided it wasn't her fault who she was kin to.

"Then, one day I drop'd in, this ole girlfriend was thaih and she had a sweet potato pie. She knowed I loved them, but I didn't want none that day.

"She had a hissy-fit, cuss'd me out, saliva runnin' down her mouth like a wild animal. Her cousin had to ax her to leave, but tole her to leave the pie. She would eat it.

"You know what she did? She throw'd that pie in the trash.

"But what did that prove, 'xcept she was mad?"

"I didn't thank nothin' of it 'til her cousin said...." he paused, embarrassed.

"Come on, said what?"

"It gon' turn yo' stomach."

"Tell me."

"Her cousin said that she prob'ly put her monthly in it to fix me and git me back. When I heard that, I rush'd outside to the toilet and threw up everythang I had ate that day. I left that house and nevah went back." He leaned forward, his hands clenched.

"Now you answer my question, Susie. Do you thank he used voodoo on you?"

"I b'lieve he did. 'Cause I don't know no othah reason why I'm with him. I sho don't like him as a boyfriend. He's the last person I would choose."

He moved, sat close to her, and held her hand. Then he whispered, "Tell me how you got into his damn mess, Susie."

Suddenly, she felt like telling him everything. After all, he was her brother and loved her just as she was. She gently pulled away from him, went into the kitchen and returned with two cups of coffee and a chaser of whiskey for him. She knew he would need it. She sat next to him and lit a fresh cigarette.

Slowly, she spilled the haunting story. She started by saying she had foolishly agreed to go with Koffee to a pea patch, twenty-five miles from Selma, after much encouragement from Mrs. Bosmun and also because he had been there for her when she had lost her husband, Nathan.

She had been tense when she started out, around 4:30 a.m., but during the ride, he had talked, mostly about his church ministries, and told humorous stories about some of his friends. By the time they arrived, she was relaxed and the day was awake.

She and Koffee were standing outside of the car, approximately ten feet away when several of his church members arrived. After introductions they set off with their equipment to find his pea-patch.

Once there, Rev. Koffee stood close to her, handed her a new hoe. Susie took it, suddenly feeling light-headed, her vision blurred. She dropped the hoe and began to stagger. One of his church members stopped and offered to help, but Koffee refused, saying he would get her back to the car and give her some water.

She remembered that he had helped her into the car, onto the back seat. His closeness caused her stomach to churn, and she felt as if her insides would come out of her mouth.

He gave her water, then left her, saying he was going back to the pea-patch but would return to check on her. Later, feeling better, but warm, she was able to join him.

But as soon as he stood next to her, she began to feel ill again. She moved to get away from him, but failed.

She fainted.

Susie stopped her story to sip her warm coffee and to light another cigarette. Augustus, shaking his head as if stirring from a bad dream, poured whiskey into his black coffee and waited.

"This part, I can only guess what happen'd 'cause I was out cold, but months latah, some thangs did come to me. I see and hear them as clear as day."

She continued. Rev. Koffee had taken her back to the car and placed her in the back seat, behind the driver's side, and driven where he could hide in the surrounding tall weeds, flowing weeping willows, and thicket of pine trees. Satisfied with her comatose position, he moved from the front of the car and leaned into the back seat. He grinned. It had worked.

His time had finally come. He would have her. He had wanted her from the moment he had seen her in church, years before. But too many stumbling blocks had been in place.

Now he promised himself, that no one else would ever have her again. Even though he hadn't anything to do with the rest of the men in her life, he certainly had a hand in getting rid of the last one, with the help of voodoo.

Susie was as limp as a dishrag, but alive. Maybe the moe-joe had been too strong. He sat next to her, pulled the odd-shaped object from his breast pocket. It was the voodoo dressing that had made Susie so ill. He rolled down the window and tossed the object backwards, then repeated some unintelligible words, four times.

The object he threw landed in honeysuckle bushes, about five feet away. Even he would have cringed if he had seen the evil, slimy venom that slid from the ripped material and into the bushes. The remaining creatures were not alive, but just as disgusting.

He took in her beauty, stroked her lovely hair, face, and lightly caressed her neck. Then slowly, he unbuttoned her dress. Finally, he had his way with her....

She had been out for hours and didn't stir until he stopped the car, later that evening, in front of her house. She had sat up from her slumped position. Her head felt as if it had been beaten by a hammer until her brains were scrambled. The least movement caused her head to pummel. She gagged, trying to throw up, but had nothing on her stomach.

Her body felt violated and bruised, everywhere.

She had turned to Koffee. "Somethang happen'd to me. What? I whispered to him."

"You faint'd after we got out the car. I couln' git you to wake up the second time, so I brough' you home."

"I feel like somebody put me in a cooker and tried to kill me. My body is bruis'd, and my head was killin' me.

'What did you do to me?' I asked him. I was so sick, I coulda died right thaih, Augustus. He tried to hide his nervousness by lightin' a cigar. He knowed deep in his heart he had committ'd a crime towards me. And I knowed, as soon I touch'd myself down thaih. The bastard had raped me. I gag'd again, but couldn' throw up. I moan'd with dread. This had happen'd to me a third time. I had walk'd with the devil and end'd up in hell.

"All I could do was moan. That's all the energy I had left in me. Then I got enough energy to git out the car and make it into the house. After I got inside, I took off the stanky, smelling clothes, put them in a garbage bag and heat'd water 'til it was scaldin' hot. I stay'd in the tub 'til my body was almost raw. I couldn' touch it for days without screamin'.

"Now, you see I got myself in hell, and hell is where I'm gonna stay." She drank her cold coffee and lit another cigarette.

Augustus drained the shot glass of liquor, sniffed back tears, and remained silent for a long moment.

Finally, he said in dull tones, "Susie, you can go to somebody."

"Augustus, I done tried, and every time, somethin' happens to keep me from gettin' thaih. It seems like a invisible wall, standin' in my way.

"Thaih's moe." She refilled their drinks. Lit another cigarette.

Augustus wished she would take something stronger than coffee, but knew she wouldn't.

"He stay'd out thaih 'til I got in bed. Then I heard his car drive away. I guess he was thankin' on what he had done or was tryin' to figure out how he would git me or even that he had almost kill'd me.

"I lay'd thaih, hatin' him and hatin' me. As the days slowly crept by and my body heal'd, I didn't have to worry 'bout killin' him 'cause he didn't come by for weeks, to my relief. I made it my bus'ness to stay away from Miss Bosmun. To this day, I don't trust her."

"So I gather'd he went back to the voodoo man," Augustus stated, rather than asking.

"Yeah. Like I said, it was weeks befoe I saw him again. He follow'd me from work. I threaten' to git my gun and shoot him. But that didn't stop him for long.

"He was determin'd alright, and to make this shitty story shorter, he came 'round again in a month, tried to git into my house, but I kept him out. He warn'd me he was goin' to git me and that I would nevah marry Miles. That's when I knowed he had somehow broke us up. The warnin' that Miles tole me 'bout when we quit, I'll nevah forgit it. He said, 'The same person who had me up at night, cryin' where I couldn' sleep gon' have you wringin' your hands...' words close to that.

"I thought I could outsmart him. I was feelin' bettah then I had in a long while. I had went back to work, so I forgot him. I spent time with my chil'ren and went to church. It had been years since I felt that good.

"Then word reach'd me that he was gon' out of town, to Lyden, Alabama. I didn't care. I guess I shoulda.

"Two weeks latah, he was at my house, 'round two o'clock in the mornin', tappin' on my window. I tole him to go away, but he threaten' to stay unless I answer'd the door.

"I did, and today, I'm still answerin' the door, Augustus."

"I cain't say I blame him for wantin' you, but the man gotta be sick to do somethang like this. You might not b'lieve this, but when he was talkin', I knowed somethang was evil 'bout him. Lawdy, Lawdy, I sho cain't b'lieve that low-down son-of-a-gun. I feel like pullin' his rotten heart out."

"Augustus, I know you all upset, and you got a right to be, but thaih ain't nothin' you can do 'bout it now." She knew that he meant every word he said. "I'll be able to handle it aftah while. I jest need to git myself together."

But he wasn't willing to let it go. "What kinda spell did he use on you? Maybe we can git it off. You know somebody we can go to while I'm here?"

"Naw, I don't want you in this mess. You could git hurt. I'll find some way, some day to git rid of him. Deep down, he knows I don't care 'bout him and all the voodoo in the world won't change that."

"I know you ain't no fool, but you gettin' kinda close thaih, Susie. Thaih's got to be a way...."

He stopped speaking because her eyes had become hooded, her face closed. He knew she would talk no more about the matter.

The room became still; the air even felt afraid to move around as Susie sat analyzing her helpless situation, and Miles. She often thought of Miles these days, although she would never hear or see him again. And even if she did, what good would it do? Once again she blocked his memory.

She bit at her lower lip. There had to be a way to get rid of Koffee, and she was determined to find one. When? She didn't know.

She peered at her loving brother. She must apologize to him. He was the best, and he needed to know that.

"Augustus, I'm sorry. I don't know what came over me. This has been such a good time with you here I don't want to spoil it with my problems." *Shit. I knowed if I let ole Koffee in, it would cause troubl'."*

"Alright, if you say so," Augustus said, feeling helpless, longing to assist Susie.

Susie did not respond, but a smile appeared on her somber face.

"What say we go back in the kitchen and find some moe of that good food you cook'd," he suggested, holding out his hand to her.

Later that evening, Rev. Koffee returned bearing gifts for Susie – inexpensive pink house shoes and a box of Whitman's candy. She thanked him and rushed back into the house from the biting cold.

In the kitchen, she found Augustus, Blanche, and Lola sitting around the table, rolling with laughter from some wild stories Augustus was telling them.

"Mama, Uncle Augustus is so funny," Lola said, her words barely audible, she was giggling so hard.

"He sho is Mama," Blanche agreed. "You oughta hear what he been sayin'," she uttered, sounding almost as bad as Lola.

Susie smiled. She was happy to see them full of merriment. It had been a long time since she had seen them this way.

"Don't y'all b'lieve everythang yo' uncle tell you. He's good at makin' up stories," she cautioned before joining them at.

Five days later they stood on the porch, watching Augustus's car drive down the street and out of their lives.

"Well, y'all. He's gon', and I'm sho gon' miss him," Susie said as she turned and walked back into the house, the girls trailing her.

27

Susie sat watching the short, brown-skinned man with his large mouth, big head, and strong hands march back and forth across her living room floor. It didn't matter how many times she saw him, it always amazed her that she was with him.

"You heard me, didn't you? I said I was mar-red last month, and I thought it best to tell you befoe somebody else did," he said in apologetic tones.

His words were like numerous needles, prickling her skin. She frowned and clenched her hands, trying to get the pain and anger in her head to leave her alone. She reasoned that she should be happy he was married. This could be the best way to get rid of him. Still, she fumed because he had deceived her. The idea that he would use and kick her aside like she was a piece of dried up shit infuriated her. Yet it made no sense to her – why was she really angry?

Seeing the flying sparks in her eyes, he stopped pacing. "Now, I don't want you go gettin' yo'self upset. Jest let me 'xplain, Madam" he said, patting his left foot as if he were trying to keep it from going to sleep.

"I don't want to hear no 'xplanation 'cause thaih ain't one. How do you 'xpect me to lis-sen to yo' lies?"

She blurted. She had never spoken to him this way. Surprise registered on his face.

"Madam, that's what I'm tryin' to tell you," he said, pretending he hadn't heard her outburst. "I met this lady a long time ago when she was dirt po' and mar-red to someone else, and I took her from him. I felt guilty. I couldn' do nothin' for her then, so I promised her I would marry her when I was able to take care of her and her little girl"

"Her and her chile?" Susie interrupted. She stood and walked toward him with clenched fists. Standing face to face with him, she lost her anger. Her head suddenly felt as if it was going to split in two. Then it dawned on her that she always had a headache every time he was near her.

And everything fell into place. Bang, just like that! He was still using voodoo to hold her. That's why she couldn't find the energy to get him out of her life. She realized why she had headaches, why she laughed too much at things he said that weren't even funny, and why she found herself mesmerized by him when she didn't even like him. And why she became agitated about things that he did when she really did not care what he did. No more, she promised herself. This time, she meant it.

Sitting again, she said, "And jest what do you thank I'm 'spose to do, Rev'end? Keep goin' with you? Man, maybe you forgot, but I didn't come lookin' for you. You came aftah me and did whatever you did to me. But then you nevah made me no promises. Not that I want any, but you cain't come here and do...."

She couldn't speak anymore. She felt as if she was going to blank out from the piercing pain in her head. She closed her eyes tightly and placed her hands over her face. She wished he would leave.

Mistaking her mood change for sadness, he spoke softly "Madam, I...I don't love her. But I made a promise, and I couldn' go back on it," he said, continuing to pat his foot.

The throbbing pain, having eased, she exclaimed ardently, "Of all the damnest thangs I heard in my life, you take the cake, Rev'end you sound like a sorry 'xcuse for a man."

Taken aback, he turned a deep brownish red, jumping from his spot to lean over her. "Naw, I ain't no fool. I know what I'm doin'," he argued as he turned and walked to the front door then back to his spot on the floor.

"Then why don't you jest leave, man?"

He didn't move or speak.

She bounced from the sofa and stalked to the door, her pain forgotten. Her eyes were boiling liquid, ready to burn into his lying flesh. "Leave."

He walked to the door and paused to gaze closely at her.

"Leave my house, you son of a bitch," she demanded, regretting the words as soon as they escaped. She knew she had sinned, but she couldn't take back the ugly words.

He left as quickly as his short legs would carry him. Confused. His moe joe was not working. He needed something stronger.

Susie was so angry, her entire body shook. She went to her room and fell across the bed. *That bastard must thank I'm the biggest fool in the world. And I must be for puttin' up with his shit. Now, I know as good as I'm layin' here, he used some powerful voodoo to git me, and like a fool, I ain't done nothin' to git it off. So I guess I deserve this mess. But, not for much longer,* she vowed.

"What am I layin' here whinnin' for and callin' myself a fool? Or am I?" She got up and strolled to the window. "Thaih's a fool for everybody, and everybody has to be a fool sometimes, but they sho don't have to stay one. And I sho the hell ain't. Not for that lowdown, no good, vile man," she said with renewed strength and determination.

Sleep eluded her as she tossed and turned that night. Finally, she sat up in bed trying to find a way to get rid of him. There had to be a way.

She felt emotionally drained, tormented, and close to a nervous breakdown. She fussed. "The bastard said he loved me. How can he love me and do hateful thangs to me? Every since he's been comin' 'round, I ain't been myself. I feel like I don't own my own body, thoughts or feelin's no moe.

"I made myself promises I would git rid of him, and look at

me, I'm still sayin' the same thangs. Sometimes I wonder if I'm bein' punish'd for somethin'." She looked around as if searching for someone or something to answer her.

Not receiving a response, she said, "I'll do it by myself." She fell back on the pillows, sleep eluding her.

The following morning, after Susie left for work, Blanche and Lola remained home to clean the kitchen before going to school.

"Blanche, I sho do wish Mama had mar-red Rev'end Miles. I sho did love him and want'd him for our daddy. Mama was so happy with him. I don't know how you can be happy and still send somebody away," Lola offered.

"I don't know either. But I wish'd we could find him and have him come back so we can all be happy. Did you hear 'bout the fine house he bought befoe Mama sent him packin', Sistah?"

"Naw. I didn't. I guess I was too young to know them thangs."

"You was not, two years ago." Blanche reminded her and laughed. "But some of the girls I know said they heard thaih mamas talkin' 'bout that fine house with all them rooms and fur-niture, and flowers and pretty trees in front of it. That it was a shame we didn't git a chance to live in it. I sho did want a daddy befoe we got grown." Tears flowed down Blanche's face as she put the glasses in the cupboard.

"I guess we won't have one," Lola said. She sat down at the table and drew patterns with her fingers.

"But I know one thang. We gon' have to leave Selma when we grow up so we can have us a bettah life then Mama," Blanche said as she flopped down, in a chair across the table from Lola, tears meeting on her pretty young face.

Lola stood and hugged her. "Don't cry, Blanche. You and me gon' have a good life. And if Mama wants to leave Selma, she welcome to come stay with us."

Susie had returned home to pick up her pocketbook and had overheard every word they uttered. Hot tears stung her face as she slipped into her room, grabbed her bag, and ran out the door. She trembled so badly she had to stop and lean against a chinaberry tree until her composure was restored.

The rest of the day, she was unable to work at her normal pace as the girls' voices rang in her burning ears.

She wished she could gather them in her arms and tell them everything would be fine, but she couldn't, not until she was sure about her future. She was relieved when the three o'clock whistle blew, signaling the end of the work day.

She took the long way home, not wanting to face the children yet. She walked and prayed. "Lawd, please have mercy on me. I don't know what to do anymoe. I don't know where to turn, 'xcept to You. I feel like fallin' down on this ground and nevah gettin' up again. My life is a complete mess, and it's interferrin' in my chil'ren's happiness. Someway I got to make it bettah, and I cain't without You. Please help me." Susie pleaded as she walked the back streets with her head hangin' unaware of the stares she received.

The following week Susie found and rented another house, one step toward getting rid of Koffee. He would look like a fool when he found her gone. She hoped he would understand the meaning. She knew the girls would be elated.

The next evening, they made two trips to Lawrence Street with the help of Girt and her boyfriend, to her new house. When all the furniture was in place, she still had plenty of room remaining.

The house was a single dwelling, her first one, and very large. It was surrounded by a fenced-in-yard with large pecan and chinaberry trees in front and two peach trees in back. Blanche and Lola were thrilled to have their own bedrooms and a real bathroom with a cast iron tub. Quite a switch from the metal bathtub and the slop jar at night.

"Girl, you sho did yo'self good when you found this place," Girt smiled and patted Susie's shoulder, breaking into her reflections.

"Sheer stroke of luck. I pray'd and then went lookin', and

Gawd let me find it," Susie grinned as she looked around the living room thankful for the blessing.

"I sho wish I could find somethin' else 'side these shotgun houses. Jest walk in and straight on out the back door. No room off the side or nice hallways. I'm gon' come visit you moe often," Girt said, her dark, smooth face showing signs of joy.

"You welcome to come often as you want, Girt. And thank you and yo' boyfriend for helpin' us move. I'll have to fix y'all a nice supper, soon."

"Anythang for you, Susie. You knows that. You like a sistah I ain't got, and I loves you and yo' chil'ren. But supper is jest fine, too. Any ole time."

"Girt you is 'bout full of shit. But me and the chil'ren is crazy 'bout you, too."

Deep down in the marrow of her bones, Susie could feel it. The simmering coldness stayed with her no matter what or how she tried to ignore it. She knew he would find her, and in doing so, she tried to prepare for his arrival, but she found herself becoming more jittery and agitated. Every night for two weeks, she sat waiting for him, chain smoking.

One Friday evening there was a knock at her door. After peeking through the living room drapes, she admitted him.

He followed her and sat across from her, but she refused to speak to him because she hated her weakness, allowing him to enter her house after she had purposely moved to get away from him.

They sat in silence for more than ten minutes before he inquired, "How you been doin', Madam?" he looked at his expensive cigar and blew smoke toward empty space.

"Well as can be 'xpect'd," she said bitterly.

He squinted his eyes and looked at her strangely, and patted his right foot. "Well, I been runnin' the last months with the church and all. I came by to see you, but Miss Bosmun said you moved. I been lookin' all over Selma for you."

"I don't know why you was lookin' for me. I ain't nothin' to you."

"Now, why you want to go an say a thang like that? I tole you how...."

She cut him off. "Rev'end, maybe I didn't make myself clear befoe. So let me repeat myself. I have wast'd two years of my life involv'd with you, and I don't know why. All you ever did was use me. I was a fool, but..." she paused, suddenly feeling sick to her stomach. Clutching her abdoman, she leaned forward, groaning in pain as a cold wave stole through her.

Rev. Koffee grinned behind his hand. "I tried to tell you the last time I saw you, but you didn't lis-sen. I don't love my wife, I'm jest oblig'd to her."

"Then she must be a fool too, 'cause you usin' her. Man, to be a preacher, you worst then a alley cat. Why don't you leave.... Oh, my Goodness. What...is happenin'... to me? I feel...sick... as...a...dog...," Susie moaned and fell on her side.

Rev. Koffee became alarmed, thinking he might have gone too far with the voodoo potion he had on him. He rushed to her side. "Susie, is you alright?"

"Sick. So...sick," Susie whimpered and passed out in his arms.

He called Blanche and Lola, instructed them to look after her until he returned. Then he drove quickly to the Alabama River, tossed the voodoo doll in it, and returned to Susie's house in less than fifteen minutes.

She was sitting in a chair, holding a hot towel to her forehead. When he walked in, she smiled, "How you doin', Rev-end Come on in, and have a seat."

The girls gazed at Susie, then at each other, totally perplexed at their mother. They knew something was amiss. As soon as Rev. Koffee entered the room, her whole demeanor became submissive.

"Y'all chil'ren can go now." Susie spoke in a high-pitched voice, as if nothing had happened earlier. Both girls gazed closely at her, nodded their acknowledgments to Rev. Koffee and skirted from the room.

Koffee sat next to her on the sofa, a wide grin on his deceitful face.

In Blanche's room, they sat on her bed and whispered about their mother's oddity.

"Nina," Lola's nickname for her sister when she was unnerved and near tears. "I heard some talk 'bout voodoo and what it can do to you." Lola paused and looked at the door, listened and continued in quiet tones.

"The way Mama acts when he comes here...I don't b'lieve in the stuff. But why do she act...You saw how she was when he first came, real sick, then he left, and she was able to sit up; then he comes back, and she start actin' all funny....I know he's doin' something to hurt Mama, and I'm scared. I want Rev'end Miles back," she wept, her thirteen-year-old voice breaking, as would a fragile glass that falls from a high fireplace.

"I'm scared for Mama, too. You right. She don't act like herself." Blanche placed her arm around her sister's shoulder, and for a few moments her tears flowed. Then she said, "All the othah times, she's so strong. Then he comes, and she smiles, and talks louder, but her eyes look sad, like somebody died."

"What can we do to help her?" Lola inquired, her tears subsiding.

"We too young to butt into grown folks bus'ness, so all we can do is pray. Pray for Rev'end Miles to come and help Mama, befoe it's too late," Blanche suggested, then blew her nose with a handkerchief.

Later, they heard the front door close, and they knew he had left. Relief flowed through them. Susie was left with a mild headache that lasted several days.

Weeks later, Rev. Koffee returned, bearing gifts: a box of Whitman's candy and a carton of Pall Mall cigarettes.

Susie took the packages and laid them on the coffee table. "Thank you." She had changed brands after deciding the Camels were too strong, hoping that she would be able to quit easier by smoking filtered cigarettes.

"You doin' alright, Madam?" He knew she probably hadn't remembered their last fight two weeks ago and hoped she never would.

"I'm doin' jest fine. I had a pretty good day at work. And yo'self?"

He smiled in relief, then for the next hour, bragged about his two churches, one in the city, the other in the country. He also boasted about his small brick-mason company, applauding himself by patting both his feet on Susie's new rug, a sure sign of satisfaction. Susie had learned.

"You sho do seem to be risin' fast, Rev'end. I'm glad for you. Would you like a cold drank?"

"Thank you. I thank I will, Madam." He watched as she glided through the door, her hips swaying slightly to the rhythm of her movements. He lusted after her and wished with all his heart he had never made his wife that damn promise, if only he had met Susie first.

Susie returned with iced-tea and set it on the table.

He picked the glass up and gulped the refreshing liquid in one swallow. "Aaah. That was good. Thank you." He stood and stretched his short frame. I guess I bettah be goin'. I got a lot of work head of me."

After he left, on a hunch, Susie threw the candy in the garbage can and kept the cigarettes to give away.

The months ahead proved busy for Rev. Koffee. He traveled to Lyden, Alabama, several times, and upon his return, he went directly to Susie's house. And each time she became more friendly towards him. He gloated as he watched her become entangled in the web that he had woven for her, a web he planned to last always. His only regret was that he had to resort to voodoo to get her. Any other woman that he had desired had always been willing. He had been the one who feared them using witchcraft on him.

Although Susie sat laughing at his jokes, presumably satisfied with her situation, she knew she was entangled in his snare. But like a fly in buttermilk, she was helpless to do anything.

Months turned into another year, and Susie's involvement with Rev. Koffee continued while Blanche and Lola watched and hoped that something would happen to change the course of their mother's life. Of course, an outsider could not look at Susie and discern that she acted unusual. Only Koffee, the girls, Girt and Susie knew. Not only did Susie know, but she also realized that her time was diminishing. She periodically believed that her mind wasn't hers. There were days that she felt so flaccid she didn't know if she could wrench herself from her bed. She had all but stopped thinking of Rev. JaRett.

She realized that evil was surrounding her and she was not capable of coping with it. Her hope had dwindled, her faith weakened.

28

She saw them several blocks away, walking quickly down the unpaved sidewalk.

"Who's that mannish boy tryin' to walk you home, Blanche? You ain't sixteen yet," Susie reminded her as she and Lola walked into the house. She went into the sewing room and folded the pattern she had ben cutting.

"That was Marshall Jacobs from school. I tried to tell him not to follow us from choir practice, but he wouldn' lis-sen, Mama," Blanche apologized, following her into the room.

"He said you weren't gon' do nothin' to him, Mama. And I tole him you would, too," Lola said, as she stood next to Blanche.

"Well, maybe I jest bettah tell him a thang or two when I see him at church on Sunday. Both of y'all know my rules. No courtin' 'til you sixteen, and that includes boys walkin' y'all home."

"Yes, Mam," Blanche said, gazing down at the floor.

"Jest where do this boy live, and who is his folks?" Susie stood facing them.

"He lives on Sylvan Street. His mother and father go to anothah church, but he said they gon' move their membership to ours. His daddy works for the railroad, and his mama works for a rich white lady. He's a year oler then me," Blanche said, her voice barely audible.

"Mama, he's been tryin' to talk to Blanche, but she ig him all the time. She walks, and he gits behind her and talks and talks," Lola intoned.

"Alright then. Y'all go on to yo' rooms."

Susie sat down and fingered the material she had bought to make dresses for the girls. She realized her girls were becoming young ladies. Lola had turned fourteen, and Blanche would turn sixteen in October. She realized Blanche's birthday was approaching quickly. She had promised Blanche a sweet sixteen birthday party. She laid the cloth aside and walked to her room, pulled a pad and pencil from a drawer, then she went into the living room to make a list for Blanche's party.

As she made the list, her mind strayed to the girls, thinking how different they were from each another, yet simultaneously very close and protective. Blanche was the color of milk with two spoons of brown sugar added. She had brown hair, bright eyes, and dimples half an inch deep when she smiled. She was studious, serious, sweet and quiet. She could be funny at times and mean when provoked. Lola was the complete opposite, deep brown skin with a sprinkling of red added. Her hair was almost black; she had mischievous, slanted eyes and a robust sound when she laughed. She was free hearted and outgoing. She loved to have fun. She was not a serious student, but did well.

Susie laid the pad down and placed one hand under her chin, the other across her stomach. She wondered how she was going to deal with two teen-age girls and the boys hanging around. She had protected them when they were younger, but now she realized it would be difficult as they became more independent.

"How you doin', Miss Norwood?" Marshall stammered as he twisted his hat in his trembling thin hands.

Susie smiled. He was the thinnest boy she had ever seen, with curly hair and brown pop-eyes which appeared larger when he was afraid. "'Bout as good as can be 'xpect'd, considerin' you tryin' to knock my door in, Marshall," she offered and fanned at the humid heat penetrating her.

He jumped, almost losing his balance. "I'm sorry, Miss Norwood."

"So you the mannish young man that's followin' Blanche from church on Wednesdays and after school. What you doin' knockin' at my door?"

"I...jest want'd to ax you if Blanche and Lola could come to my birthday party next week, Miss Norwood."

"When next week?"

"Ju-ly twenty-sixth, Miss Norwood."

"Is yo' mother and father goin' to be thaih?"

"Yes, Mam. And my sistah Marie, too," he offered, bouncing his head up and down like a mattress spring.

"I tell you what. I'll talk to Blanche, and she'll let you know at choir rehearsal."

"Mam?"

"You heard me. Now git out of the sun befoe you die from this heat. Good evenin'," she said and closed the door.

Susie walked into the kitchen, a half smile on her face, and put coffee on to perk. It didn't matter that it was more than ninety degrees outside; she loved her coffee year round.

Boys sho done changed since I was a young girl, she thought. *But then I wasn't nevah a girl, really.* A single tear fell into her mouth. She frowned and brushed the salty taste away.

She knocked and entered Blanche's room. "That was Marshall at the door 'bout half-hour ago," Susie said, sitting in a rocking chair next to Blanche's bed. "He want'd to know if you and Lola could come to his birthday party."

"He's havin' a birthday party?" Blanche blinked several times, then looked at Lola who was lying at the foot of the bed.

"Seems that way," Susie said. "Y'all want to go?"

"Yes, Mam, if we can," Blanche smiled.

"Y'all know his sistah?"

"Yes, Mam. She's a real nice person. She gra'uated last year and she workin' at the cigar factory," Lola said, her eyes twinkling with excitement.

"I'll thank on it and let y'all know my decision," Susie said as she stood and walked to the door. "Is yo' room clean, Sistah?"

"Yes, Mam. I clean'd it up this mornin', real good."

Susie nodded, slipped from the room and closed the door.

They jumped into each other's arms. "Do you thank she'll let us go?" Lola questioned.

"I don't know, but we ain't been in no troubl', and we had good grades all year," Blanche reasoned.

"We don't nevah go nowhere and have fun like othah girls do. All we do is go to church, work hard in school, and work at home. Work, work, work..."

"Sshh, Mama will hear you, Sistah. And that ain't true. My friends do the same thangs as we do."

"I don't care if she do hear me. And yo' friends is stuffy like these here pillows. Mine like to go out and have fun."

"Lola Morton. Shame on you! If Mama knowed you was hangin' 'round with Charlotte, she would kill you. That is a grown woman, and she is fast as they git."

"I don't hang 'round her. And she's only eighteen. Don't you want to have some fun, Blanche?"

"I will on my birthday. And she is grown. Mama said no friends moe then two years o-ler then us, 'member?"

Lola fell across the bed. "But yo' birthday is way in October. This is only Ju-ly. You act too ole-fashioned sometimes, Blanche. Don't you want to have fun befoe you git ole?"

"Yeah. I want to have fun, and I will. You know how Mama is 'bout us bein' round boys and you only fourteen. I don't thank we got a chance to go to this party."

"Why you change yo' mind so much? Sometimes I thank you confus'd as Mama."

"Lola Amelia Morton, shame on you! You take that back!"

"I do. I'm sorry, but you gots to promise me you'll keep yo' fingers cross'd."

"I promise," Blanche said as she fell across her bed.

"Okay. Then I'll stay away from Charlotte." Lola smiled and hugged the sister she loved so much.

Two days later, Susie, after much soul-searching and against her better judgment, agreed they could attend the party. But she would take them and pick them up.

When Susie left the room, they hugged each other.

"See, Blanche. See. All you got to do is hope."

"Ain't it jest great! We're goin' to a party." Then they danced and giggled so hard they fell across the bed holding their aching sides.

29

They laughed and teased each other as they hung up the streamers and tinsel for Blanche's sweet, sixteen birthday party. Mary, Lola's friend, and Mattie and Girt, Susie's friends, all helped with the last-minute preparations.

Susie had met Mattie through Girt and liked her from the beginning. Mattie was light-skinned, like Susie. Girt was as dark as midnight, but with beautiful, smooth skin, and long, straight hair. Susie enjoyed being with them whenever she could. She had become close to them.

"This reminds me of myself when I was turnin' six-teen," Girt remarked as she tacked a purple streamer in a corner with the hammer.

"You ain't nevah been sixteen. You was grown when yo' Mama had you," Susie teased.

Girt made a face, and they all laughed, then returned to their chores, looking forward to the party almost as much as Blanche and Lola.

Half an hour later, Susie yelled from the top of the ladder, "Y'all hurry up and git ready, Blanche and Lola. We can git the rest of this finish'd."

Blanche and Lola retreated happily to their rooms and pulled down the lovely dresses Susie had helped them design and make. Blanche's was a simple, river blue, straight line with a flair tail. On the other hand, Lola's was a pale peach, square neck, fitted bottom, and a tight belt.

After bathing, they spread Jergen's lotion over their bodies and added Mum deodorant and Johnson's baby powder. They weren't allowed to wear makeup. Then they pulled on their frocks and combed their hair.

When the girls walked into the living room, Susie hurried down the ladder and stood looking at them as if they were two beautiful flowers.

"Y'all look so pretty, and them dresses fit perfect," she beamed, her face displaying joy and pride, marveling that she had given birth to them so many years before.

"They look like African queens; don't they Susie?" Girt praised.

"They the prettiest and sweetest girls Selma ever saw," Mattie agreed.

"You best be ready to hold that shotgun on them boys tonight," Girt advised and patted Susie's back.

"I might jest have to do that, Girt," she said as she hugged her daughters, holding each longer than necessary. But they didn't seem to mind.

Susie's smile wouldn't let go as she said, "Y'all come on and help me move the rest of this stuff out of here. Mattie, you and Mary finish pulling the rug out of the hallway and put it in the study. Girt, you help me take this ladder out. Blanche, y'all jest sit down and look pretty 'til yo' friends git here."

Shortly before the guests arrived, Susie brought out fried chicken, ham, potato salad, coleslaw, homemade rolls, and vanilla and chocolate ice cream, still in the churn.

Blanche's cake was beautifully decorated with light blue frosting and tiny yellow and blue roses and seventeen candles. The extra candle was a tradition, one to grow on. The expense for the party had come from the savings Susie had managed to put away for the house she wanted to buy one day.

"Wow, the cake is too pretty to eat, Mama." Blanche remarked.

"But we have to eat it. We'll jest have to 'member how it looked," Lola offered.

Susie smiled as she stared at her five feet, three inch, beautiful, slim daughter standing before her. Her brown eyes showed the happiness she felt inside as she looked at her mother.

Susie hugged her. I'm so proud of you. Happy sweet sixteen birthday, Blanche," she said and brushed a tear aside. It seemed just a few years ago she was rocking Blanche in her arms.

"Thank you, Mama. Thank you very much for everythang."

"You're welcome, baby. You deserve every bit of it. You nevah gave me much troubl' since you was born. And the way it's lookin', you should have a good future. So keep on gettin' them A's and doin' everythang I tole you," she advised.

"I will, Mama," Blanche promised and dabbed at her teary eyes.

"You go and dry yo' face befoe the othahs git here." Susie turned to Lola, her eyes warm, voice firm. "I want you to 'member this is yo' sistah's party, young lady. You do look as pretty as you can be. Jest act it, too."

"I will, Mama," Lola promised, looking forward to the party and all the attention she could get from her friends.

Susie saw her friends and Mary to the door, promising them she would save them each a plate.

The party was a great success. All who were invited, attended. Everyone had arrived on time. Susie was surprised when she opened the door and found twenty youth standing before her.

She greeted each of them as they entered and told each one what she expected of them.

When she saw Marshall, she pulled him to the side and said, "You bettah be real good 'cause I'll be watchin' you."

He gulped and shook his head in silent agreement. Everyone danced, talked, and laughed and put the food away as if they hadn't eaten all day. It was like a dream come true for Susie as she stayed out of the room and out of sight, but close enough to keep a handle on what was going on.

She overheard several of them talking among themselves

about the good food and how they would like to live there just to eat. She laughed and lit a cigarette. Then she pulled her shoes off and laid across the bed.

An hour later, Susie replenished the empty dishes. She noticed they were doing the same kind of dances they had done when she was about their age. A few more steps had been added or taken away, and given new names.

She hadn't gotten the opportunity to dance much, but she could cut a rug with the best of them, she reminisced. She giggled and put her cigarette in an astray and stretched across the bed again.

Twenty minutes later, it was too quiet. Slipping from her bed, she went to stand next to the wall outside of the living room.

"Come on, Blanche, let them stay off for one dance."

Naw, I ain't neither. Now turn the lights back on," she demanded sternly.

"Yeah, Marshall," a friend of his said, "What you tryin' to do, git us kick'd out or somethin'? We havin' fun with the lights on."

"Awww, man. Ain't gon' be no troubl' if you don't start tellin' Miss Norwood."

"I guess I'll have to teach him a lesson," she said to the wall.

"Did you hear them tell you to turn the lights back on, boy?" Susie said in a deep, growling, masculine voice. She had always been good at changing and throwing her voice, and the children had always loved it when she told them stories.

Marshall jumped back against the wall as if someone had struck him. His popped eyes looked as if they would leap from his head. His mouth gaped open as he turned to look for the voice.

Susie resumed. "You got five seconds to git them lights back on or I'll break every bone in yo' fingers! One, two."

Before she could say three, he regained enough movement to do as she demanded.

Blanche and Lola knew it was their mother scaring him and the rest of their friends, but they weren't telling. They were having too much fun. When Marshall turned the lights back on, the voice continued, "I got my eyes on you, boy, so watch yo'self. And all y'all othah chil'ren go on and have some fun. If this mannish boy

Marshall tries anythang again, he'll be sorry." The mention of his name caused him to turn to see what wall the voice was coming from. And I repeat. If Marshall give y'all any moe troubl', I will break all his skinny fingers and toes too, so be warned."

The teens stood silent for a few minutes then started dancing again. Marshall sat down, scared motionless. Blanche and Lola looked at him, trying to keep a straight face, then left him to squirm alone.

Susie waited a few minutes then walked into the room. Over the music she said, "I thought I heard somebody talkin' in here with a heavy voice. Did somebody call me? What's goin' on in here? Is everythang alright?" She stood looking at Marshall who remained on the sofa looking like a frightened child whose mother had left him alone in the dark.

He looked at her as if he wanted to run, but couldn't. He squeezed his legs together as if to prevent himself from wetting his pants. It had been bad enough hearing that strange voice from out of nowhere, but he felt like running and hiding upon seeing her.

Susie looked as if she was reading his mind as she peered into his large, frightened eyes. He lowered them and held his hands tightly.

Susie turned to the others, "Is somethan' wrong with him? Is he sick?" she asked with concern.

Lawrence spoke up. "No, Mam. I don't thank he's sick or nothin'." He paused for a moment. "Uhh, maybe he a little scared from that voice who was talkin' to him outta the wall."

"Scared? A voice in the wall talkin' to him? We ain't got no haints here. All y'all heard the voice?"

"Yes, Mam," everyone echoed except Marshall, who was turning various shades of reddish browns.

Susie decided to continue the fun for a while longer. "Who was the voice talkin' to?" she asked.

"Marshall," several girls cried in unison.

She turned to Marshall. "Left you speechless, didn't it, son. First time I ever saw you with yo' mouth closed." He shook his head in agreement.

His friends snickered.

Susie turned back to the others, "What was he doin' so bad to make this voice come out the walls at him?"

"He turned the lights out and didn't turn them back on when I tole him to, Mama," Blanche offered.

"Oh. So you was bein' hardheaded and mannish again, huh? Maybe you deserved the voice comin' out of the wall aftah you. Do you 'spose you'll be able to sleep tonight, or will the voice keep you company?"

"Co...co...com...come...talk to...to...m..me?" Marshall stuttered and closed his eyes, visibly shaking.

The room suddenly became completely still. Susie decided he had suffered enough. The big, little, brave boy who thought he was so much a man was still a child in so many ways, still wet behind the ears with a great deal more to learn if he was lucky to live and reach manhood.

Shaking her head in slight annoyance, she warned, "Marshall, I'm gon' let you in on a little secret. And only 'cause I don't want you to go home tonight and have bad dreams, and 'cause I know my daughter likes you, but for the life of me, I don't know why. Chile, it was me behind the wall, throwin' my voice like a man to scare you and teach you a lesson. If you had done what I tole you to when you got here, this nevah woulda happen'd."

He gasped and sat up on the sofa. "You...you...it was you, Miss Norwood?" he asked, disbelief clouding his face.

All his friends looked at him, exploding with laughter. Some slapped him on the shoulder. Others laughed so arduously, tears sprang forth. Marshall finally joined them.

When they settled down, Susie let them stay on an extra forty-five minutes and sent a note home with each of them.

30

"How you doin' this evenin'?" Koffee inquired, raising his pants before sitting, displaying shapely legs and silk socks.

"I'm doin' fine. Make yo'self comfortabl'," Susie said, politely when she didn't feel that way. She hadn't seen him for a while and had been encouraged when he hadn't shown for Blanche's party.

She could see that he had changed since she last saw him. He sported more confidence than before. And his clothing was definitely more expensive. She hoped he wasn't trying to impress her.

He smiled. "I jest got back in town from a convention. While I was gon', I kept thankin' 'bout you, and 'cided I need'd to show you somethin'. You don't know much 'bout me and maybe this will help you. I need you to come for a short ride with me."

"Where?"

"Jest over on First Avenue and back."

"Cain't it wait?" she asked, feeling uncomfortable.

"I need to show you now."

"Alright," she said reluctantly. She informed the girls she was leaving, grabbing a sweater and following him.

He stopped the car in front of a run-down gray house and turned to Susie. He spoke for more than five minutes about his churches and his brick mason business before finally saying, "Do you want to go in and see my house?"

"Man, if you crazy enuf to thank I'm goin' inside yo' wife's house, you need to have yo' head 'xamined. The best thang for you to do is take me back home. Or bettah yet, I'll walk," Susie hissed as white anger exploded in her. She reached for the door.

"Naw, Susie," he said as he gunned the engine and pulled away. "I jest want'd you to see what I have, which ain't much. But one day I will be a rich man," he pledged as his knuckles strained against the steering wheel. "I knowed you wouldn' 'xcept me without havin' somethin'."

"How in the hell do you know what I woulda done if you nevah tried to find out or give me a choice? You don't know me well enuf to say that. And you don't know what kind of life I had growin' up. You don't know nothin' 'bout me, Rev'end. Don't ever try and second guess me."

"I didn't take you thaih to upset you, Madam," he apologized, causing Susie to turn and look at him again. The man had never said he was sorry about anything.

Susie lit a cigarette, fighting the urge to get away from him and his crazy talk. "Why then? Ain't it bad enuf what we doin'?" she asked bluntly.

Ignoring her questions, he told her about his life as a youngster. He had been dirt poor. He had been raised by his mother. They had lived in a run-down house in the country. "I tell you, Madam, the place was so bad, yo' dog woulda ran away from it," he stated emphatically at that point. He had worn hand-me-down clothes and worked for a living since he was a small child, to help his mother keep food on the table. Some days, they had to look for potatoes in the frozen earth to feed him while she went hungry. He had promised himself that one day he would complete his education and become wealthy and take care of his mother the way she deserved.

When he was around fifteen or so, he had been called by God to become a preacher, but had failed to listen. His mother became very ill, and in the process of caring for her, he forgot his calling. A few years after her death, he was reminded by a strong voice that he had failed the Lord.

He then begged and scraped every brown cent he could and moved from the country to Selma. He had managed to get a job and live in a boarding house, finish school, and finally go on to the seminary at Selma University.

He confessed that he was still poor, but much better off than he had been. He still had a long way to go, he admitted, but he would have plenty of money one day. His voice had cracked several times during his declaration.

His story saddened Susie. She felt pity for him, momentarily forgetting all that he had done to her. She found herself reaching to touch him, but stopped. Her mind wandered.

Look at him Susie thought. *He seems so sad and miserable, like a good and understandin' man. I wonder how he could seem that way, then turn 'round, and use voodoo to git me?*

You already know the answer to that or you wouldn't be sitting in his car. The voice said.

She jumped slightly, covering her mouth to keep any sound from escaping. Then she felt a bit dizzy. She turned her head toward the window and closed her eyes as the glow appeared in them.

The voice persisted. *A good man would not do to you what he has done. Don't make excuses for him or yourself. Just hurry and get rid of him. Your time is running out. You know what you need to do.*

When the voice faded, her eyes returned to normal, leaving her totally shaken. "What do you mean?" she whispered.

"Did you say somethin', Madam?"

"Take me home, Rev'end."

"Is thaih somethin' I said?"

"Nawh. I have to git home."

BOOK III

MIXED BLESSINGS

*Mixed Blessings come
in all shapes and forms.
Filled with joy, hope,
pain and even fear.
Mixed Blessings can warn
of coming events
that only the receiver may
or may not understand....
One must pull the veil from
one's eyes, force the cob webs
from the mind, open wide
the door, and destroy the evil
that lurks.*

Carolyn V. Parnell

31

Susie strolled slowly down the street towards home. Tired and hot, she longed to get out of the scorching July weather, but her depression outweighed her desires. She kicked at a rock and squinted from the glaring sun, thinking back to the past.

It seemed in a matter of minutes, her life had gone from worse, to worse, to worse. After Rev. Koffee had dropped her at her door that awful evening, last November, she had made herself the second or third promise to rid herself of him, and when she went to bed that evening, she assured herself that tomorrow would be a new beginning, that she would finally take the first and final step necessary to rid herself of him.

But, the following morning proved her wrong. Susie had awakened and discovered the most heart wrenching news. As she walked toward the bathroom, she heard someone throwing up, and she knocked at the door. She saw Blanche leaning over the toilet seat.

She knew the answer even before she demanded an explanation, but she needed to hear it to believe it. Blanche tearfully admitted that Marshall had gotten into their home while Susie was away and attacked her. Blanche had been too ashamed to tell her, and had made Lola promise to keep quiet as well.

"But why didn't you tell me when I ax'd you 'bout missin' yo' last period, Blanche?" Susie had moaned, holding her splitting head, seeing all Blanche's dreams washed away as in a bad rainstorm.

"Mama, I jest couldn' bear to have you go through moe pain. You always in some pain. I was hopin' my period would start" Blanche gagged.

Susie had stood there for the longest time, staring. Her mind raced with cold anger and fear. Finally, she took Blanche's hand and walked with her back to her room.

She had wandered downtown for several hours, fighting the desire to scream from the piercing pain that grabbed and twisted at her heart, fighting the urge to fling herself into the Alabama River and leave the misery behind.

But that awful feeling had finally been pushed aside as she considered all the pain and horror her child had endured and was coping with.

Susie had pulled strength from her boots and courage from her burdened soul, sat down, wrote and told her mother about Blanche's dilemma. Then begged her not to come to her rescue this time.

She had also confided in two other friends, Girt and Mrs. Turner, an older friend and next door neighbor. Their advice had been to give Blanche some kind of tonic and sugar to start her period. But Susie's religious beliefs had kept her from taking that route. Instead, she had wrapped her child in her arms and promised her all would work out in the end.

Unfortunately, Blanche's devastating news caused Susie to put aside her plans to free herself of Koffee.

As the weeks slowly merged into months, Blanche's slim body turned into one that made her ashamed and withdrawn. She hid from everyone except her family, but on warm days she would sneak on the porch and sit in the swing until she saw someone approaching.

Now, Susie saw Blanche's bulky outline as she turned the corner and approached her house.

Blanche's face always lit up when she saw her mother. Since

becoming pregnant, Blanche sat in the old swing, and waited for her like a lost child.

"Hi, Mama," she said softly, watching her mother walk up the steps and onto the porch.

"Hi, Blanche, how you feelin' today, baby?" Susie asked her usual question, opening the screen door and waiting for Blanche to pull her bulky weight from the swing and follow her.

"I'm doin' okay, Mama, jest hot."

"Yeah, it's a hot one alright. We sho could use some rain to cool it off a bit," she commented as she continued walking toward her bedroom to change from her sweaty work clothes and into a housedress so she could prepare dinner.

As she washed her face and hands, Susie thought of the promises she had made to Blanche about getting her back in school. Each day she prayed that when that time arrived, the Good Lord would be in the principal's heart so that he would bend the rules, under the awful circumstances.

R. B. Hudson High had very strict rules. No pregnant girls could attend before or after giving birth. Girls were considered women after giving birth and weren't allowed around innocent girls.

Marshall had found the courage to come forward. Susie saw fit to let him in, and sat in the living room with them while he repeatedly begged Blanche to forgive him, pledged his love to her, and, finally, asked her to marry him a dozen times. In the end, Blanche refused him, telling him to go away.

Susie splashed the lukewarm water on her face and let her mind become blank. She walked into the kitchen to prepare dinner, Blanche poking behind her. Blanche dropped down in a chair at the table and fanned her flushed face.

"Mama, I heard that girl Anna Belle was taken to the hospital this mornin' to have her baby," she said frantically, her eyes glassy with tears.

Anna Belle was another girl pregnant by Marshall, under diffrent circumstances.

"Who tole you that?" Susie demanded as she walked to the icebox and took out some whiting fish to fry.

"Sistah did when her friends stop'd by this mornin'. She didn't let them in, though," she added quickly.

"I heard she wasn't due 'til the end of the month, and neither is you for that mattah, accordin' to what the doctor said, 'round the twenty-fourth. You not gon' let her beat you and have hers first?" Susie inquired as she prepared the cabbage for making coleslaw.

"No, Mam. I don't thank so," Blanche answered, tears streaming down her cheeks.

Susie stopped chopping the cabbage and put her arms around Blanche. "Don't cry, baby. Everythang's gon' be fine, jest you wait and see. Yo' baby will be born first, I jest know it."

Her reassuring words calmed Blanche immediately. Susie finished and placed the slaw in the icebox, and prepared the fish to fry. After dropping the fish into the hot grease, she walked back to the table and sat down with Blanche.

"Well, baby. I thank aftah dinner, when it's dark, the three of us will take a long walk. That'll help relax you and make you sleep bettah. So don't eat too much, alright?"

Blanche nodded her head and touched her heavy stomach. She thought about the other girl. She knew Anna Belle by sight only. Rumor was she ran with a fast group of girls. That didn't matter to her. Not even the rumor that the girl wanted to marry Marshall. It was the bragging – that Marshall had been with her – Anna Belle first.... Yes, she was willing to do anything to have her baby first.

Susie returned to the stove to finish dinner, and Lola slipped into the kitchen.

"Hi, Mama. Hi, Blanche," she offered as she flopped down in a chair.

"Hi, Sistah," Susie replied. "Go wash yo' hands and come take the dishes down for dinner. We gon' eat soon."

When Lola returned, she set the table. "Blanche, what do you say 'bout Anna Belle? Do you thank it's true she gon' have her baby first jest so she can git yo' goat?"

"Hush up, Sistah, and do yo' work. The chile don't need to hear none of yo' mess," Susie ordered as she brought the food to the table.

The sky had started to lighten, turning a beautiful orange-red as dawn turned into daylight. Susie was finally dozing after staying awake most of the night praying for Blanche when a shriek jerked her from her bed.

"Mamaaaaaaaaaa!" Blanche wailed.

Before Blanche finished calling out to her, Susie's feet were on the floor, running toward her child's room. But Blanche wasn't there.

Susie turned and ran into the bathroom and found Blanche sitting on the toilet. Her eyes filled with terror.

She shrieked, "Mama! I got to go to the bathroom, but I cain't! It hurts too much!"

Susie knew immediately Blanche was in labor, that she was experiencing pressure from the baby where it had dropped down into the birth canal, waiting for the right moment to enter the world.

Not wanting to alarm her any further, she coached gently, "Blanche, git up. The baby is ready to be born. You in labor."

Blanche's eyes filled with more alarm than before. She reached for her mother.

"Wait, baby. Stay here for a minute and try to breathe slow and even. Do you hear me, Blanche? Don't push."

Blanche nodded her head rapidly, understanding. "I'll be right back." She fled to Lola's bedroom to awake her. "Go quick and help yo' sistah off the toilet, she's in labor."

Lola's eyes were opened, but she wasn't fully awake. "Come on, wake up. Yo sistah needs you. She's in labor." Lola's eyes widened in surprise, fully awake.

"Now you go in the bathroom and help git Blanche to the bed and have her lay down on her side. I have to go and call the doctor so we can git her to the hospital."

"Mama, naw." If I go to the hospital, I'll die! Mama, please don't make me go. I know I'll die for sho. I won't make it, I won't!"

Susie swung around and looked into her daughter's terrified eyes and saw the truth written in them. She knew Blanche meant every word, her heavy bulk leaning against the doorway. She couldn't take a chance and send her to the hospital and maybe

STILL MY TREMBLIN' SOUL

lose her. But what if there were complications and she needed to be in the hospital?

Lawd, I guess I could call Doc Walker to come out here; the rest is up to You, she prayed.

Dr. Walker was a colored doctor who delivered babies at Good Samaritan Hospital in the colored section, and also delivered babies at home for twenty-five dollars.

"Lola, come help yo' sistah," Susie ordered as she took one of Blanche's arms and waited for Lola to get the other before moving toward Blanche's bedroom.

When Blanche was in bed, Susie said, "You try to breathe with each pain while I go and call Doctor Walker to come out here to deliver yo' baby. Sistah, you git the ironin' board out." Then she left the room to call the doctor, hoping he could get there in time.

The call made, Susie returned to Blanche's room to start preparing her for the delivery. She changed the linen on the bed, and placed an ironing board under the sheet so Blanche would have something to bear down on. Blanche suddenly had a contraction, causing her to jump from the straight chair she was sitting in onto Susie's back.

Susie's mind shrieked in pain, but she gritted her teeth to keep from crying out, afraid of frightening Blanche.

Every attempt to release Blanche's iron grip failed. Susie felt all her muscles strain against her 160-pound daughter's weight.

When Blanche's pain passed, Susie said, "Sistah, help me git Blanche back into the chair so I can finish the bed." She pushed aside her back pain, wondering what was keeping the doctor.

"Come on, baby, and let's git you in the bed so you can git comfortabl," Susie soothed, as she and Lola struggled with Blanche, finally getting her into a more comfortable position.

Susie had just put water on the stove to boil when Dr. Walker arrived, pulling his bulky form into the living room.

"Where is she, Susie?"

"Follow me, Doctor," Susie said, happy to see him.

When they reached Blanche's room, she was having another contraction, followed by another and another. With each occurrence she screamed so loudly their ears hurt!

Afraid for her, Susie went to her.

"Go and git the hot water. She ready," the doctor ordered.

"Git the hot water, Sistah," Susie said as she sat next to the bed, but Lola was rooted to the floor, her eyes transfixed on her frightened sister.

Susie started to repeat her request, but the doctor interceded. "It may do her some good to see this," he suggested.

Susie agreed and brought the water to the doctor. It's not hot yet, doctor."

"We cain't wait, this baby's comin', see her head. Anyway, it's warm enuf," he said, testing the water with his finger. "Cain't hurt her none."

"Mamaaaaaaa!" Blanche wailed, twisting her face in agony. Susie grabbed her hand. "I'm here, baby. It's gon' be alright."

The baby's head was there, but it couldn't move forward. Blanche was turning red and sweating profusely, gasping for breath.

Susie, scared for her daughter and the unborn child, turned to speak to the doctor, but at that moment he reached into his black bag, pulled out a pair of scissors and cut Blanche like she was a bolt of material, causing her to screech in horrible anguish.

The baby's head pushed forward; then her left shoulder and the rest followed. Blanche fell back against the pillows like a sack of flour as the doctor caught the screaming baby.

Susie let go of the breath she had been holding and cleaned the perspiration from her forehead. Lola's mouth had formed a permanent o-shape as she remained rooted to the floor.

"It's a girl." The doctor stated.

"Why did you do that, Doctor?" Susie asked, looking at her daughter's bleeding bottom while the doctor lay the hungry baby aside to thread his needle.

"Had to, or she wouldn' a made it. The baby was too big to come out the birth canal. Couldn' give her no shot neither. That woulda kill'd her. Don't worry, she'll be alright," he advised as he finished threading the needle and pulled his gloves on.

"You ain't gon' sew her without givin' her somethin', I know," Susie whispered.

"It'll hurt some, but not as bad as what she jest went through, and latah I'll be back to check up on her."

Susie didn't like it, but there wasn't anything she could do about it. She looked at the baby, who was sucking her bloody fists. Frowning, Susie offered, "Doctor, the baby's eatin' her own blood. Cain't you hurry and take care of her?"

"It sho cain't hurt her none. She jest came out of it," he stated and stuck the needle into Blanche's tender skin, causing her to faint from the agony.

"She need the rest anyway," he uttered before Susie could protest.

The hot August sun bore down on Susie's head, causing her to feel as if her hair would catch fire any minute. The perspiration and hair grease rolled down her face as fast as she patted it with her handkerchief. She hoped the grease hadn't streaked her powder, which was too white for her high yellow skin tones. She often wondered why they only made two shades, corn silk white and dark brown, conveniently forgetting that colored people came in many tones.

Susie quickened her pace, determined that the heat and nothing else was going to keep her from this appointment. Blanche's future rested on her, and she couldn't, wouldn't fail her. Even though she had no idea what she was going to say to the man when she got there.

She greeted him and sat down only after he asked her. She got right to the point.

"Mr. Stonner, I know what yo' rules is at school 'bout girls who git pregnant. You don't let them come back.

"What I'm sayin' is, my daughter is in the same situation, but she's a good girl, and she didn't brang this on herself. She's nevah been in any troubl' and always mind'd her own bus'ness," Susie stated in a clear, strong, and confident voice filled with quiet conviction.

"As far as her bein' pregnant, nobody knowed 'bout it 'xcept a few of the teachers and two close friends of the family. We ain't the kind of people who throw somethin' like that out in the wash. We consider it a disgrace for a girl to git pregnant 'til she marred, even under these circumstances.

"You was kind enuf to let her brang her homework home aftah she stop'd comin' to school in February so she could keep up with her classmates. And by takin' her out of school, it help'd save her shame and show'd respect for the school and herself."

Mr. Stonner sat looking at Susie for several long seconds causing her discomfort, but she didn't let it show.

He was amazed at how direct and assertive she was, speaking to him as if she was an equal to a white woman, or more so, a white man.

Even though he had been caught totally off guard, he wasn't insulted or angry by this colored woman. Quite to the contrary, he found her fascinating and sincere.

"Now, I'm axin' you to give yo' permission for her to have the chance that she woulda had if she hadn't been ravish'd. I can promise you the boy is gon' that did it and won't be comin' back. She needs this chance to turn her life 'round, Mr. Stonner."

Finding himself drawn to her, Mr. Stonner leaned forward and peered closely at Susie.

"Well, Miss Norwood," he spoke as if speaking to a white woman who had clout. "I have to agree with you; Blanche is a good girl from what I have observed since she's been goin' to school here. And an excellent student."

Susie smiled slightly.

"From what I can tell, the teachers say she was a model pupil, and was rootin' for her to come back here and teach aftah she finish'd college. And I must say, I was truly taken back when I found out she was in the ah, situation. I would have expect'd yo' othah daughter, Lola. She's always runnin' up b'hind the boys."

He paused and dabbed at his flushed face with a handkerchief. "Whew, it's hot in here today. Must be a hundred outdoors."

Susie waited.

"Well," he continued, clearing his voice. "The only thang I can say is I'm sorry it had to happen to her. Sometimes thangs happen, and we jest cain't control them..." He stopped abruptly, picked up a pencil, and started writing.

Susie waited, thankful for his understanding, praying he would say the words she and Blanche desperately needed to hear.

A few minutes later, he looked up from his paper. "I tell you what I'm gonna do, and it goes against all the rules. But I'm gonna bend them a little and allow Blanche back in school. So you go on back home and tell her she can come back next month." He stood, walked around the desk, and sat on top on it.

"Have her come to the office, and I will have her schedule ready for her jest like she nevah left. And if she still do as well as she had been doin', she'll be a good candidate to come back here aftah she finish college. We'll be proud to have her teach here."

Susie wanted to grab and hug him, but she knew that was impossible. Instead, she held her hand out to him in gratitude. He shook it and smiled at her.

"I don't know how to thank you, so I'll jest say it. Thank you from the bottom of my heart, Mister Stonner. My daughter will be most grateful to you, too."

He nodded and released her hand. "Befoe you leave, I want you to take a message back to the othah one. Tell her she bettah be careful 'cause I'm watchin' her. If this had been her I wouldn' let her come back."

"I sho will do that, Mr. Stonner," Susie promised, knowing he was speaking truthfully about Lola. She was a people person and loved being the center of attention, especially with boys.

"Enjoy the rest of yo' summer, Susie," he said, walking her to the door.

"Thank you. I sho will try." She slipped through the door.

As hot as it was, she didn't feel the blazing sun as she walked from the building. She felt like doing the jitterbug, she was so estatic but decided against it.

Susie had been home for hours. They sat in the living room, the warm breeze floating through the window, shuffling the newspaper Susie was reading. Eventually, she laid the paper down, looked at Blanche and smiled.

"Well, young lady, you been waitin' long enuf, so I guess you bettah start weanin' Carolyn, 'cause you goin' back to school next month."

"Mama. Oh, Mama. Thank you so much. I knew you could do it," Blanche screamed, throwing her arms around her, happy tears gushing forth.

Lola sat looking, amazed. She bit at her nails.

Susie looked at her. "Close yo' mouth and keep doin' what I tell you and you won't have to worry 'bout goin' through this. And by the way, Mister Stonner sent you a message. He said, 'You bettah watch yo'self'."

"Mama," Lola's voice shook as she jumped from her chair. "What do he mean watchin' me? I ain't doin' nothin', Mama."

"What's done in the night comes to the light, I always heard Mama say to her friends. Make sho yo' nights is at home in yo' own bed by yo'self, and thaih won't be no surprises, Sistah." She picked up the newspaper.

Lola sat playing with her hands, biting her nails, patting her hair and chewing her nails again. She picked up the comic book from the table, but did not read it.

Susie looked up from the newspaper and shook her head. She hoped this daughter could understand what harm she could do to herself and her future by having a child out of wedlock. *How can I make her understan' befoe it's too late?*

Baby Carolyn screamed, demanding to be fed and Blanche who was reading, went to see after her.

"You sho is quiet, Sistah. Anythang wrong?" Susie inquired.

"Nome." She pulled the comic book closer to her face, and nibbled her nails.

"Don't eat yo' fingernails off, and you must have read that funny book 'bout twenty times." She paused for moment, then said so quietly that she was barely audible, "I know somethin' is botherin' you."

Lola started chewing at the end of her fingers, "Nome. I'm

alright." But she wasn't. Her mother's tone had sent an electric charge through her.

"In that case, I want you to know that everythang I tell you and yo' sistah is for yo' own good. I want y'all to have a good life, and you cain't do that unless you have a education and respect for yo'self.

"You know how hard it is for us, even when we got one. The only jobs out thaih for most us is a maid, cook, or janitor. Unless you want to take in washin' or sewin'. And for us who is educated, we lucky to be a nurse's aide, teacher, preacher, and Lawd knows 'bout the doctors. Them that own thaih own cafe, barber shop, co'ner grocery stoe's and undertakers is lucky. And only 'cause we ain't allow'd in thaih places for none of them services. So they have to be hu-mane and let us have somethin' of our own since we gon' be in and out of thaih homes, workin' for them and all.

"You know, by seein' what Blanche done gon' through, that life ain't no soft bed to lay in. That chile has gon' through too much to be her age, and I don't know if she will ever be the same. I don't want that for you. So please, please lis-sen to me and git yo'self through school."

"I'm gon' finish school, Mama."

"Alright then."

32

Susie sat on the sofa looking at Blanche's report card, a pleased smile on her tired face, while Carolyn, now nine months old, stood at the screen door, looking at the empty street.

"Mama, Boo," her tiny voice squealed in delight as her chubby finger pointed toward the screen door. It was Rev. Koffee, the only man she knew in her short life.

Susie's smile faded as she moved toward the door to allow him in. He annoyed her so badly that she wanted to tell him that both of them were probably the biggest, damnable fools that she had ever known. And she was the worst for not ending their sick relationship.

Koffee smiled at Carolyn, bent over and squeezed her fat cheeks, "Hi, Boo, how you?" he said, using the nickname he had given her because she was quick to repeat simple words he said to her. She especially liked "boo". After hugging her, he sat and began speaking to Susie.

Carolyn giggled and clapped her chubby hands, toddled to Susie and climbed on her lap.

Susie refused to speak to him, only bowing her head in acknowledgment. *Why don't you tell him to go and nevah come back and do somethin' to keep him away? But what if he goes to the voodoo man again? How did I ever git in this mess?* She questioned herself.

He sat for a few minutes, no words passing between them. He patted his feet and then uttered in a small voice, "Well, I best be goin'. I got a club meetin' to go to."

Smiling slightly, Susie said, "You belong to a club? I got a club meetin' to go to myself." She pulled Carolyn's heavy bottom from her knee, placing her next to her on the sofa.

"Where's yo' club meetin'?" he said.

"The same place yo's is," she responded.

He looked at her strangely, stood, and stretched. "Well, I gotta go. I'll be seein' you latah on, Madam."

"It's accordin' to when you git out yo' meetin'," she replied and watched him walk down the steps, an angry smirk on her face. She hated liars. She knew his club meeting was probably on Small Street or down in the bottom with another woman.

She certainly didn't belong to a club, but she couldn't resist taunting him. She found herself enjoying it. He deserved it.

After bathing, Susie sat playing with her makeup at the vanity dresser. She ran a powder puff across her face and put a dab of lipstick on her shapely, thin lips.

"Well, Susie, ole girl, you sho the one for tellin' people what's right and wrong, but you bad when it comes to takin' yo' own advice. So this time you gon' do it. You gon' git rid of that sorry, no-account, women chasin', lyin', voodoo man befoe you don't have a life left.

"Look at you. What have you done in yo' life to be happy 'xcept have yo' chil'ren? And even then it was done all wrong."

She walked to her modest closet and examined her clothing before pulling out a striking brown suit with a fur-trimmed collar. "Well, I guess I can git away with this bein' it's kinda chilly for March. Humm, maybe I should go out to a club or somethin'."

She slipped into the suit and studied her figure. "Not too bad for a grandmother of almost thirty-six," she smiled and turned sideways, smoothing the material on her round hips, placing hands on her small waist and squeezing it.

She thought suddenly of Miles and became melancholy. She covered her face and cried until her eyes stung. She hadn't brooded about him for years. Thinking of Miles troubled her because she realized by sending him away, she had sent her heart and spirit with him.

Pulling herself together, she walked into the living room to get Lola. She glanced through the curtains and saw Koffee's car pull up and stop.

"Sistah, tell him I'm gon'. Hurry up, I'll git b'hind the door," she whispered. Lola was always quick on her feet, and understood what her mother wanted her to do.

"Hi, Rev. Koffee," Lola greeted him as he walked up the steps and stopped at the locked screen door.

"How you doin', young lady?"

"Fine, thank you. Mama ain't here."

"She ain't?" he frowned.

"Naw, Suh."

Susie smiled as she peeped through the crack of the door and saw his angry face.

He had turned to leave when Blanche said, "Aaah, Mama, come from b'hind the door."

Susie frowned and shook her head as she faced Blanche. You know, you nevah could keep nothin," she whispered.

Lola opened the door and let Koffee in. She excused herself and Blanche.

He stood, looking around as if searching for someone else, then he turned and walked out, stomping down the steps like an angry jackass. He opened and slammed his car door after getting in. He sat puffing furiously on his cigar before finally pulling away, leaving dust flying behind him.

Susie laughed to herself and shrugged her shoulders before dismissing him. "Sistah, let's go," Susie called out to her.

Lola was in Blanche's room, trying to get her to understand that she must always do what Susie asked her to do. "You nevah betray her, no mattah how you feel. It's her life."

"I know that, but he was lookin' so mad. I didn't know what he might do."

"Blanche, you jest 'member, always lis-sen when she says to do somethin' for her. Anyway, you don't like the man, and you ought to know, Mama don't want him hangin' 'round."

"You right. I shoulda stay'd out of it. I'm sorry, I wasn't thankin'." Tears welled in her eyes.

"Don't go cryin'. It's alright. Now, I got to leave with Mama. Bye."

The following day Koffee returned. Susie observed his small eyes, smoldering in anger, looking mean like he was itching for a fight.

Susie glared at him in defiance. He didn't own her.

"Did you git that ice cream you want'd so bad?" he asked as he patted his right foot like a cat does its tail when it's getting ready to attack.

"Yeah. I sho did." *So you follow'd me. I shoulda knowed it. You scoundrel.*

"Well, I thank I came back a little too early for you," he charged. "You look'd like you was fixin' to go out."

Before she could respond he darted across the room as quickly as a snake, and slapped her hard, across the face, causing her unlit cigarette to break and the tobacco to stick to her lips.

Susie saw red stronger than any fire could make. She shook her head slightly and shot daggers at him. "I know you didn't mean that, Rev'end, but b'lieve what you want," she said in a calm voice, using her teeth to remove the tobacco from her stinging mouth.

Quite suddenly, in one swift movement, she shoved him off balance so that he was straddling the gas heater. He didn't realize it was on until he felt the intense heat crawling through his trousers, brushing at his legs.

"Damn you!" he bellowed out in pain as he bolted out the door, leaving a burning smell trailing him.

Before Susie had a chance to lock the door behind him, he rushed throught it with his .45 and pointed it at her.

She didn't panic, she pulled a large, heavy glass ashtray from the coffee table and held it in the air, knowing she could intimidate him. Damn if she would let him kill her. Her dark eyes danced in her face.

Mrs. Turner, a friend and next door neighbor had been hanging out clothes when Koffee ran out of the house, drawing her attention. She stopped and glanced at him as he charged back up the steps with something in his hand. She had stopped her task and stood staring into Susie's living room.

A look of pleasure on his face, Koffee stood, waving the gun at Susie.

"Shoot me if you gon' shoot me," she said in an unrecognizable voice. "But I'll be damned if you shoot me; you sho cain't eat me. If you do', I'll lay mighty damn heavy on yo' stomach. And you bettah make sho you kill me, 'cause I sho as hell will kill you," she warned, meaning every word.

His nostrils flared, and saliva dripped from his slackened mouth. She saw hesitation appear in his dead eyes, but her fiery eyes didn't waver.

He turned the butt of the gun around and stepped towards Susie.

"If you hit me, I'll kill you. I ain't yo' wife, yo' possession, or yo' dog, man," she warned in a deadly, calm voice, her eyes piercing his, causing him to become a statue for a moment.

He could feel the deadly tones, and see the hot flames in her eyes. He knew that she would do exactly as she said, if she was forced to. He had never seen her this way. She wasn't meek or passive. His voodoo wasn't working. He was losing control over her. He blamed his voodoo man.

"Oh, I forgot," he blurted, lowing the gun to his side. "I was 'spose to pick her up from the hair dresser." Then he fled through the door and to his car.

"That's what you shoulda been doin' all along," Susie yelled before he sped away, leaving dust behind him. When his car disappeared, Mrs. Turner who had been hiding behind a tree, dashed to Susie's house, knocked, and slipped through the door.

"You sho stood up to him, Susie. Is you alright?"

"And you sho didn't make it yo' bus'ness to offer any help, Miss Turner. Yeah, I'm fine."

"Honey, stray bullets don't care who they hit. But I was rootin' for you," she said as she laughed and followed Susie to the sofa and sat down, glad to relieve her trembling legs.

"He might whup othah women's butts, but this one he sho won't. And if he make the mistake and try, b'lieve me, we gon' whup each othahs butts, if any gits beat 'round here," Susie promised as she replaced the ashtray, sat down, and lit a ciga-rette with steady hands.

"I hear you, Susie, I sho hear you."

That night before going to bed, Susie prayed and cried for hours, desperately seeking answers to rid herself of Koffee's voodoo spell.

If she had listened just a bit more carefully, she might have heard what she needed to know.

33

Three months had passed since her blow up with Koffee, and she hadn't heard from or seen him. But this day, her anger was just as fierce as when she last saw him. As she pounded on Mrs. Turner's door, she ignored the sunny morning and chipper birds hanging about on her magnolia trees.

At sight of Mrs. Turner, Susie swept through the door, hands on her hips. "Miss Turner, I was right. That heifer, Sistah, is pregnant. But you know what the sad thing is? She stood in my face, look'd me in my eyes, and outright lied to me when I ax'd her 'bout it, months ago!" Susie exploded, hot liquid clouding her mysterious eyes.

"Susie, I'm sorry. I know you hurtin'. Come on in and have a seat."

Susie sat in a comfortable chair, lit a cigarette, her hands shaking. "It's killin' me, Miss Turner. Aftah all that talkin' I did all these years, the ravishin' of her sistah and seein' how it's changed her life, the heifer goes and take her tail and do somethin' like this. I jest cain't b'lieve it, but I shouldn' be surprised. I feel like wrangin' her neck."

"I know you do, Susie, but you have to thank 'bout yo'self too. If she gon' do somethin' like this, she ought to have to pay for it. She knowed bettah."

"If you mean put her out," Susie groaned as she stood and paced the linoleum floor, "I jest cain't throw her out in the streets. She don't have enuf education or a job to raise a chicken, let alone a chile. And I sho ain't goin' back and face that white man again. Not on my life.

"I jest don't know why she did this when she knowed she would git caught. Mess her life up. I jest don't understan' the chile, Miss Turner."

"Susie, honey, don't take it so hard. Everybody knows you done a fine job raisin' yo' chil'ren. What done happen'd you cain't do nothin' 'bout, so don't go blamin' yo'self. Now you jest come on and sit down and I'll git you some coffee," she said, patting Susie's back, leading her back to the chair.

Susie lowered her head and closed her eyes; tears flooded her face. "Lawd, I don't know why this happen'd, and I don't know how much moe I can take. It seems like the moe I try, the harder it gits. But...maybe this is my fault for not bein' thaih for them when I had all my troubl's," she whispered.

Mrs. Turner returned with the coffee and placed it on the table and waited for Susie to compose herself.

"Susie, no mattah how much you try to talk yo'self into bein' at fault, you ain't. You did the best you could. Now you take a minute and drank some of this strong coffee."

"Thank you, Miss Turner."

"You welcome. You 'bout the only person I know that no mattah how hot it is outdoors, you gots to have yo' coffee."

But Susie didn't hear her. "Sometimes I wonder if I'm put here jest to suffer. All my life it's been one thang aftah another. Gawd knows, I've tried to keep the faith, but it seems the devil keep havin' his way. And 'cause it's so hard, I know I cain't lose my faith, but I'm gettin' weary. Ain't life somethin?" she finished bitterly.

"Susie, you make me want to break down and cry. That's a awful thang to say 'bout yo'self. You a good and strong woman that done been dealt a lot of problems, but with yo' faith I know you gon' be alright. And I know deep down, you do too. You jest need to search deep down, and pull up the rest of yo' faith. Jest know you have all my sympathy and prayers. And if thaih's anythang I can do, you let me know."

"You know, Miss Turner, I always figured my chil'ren would grow up, court, finish school, go to college, and then when they 'cided to, git mar-red and have a family. I always want'd them to have moe then me. Do moe then me and have the chilehood I did-n't have.

"I got one chile who mind'd me, and it didn't do no good. And I got one who thought she knowed moe then me, went her way 'til she got caught. Now, I'm gon' be a grandmother for the sec-ond time when I ain't had time to git my own life together."

Susie stopped and sipped the cold coffee and lit another cig-arette and then she looked at Mrs. Turner with a bitter smile, new tears flowing unnoticed.

"I'm sorry, Miss Turner, I don't mean to burden you with my troubl's."

"You know you can always talk to me anytime, Susie. You like the daughter I wish'd I had."

"Thank you, Miss Turner. I guess all the talk in the world won't take the baby away or change my daughter. I know that Blanche is goin' to be awful hurt when she finds out. I bettah be gettin' back." She smothered the cigarette in the ashtray removed a hanky from her dress pocket, dried her tear streaked face and stood.

"Susie, you know if anythang happen'd to you, the chil'ren won't be able to make it," she warned as they neared the door.

At the door, Susie turned and looked at her friend strangely, nodded, and slipped out.

"Why did you do it? Why, when you had a choice, Sistah? Why?" Blanche cried before fleeing to her room where she wept for days, refusing to speak to Lola.

Finally, they reconciled. Lola apologized, but never offered an explanation, and Blanche didn't press her.

It took Susie much longer to be civil to her daughter. Every time she looked at Lola she wanted to lash out at her. Therefore, she avoided or ignored her as much as possible. Susie remained in her room where she cried, prayed, and talked to herself for several weeks.

The months crept by slowly, each of them caught up in their own problems. Finally, Susie was able to look at her child without malice. Inwardly, she hurt badly.

On a still, frigid January night, to everyone's relief, Lola gave birth to a daughter, Patricia. All Susie's anger took flight when she saw her second grandchild in the hospital.

Koffee had returned three months after that awful night – he had pulled a gun on Susie.

While he was kind, he did not ask Susie to forgive him for the way he had acted when he was there the last time.

He tried to be generous with his money and gifts, but she refused them, saying she would manage on her own. He was surprised, but didn't push her. Since Susie was colder toward him, he stopped visiting her as often as he used to. His visits were weekly and short. Susie never told him about Lola's pregnancy. He learned only after hearing the infant cry one day while visiting. He was hurt, but Susie did not care. She would take care of him soon, she vowed.

Meanwhile, Susie kept busy by concentrating on the baby's needs and Lola's recuperation, and soon the dreaded time arrived.

Even though she had promised herself she wouldn't help Lola return to school, she decided she had to give her a second chance as well.

But, as she had stated almost two years before, she would not face Mr. Stonner for her. However, she sent Lola with a letter, pleading with him to allow her another chance.

Mr. Stonner responded, saying he would allow Lola to return, but only because of Susie. Lola would be placed on probation and would have to maintain a 'B' average or she would be expelled.

"This is the last time, Lola. If you 'cide to go out thaih and do this again, don't even come my way."

"Oh, Mama, I won't do that. You jest don't know how much this means to me. I won't let you down again."

"You worry 'bout lettin' yo'self down. It's yo' life, not mine. I done talk'd out of words now. But thaih's one thang I want to ax you. Please don't brang no moe chil'ren in my house. We done had enuf disgrace."

"I won't, Mama."

When Lola re-entered school, Blanche, in her last year, had applied to several colleges and was anxiously awaiting a response.

Finally, Susie had started to feel as if the heavy darkness covering their lives was finally lifting, giving her a ray of hope to help pull her through so that she could finally move forward with the flicker of life that remained within her.

Still, Susie couldn't erase the glow from her face as she sorted through Blanche's clothes, getting her ready for her trip to Seattle, where she would be going to live with her father and attend Seattle University.

Over the years, either Blanche's father or his sister had always kept in touch with Susie, whenever he moved. Susie had always known that he loved his daughter, but, as in the past, she refused to have anything to do with him or accept anything from him. Now, she was glad for her child's sake that she had kept his last address. She had been in contact with him over the last six months to arrange Blanche's future.

Blanche's graduation was one of the most special moments in Susie's life as she watched her march across the stage, her head held high, her pride in tact. When the principal praised her and said what a smart and brave student she had been, he presented her with an award for being one of the top ten students. And then, he welcomed her to return as a teacher and handed her diploma. Susie's tears flowed, matching Blanche's.

Later, Susie's smile had been as wide as Blanche's had when her daughter placed her diploma, and her award, in her hand and said, "Mama, this is for you as well as me. Thank you, Mama." The two of them had embraced and cried in each other's arms. Rubye Mae grabbed them both and joined in.

They celebrated the happy event by having Blanche's close friends over for dinner. Afterwards, the four of them....Susie,

Rubye Mae, Blanche, and Lola….sat around until past midnight, enjoying each other's company. Three generations, each having added a bit of history to their family tree.

Three days later, Blanche wept openly in Susie's arms, held her sister for a few minutes; then Carolyn and Pat before she held her mother again. Susie gently withdrew her, and watched her stumble up the steps and onto the train.

Blanche turned when she reached the landing, her face streaked with uncontrollable tears, "Goodbye, Mama," she whispered. "I'll…I'll write as soon as I git thaih." Then she turned and was gone.

Long after the train had disappeared, Susie still stood waiting as if it would return and release her daughter because it knew her pain.

Lola stood holding Carolyn's hand and Patricia in her arms, her feelings mixed. She would miss her sister dearly, but she was glad Blanche had a chance to get out of Selma. She hoped one day she would do the same.

Susie found it difficult to adjust to Blanche's departure, but the letters she received helped make her absence easier. Her letters were filled with the beauty of the city and its varied people.

"Mama, I never saw so many people befoe.
And thaih's moe then colored and white.
They have Indians, Scottish, Swedish,
Norwegian and othahs, too. But they all look
about the same to me,'xcept the Indians.
The streets are wide and filled with tall
trees every which way I turn. Dad said
that most of them stay green all year long.
But they don't have pecan and chinaberry
ones here like we do in Selma.
The mountains are so big, you can see
them for over a hundred miles away. And the
houses are mostly two-story, like where

*Dad lives,'except he has three floors, Mama.
Imagine that, with fifteen rooms to clean
every day. Whee!
My father has taken me to dinner to several
restaurants where colored people can go.
The food is so good, I nevah want to stop
eatin'! Thaih's so many kinds, I could eat
for a year and not have tasted all of them..."*

Each of Blanche's letters filled Susie with new life as she became caught up in them, putting herself in her daughter's position. Through Blanche's description, Susie could picture Pike Place Market, located on the Seattle's downtown waterfront where one could see displayed its various foods, fruits vegetables and flowers; its many rooms and stands filled with jewelry, clothing, furs; people moving in and out, touching, smelling and eating.

She longed to be there, even if only for a few minutes. Blanche described Seattle University as being so overwhelming the first time she saw it she had to run to the little girls' room. Susie laughed out loud when she read that. She could see Blanche doing just that.

Susie laid the letter down and smiled. It had only been a matter of months since Blanche left, but she could read and hear the changes in her. Her child was now a woman and growing every day. She was very happyand proud of her even though she missed her something awful.

Surprisingly, months later, Susie found out Lola was expecting again. Without a word, she turned, walked from the room, out the door, and down to the river bridge where she sat until it was too dark to see her hand before her.

During those dreadful hours, her mind wandered back to the moment of Lola's birth. She had loved her from the beginning, forgetting how she had been conceived. Now, she wondered if Lola carried some of her father's genes. And then she violently cast that horrible notion aside. But why? Why did the chile do this?

When Susie returned home, her questions were still unanswered. She cooked dinner, fed Carolyn, took her with her into her room and went to bed.

That night, she started having nightmares that continued for weeks, causing her to develop large purplish circles beneath her eyes. When her friends asked what was wrong, she waved them away, refusing to tell them that her daughter had done about the worst thing she could do, next to killing her.

Even Blanche's letters had lost their glamour, no longer comforting to her. She lay this one aside she had received today, and took a deep sigh, her mind straying to Lola.

She had thought several times of writing and telling Blanche, but she knew it would hurt her too badly and possibly cause her to return home. She couldn't chance that and have Blanche ruin her future as well. Koffee arrived and she put her brooding aside.

Susie didn't know if it was because she was feeling lonely and lost or if her final nerve had been pulled to its breaking point. Whatever the reason, she attacked Koffee almost before he had a chance to sit down, stretch his short legs, pat his feet and light a cigar.

"You know, Rev'end, every since I been involv'd with you, my life's been nothin' but hell. I don't know why in the hell I got myself mix'd up in this shit, and you. And for the life of me, I cain't seem to git rid of you.

"You...you like a bad disease, Rev'end. A disease I need to git out of my system so I can go on livin', and do what the Lawd intend'd me to do with my pitiful life." She paused, her piercing, dark eyes penetrating his.

He moved, uneasy in his seat, startled at her outburst and terrible language, but couldn't find the words to tell her to hush. It was as if Susie's eyes reached out to him and held him motionless and speechless.

"You know, I thank I'm bein' test'd and Gawd is gettin' tir'd of me not figurin' it out. So He's givin' me moe rope to hang myself. Do you thank by me goin' with you, and you bein' mar-red, and prob'ly doin' much moe then that, that Gawd is grinnin', sayin' it's alright? Naw, Rev'end. You know He ain't. He's gon' punish the both of us.

"I been weak in the past, but now I'm gon' pull the strength from the bottom of my flat feet and tell you to jest have the decency to stand up and walk out of here and nevah come back. Leave me so I can live." She lit a cigarette and blew the smoke toward the ceiling, more relieved than she had been in years.

"Woman, you sound like you done lost yo' mind," he accused as he leaped to his feet and stood next to her, shaking his forefinger at her as if she was a child being scolded for misbehaving. "You talkin' crazy. Jest plain crazy. I don't know where you git yo' information from 'bout some othah women. I ain't got no othah women." He returned to his chair and puffed at an unlit cigar.

Susie looked at him and almost laughed. "You ain't heard nothin' I said, is you? We sinnin', Rev'end, sinnin' against Gawd and His commandments. I don't want to live this way no longer, so git the hell out my life," she demanded with the intensity of a cobra snake.

Rev. Koffee jumped from his chair, slammed the door in a fit of anger and practically leaped down the steps to his car.

That night Susie's nightmares occurred.

People with large, yellow eyes were chasing her, ripping
at her clothing, pulling her hair, taunting her, hurting her.
She tried escaping, but all the doors were sealed.
They chased after her with butcher knives. And those
blazing yellow, sinister eyes. She tried desperately
to kick one of the doors in, but the hands pulled at her,
causing her to scream and run. Then she was floating
in the air on what seemed to be a cushion.
Suddenly, the moon appeared, shining on the muddy
water; then it disappeared. Susie was horrified. She was
over the Alabama River. She had always feared water,
but muddy water was a sign that death was near,
knocking at the door.
Frantically, she looked around for someone to help

her as she continued to float further down the river,
moving with the waves, and shaking so violently
her teeth tapped together.
A coiled hand with blood red nails burst from the
water, reaching for her, grabbing at her gown,
seizing her, drawing her into the dark, cold wetness.
She beat at the hand, but more hands came toward
her until she could no longer fight them.
Slowly, the heads belonging to the bodies started to
rise from the river, their eyes matching their burnished
red nails. Their thick black hair resembled butcher
knives pointing toward the darkened sky. Their mouths,
filled with sharp, rotten teeth, came so close to her
face that their smell devoured her, causing her to
lose consciousness.
Seconds later, her eyes flew open, and she tried
screaming, but one of them covered her mouth with its
twisted crude hand and stuck out its snake like tongue at
her. It was clear that they would pull her into the water
and she would die. She cringed, closed her eyes tightly
and tried to pray, but words failed her.
They were all around her, pulling her hair and arms.
She gagged as they flicked their snake tongues toward her.
She started to quiver, realizing there was no help for her.
They would pull her soul to its horrible death in the evil
water. She slowly gave up the ghost.
Her neck was just above the water when suddenly her
body shook as if being awakened by someone.
Her eyes opened slightly. She saw a tiny pinpoint
of light glowing through the darkened clouds,
its glory seeming to send her some
sort of message, but she couldn't read it.
Her shoulders were slowly being pulled under again.
One of them yanked her head, causing her to cry out
in pain. Abruptly, her body shook so violently,
the demonic beings released her.

She flung her arms toward the heavens, eyes dilated,
and cried frantically, "Lawd, Still My Tremblin' Soul!
Lawd, Still My Tremblin' Soul! Sweet Jesus, Please!
Her body became still. The demons released a piercing
scream, then vanished beneath the black water.

Susie, startled from her sleep, looked around for the demons. Feeling wet, she looked down. She was on the floor, surrounded by a puddle of muddy water.

She hugged herself to keep from shivering from the breeze that entered the room, causing her to feel the wetness of her gown. "Lawd Jesus, my po' soul. Please. Still my tremblin' soul. Please make me whole again. Keep the devil away!" she cried," realizing she had screamed the same words in her nightmare.

Later, when the roosters crowed the dawning of the day, Susie was wide awake, having been that way since the nightmare. She had smoked two packs of cigarettes, and her mouth was parched dry.

Finally, she decided to get up and make coffee. She returned to her bed, feeling so mixed up she couldn't bear to think of going to work.

Mrs. Turner watched the children while Lola delivered a note to Susie's boss stating that she was ill and wouldn't be there for a while. Lola didn't like the glazed look in Susie's eyes. She remembered seeing that look before, when her stepfather had died and her mother had almost lost her mind.

After Mrs. Turner left, Lola took the children and went to her room and told them they had to be quiet so their grandmother could get well again.

Meanwhile, Susie sat on the edge of her bed, pulling at the sheets, running her fingers over them like a cat clawing a tree.

She paced the floor and smoked cigarettes until she coughed, and she sipped cold coffee. Then, after tossing most of her clothes onto the floor and stepping on them as if they weren't there, she pulled an old faded housedress over her head, slipped her feet into some old shoes, patted her hair, sat down at the vanity. She rambled through the drawers, throwing out stockings and more stockings on the floor.

And then she stood and walked from her room, leaving it looking like a hurricane zone. She slipped into Lola's room without knocking on the door. Lola gasped at the unseemly sight of her mother, her unruly hair and those strange, lifeless eyes. Suddenly frightened, she asked, "Mama. Can I do somethin' for you?" she paused then asked in a shaky voice. "You alright, Mama?"

"Naw. Naw. I'm leavin' now," Susie answered in a flat, lifeless voice before walking out the door, down the steps, headed toward downtown.

Lola stood at the front door, watching her mother, not knowing what to do.

Susie stopped in the center of the Edmund Pettus Bridge, known to them simply as the Alabama River. She stood looking down at the muddy water rushing beneath the bridge on its way to the Mississippi River. Steamy tears raced down her face, blurring her vision.

The river seemed to be stretching out its watery image calling out to her in its whooshing sound as she leaned over the edge, her fear of water forgotten. She straddled the safety guard and leaned over it. Leaning even farther, seemingly hearing something, she cocked her head to the side and smiled as the water turned bluish-green. Waves rippled through it, and then the waves turned into a finger, beckoning her to come in and soak up the magic of its wetness.

Susie squinted her eyes and returned the wave of the person in the water. She smiled and leaned farther over the stone wall, causing her body to bend in half, almost losing her balance.

"It sho is pretty down thaih. But I ain't got nobody to take me in 'cause everybody done left me and let me down. Can you come up here and git me?"

The grayish shadow only beckoned toward her and shook its head.

"Oh, you want me to jump?" Susie let herself slip to the landing and pulled herself up higher on the railing until she was almost high enough to straddle the side. She waved at two people who were frantically inviting her to join them although she did not recognize them. She failed to see their bright fingernail polish and their sharp, long, blackish teeth.

She was going to jump in and join them. Susie forgot she could not swim as she straddled the inside railing and prepared to jump.

At this time, a voice spoke softly "Susie." But she didn't hear. She was straddle the safety railing now and couldn't wait to get into the cool, inviting, blue water and be with her friends.

Again, the voice said faintly, but with urgency, "Susie, Susie, please. What you doin' up thaih?"

Annoyed at the voice, she turned to see who it was. It took her several moments to recognize him; then she laughed. "You. What you doin' here? You ain't no friend. You cain't swim with us?"

"I don't want to swim with you, but I'll take you down the side. It's too high up here to dive in," he said, quickly looking over the side, seeing no one else down there.

"Oh, I kinda like it from here, and they're waitin' for me."

"It's too high up here, Susie."

"Who you callin', Susie?" she giggled.

He knew he had to get her down and quickly. Slowly he moved until he was standing next to her. Frightened, he grabbed her hand, and at the same time placed his other around her waist and in one swift motion, pulled her down. She looked blankly at him, but didn't speak, her friends forgotten.

As they walked away, the hands stretched to the top of the bridge and reached for Susie, its red claws just missing her blouse. Then it shrank back into the water causing the area around it to turn a black-red as it howled in defeat before disappearing beneath the now boiling inferno. Again, the river was again as it should be, full of catfish.

He led her to his car, drove home, ran into the house, told Lola to pack a suitcase for Susie. And then he rushed back outside and waited until Lola brought the luggage to him.

"I'm gon' take her to her uncle's in the country. I'll be back and let you know how she doin'."

34

She's sick. I found her on the bridge and brought her here," Koffee explained to Tom as he stood, gaping in surprise at seeing his niece looking like some crazy, wild woman.

"What did you do to her?" he accused.

"I ain't done nothin' to her. Found her gettin' ready to jump off the Alabama Bridge and brough' her here."

Tom pulled Susie to him and guided her to the sofa. "Here, chile. Sit down here," he said gently, then sat next to her.

"You look tir'd. How you doin', Susie?" he questioned with concern, gazing into her sad eyes and drawn face. She didn't speak. He threw an accusing look at Koffee, causing him to gaze down at the floor, and pat his foot uncomfortably. They sat in silence for nearly an hour before Tom asked, "Do you want me to git you somethin' cold to drank, Susie?"

Long minutes passed before she spoke. "It's hot. You got a cold drank, Uncle Tom?" she asked in dull tones.

He smiled with relief. "Why sho I do baby. Hold on, I'll be right back with one." He went into the kitchen and returned within a few moments. "Here, baby girl," he said as he handed her the ice-cold coke-a-cola.

She drank several long sips and breathed deeply.

"Thank you, Uncle Tom."

"Any time, Sue." He patted her on the shoulder with affection.

"How did I git here?" She asked, not bothering to look at her uncle.

"You mean you don't 'member, Susie?" he asked, and looked in Rev. Koffee's direction.

Koffee hunched his shoulders and patted his foot nervously, hoping his voodoo wasn't driving her crazy. He knew it could do that to some folks, and they never were the same again, just walked around grinning most of the time.

"He said you ain't feelin' good and thought you need'd to come to be with me for a spell."

Her eyes brightened as she turned them on Koffee, staring at him, seemingly looking through him, then dismissing him, her eyes turned lifeless again.

But he had felt her scorn and something else from across the room and rose immediately to leave.

When he left, Susie seemed to relax. They sat for hours with no conversation between them. Tom was afraid and didn't know what to do; he prayed. While he waited, he made coffee for her, then sat whittling a piece of wood he had gotten from one of the trees in the woods.

He put his work down when Susie stood and stretched then sat down again. "I thank I bettah git a bit to eat. I feel gas 'round my chest."

"I got some greens and hoe-cake corn bread I made up. It ain't much, but it'll fill you up. I'll get some for you."

He brought the food and watched Susie pick at it, only eating a child's portion before pushing the plate aside.

"You got a cigarette, Uncle Tom?"

He handed her one of his camels and lit it for her. Slowly, she let the smoke escape from her mouth and glanced at her uncle. She finished smoking the cigarette.

"Give me anothah one, please."

But she didn't light it. She simply squeezed it in her hand.

Then she bowed her head and bellowed, a thin, piercing sound, filled with pain, torment, and confusion.

Tom jumped straight up in the air, and ran over to her.

"They done stole my life. All my life is gon' and I don't want to live. Please let me jest lay down and die in peace. Ain't nothin' left to live for," Susie whimpered, slipped to the floor and rolled back and forth while Tom sat on the sofa, bewildered.

Consequently, Susie spent the next month with her uncle. She had suffered a breakdown and was examined by one of the white doctors Rev. Koffee had sought out and brought with him.

After several sessions with her, Dr. Jaffe ordered Koffee to stay away from her as he seemed to be part of the problem.

Koffee was angry, but he loved Susie in his own sick way and did what was expected of him. Tom, constantly by her side, took care of her, helping to feed, cook and bathe her. During the day they went for long walks, and sat on tree stumps while he told her stories about his and her father when they were young boys. Those stories always made her smile, taking her back to her childhood when her father had returned home to them.

He took her fishing, and sat for hours listening to nothing or the sounds of the country animals.

During the evenings and into the late nights she would lie in bed and listen to the sounds of the crickets and the popping sounds of the lightning bugs, and once in a while she heard the sounds of wise old owls. Those sounds helped heal her, replaced some hope in her tormented mind, and relaxed her.

Slowly, life began to seep back into her broken soul. First came the hearty laughter, the twinkling in her mysterious eyes, next the physically fading of the bags beneath her eyes and the straightening of her shoulders. Finally when she volunteered to cook, Tom knew she had come around.

One day they were sitting on one of their favorite tree stumps when Susie said, "You know, Uncle Tom, I thank it's time I git on back home. I thank I can deal with the mess thaih now. I have made some decisions in my life, and I plan to stick to them. I pray'd and ask'd Gawd to stay with me, even in my weakest moment, and deep in my heart, I knowed somehow He would pull me through this. Only Him. That doctor couldn' do much to help me.

"I know Carolyn and Pat miss me and Miss Turner is gettin' tir'd of lookin' aftah them. And I need to git back to my job, if I still have one."

"You right sho you don't want to stay a while longer, Susie?" He was so pleased that she had almost healed and would continue. He had enjoyed having her with him and taking care of her.

"Yes, Suh. But I want to thank you for listenin' to the rantin' and ravin' I know I did. Takin' care of me like I was a chile. You always been thaih for me, and you still is. Maybe one day I can do the same for you. I love you, Uncle Tom."

"I love you too, Susie. You was a good chile, and you a good woman, mother and father to yo' chil'ren. Gawd always gon' be with you. And you stay away from Rev'end Koffee. I don't care if he did save yo' life. He done enuf to you to owe you that much."

"Oh. I got somethin' in store for him that will fix his little red wagon, don't worry, Uncle Tom." Then she smiled and hugged him.

As soon as she walked in the door, the children were all over her. They climbed in her lap and gave her wet kisses. Lola hugged her, then broke down and asked for forgiveness.

35

Susie stood at her bedroom window, watching the children outside play Little Sally Walker while some of the parents sat on their porches talking and laughing with each other.

She smiled and closed her eyes, letting the warm breeze caress her face. She felt good. She wanted nothing more than to live and be happy. Find a man, a good, decent, and caring man to love. Yes-suh-ree.

She floated on clouds of velvet softness of many colors and shapes. Someone was fanning her with a rainbow of feathers. She couldn't see their faces, but they wore white, billowing dresses and gold sandals with long laces around their ankles.

She sensed someone on the clouds with her: a man, tall, dark, and very handsome. Turning her head, she saw a shadow of him, and was able to make out a smile.

She felt his eyes move over her, stopping then moving again. She became excited as well as nervous. But she wanted to see him, speak to him. Touch him. A beautiful woman appeared wearing a silk gown made of many colors, her head, adorned with a strange silk headdress, trimmed with gold and flowing to the floor. She approached Susie with a tall, cool drink, then turned and handed one to him. She sipped at the cool exotic drink, tasting coconut, pineapple, thick sweet cream. She closed her eyes, feeling almost sensual. Her eyes fluttered open just in time to see the lady who had served them disappear into a puff of clouds, her many golden belts around her waist with no beginning or ending, floating behind her.

Susie sensed the man's gaze upon her and knew he was closer. She smiled as her heart began to fill with a feeling of passion that she had never known.

He kneeled before her, his presence, those magnificent brown eyes, his dark, honey tone handsome face, caused her heart to quiver. He smiled and raised his glass in a toast, then took her hand and went down on one knee.

"Susie," he caressed her name. "You are the most beautiful lady I have ever set eyes upon. Your soul cries out to me, makin' me long to be near you, to hold you in my arms forever.

"If you let me, I will make up to you all that you have miss'd and you will nevah long for completeness again."

She attempted to pull away.

"Don't be frightened. I would nevah let you be hurt again as you have been by othahs. Now is the time to love again, sweet Susie."

She felt as if he was casting a love spell over her, and she didn't want him to stop as she gazed into his seductive eyes. She felt a kindred spirit to him.

His powerful arms took hold of her and held her to him for a moment. Then he caressed her soft face with his hot lips.

Oooohhhh, he feels too good. He's makin' me lose my mind. She felt herself slipping, becoming weak, drowning in his love as they fell into the softness that continued to float...

"Mama. Mama, are you alright?" Lola asked as she stood behind Susie with a concerned look on her face after calling out to her for more than a minute.

Susie didn't hear her.

"Mama," Lola tried again, facing her, she gently placed her hand on Susie's shoulder. "Mama, are you alright?"

But Susie, swept away in the web of her daydream, her hips swaying slightly, eyes closed, was totally unaware of Lola.

Unable to get her attention, Lola quietly slipped from the room with a perplexed look on her face. She had never seen her mother like this. It was as if she was in a dream world and refused to let go.

She smiled, realizing her mother's face had been filled with unadulterated happiness and surrender. Breaking her fantasy would have been cruel. In her bedroom, she flopped down on her bed. "She must be havin' a daisy of one. Wow," she said, and picked up a funny book.

Hours later, when everyone was in bed, Susie sat at her bedroom window, looking out at the darkened night, trying to recognize the man in her fantasy.

Then she sat up straighter as her mouth formed an O-shape. "It was Miles," she whispered, placing one hand over her mouth and the other on her heart, as she realized she still loved him and always would, that she had forgiven him for their problem with Uleena. She was finally over the hurt.

She frowned briefly, "Some friend she turn'd out to be. I wonder if she's still in Selma?" She questioned the empty space.

She stood and bit her bottom lip, her mind slipping back to Miles. "I guess I'm jest a little too late to want him back now. I don't even know where he is and if he'll want me back, anyhow. Somebody else prob'ly snag'd him anyway," she whispered.

Feeling depressed, she lit a Pall Mall cigarette. She blew the smoke from her mouth, slowly shaking her head.

A thought occurred to her. *I should try to find him anyway. I need to see him, if only one more time.*

She desperately needed to apologize to him if nothing else. Another thought crossed her mind. *Maybe Miles can help me git this stuff off me and help me with my Gift. Now wouldn' that be somethin', Susie, ole gal?* She bit at her nails.

That Koffee's like a sore that nevah heals. Always with you no mattah what you do to git rid of him. I ain't sho what he gon' do this time, but I know I'm gon' need somethin' awful powerful to git rid of him. And I'm sho gon' need my Mama, this one last time.

Susie pulled stationery from the drawer next to her bed and

sat on the bed to write Rubye Mae a long letter. She explained her dire situation, telling her now much she needed her.

Susie smiled as she watched Lola march across the stage to receive her diploma. She was relieved that only Mr. Stonner and no one else knew about this second pregnancy. She thanked God Lola wasn't showing and this was finally over, and that Lola had kept her mouth closed.

Later that evening while Susie watched Pat, Lola went to the colored Elk's Club to celebrate her graduation with her friends. When she returned home the next morning at four, she met her mother's fierce eyes.

"Now you git yo' ass 'round to the front door and walk through it like a decent young woman is 'spose to," Susie ordered, slamming the window shut and latching it.

She opened the door and let Lola in. "Sit down," she demanded. "Now, you tell me why you actin' like a street walker?"

"Mama, I was jest havin' fun, and it got late. I didn't want to wake you up," she said, lamely.

"That's 'bout the sorriest 'xcuse I ever heard, Sistah. I don't know where you git yo' ways and all, but you bettah nevah try and crawl in my window again, that is, if you want to keep yo' head. Now you grown, got a chile and anothah on the way. But you still livin' under my roof.

"So if you thank you cain't follow my rules, then it's time you go find yo'self a place of yo' own to live and raise yo' chil'ren."

Lola was stunned at her mother's harsh words. "I'm sorry, Mama. I won't do it again. Time jest got away from me aftah we left the club and went somewhere else."

"Next time I suggest you know when to stop and come see 'bout yo' chil'ren. Try and show some respect for yo'self. And by all means, don't go 'round Selma and completely ruin yo'self."

"What do you mean, Mama?"

"Try actin' like a woman, not a animal, and the men will respect you." Susie walked from the room, leaving Lola with her mouth hanging opened.

36

Susie was on her way out the door to see the spiritual healer, Mr. Windmore, in Montgomery, when she brushed against a sticky, yellow substance on her screen door. She frowned, and shook her head; her mind raced.

Why is it the devil is always standin' in my way? Now I bet ain't nobody put this stuff here 'xcept one of his women. The po', lost, damn souls, don't even know I don't want him and nevah did. And he lyin' all the time tellin' me he ain't messin' with nobody. The man coulda gave me some vile disease if I had kept goin'... She knew she had to try and do something about the mess on her screen.

So Susie boiled water, mixed it with saltpeter, Clorox and tossed it on the screen door, porch, and steps. Five minutes later, she swept the porch then placed the broom in the Clorox solution to soak. Afterward, she left for her appointment.

She was walking swiftly toward the bus station when an acquaintance of hers saw her. "Hey, Susie. Where you goin' so early in the mornin'?"

"I have an appointment in Montgomery, and I cain't miss the bus, Quelus. What you doin' out this early?"

"Oh, you know me. Always lookin' for somebody to ride in my

cab. The wife insist I work my bones into the ground. But it's slow right now. I could give you a lift to Montgomery, Susie."

"Naw, thank you. I don't want to take you outta yo' way, and I cain't afford to pay no taxi fare for fifty miles. Now, I gotta go befoe I miss that bus."

"Susie, would you jest wait a minute. I know you cain't pay that much to git thaih. What colored person in Selma can? But since it's slow, I can take you thaih and back for two bucks. It that a deal for a friend?"

"Oh, alright. I do need to git thaih in a hurry. My arm is startin' to hurt somethin' awful, and the bus ride will be long. Thank you, Quelus."

When Susie finally stepped into Windmore's office, her right arm was swollen almost twice its size. The pain had moved upward, to her throat, leaving her almost paralyzed.

Windmore looked closely at her from behind his desk, pulled something from his drawer that she couldn't see, leaned toward her, and placed his hand over her forehead and pressed hard, causing her to scream inwardly. With his hand still on her head, he mumbled to himself for more than five minutes. Susie started to feel the pressure leave her throat and the pain in her arm subside.

The tenseness in her body decreased, allowing her to breathe freely. She moved her shoulder up and down, without pain then looked at him. "Thank you, Mister Windmore. I feel much bettah."

"Well, you sure got here in time," he laughed. "You'll be alright. The arm will be good as new."

She believed this short, proper talking, honest looking man with intense, darkish blue, intelligent eyes.

"I would have thought you had long started to do yo' own business by now," he said, throwing her completely off guard.

"What bus'ness, Mr. Windmore?" *Not the Gift. Not now, please,* she thought.

"I'm not getting into that with you, not right now," he said gently.

Susie was visibly relieved. "Good." *'Cause I'm not ready for this. I need a little moe time.*

He gave her a curious look and said, "So you came to rid yourself of the demon preacher, huh? It's 'bout time you came to your senses, Susie. The man can't do you any good, no matter how much he cares for you. You don't know it, but he can cost you your life."

"What!" she screamed and attempted to stand. He waved her back in her seat, leaned back in his chair, and tapped a pencil on his desk. "The way he keeps you is by going to Booth, Alabama, once a month and taking something of yours from your body. It could be hair, panties, stockings, fingernails, anythang that's personal.

"So what you have to do is keep away from him for at least a month to six weeks. Don't even let him get to your doorsteps.

"All those times you experienced feeling sick and dizzy, that you nevah told anyone 'bout, well, it only happens every month or so when he comes 'round, for a few days straight. That's the stuff that's taking effect on you.

"And the times when he stayed away for a spell, the stuff wore off, so you started to go back to yourself; and then, up he comes, and puff, you're under his spell again. You always knew deep down that he was bringing something 'round, but you didn't want to admit it 'cause you felt you were partly to blame."

Susie shook her head in agreement, impressed by this man and his foresight.

"Susie, there's a lot 'bout you that even you don't know, and you have been afraid to let yourself find out. You have been running away so long, you thought you got away, but you haven't. You nevah will."

She looked at him as if he was speaking a language beyond her understanding.

"You know exactly what I'm talking 'bout, so don't give me that you-must-be-crazy look. It's 'bout time you get started, isn't it, Susie?" he asked softly.

"Start'd with what?" she asked, playing it off.

"You know exactly what I'm talking 'bout, Susie."

She shuddered, remembering the horrible nightmares she had experienced.

"Susie."

She glared at him.

He ignored her and continued. "This Gift is no burden. I undertake it everyday, sometimes at night or in the middle of the witchin' hours," he said softly, springing from his seat and sitting next to her.

She turned and look toward the door. She didn't know what to do, run or stay. She swallowed. She felt trapped. Windmore waited while she gathered her thoughts.

"You stop making excuses and start praying. You need to open your mind and heart to everythang and be willing to accept your duties. It's not frightening at all. It is easy. It has always been that way for me, but I nevah fought it. Maybe 'cause I didn't start 'til I was older.

But you're older and wiser now, and you know the Lawd bettah than when you were a chile." He finished abruptly and stood again.

"Now, I must go to those people who need me more than you."

She stood, and he walked her to the door, handed her an envelope, said good-bye, and watched her walk away.

There had been so much more he had wanted to tell her, but he had been warned against it.

When Quelus dropped Susie off in front of her door, she thanked him, ran up the steps, unlocked the front door and went straight to her bedroom. There, she removed Windmore's instructions from her pocketbook, read, and re-read them before carrying them out.

She stood watching the voodoo disappear from her screen door as if by magic, shaking her head at the knowledge and wisdom God had given Windmore, and possibly her.

She shuddered, moved away from the door, went into the kitchen and slumped into a chair. She felt a sense of dread and wondered what it could be.

The next morning, when Susie rose, it was so cold her nose was icy. She raced from the bed. Rather than going to the bathroom as usual, she made a fire to heat the ice-cold house as quickly as possible. Then she peeked out the window and saw icicles hanging from the windows.

"It's a cold one today," she shivered as she ran into the bathroom. Right after breakfast, Susie started dinner, deciding they could do without her at church. Lola wasn't feeling or looking her usual self, and she wanted to get everything out of the way just in case she went into labor.

Hours later, Lola, feeling better, sat with her legs pulled under her on the sofa, laughing and talking with Susie when a strange look appeared on her face.

"You alright, Lola?"

"Yes, Mam. I jest had a little pain in my stomach, prob'ly from eatin' too much. I thank I'll go and take a nap."

"You already did that. You sho you ain't in labor?"

"I'm sho. I 'member the last one."

"All labor ain't the same, Lola."

"This do feel differen'. I don't know, Mama."

"I'll go and fix you a bath in the tin tub so you can take it in the kitchen where it's already warm."

She pulled the round tub in from the washroom and poured hot water into it. While Lola bathed, Susie prepared her things to take to the hospital.

"Lola, you sit thaih, and if you have any pains jest 'member to breathe real quick, in and out 'til they pass.

I'll be right back."

As she walked into the room to wake the children to take them to her ex-sister-in-law's, a voice said, *Susie, wouldn't it make more sense to bring her here instead of taking the children out in the cold weather?*

"Yeah, it sho would," she answered. She pulled a heavy coat from the closet, hastily tied a scarf tightly beneath her chin, jammed on thick gloves, and rushed to Stella's.

Susie returned in less than five minutes with Stella at her heels, almost out of breath, trying to keep up with her pace.

Susie rushed into the kitchen just as Lola was having another pain. "You sho in labor. Come on and let me help you git out. It's cold out thaih, and you need to be dry befoe we leave for the hospital."

Since Susie couldn't reach either one of the colored cab drivers, she and Lola left on foot. Each time Lola had a contraction, she leaned against Susie until it passed.

Fifteen minutes later, they reached the hospital, shivering from the fierce weather.

The nurses immediately took Lola upstairs to the colored ward of the delivery area. Susie couldn't stay.

After arriving home, Susie called the hospital several times before being informed Lola had given birth to a healthy boy and both were doing well.

"Please, Lawd, let this be the last one," she whispered.

37

Susie was reading the book of Proverbs when someone tapped softly at her front door. She answered the knock and was taken aback to see Koffee. She hadn't seen him for months and had hoped he had decided to leave her be. While she stood, trying to get over the shock of seeing him, he slipped through the door, grinning, his mouth spreading almost to his ears. He followed her into the living room and made himself comfortable.

"Well, they been keepin' me so busy, I ain't been able to come 'round for a while. My membership is growin' at Mornin' Star, and they keep me runnin' at my church in the country," he bragged, then stuck a match to his cigar.

Susie lit a cigarette and looked at him. "That's nice. I'm glad to see you prosperin'." She thought to herself, *I don't thank he gits it. Is he crazy or what? How many times do I have to tell the man that I don't want him?*

"Yeah," he said, his chest expanding with pride. "My bus'ness is pickin' up so fast I got to hire another boy."

He lowered his voice. "I done tole you befoe, I would help you with yo' bills and buy yo' food, but you so stubborn, you jest won't let me help."

274 CAROLYN V. PARNELL

"You talkin' crazy man. I thank you forgot what I said to you the last time 'bout us."

"See, thaih you go, iggin' me again."

"Naw. You the one. I thank you bettah leave. We ain't got nothin' moe to talk 'bout."

He leaned forward and touched her flawless face, his eyes revealing his desire.

She stood up. "I said I thank you bettah leave, Rev'end."

"It's been a long time," he said hoarsely. "You 'bout the most temptin' young woman I ever knowed, Susie," he whispered, then grabbed her breasts and squeezed them.

She felt repulsed and became very angry. "Don't touch me," she demanded with composure and walked toward the door.

"Hey, come here," he groaned, moved across the room and forced his hand up her dress and on her private part before she could stop him.

She jumped away, shocked. "What in the Sam Hill is wrong with you?" she seethed, saliva touching the corners of her mouth.

But he ignored her and yanked her to him, slobbering over her mouth and down her neck, running his hands under her dress, fumbling. "Oh, Susie, you drive me crazy. I cain't help myself. Please let me love you."

Susie shoved him from her and slapped him hard as she could across his face, sending him reeling back in the chair where he had sat earlier.

He grabbed his burning face, his dark color turning a deep, brownish red. As he shook his head, his eyes became liquid pools of naked lust and anger. He grinned and came back at her, grabbing her by the shoulders and squeezing her to him until she gasped for breath.

Enraged, she managed to pull her foot up and kick him in the shin, causing him to yell and grab his wounded leg.

Then she backhanded him as hard as any man, sending him to his knees, causing him to reel backwards.

He sat stunned for a few minutes, tasting his blood, a look of disbelief on his face.

Susie's fists were balled into hard knots, her eyes lethal.

He pulled a clean white handkerchief from his breast pocket and patted his wound before saying, "Nobody hits me and gits away with it, bitch."

White, hot anger burst forth. "Man, you must be losin' yo' mind, or you been drankin' and it's gon' to you head, but as long, and I mean as long as you live, you bettah nevah try nothin' like this with me again, or I will kill you! Now git the hell outta my damn house."

"Susie, I'm sorry, I don't know what came over me. I ain't nevah act'd liked this befoe. Must be the medicine the doctor gave me..."

She cut him off. "I said git the hell outta my house. We ain't havin' no friendly conversation. Git!"

He glared at her, his face swelling with anger. He moved from his position and stood face to face with her, his nostrils flaring like a bull's.

"Don't nobody tell me what I can and cain't do. Not even you."

Standing flat-footed and hands on her hip, she whispered, "I'm sho you don't won't nobody to find you layin' here on my livin' room floor dead, do you? How could yo' po' wife stand it?"

"Why you...." he slapped her across the face, sending her backwards, but she regained her balance and backhanded him in the center of his face, breaking his glasses in half.

He caught the pieces in his hand. "See what you did to my glasses," he yelled, his hands going toward her neck, but she jumped aside, and he fell against the wall. He turned and came back at her, but she had a poker in her hand, ready to strike.

Angry tears ran down her face. She didn't want to kill this man, but he was begging to die. "I guess you don't b'lieve rain comes from the Heaven, do you? If you do, you bettah leave befoe I send you to hell."

He backed his way to the front door, but before he ran out, he promised, "You cain't git rid of me jest like that. You will see me when I git good and ready, or I'll see you dead, first," he threatened before fleeing.

Susie closed and locked the door. Her anger was so profound that when Lola entered the room and saw her face, she turned and walked out again.

Susie sat in the dark for hours, pondering how she would get rid of Koffee. Now that he had threatened her, she believed he would kill her if she quit him. She realized that he was a sick man in many ways.

She decided it was time to call her mother because she needed her help and protection. She also wondered why Rubye Mae hadn't answered her letter. It wasn't like her; Rubye Mae loved writing unless she was ill.

Suddenly, she shivered violently. *I wonder who's walkin' over my grave.* She hugged herself and moaned Miles's name and pictured his face, which comforted her.

Then she walked into her bedroom and prepared for bed. She tried to fall asleep, but Koffee's face kept reappearing before her. Each time she saw him, her skin crawled. Something was wrong, and she didn't know what it was.

Daybreak arrived before she finally fell into a fitful sleep. Susie's morning had started out badly from lack of sleep and disgust with herself. But she had received a letter from Blanche that helped to lift her spirits. She didn't make that crucial call to her mother as she had promised herself.

She smiled as she bent over the tub, washing her delicate underwear, not trusting the wringer washer since it had ripped several pieces of clothing.

Her mind drifted to Blanche. It had been three long years since she left home. Three years. But this summer as she had written, she would be returning to stay for several months.

A sharp pain suddenly hit her in the center of her forehead, causing her to lose her balance. She grabbed the water faucet to keep from falling into the hot, soapy, Clorox water.

Her sight went blank for a moment, then she pulled herself up, dried her hands and sat on the toilet seat until she felt better.

Days later, Susie picked up the phone to call her mother, but couldn't. She felt tired and nervous. "Prob'ly need to take some Geritol to build my blood up," she said as she walked to her room and stretched across the bed.

But the following days proved her wrong as she became alarmingly worse. She finally visited her doctor who seemed baffled by her condition and recommended she see an internist. But he, too, seemed stunned and uncertain about her condition.

She felt so desperately ill she thought she would die anytime. Realizing that Lola was struggling with the children, she sent for Mrs. Turner, who came right away.

When she saw Susie's pale, thin face and body, she screamed and hugged Susie to her as one would a child. Then she said, "Honey chile, you look awful. What did they do to you?"

"Miss Turner," she breathed hard several times, before speaking, "I don't know what's wrong with me. I been to two doctors, and they ain't help'd me. The second one I went to wants me to come back tomorrow, but I'm so tir'd and weak, I don't know if I can make it."

"Baby, you gots to git somebody to help you. What 'bout Rev'end Koffee. He's the one who prob'ly know what to do."

"Naw!" she said forcefully, "I'll wait and see what the doctor says. I'm jest thankful you could come to my rescue."

"I tole you anytime you need'd me I would be here. Come on and let's put you to bed."

"Susie. To be frank, I jest can't find nothin' physically wrong with you," the Dr. said, totally puzzled by Susie's condition.

"Doctor, don't you see all this weight I done lost, and these black circles under my eyes. Somethin's wrong, Doctor, and I need to know what I can do to git well."

"Susie," said the white doctor, scratching his head, "What's wrong with you is a mystery to me. Nothin' I learn'd in medical school nevah prepared me for what's wrong with you. I jest don't know what to tell you; 'xcept you bettah go see another doctor."

"What doctor, Doctor? I already been to see three, includin' you, and I'm gettin' worser by the day."

"I'll send you to another internal one," he said as he wrote the name on a slip of paper and handed it to her.

After leaving his office, Susie tore the referral up and threw it in the garbage.

She prayed as she sat in the taxi cab, desperately asking God to save her life.

Quelus, the cab driver, helped her up the steps and into the house. "Susie, please call me if I can help you," he said before leaving.

The children ran to greet her when she arrived home, but she couldn't play with them. "Mama's sick y'all. I'll have to play with y'all when I git well. Y'all go on back with Sistah now."

Mrs. Turner who was helping take care of the children, helped her to bed and suggested she call Rev. Koffee.

"Naw. Please don't, Miss Turner," she pleaded as she lay against the cool sheets.

Soon, Susie became so weak she had to be assisted to bed and flinched with pain whenever touched. She developed a fever that was hard to control and she soon became delirious.

Forgetting Susie's plea about Koffee, Mrs. Turner called for his help when Susie complained that the rubber around her brassiere, that she insisted on wearing, even in bed, smelled as if it were burning.

He arrived within ten minutes. He took one look at the horrible sight of her. "Git some clothes on her, quick," he demanded.

I'll do it," Mrs. Turner offered and sent Lola from the room.

"Do you know what's wrong with Mama, Rev'end Koffee?" Lola asked nervously while they waited in the living room.

"Naw, Sistah. I sho don't. But I'm gon' take her to Montgomery so she can git well."

38

At the intersection between Broad and Jeff Davis Streets, he briefly glanced at his watch. Time was of the essence.

He exceeded the speed limit as he raced down the Old Montgomery Highway, heading east. In his desperate attempt to reach his destination he was unaware that his foot continued to bear down on the accelerator.

The early morning had predicted the blistering day to come as the sun rays forced its way through the windows, which caused him to unbutton his collar and loosen his tie.

Finding no relief, he quickly scanned the air conditioning, only to find it already on high. The sun caused him great discomfort as it seemed to follow him. Its glare almost blinded him as its luminous light played games on his eye glasses, causing geometric patterns to appear before him. Alarmed, he reached to remove them but realized that if he did, he wouldn't be able to see.

His heart raced. He said a silent prayer, asking God to get him there on time.

Finally he saw it. The last landmark. He quickly made a sharp left turn, causing Susie to moan softly.

"Hold on Susie, we almost thaih," he choked.

He stopped before the house on the hill, larger than life, radiant rays flowing from it, sending out welcoming warmth. His breath caught in his throat at the tranquility.

He rubbed his eyes and blinked. Immediately he dashed from his black Cadillac, perspiration beading down his already drenched face. He knew he was being propelled by some supernatural force.

Nervously, he opened the door, took a weakened Susie in his arms, and gently assisted her from the car. Too lifeless to walk on her own, she faltered. He quickly steadied her and then half carried her toward the magnificent house.

When they reached the wide brick steps, a lady dressed in a white flowing dress was smiling and waiting. Even from where she stood, Koffee could feel the same illuminating warmth from her that he had felt earlier.

The lady reached out her hand beckoning them to pass the crowd of people waiting patiently to see her. The lady rushed down to meet them, took Susie's hand in hers, signaled for him to wait, then hurried her inside the house.

Still stunned and angry after being dimissed like a child, he found a place beside the stone wall that ran along the side of the white mansion and waited with the others, hating every passing moment.

Slowly he turned and saw at least a hundred people waiting. Women, men, old, young, from all walks of life. All seeking ends to their problems that doctors couldn't solve or predict, but fortune tellers could.

Satisfied that he recognized none of them, nor they he, he breathed a sigh of relief. He pulled a handkerchief from his pocket, dabbed his wet face, removed a cigar from his coat pocket, lit it, and leaned against the wall to wait with the others.

Susie was led into a sparsely, yet beautifully furnished study, dimly lit with Roman candles. The lady gently assisted her into a lovely, hand carved chair.

She sat facing Susie. Susie had grown weaker, her breathing shallow. Her time was running out. The lady placed her right hand on Susie's forehead, her other on Susie's shoulder, close to her neck, applying slight pressure to the artery. She waited a few minutes.

The lady bowed her head and closed her eyes. Her face went through several changes: peaceful, painful, haunting. Her breathing became forced, as if someone were gasping for breath. Long moments later, it seemed as if the lady no longer breathed.

On the other hand, Susie's breathing became slightly stronger. Her eyes fluttered, and were still again. Tick. Tick. Tick.

The lady shuddered suddenly as if being shaken from a nightmare. She opened her eyes and removed her hand from Susie's shoulder and left the room.

The lady returned in a matter of moments and sat before Susie. Susie opened her eyes and gazed intently into the lady's. She tried speaking, but words failed her. Her eyes closed again, and she slouched over on the chair.

Abruptly, Susie sat upright in the chair, gripped the sides so firmly her veins protruded, threatening to break through her pale skin. Her eyes fluttered rapidly, then stopped. Very slowly, a pulsating movement began creeping across her forehead, causing her skin to expand like elastic. The throbbing sensation exploded throughout her body, violently shaking her lifeless body for several moments.

She slumped forward as the entity continued to inch to the center of her forehead, slithering, searching, probing, seeking an exit.

The entity moved to the bridge of her nose, causing her great stabbing pain. Susie suddenly awakened, wailed like a wounded, wild animal and fainted as her nostrils expanded three times their normal size to allow the creature to force its way through her passage.

The lady had been waiting with a can containing a strong potion mixed with devil lye to kill the snake-like object which was the size of a hen's egg. She shuddered when she examined the darkish red, white, speckled viper as it twitched about, fighting against its death until the solution consumed and destroyed it.

Shaking her head in disgust and sadness, the lady praised

the Lord that the silly woman had made a mistake or Susie would not be alive.

She left the room with the can and soon returned with hot cloths and several bottles of herbs and roots that smelled of coconut cream. The lady rubbed some on Susie's slackened face and neck, then gently removed the solution with the hot cloth. She repeated the process, carrying her hand in a circular motion, then upwards, mumbling beneath her breath.

Afer removing the substance from Susie's face, the lady held a bottle of strong herbs neneath Susie's nose, drawing almost black blood. Then she placed the can aside to be buried.

Half an hour later, Susie's eyes opened as she regained conscious. She stared at the lady sitting in front of her.

"Wha..What...?" She sat up in her chair. "What am I sittin' here for? Who are you?" Susie asked in a strong voice.

"Chile, you in Montgomery at Mis Para Lee's. Don't you 'member me from befoe?"

"I thank so. How did I git here?" she squinted her eyes. "How did I git here?" she repeated.

"Koffee brought you. I made him wait outside. This ain't his business."

"Oh." Susie said and frowned as if tasting something she did not like.

"You feelin' any pain, Susie?"

"No, Mam, but I do feel like I could sleep for a week."

"Aahhh, that's good. You need to sleep and eat plenty in the next three weeks. I'll give you somethin' for that. Meanwhile, I'm glad you still alive, Chile. What do you 'member from befoe?"

"That I was sick as a dog unto death."

"Chile, you was so close to death, all you had to do was push open the gates and walk right into Heaven. It's by the pure Grace of the Good Lawd that He weren't ready for you yet."

"And I thank Him for that. But I sho wish somebody..."

"Else had brough you," she finished for Susie. Shaking her head sideways, she added, "If that man had been just a little bit latah getting' here you would sho be layin' somewhere in a funeral home by now. I jest cain't git over this, and b'lieve me, I've seen a lot of bad voodoo spells, but honey, yo's ...." She trailed off, not wanting to upset Susie any more than she was.

"What was it? Somebody had me dress'd or something?" The lady hesitated.

"I need to know, Miss Para Lee," Susie pressed her.

"Someway and somehow, somebody not only had you dress'd, they want'd you stone, cold dead, chile. The only thang that saved you was they miss'd one of the steps. Seems always to be that way with you," she said almost to herself, then continued. "The person that did this to you hates you. And the sad thang is, it ain't even yo' fault."

"Who was it?" Susie asked quietly, realizing it was the bright-skinned woman with long, wavy hair that lived down the street and around the corner from her. She had heard that the woman was crazy for Koffee, but he hadn't paid her any attention.

"You already know the answer. You have to git rid of him. And even then, you have to watch who you 'sociate with. Where you eat or drank and by all means, don't let anybody git hold of yo' hair or any of yo' under drawers."

Susie sat straighter in her seat, rubbed her hands over her face, fighting her anger.

"Honey, some people can be so hung up on a mna or so jealous of a woman they will do anything they have to rid themselves of that person. And at thie risk of repeatin' myself, somebody got somethin' into you or from you' cause that's the only way you got that thang in yo' head. It was 'spose to kill you, but it jest weren't yo' time."

"You don't thank...."

"Naw. He's done some awful thangs, but he ain't tried to kill you... in his own sick way, he loves you moe then he does anybody else, but honey, he can snap like a pencil and that'll be it."

Susie shook her head in understanding. "What was in me?"

"Somethin' that you nevah want to know 'bout."

"I need to know."

"It was a voodoo snake."

Susie leaned forward to throw up vile, and Miss Para Lee held a bucket under her.

The lady placed her hand on Susie's should and said, "Next time I tell you somethin', you lis-sen. You one stubborn lady. Now, I want you to sit here and pray while I see 'bout some of my customers. I'll be back 'cause thaih's somethin' real importan' I need to tell you."

Koffee shifted positions for the tenth time, walked back and forth, then returned to his position against the wall.

Suddenly losing patience, he went to his car to wait. He relieved himself, slipped into his car, grabbed one of the water jugs and drank from it, almost choking. Then leaning back on the hot seat, he let the window down and removed his suit jacket, yanked off his tie, lit his cigar and waited.

Susie was asleep when the lady returned.

"I see you're feelin' much bettah. That's good."

Susie opened her eyes and gazed at her.

"Now, I don' have much time, but I have to tell you this."

"What 'bout Rev'end?"

"Nothin'. He's been waitin', and he can continue to wait 'til I'm through with you, then I'll talk to him."

She sat down and took Susie's hands in hers. "Susie Norwood, you are one of the most stubborn people that Gawd done created, yet you are also one of the most forgivin' and lovin' ones, and you don't give up on yo' faith though you may stumble sometimes. You was born with and have been runnin' from yo' Gift for moe then twenty some odd years and you got to stop that. Yo' time is runnin' out. I see that some of the thangs that's happen'd to you was partly due to yo' own disobedience and bein' stubborn. You know the Lawd loves you. He's yo' Father, and you got to obey Him or He will punish you, 'specially when He knows You know bettah. I know the othah person you went to tole you to start doin' what

STILL MY TREMBLIN' SOUL

you was 'spose to do and you ig'd him. You cain't afford to ig' me. The message I got is strong, real strong and not to be push'd aside. All them bad dreams you had was 'spose to warn you, but you din't take heed, but you must."

"Here. Take these, and follow my directions to the letter," she said giving Susie a brown bag filled with herbs. "You will find that in a few weeks you will feel like new. Try to stay that way, and Gawd bless you child," she said. And then she gave Susie the directions on how to take the herbs.

"You stay here 'till I send him in to git you." She left the room.

Fifteen minutes later, Rev. Koffee knocked at the door and entered it like a little boy who had been whipped. His face was swollen and his eyes hard.

Susie knew that Miss Para Lee had blessed him out. She felt like laughing and covered her mouth to hide a smile.

"You 'bout ready to go?" he asked, trying to hide his anger. The woman had gone too far, telling him to stop using voodoo on Susie. He wasn't hurting her, jest keeping her for himself.

"I'm so glad you alright, Madam," he offered as he attempted to help her from the chair.

"I'm glad myself. Thank you for brangin' me here," she said, avoiding his hand. "I understan' you saved my life."

He grinned proudly as they slowly walked to the door, down the long corridor and out the front door of the mansion. They had been there more than three hours, but to Susie it felt as if she had just awaked from a horrible nightmare and left it behind.

When Susie arrived home, Lola, Mrs. Turner and the children were waiting anxiously and cried with relief when Susie walked in the house. She smiled and hugged them all before being put to bed by Mrs. Turner.

Koffee left begrudgingly, promising himself he would return soon and she would always belong to him.

39

Three days after Susie's return from Montgomery, Lola was helping her into a nightgown when they heard persistent knocking at the front door.

"Go see who's tryin' to break the door in, Sistah. I can manage," Susie said as she sat on the bed and finished pulling on her gown.

Lola smiled from ear to ear as she unlocked the screen door and let her grandmother enter.

After hugging her, she exclaimed, "Oh, Mama Rubye Mae, I'm so glad you could make it. Mama sho do need you." She tried hard to hold back the happy tears gleaming in her eyes.

"From the sound of yo' voice over the phone, I knowed she did. You a smart girl for callin' me, baby gal. How you makin' out with the chil'ren and all?"

"It was hard 'til Mama had Miss Turner come and help. She's a good friend of Mama's."

"Yeah, I know. Susie wrote me 'bout her. A good woman. Now where is my chile?"

"She's in bed. I'll take you to her."

Lola stood back when they reached Susie's room. Rubye Mae knocked quietly on the door.

"Yeah. Who is it?"

"It's me, Susie, yo' Mama," Rubye Mae whispered as she stepped into the room.

"Mama. Mama. Oh Mama! I'm so glad you came," Susie cried, reaching for her mother, hugging her as she had when she was a small child.

Tears of satisfaction flowed down Lola's flushed cheeks as she backed away and went to look after the children.

"Baby, why didn't you let me know you been so sick and all? You knowed I woulda come to see aftah you."

"I know that, Mama, but you raisin' Mae Frances, and I didn't want to bother you." She assumed her mother never got her letter, that Koffee had somehow got his hands on it. It wouldn't do any good to tell her mother.

Rubye Mae released her. "You know you nevah bother me, Susie. And yo' sistah Willie Mae got Mae Frances now. Don't you 'member I wrote and tole you? Oh, nevah you mind. I'm here to help git you well. I jest wish you lived up Nawth with us."

"I know, Mama, but I don't want to live in De-trot."

"Alright, we gon' let that pass for now, baby. You jest tell me what you want, and I'll make sho you git it."

"Right now, Mama, jest havin' you here is good enuf for me." Susie felt like a small child again when her mother called her baby. For a brief moment she wanted to climb in her lap, lay her head on her shoulder, and tell her to take away the pain. But she would settle for her just being here, and her love.

"Susie, Susie, my wonder chile. Always been differen', and my best. You make me feel good to be sayin' thangs like that," Rubye Mae smiled, patted her on the shoulder, and rubbed her head.

Susie thought she saw a tear in the corner of her mother's eye, but she couldn't be sure.

For more than an hour, Rubye Mae sat on Susie's bed, updating her about their family and rubbing her head now and then.

"Yo' brother, Augustus done gon' and bought a house for me and Boy. Said he ain't nevah gon' git mar-red. Said he don't want to take no chances on no gals doin' to him what he done did to them."

Susie smiled. "That's Augustus alright. But he's right
for not wantin' to git the same thang from women he put
them through. So he's scared to take the chance on findin' a
good woman."

"You know him alright. Here. You lay back against these pillows while I go and fix you some supper. Will collard greens be
alright?" Rubye Mae asked and slipped out the door before Susie
could answer.

She settled back against the feather pillows that Rubye Mae
had fluffed for her, thrilled that she would be making her favorite
food. Every time her mother said "collard greens," Susie knew
she would cook hoe-cake cornbread, fried chicken, mashed potatoes, yams, and biscuits. She could almost taste those wonderful aromas, and her stomach growled in anticipation.

She realized her mother would be her best medicine. She
had become very strong, living up to the hardship that had been
planted in her path over the years, including the sudden death of
her husband because of a mysterious illness, the loss of her
young daughter in child birth, and other heart-rendering situa-
tions. But she had pulled through without the bitter scars of the
heart and soul, not becoming a cynical, useless woman.

The next weeks almost proved that Susie had never been
deadly ill as she made remarkable progress.

She realized she had Lola and her mother partly to thank.
Lola for caring enough to know that she needed her mother. And
her mother for being there, spoiling her, keeping all worries and
obstacles from her, including Koffee.

Meanwhile, Rubye Mae had questions of her own and only
hoped that Susie would speak to her soon.

After dinner one evening, Susie closed and locked her bedroom door.

"Mama, I know you been wonderin' what's been goin' on.
Thaih's jest so much I don't know where to start. The only thang
I can do is tell you I been the biggest fool you ever gave birth to
and I almost lost my life 'cause I been too weak to pull myself up
by the bootstraps and put all my faith in Gawd.

"I'm 'shamed, but I feel I have to tell you how Rev'end Koffee and me got start'd." She told her about the voodoo doll and the spell he put on her when they went to the county to plow his crops, leaving nothing out.

"But I didn't do nothin' 'bout it, Mama. Nothin', 'xcept I got mad with him for a while, then befoe I knowed it, BAMB, we was goin' together, and I couldn' seem to git rid of him.

Even when I knowed we both was sinnin', it was hard.

"All these wasted years with him, and now I got a big problem on my hand 'cause he don't seem to understan' I don't want him here, that I nevah want'd him, Mama. I nevah liked the man from the time I met him.

"He's possess'd. He's sick, Mama." Susie picked at the blue spread on her bed and brushed a tear from her eye.

"You po' chile. You done car-red all this on yo' shoulders and ain't tole nobody. Not even yo' friends?"

"I couldn', Mama. I didn't even b'lieve it was happenin' at first. And when I finally xcept'd it, I was too 'shamed to tell them."

"And here I was, thankin' he was such a fine man, and crazy 'bout you. Now, to thank back on it, Augustus nevah talk'd much 'bout him aftah meetin' him. I shoulda knowed somethin' was wrong then. He's good at judgin' bad men.

"And you right, he sick, honey. He want to posess you like a wagon or mule.

"A preacher man, usin' voodoo, practicin' that ole timey mess that came over from Africa." Her eyes were like saucers as she stared at the wall, seemingly seeing something there.

"Susie, chile. You gots to git rid of him, fast." she whispered hoarsely.

"Now, I know that, Mama. But how? Every time I try, somethin' seems to block my way." She paused before saying, "That one time Augustus was here for Christmas, we talked, but I told him I didn't need no help." She hesitated then said, "This stuff is hard to fight."

"I know you ain't got no plan, but I'm gon' try and help you with the little bit I know."

"You, Mama? I thought you jest said that...I didn't know you b'lieved in voodoo. You nevah said nothin' 'bout it when we was chil'ren or when we got o-ler."

"Ain't nothin' chil'ren need to know 'bout. Or brag 'bout. Thaih's enuf evil in the world as it is. But I did a learn thang or two from a good witchcraft person."

She stopped to sip her coffee. "This been used by some peoples I know, and it work'd for them. Now what you got to do is git some devil lye and put it under yo' bed and bury a couple cans upside down in yo' yard and 'round yo' house."

"What? That stuff is used only to unstop sinks or eat the pipes up if you put too much down the drain," Susie exclaimed.

"Honey, everythang they make can be used for moe then one thang, and you know that, but you said the words, 'Eat it up'. That stuff is so powerful it will kill most anythang. And it will show keep him from gettin' to yo' house. The person he's goin' to ain't so good as he thanks he is or he wouldn' have to go back once a month to do it again."

"Mama, you full of surprises, but if you say it works, then we sho gon' try it. I'm determin'd to live a life that I have some control over."

"Now you soundin' moe like my Susie," Rubye Mae smiled and hugged her with affection. "Tomorrow night we will do what needs to be done, and then we'll wait and see what happens." She winked, and Susie returned her mischievous smile.

The following evening, Susie and Rubye Mae sat on the bottom steps, carefully opening four cans of devil lye, thankful to the quarter moon which lent just enough light to let them see what they were doing.

Their hands were wrapped with cloths and covered by gloves. They had placed several cans under Susie's bed in a wash basin. Just before going outside, they covered their shoes with clean rags.

They dug two holes, approximately twelve inches deep, one

on each side of the steps and buried the cans upside down; then they walked slowly around the house, carefully sprinkling devil lye from the remaining cans before sitting on the steps again.

"You be careful not to git that poison on you, Susie. That stuff will eat you quicker then a snake can swallow a hen's egg," Rubye Mae warned as she pulled the rags from her shoes.

"I will, Mama. How long do you thank it'll take befoe it starts workin'?" Susie asked anxiously as she pulled her nose downward to keep from inhaling the strong odor surrounding the house.

"I don't rightly know that, chile. But I guess as soon as somebody come 'round with they mojo, the stuff spurts out. And if you got somethin' in yo' mattress or in yo' room, we'll know that soon too.

"The wind is pickin' up. We best git in the house foe we inhale the stuff and they find us all dried up out here," Rubye Mae said.

They pulled the gloves and rags from their hands and discarded them along with the ones from their shoes in the garbage can, then they rushed into the house and washed their hands in Clorox and lye soap before taking hot baths.

Five minutes before midnight, Susie and Rubye Mae sat on the sofa laughing, talking, drinking Coke-a-Colas and eating skins with hot sauce.

"Chile, I sho hate to see Koffee's face when he tries to come here and cain't even walk up the steps. He gon' be fit to be tied," Rubye Mae said, slapping her thighs and throwing her head back in pleasure.

Susie put her Coke down and looked at her mother intently. "Mama, you sho that stuff gon' stop him?"

"Jest like that," Rubye Mae snapped her fingers sharply. Then added, "If it don't rain befoe it settles in the ground."

"I ain't smelled it in the air. I don't thank it'll rain befoe mornin'. And I sho cain't wait to see it work. Maybe this will teach him a les-son in voodoo." Susie shook her head and lit a cigarette. "All this is like a bad dream come true."

"You bettah b'lieve it. The sooner you do, the bettah off you gon' be. That man is so full of the devil I can almost see a tail hangin' outta his pants. I don't care if he is a preacher man."

"That's the sad part. He's such a good preacher. I b'lieve he was call'd to preach." She held her hands up in defeat. "I jest don't understan' it." Susie shook her curly head sadly and folded her hands in her lap.

"Thaih's them that's call'd and know what to do and them that's call'd and ignore what's right and wrong. He one of them."

"I was a bigger fool then I thought, and I almost lost my life cause of it." She looked at Rubye Mae who seemed to be lost in thought for a moment. "I feel like eatin' all these skins and maybe gettin' a hot link too. How 'bout you, Mama?"

"Sounds good to me," Rubye Mae said and pushed another skin into her mouth to prove her point, deciding not to pursue the subject of Susie's claim to being a fool.

Two days later, Susie looked under her bed and was surprised to see the white substance that had spurted out of the cans, and was threatening to spill over the edge of the wash basin.

Susie batted her eyes quickly in amazement, and turned to stare at her mother who was next to her, smiling with satisfaction.

"Well, he sho had somethin' in here, alright. But that stuff eatin' it up. He cain't git at you in here no moe. But you gotta throw away yo' mattress anyway."

"Well, I'll be," Susie said, now visibly upset, tears bumping down her high cheeks. He sho must hate me to do this to me." She sat on her bed.

"Naw, chile. He don't hate you. He's possess'd like the devil and won't nevah give up. He wants you moe then anythang else, or he wouldn' do this. Now come on and cheer up 'cause you gon' start improvin' real fast now. But we got to git this stuff outta here and put some moe in and see 'bout gettin' you some new mattresses."

Susie followed her mother's instructions, thankful she was here to help her through this awful mess. This was evil that couldn't be seen, yet it was deadly. It just sat there and waited for you, ate at you like a terminal disease, killing you when it got the chance. *How can human bein's be so evil?*

Some days later, they sat watching as he drove up, got out of the car, and moved quickly toward the steps, then stopped.

He raised his foot and tried putting it down, but it wouldn't behave. Instead, it paused in mid air as if it had a mind of its own. He tried several more times, but he just couldn't get his foot to touch that step.

So he tried with the other. He went on for at least a full minute with the same results. Susie and Rubye Mae watched, amused. They covered their mouths to keep from laughing out at him as he turned several shades of ash brown, then black. He planted both feet on the ground, glanced in their direction, his face full of anger, turned and skirted back to his car on his short legs, slammed the door, and sped down the street, leaving them rolling on the floor in uncontrollable laughter.

"Serves him right," Susie said when she stopped laughing.

An hour later, Koffee yelled, "What in the hell is you doin'? Tryin' to make a fool outta me? I couldn' git up the steps. The shit ain't workin'," he ranted, throwing his short body around like a yo-yo in the small office.

"She must be blockin' it with that damn devil lye. That's the only thang that can keep you from gettin' up them steps," the old man said, scratching his weathered face.

"Then damn it, you shoulda tole me that befoe. Maybe we coulda done somethin' to stop her. What kinda voodoo man is you when you cain't help me?"

"I cain't work no miracles."

"Then I cain't use you no moe." Koffee screamed and fled from the house, his mind racing, trying to figure out who could help him. "I'm gon' have her or else," he vowed.

Without a doubt, people who were brave enough to be around Koffee for the next two weeks were putting their mental health at risk. If they made the mistake and said one word Koffee didn't like, he went into a rage. And his poor wife was so fearful of him, she almost ran from the room when he entered.

The wrath he directed at others was to keep him from becoming angry at himself. He had known from the beginning that she wasn't meant for nor interested in him, but he had been so determined to have her he sought to use voodoo to get her.

Even when she was under his spell, most times they hadn't gotten along as well as he thought they should have. She was still unruly, but he kept thinking it would take more time for her to succumb to him and kept returning to the voodoo man.

Even now, when he should have given up, he vowed, "She'll be mine or else," knowing he was wrong. That it went against the way he had been raised, his ministry, and his marriage, didn't seem to matter to him any longer.

Six weeks after her near bout with death, Susie strutted from her room looking like a young woman of twenty-five. Her color had returned, her face clear and smooth. Her body projected a youthful sex appeal of which she was totally unaware. And her mysterious brownish-amber eyes smothered hidden secrets.

Lola's head jerked several times as she stared at her mother when she walked into the kitchen and pulled a cup from the cupboard.

"Mama, what happen'd to you? You... you sho do look differen'. I don't know what it is, but you seem kinda like a angel or somethin'."

"Thank you, Sistah. I can a'sho you I'm far from the angel part, but I do feel bettah then I have in years. Even my walk feels lighter." She poured coffee and sat down at the table to add Pet Milk and two teaspoons of sugar.

"Mornin', Mama. How you doin' this mornin?"

"I would give you a thousand dollars to look like you do."

She smiled. "Gal, you look like a young girl again. Don't she, Sistah?" Rubye Mae praised her as she sat a plate of food in front of Susie.

Susie laughed. "Since y'all thank I look so good, maybe I'll start lookin' for me a young boyfriend then."

"Mama!" Lola exclaimed.

Susie's eyes twinkled with mischief. "Maybe I'll take one of yo's from you. You got plenty to go 'round, don't you?"

"Mama!" Lola looked at her grandmother, her eyes begging for help.

"Ah, chile. Yo' Mama is jest tryin' to git yo' goat." She turned to Susie and said, "And you right, you outta start lookin'," she winked and sat down to eat.

Susie covered her mother's hand. "Mama, I owe you a lot for comin' here and takin' care of me like I was a baby when Sistah call'd you. I wouldn' made it this far without you. Thank you, Mama." She had already thanked Lola, privately.

Rubye Mae fidgeted with her eggs. "Thank the Lawd for all His blessin's. He's the one that paves the way; we jest have to know which way to walk, and this time we walk'd the right road," she said as she looked into her daughter's eyes, sending her a message.

Susie understood. It was time to start preparing to do what she was born to do. "Ain't that the truth? Ain't that the truth."

Grace was said, and they ate heartily.

Too soon, Rubye Mae left, knowing that Susie would be fine if she went forward with her decision. She would be on the right course to a better life.

40

Susie sat, lost in thought as she placed Blanche's letter in her dress pocket. She lit a cigarette and glanced out the window at the growing dark. It was quiet, silent, filled with untold stories. Matching her mood, it reminded her of the unsaid words in Blanche's letter.

Blowing smoke toward the window, she reflected on the letter. Behind all Blanche's exciting words about coming home, Susie sensed pain. And it was Paul, the man Blanche had been writing about for more than a year.

"Oh, Mama, he's not jest the best lookin' man I've ever seen, but he's sensitive, smart, and fun to be with. Always makin' me laugh, sometimes 'til I cry. His family is from here and very nice. They are rich, Mama. But they don't act uppity," she had written.

Each one of Blanche's letters had been filled with her new life and Paul. When they had turned serious, Susie knew she was falling in love with Paul and was delighted for her.

But this letter left Susie feeling discouraged. There was trouble in Blanche's relationship. "It's got to be the chile."

She turned on the light in the darkened room and examined her hands and nails, covered her face, and massaged her eyes.

"Lawd, sometimes wanting the best for yo' chile jest don't make it happen. They got to want the same too. All these years I done tried to help Blanche so she could go on and have a good life. But thaih's somethin' in her that makes her thank she ain't worthy. That hurts her, and it hurts me 'cause she is deservin' of havin' a happy life. The Lawd knows I couldn' asked for a bettah daughter.

"Sometimes I feel like a pure failure as a mother." She shuddered then stood up, glanced at the clock on the table. It was past midnight, and she had to rise at five o'clock in the morning to wash and have her clothes on the line by eight.

After dressing for bed, she fell to her knees in prayer, knowing God already knew what she wanted, but she had to ask Him anyway.

Susie was ironing the last sheet when Miss Maggie, the neighbor who lived around the corner, and a member of Rev. Koffee's church, banged on the door.

"How you do, Miss Susie? I was on my way home from work and thought I'd stop by and see you for a minute," she grinned, showing false teeth with bluish-pink gums.

Although Susie didn't want company, and Miss Maggie didn't know what a minute was, Susie let the older lady in and asked her to sit down, especially since she had made it past the buried devil lye. She knew the woman didn't have any voodoo on her.

"I'm doin' jest fine, Miss Mag. And you? I didn't know you work'd on Sad-days."

Miss Maggie removed her glasses and squinted her eyes at Susie as she sat down. "I don't usually, but the folks got a family git together tomorrow, and they need'd me to cook extra food," she said as she sat down and fanned herself with her hand.

Susie handed her a church fan.

"Thank you. Chile, I don't know if it's my eyes or what, but I could swear you look like one of them young girls runnin' 'round. You look good. Real good," she complimented, pushing her false teeth forward with her tongue.

"Thank you, Miss Mag. I finally feel like my ole self again," Susie said as she sat facing the woman. You lookin' mighty fine yo'self."

"I'm doin' alright for a ole woman," she cackled, moving her teeth up and down, making them click. She leaned closer to Susie. "But me and some of the othah members is scared for our preacher. Honey, let me tell you, Rev. Koffee is actin' so funny we thank somethin' is wrong in his head." Her eyes became large behind her glasses.

Shaking her head sadly, she continued. "He done changed so much we hardly know him. His temper is worser then a man who caught his woman with anothah man. He hollers at everybody that gits in his way. He don't go to see his sick members like he used to; he don't preach with the spirit, and he look awful most of the times. He done gon' down, Susie."

"Maybe y'all ought to take him to see a doctor," Susie suggested, almost feeling sorry for him.

"His deacons and members done tried tellin' him that, but he says he alright. But lis-sen to this, Susie. I hear tell he only gits that way when it's a woman givin' him troubl', and I don't mean his wife. Most all his members know he got women problems, but he's a man, no mattah how good he preach. So we forgives him as long as he don't take it home. And he don't allow that.

"But this thang is worser then when him and that othah woman fell out. Chile, the man went insane, I hear tell. Nobody could do nothin' with him. He beat the mess outta her for leavin' him, then sent her runnin' outta Selma, and we ain't seen hair nor hide of her since."

"Well, I declare," Susie said quietly. "I nevah heard none of this befoe. It's sho amazin' how this small town can keep secrets, if need be."

"Only his members knows this stuff 'bout him. And we don't usually tell no outsiders, but seein' that you one of his friends, I want'd you to know."

"Oh. I see," Susie managed to say.

"But I gots to ax you a question. Is you noticed anythang unusual 'bout my preacher?"

Susie looked at her, wanting to tell her how dirty and low-down he was, but she couldn't find it in her heart to try and destroy the woman's love for her minister. "To tell you the truth, Miss Mag, I ain't seen him in a while. I guess he's been too busy to stop by. I sho do wish him well, though." Susie stood and walked her guest to the door.

"I jest hope he git help soon. Well, Susie, I'll be seein' you, and you keep me and my family in yo' prayers."

"I sho will do that. And you do the same, Miss Mag,"

Susie closed and locked the door and walked to her bedroom. She sat by the window, gazing out at nothing while her mind raced in various directions.

"Oh, Lawd Jesus," Susie moaned as she fell to the throw rug next to her bed and closed her eyes. "I know I jest left prayer meetin' and all, but I feel the need to pray to You again by myself. I feel the need to come to You so that You may make me understan' myself bettah, that You may give me the wisdom and the strength to go on with my deed in life. Give me the courage to take on whatever my load is and do it with cheerfulness.

"Dear Lawd, my Savior in Jesus Christ. I love You with every-thang that is in me, and I know You love me. I know that I have run away from my Gift that You saw fit to bestow on me. I ask You to forgive me, a saved sinner, for everythang I have done to turn away from You. Please make me the person I am to be so that I may rise up and do what is intend'd to do for You and Yo' Kingdom.

"And lastly, Dear Lawd, I want to thank You for all Yo' grace, wisdom, and mercy that Thou hast bestow'd on me. I thank You for my chil'ren and thaih chil'ren, for our health, strength and love in our hearts, for the tribulations that I encounter'd and the thangs I have learn'd. In the name of the Father, Son, and Holy Ghost, I pray. Amen."

Susie stood slowly, pulled the covers back and slipped into bed. This night and many more was spent praying. And each time, she felt a change occur in her.

One Monday morning, she woke to muddy streets and a steady downpour. "Oh Lawd. I wonder if this is a warnin' or what. I sho don't need that man comin' back 'round here tryin' to git in my house and do only Gawd knows what to me."

"Did you say somethin', Mama?" Lola asked as she and the children walked into the room.

Susie turned from the window and looked at Lola and her two children. Pat was three and Ronney one. She went over to them and patted their heads, then turned to Carolyn who would be turning five. How y'all chil'ren doin' this mornin'?" she asked, smiling at them.

"We doin' good, Mama." Carolyn answered for all of them, pulling at their hands. "We ready to eat now, Mama," she said.

Susie smiled and turned to Lola. "You go fix them some oatmeal. I'll be in shortly."

Susie peeked out the curtains again. "Lawdy, I hope this ain't no sign."

Well Susie, you finally found the right road. It took you long enough, but you made it, and just in the nick of time.

"Don't I know it. I feel like I done lived for moe then a hundreds years and now bein' born again." Susie answered the voice as it had been a part of her since she was a young girl. "You been gon' for moe then six years. Where you been? I thought you was nevah comin' back."

I been right here all the while. You just didn't want anything to do with me. Now that you do, I can help you with certain things.

"Like what?"

Be very careful at church Sunday. He hasn't given up.

"He what!" Susie exclaimed. But the voice had faded. "You know what it means," she moaned to herself.

Following service, Susie stood talking with several church members when she suddenly felt ill at ease and turned around. Koffee was glaring her way. She could feel his indignation. She turned from his view. Her legs felt like rubber as she desperately tried to conceive a way to slip away.

"Susie, I'm goin' yo' way this evenin. Why don't I give you a lift home," George, one of the deacons offered.

"Thank you, brother George. I'll take you up on yo' kind offer," she said, relief flowing through her. Although she didn't normally ride with married men because she didn't want their wives accusing her of coming on to them, this was one time she didn't care what they thought.

The next morning, Susie opened her door and gasped at the brown, sticky foot-tracks someone had deliberately traced up and down her porch and steps the night before.

"Well, I'll be."

Warning the children and Lola to remain inside, she placed a clean cloth over her mouth, tied a rag around her head, pulled gloves on, then mixed devil lye with Clorox, walked to the door, and tossed it on the porch.

Within ten minutes, the porch and steps were bleached almost as white as sand on the Caribbean beach. Susie smiled. "You didn't git me this time, and next time I'll be on my guard too."

That evening right before dusk, she took Lola outside, and they sprinkled more devil lye around the house and buried more cans, replacing the first ones that were completely empty.

After cleaning up, they sat in the living room, Susie reading, Lola fidgeting.

"Mama, why did we put that stuff down like you and Mama Rubye Mae did when she was here?"

Susie laid the newspaper aside. "Cause thaih's evil people in the world who practice voodoo to git people to do thangs they want them to do. If people don't do somethin' to protect themselves, then it could mean thaih life."

"I nevah heard of that befoe. It don't sound right to me. What 'bout Gawd. Cain't He help do somethin'?"

"Gawd do help. He don't make the voodoo; the people do. What He does is give special people the Gift of healin' and insight to help fight the voodoo," Susie tried to explain.

"Well, I sho don't b'lieve in the stuff."

Susie wanted to tell her how much she detested the thought

of believing in something so evil. But after all the experiences she had endured, she wasn't about to turn her back on the stuff and let it kill her. She would fight the devil on his own grounds, until she got rid of him.

"Well, chile, I didn't either 'til I had problems. I hope you won't encounter none. Jest beware. Watch what you eat, don't sit with yo' back turn'd at them clubs, and nevah git involved with a marred man. And nevah with a man who wants to possess you so bad, he'll do anythang to have you."

"I won't, Mama," she promised, then excused herself to her room and fell across the bed. She was confused about the voodoo, but she understood the rest of her mother's warnings.

41

Lawd Jesus, I'm so tir'd of that man followin' me. It's gotten to be that everywhere I turn, I see his face. The only time I find peace is when I'm sleep," Susie wept on her knees a month later. "Lawd, he's worst then the red-head'd devil, ridin' my back. Please tell me what to do to git some peace from him. Please, dear Lawd. In Jesus' name I pray, Amen."

She pulled herself slowly from the floor and slumped down in the chair next to her bed. She had been praying so long, her legs were numb and her knees had indentations in them from the throw rug.

As she sat rubbing her lifeless legs, the voice spoke to her.

Remember, I warned you he wouldn't go away.

"Yeah, I sho do. But least you coulda warn'd me how long it would take. And you sho didn't tell me he was this possess'd. I ain't the only woman in Selma."

He's doing it because he wants to own your body and soul. He wants to feed from you like a baby his Mama. Without you, he feels unnourished, seeing no true meaning to life because to him, you are his life. But the thing that he's forgotten is that he chose his destiny long before you, and you will not be a part of it.

"I'll be mighty glad when he finds out I won't be. In the mean-time, I have to watch my back all the time, and I'm almost scared to go to work anymoe. If I still work'd nights, I would lose my job cause of him."

Do this. Send word by people you know that will give him the message almost the way you tell them. Specify that he or she must tell him directly or it won't work. Tell them to let him know that if he keeps following you or have you followed, you will per-sonally call his home and tell his wife.

That'll make him mad as a pistol, but it will also stop him for a while because more than anything, he can't tolerate anyone dis-respecting his home. His wife is a very kind but weak woman, unwise to his second life outside the home. Knowing what he do would cause great turmoil to her. So while he leaves you alone, you can think of something to do to get him away from you.

"I don't know how I'm 'spose to git him off me."

"Oh, yes, you do. You just need time to think about it.

Slowly, Susie shook her head in understanding. Slowly she stood and walked to the mirror, looking deeply into the reflecting glass, focusing on her inner knowledge, not seeing her reflec-tion. She knew she had the spiritual power to do many things, but as yet, she hadn't learned how to use them.

She closed her eyes and contemplated on what she should do, remaining in front of the mirror for more than an hour. Then she opened her eyes, and gazed at the woman looking back at her. She had physically changed. Her eyes had taken on a pene-trating look of one who had received knowledge from another orb, yet at the same time they were consoling.

Unafraid, Susie left the room to make coffee, stopped briefly to speak to Lola who was sitting in the living room, reading a comic book while the children played on the floor.

Lola spoke, barely looking up from her magazine, "Hi, Mama, I thought you was sleep."

"Naw. I jest need'd to git away for a while. Sistah, don't you thank you can find somethin' else to read 'sides that funny book. You got two chil'ren. Time for that is over," she advised then bent down to play with the children for a moment before going into the kitchen.

Lola blinked several times when her mother left the room, a chill skirting down her spine. Those were the strangest yet most intriguing pair of eyes she had every seen. They seemed to burn into her mind, reading her thoughts, yet gave her comfort at the same time.

She picked up her comic book, looked into it, saw nothing, laid it down again, and started biting her nails.

Susie poured two cups of fresh, perked coffee, added Pet milk and sugar, then carried them back into the living room and handed one to Lola. Lola thanked her and shifted around on top of her comic book.

"You don't have to hide the book under you, Sistah. I jest ax'd you to stop readin' it so much. Thaih's othah books to read."

"How did you know I was sittin' on it, Mama?" Her eyes almost doubled from fear.

"I jest knowed; that's all." Susie answered honestly, just as naturally as she had been doing this all the while. "And you don't have to be 'fraid of my eyes. You noticed the chil'ren ain't."

Lola removed the book, placed it on the table and sipped her coffee. "Yes, Mam."

She cleared her throat nervously. "Mama. I know I should be doin' moe 'round here. You workin' and takin' care of us. I feel bad, so I was wonderin' if I can help out by sellin' life insurance part-time. I can go when you git home from work."

"So when did you 'cide you want'd to grow up?"

"Mama."

"I jest want to make sho you serious. I don't thank that's a problem, Sistah. You need to start thankin' 'bout yo' future and how you gon' take care of yo' chil'ren."

"We talk'd 'bout this moe then a year ago, and if I 'member right, you was 'spose to be on yo' own by now, but then thangs did happen, and I need'd you here, so I didn't say nothin' to you. Now that you serious, I will talk to Crenshawe since he's the only one I know that can hire you. Then I'll let you know."

"Thank you, Mama," Lola said, avoiding Susie's eyes.

"Are you gon' be happy sellin' insurance? That's what you have to ax yo'self. In a little over a year, yo' sistah will be finishin' school; then she can come take her chile. I want both of y'all to take them at the same time."

"I don't know. Thaih's not a lot to do in Selma, I may like selling insurance."

"Have you ever thought 'bout leavin' here, Sistah? Goin' Nawth to make a bettah life? Or is you waitin' for John or Lawrence to come and sweep you off yo' feet? I wouldn' depend on them too much if I was in yo' shoes."

"I ain't dependin' on them, Mama."

Susie changed the subject. "You know yo' sistah is comin' home soon, and I ain't tole her 'bout Ronney. I didn't have the heart to, and I don't thank you have neither. I know she's gon' be hurt and disappoint'd with you, but that's up to y'all to take care of. "Anyway, I'll be glad to see her, and while she's here, I'm gon' tell her my plans so she'll know and understan' she's got a chile here that needs her too."

Lola looked down at the floor. "Yeah, it'll be nice to see Blanche again," she said, but in her heart she didn't want to face her. She knew Blanche would be angry and hurt. She didn't want her to know she had messed up a good relationship with a man who loved her because she was too busy flirting in another's face and when she decided she wanted him, he had left her, cold.

Not wanting to think about her past mistakes or have her mother whip her butt with her mouth, Lola said, "Mama, if you don't mind, I have a headache. I need to take a Stanback and lay down for a while."

Lola fell across her bed, glad to escape her mother's probing eyes and the turn of the conversation. Sometimes she wished she could be half as strong as her mother seemed to be.

She rolled over and stared dismally at the wall-papered ceiling, wishing she had listened to her mother's advice.

She cried and cried until her head did indeed ache, and she really needed a Stanback.

The following morning, Susie called Miss Mag over. She knew that if anything was going to happen, she would be the person to tell.

"Miss Mag, I call'd you over 'cause thaih's somethang I want you to do for me, if you don't mind. I know that you and all the neighbors round here been wonderin' what been goin' on with me and Rev'end Koffee. Why he ain't been comin' 'round here no moe. Well, it ain't nobody's bus'ness, but I can tell you this much. He won't be comin' back.

"So, if you would do this for me, I would be most grateful. You or somebody that you know tell him if I as much as see his car or anybody's car that look like they hangin' 'round on this street, I'm gon' personally call his wife and tell her 'bout us."

"Miss Susie! You wouldn' do that, would you?" Miss Maggie asked in shock.

"Miss Mag, as Gawd is my witness, I sho will do it if he don't leave me alone." As much as it went against the grain in her, she would do as she promised. The man had to go.

"Miss Maggie clutched her chest, "Well, I sho will tell him or see that he gits the message this day. But he ain't gon' like it, not one bit. Naw, he sho ain't. Lawdy, the man gon' have a fit on somebody." She stood and walked to the door.

"You mean it too, don't you? Miss Susie?"

"Every last word. And you make sho he gits it, word for word. And thank you, Miss Mag. I knowed I could count on you."

The older woman walked to the bottom of the steps, shaking her dyed reddish hair. "You sho welcome, Miss Susie, but Lawdy, this a mess if I ever heard of one." Then she quickly walked down the street, glad to get away from Susie's eyes.

42

Susie's nervous foot tapping ended as soon as she saw Blanche descend the train steps. She moved closer to the platform and waited, glad that she had come alone.

Blanche saw her and ran to her. "Mama, oh Mama. It's so good to see you!" she cried as she hugged Susie, almost squeezing the breath from her.

"It's good to see you too, baby," Susie said, pulling away from her daughter and taking a good look at her. "My, you sho do look pretty, real pretty. Quite a young lady," Susie praised proudly, hugging her daughter again, trying to hold back her tears.

But Blanche made up for both of them as tears flowed from her eyes like water bursting from a dam. "Oh, Mama. It's so good to finally be home again. I miss'd you so much."

Susie smiled, squeezing her hand. "I know, baby. I miss'd you too. Let's go and git yo' suitcases. Sistah and the chil'ren is waitin' at home." She choked back the tears that tickled her throat.

Blanche examined the scenery through the dusty windows as the taxi drove toward Selma, seeing colored people bent over in cotton fields, pulling at the white puffs so quickly one could barely see their hands. Some pushed plows with mules behind them, while others planted seeds. From time to time they pulled their tired and strained stiff backs up to wipe the sweat from their brows with the back of their hands; then resumed their jobs.

Farther down the road, she saw young boys and men lifting hundreds of pounds of cotton, throwing it across their backs, carrying it into the gin house where the cotton would be processed before selling.

She frowned at the houses that leaned so badly; a swift wind would tumble them over and leave splinters behind.

Feeling suddenly dejected, she turned from the sad picture as she realized her old world which she was actually witnessing for the first time, shocked her deeply, making her realize just how her people had suffered the last hundreds of years and how they continued to suffer. She wiped the fresh tears from her eyes and pulled her gloves off, deciding she could never live here again.

"Is you alright, Blanche?" Susie asked.

"Yes, Mam. She looked thoughtful then said, "Mama, where's Rev'end Koffee? I thought he would be at the train station with you.

Susie's back stiffened, and a hard look touched her face. "It's a long story. I'll tell you 'bout it when we git home," she said, noticing the cab driver's eyes and ears expand at the mention of Koffee's name, hoping to hear gossip and spread it throughout Selma. *But not today, buster.*

She smiled at the disappointed look on the driver's face. Lola saw the cab stop in front of the house and quickly threw the door open when they stepped on the porch.

Susie paused to let Blanche in and waited for the cab driver to drag the heavy trunk up the steps and on to the landing.

When Blanche walked through the door, Lola grabbed and hugged her with one arm while holding Ronney with the other. "Oh, Nina, it's so good to have you home!" she cried, reverting back to her childhood name for Blanche.

Blanche pulled away from her, fresh tears flowing as she looked at her sister and then her son, her eyes questioning.

Lola glanced downward for a moment then looked at her sister and declared, "He's mine, and I love him."

Susie entered, waited until the trunk was brought into the house, and paid the cab driver. She glanced at her daughters and smiled before going into the kitchen to prepare refreshments.

The two sisters sat looking at each other and then Blanche moved next to Lola and hugged her. "I'm just sorry you didn't keep yo' promise 'bout havin' anothah one, but he's a very pretty, little boy. May I hold him?" she asked, reaching for Ronney.

Lola handed him to her and said, "Yo voice sho done changed. You sound all proper."

Before she had a chance to respond, Susie returned with refreshments and Carolyn and Pat from their naps, holding hands, trailing her. Blanche was surprised to see how much Carolyn had grown and held her arms out to her, but Carolyn ignored her and went to Susie.

Disappointed, Blanche dropped her arms, a sad expression clouding her face.

Susie took Carolyn's hand and pointed to Blanche. "Baby, it's Blanche, yo' mother. She's come a long ways to see you. Go give her a hug; won't you?"

Carolyn gave Blanche a real hard look and planted her feet to the floor.

"Go on, Carolyn, she won't harm you," Susie coaxed.

Carolyn slowly made her way to her mother and stood, twisting her hands.

Blanche gathered her in her arms and held her for a long moment before releasing her. The feelings she had hoped to experience weren't there. She smiled to keep the tears away. "Hello, Carolyn, I know you don't 'member me 'cause you were very little when I went away. But I miss'd you very much."

Carolyn looked at her and eased back next to Susie and stuck her thumb in her mouth.

"It's gon' take some time for her to git use to you, but she'll come 'round," Susie offered, hoping it was the truth.

Blanche managed a smile then turned to Pat who was sitting next to her, looking into her face, all smiles.

Blanche hugged her for a moment, and when she released her, Pat moved to sit next to Susie also.

Susie was beside herself the next few weeks, enjoying Blanche's company, cooking dinner for her and her friends that were also home visiting their families for the summer.

In the evenings when Blanche wasn't with her friends, the three of them would sit on the porch in the swing hoping for a warm breeze. They would swing and watch the lightning bugs bump and make popping sounds. Susie, Blanche, and Lola would laugh and carry on about someone or something that had happened in Selma or Seattle.

One evening, Lola put an end to their temporary, untroubled lives. "Hey, Blanche. You ain't talk'd 'bout Paul, 'xcept in yo' letters. Tell us 'bout him."

"Thaih's nothin' much left to tell, Sistah."

"But you ain't said nothin' 'bout him since you been here. You still do court him, don't you?"

"Yes, Sistah, I do."

"Then tell us 'bout him?"

Having heard enough of Lola's demands, Susie abruptly stopped the swing, causing them to catch the armrest to keep from tumbling forward. "Sistah, I don't want to hear you talk to yo' sistah like she's on trial and you the judge. If you want to know somethin', I suggest you act the way you was brought up."

Lola said in a softer voice, "I didn't mean nothin', Mama."

Turning back to Blanche, she pleaded," Tell us some moe 'bout him again, please."

This was the moment Blanche had been dreading and wished she could avoid. Glad for the darkness that hid her pain, she told them as much about Paul as she could, in a calm voice.

"It sho sounds like a fairy tale to me, but if it's true I want to go back with you when you leave," Lola said in serious tones.

"Everythang I've said is true," Blanche said softly.

Sensing Blanche's discomfort, Susie asked Lola to leave them so she could speak privately to Blanche. Lola left but tried to stand next to the wall to listen.

"The walls ain't' got no ears, Sistah," Susie said, and then turned to Blanche.

Lola tipped-toed to her room, almost tripping over the table in the hall.

"Now that we alone, won't you tell me what' goin' on with you and yo' young man. I knowed thaih was somethin' goin' on a while back."

Blanche's eyes grew large at her mother's words, but she was relieved. She needed her mother now more than ever.

When Susie held her hand, Blanche could feel Susie's love flow to her, and her mind opened up like the earth to rainwater. She told her mother everything about her relationship with Paul.

Susie patted her hand. "Baby, I know you been goin' through a lot and yo' burden seems hard to bear. Yo' troubl' is not so much 'bout yo' chile, but how you feel 'bout yo'self. Befoe you can love someone else, you got to like you, and then you can handle anythang that comes along, even rejection.

"Yo' Paul sounds like he would understan' anythin' in yo' pass and would love you no mattah what." She stopped and hit at a mosquito. "Let's go in the house. These thangs is bad tonight."

She sat next to Blanche, held her hand in hers, turned it over, and examined it, not realizing what she was doing until Blanche questioned her.

"Mama, why you lookin' at my hand like that?"

Susie hesitated for a moment, seemingly puzzled, then said, "Readin' yo' palm, now be still."

Blanche's expression became anxious. "When did you start doin' this, Mama?"

"I jest start'd," she answered as if this had always been a natural part of her. "Sit still and hush." She saw Paul and his pain, his pleading with Blanche to be honest with him about her past. Susie closed her eyes to keep from seeing more.

You must finish seeing her future and tell her.

"Is you sho?" Susie asked.

"Bout what, Mama?" Blanche asked in a nervous voice.

"Not you, baby."

When she finished, she looked directly into her daughter's eyes. "Blanche, what I see is not good, but you can turn it 'round. Paul loves you jest like he tole you. He loves you so much it hurts him to his heart when you lie to him. Chile, he wants to marry you. But he won't ax you again, not 'til you open up to him.

"Yo' pass won't make him leave you or make him thank any less of you. He's slippin' from you, but if you open up, y'all can be happy together. He's a good man, and he loves chil'ren and people. He's gon' be a big success one day. "

Blanche sat silent, her eyes frightened. She wanted to run, but couldn't feel her legs. Speak, but her tongue was paralyzed.

"Chile, is you alright? I didn't mean to scare you. I was only tellin' yo' fortune."

"But, but...Mama...you...", her small voice faltered.

"Don't you 'member?" Susie asked, trying to calm her. I tole y'all a long time ago that I had a Gift. Well, now that I finally 'xcept'd it...this is part of it. And I cain't do nothin' when it crosses my mind. I jest follow it." She paused and studied Blanche for a moment then said, "Baby, it's alright. I'm still the same person. I'm still yo' mother."

"Oh, Mama. I...this is so strange, and what you tole me is so real. But I thank I'm too much of a coward to tell him 'bout Carolyn. I couldn' bear his scorn."

"I jest tole you, he won't feel that way. The man loves you, Blanche. Don't throw this away baby. You got a chance to have a good life and raise yo' chile by someone who will love the both of you. Don't let it fly away from you. Blanche didn't answer. Susie waited for a few minutes.

"Do you want somethin' from the kitchen?" she asked as she released Blanche's hand, stood, and patted her on the shoulder.

"Yes, Mam, but I'll come with you." She attempted to rise.

"Naw. You stay here 'til I come back," Susie said, slipping through the door just before the light appeared in her eyes. She didn't want to frighten Blanche as she had Lola who had almost passed out and, for several days, stayed away from her before timidly coming near her again.

    She couldn't explain why it happened or when it was going to occur until seconds before when the pressure behind her eyes made her feel drowsy and tingly, and she got a woozy feeling in her head.

    Now, she sat at the table until it passed and rose to pour the iced-tea for them. She felt the voice, waiting.

    "Alright, what's goin' on?" she said.

    You don't need to question what you already know. It's happening. It's just the beginning, Susie. Then the voice faded.

    Susie shook her head slightly as if to clear it, picked up the iced-tea, and carried it into the living room.

43

While Carolyn, Pat, and Ronney were snoring in their beds, Susie, Blanche, and Lola sat around the kitchen table, shelling crowder peas Susie had purchased from the colored farmer who came to town to sell his crops every Saturday during the summer.

"Whee, it's a hot one. Must be a hundred in the shade today," Susie commented as she laid down the purple-hulled peas and patted her face with a damp washcloth.

"I had forgotten how hot it could get here. I must have lost ten pounds since I've been back. 'It's cookin' in here', as Mama Rubye Mae would say," Blanche offered with a smile.

"Yeah, and Mama Rubye Mae would say, 'I ain't gon' stay in here and fry like a fool with no sense, but y'all can if y'all wants to,'" Lola mimicked.

Susie threw her head back and laughed. "Y'all sho right. Mama always hated to cook, and when we got ole enuf she left most of the cookin' to us, 'specially in the summer."

Suddenly somber, Blanche blurted, "Mama, I have to leave sooner than I plan'd. I have some unfinished business to see 'bout befoe school starts in September."

Lola's face dropped a few inches, and so did the peas from her hands. She stared at her sister as if she had slapped her. "But Blanche, you said you was goin' to stay two months. You barely been here one." Her mouth quivered as she tried to hold back tears.

Although disappointed, Susie had been expecting this since reading Blanche's palm. Susie shelled several more peas. "Well," um, um. I hate to see you leave so soon aftah all these years, but I understan'," she stopped abruptly and cleared her throat again.

Lola gazed at her mother strangely, trying to understand what she was rambling on about.

Blanche understood. Tears formed in her eyes. "I know I promised to stay 'til August, but this is urgent."

Susie stood abruptly. "I have a headache. I thank I'll go lay down with the chil'ren for a spell. Y'all finish these peas." She turned and left the room, her eyes filled with sadness that she didn't want either of them to see.

"I'm gettin' tir'd of Selma. I sho wish I could go somewhere and start a new life. Thaih's nothin' here to do but teach, preach, and have chil'ren. I got my share of chil'ren, and I sho don't want to teach no school, and the Lawd ain't callin' no women preachers," Lola said.

Susie turned and looked at her younger daughter with peeked interest. "When we talk'd befoe 'bout you sellin' insurance. I 'member axin' you if you want'd to do somethin' else. You nevah said nothin' 'bout leavin' Selma, Sistah."

"I jest made up my mind. Look, Blanche, thaih's yo' train pullin' in," she pointed.

"I know. I wish we had moe time to talk. I wish you had tole me, Sistah. Maybe we can write each othah 'bout yo' plans, huh?" Blanche suggested and hugged her sister.

"Yeah. Maybe we can do that." Lola held her tightly for a moment then pushed her away.

Blanche grabbed her mother, the tears flowing onto her Peter Pan collar. "I sure wish'd we lived closer so we could see each othah moe often. I'm goin' to miss you all so much, Mama."

"I know. We gon' miss you too, Blanche." Susie held her child to her as if it would be the last time. Then she pulled away and pushed her toward the train. "They callin' yo' train."

Blanche grabbed Susie's hand and held on to it until she reached the steps. "Mama, please take care of yo'self. I'll write you once a week. I love you, Mama."

"I love you too, baby," Susie said as they hugged for the last time. "You be good and try to have a happy life. We ain't promised no certain time on this earth, you know. You try to work yo' problems out. You deserve a good life; 'member that."

Blanche's eyes grew large as she realized her mother knew why she was leaving Selma. "I didn't want to say..."

"Hush, it's alright. I understan'."

"Bye, Mama. Bye, Sistah." Blanche waved before disappearing into the back of the train.

As she stood watching the train take her daughter away, the strangest thought occurred to her. She had forgotten to speak to Blanche about Koffee. *I ain't saw him in moe then a month and it's been like bein' free. Maybe he done gave up.*

"Let's go home, Sistah."

Shortly after Blanche left, Susie watched Lola sink into a funk deeper than the well that used to be in her parents' backyard, way years ago.

Each day Lola played with her food, refused to socialize with her friends when they stopped by. She paid no attention to her children or Carolyn whom she loved frolicking with daily, and she didn't pick up a comic book.

One evening Susie asked, "Sistah, chile, won't you tell me what's bothin' you? You been draggin' 'round here like all the life drainin' outta you. Maybe I can help."

Lola hunched her shoulders. "Ain't nothin' wrong, Mama."

"Don't tell me that. Look at you. Nothin' but skin and bones 'cause you ain't been eatin' like you 'spose too."

Lola did not respond.

"Well, when you ready to talk, I'll be here, that is if you still livin'." Susie left the room.

One night, Susie and Lola sat in the living room, Lola holding a comic book but not reading it. Susie moved to sit next to her. "You know, Sistah, I thank you have the smallest hands in the family. Maybe you got them from Mama. Let me see them."

Lola laid the book aside and let Susie take her hands, thinking nothing of it. Nor did she think anything of it when Susie focused on her left hand, turning it over, then back again, gazing at her fingers, nails, and then the middle to read her future.

It only took about a minute to see Lola's past with John and finally Lawrence. Either man could be her future hope and dream.

The last argument between John and Lola was revealed. John was very hurt and angry. "But you said you loved me, John. You said you want'd to marry me."

And John responded, "Yeah. I did say that, and I meant it, but you didn't want nothin' to do with me 'til you found out you was pregnant. You ain't gon' play me for the fool and then use me like this, Lola; I ain't marryin' you, even if this is my baby."

Then Susie saw Lola returning home after her and John's first fight. Lola was looking wild. She said she had broken up with John, was hurting badly, regretting all the mistakes she had made with him. Then she saw that Lola had gotten John to stay with her for more than a year with her empty promises. And he, taking more of her flirting and mental abuse before finally transferring from the Air Force base outside of Selma, to some parts in New York.

Next, Susie saw Lawrence's face, the handsome, light-brown skinned man Lola had met after John, also stationed at Craig Field Air Force Base. Lawrence had showered her with flowers, candy, and other small gifts, but Lola, forgetting why John had left her, fell into her same pattern with Lawrence.

The girl couldn't stop flirting her tail.

Lola found herself pregnant soon after she started courting Lawrence. He stood by her until after the baby was born, accepting all her outbursts, and accusations, and insecurities even though the child wasn't his.

She didn't change after the baby's birth. He left Lola, Selma, and a letter, stating how much she had hurt him, but he still loved her. He wrote that if she decided she ever wanted to grow up and become a responsible woman, he would be willing to take her back.

Now Susie knew why Lola had started smoking. She saw that Lola strongly desired to leave Selma, but she didn't know where to go or how to ask her for help, again. Her reading also revealed Lola sobbing in her room many a night begging someone to help her get out of Selma.

Lola believed that if she didn't leave, her life would be over. And when the morning arrived, she had held damp towels over her puffy eyes to relieve the swelling before facing her mother with a cheerful smile on her face.

Susie closed her eyes briefly. "Well, I can see yo' hands is like Mama's. They small but good and strong." She released Lola's hand, finding it difficult to control her emotions. What she had seen was a side of her daughter that she hadn't known. Her child, in her own way, really wanted to make something out of herself; she just needed help in the right direction.

Before Lola had a chance to speak, Susie said, "You 'member that day at the train station when you said you want'd to leave Selma? Do you still want to go?"

Lola's eyes widened as she laid aside the comic book that had been in her lap. "Why you ax that, Mama?"

"Nevah mind why, jest answer my question. Do you?"

"Yes, Mama. Moe then anythang, I want to leave here."

"Maybe I can help you. I was readin' in the paper 'bout a job in New York. The lady is lookin' for a live-in-person to help out, and she willin' to pay a round-trip bus fare, if necessary. You still interest'd?"

"Yes, Mam!"

With a mischievous smile, Susie stood and walked to the sofa and retrieved the newspaper. "Sistah," she said as she put the newspaper under her arm.

"Yes, Mam," Lola answered, almost panting with excitement.

"This is yo' chance if you want it. I was plannin' on tryin' to git the job myself, but since you want out so bad, I'll let you go for it. Yo' happiness is importan' to me."

Lola grabbed her mother and pulled her into her arms. "Oh, Mama. You amaze me. Every time I thank my life is a shamble, you straighten it out for me.

"This is for real," Susie warned, gently pulling away.

Lola's face became somber as she looked at her mother. "But the chil'ren?"

"You don't have to worry 'bout the chil'ren. I'll take care of them 'til you git settl'd. The ad also say the pay is up to you, so I would suggest you make the best of it."

The following weeks were hectic, yet exciting for Lola as she made arrangements to leave Selma, bragging to her friends about the job she would be getting.

Susie wanted to tell her to hush her boasting until she had the job, but didn't want to spoil her excitement.

Unfortunately, Susie's enthusiasm was spoiled. She had started to sense Koffee's presence again, and each time, turning quickly to look for him, but never seeing him.

One day when she was walking downtown to the bank, she had that eerie, uneasy feeling. She turned around and saw him dodge inside a drugstore. She quickened her pace to the bank and later, took a taxi cab home.

Since that time she hadn't seen him, but she knew he was somewhere, lurking about. She decided that after Lola was gone she would get rid of him, no matter what methods she needed. She would worry about forgiveness later.

The moment finally arrived. Lola sat nervously, puffing on a cigarette, waiting for the taxi that would embark her on her new journey.

"Oh, Mama, this is so hard," she cried.

"I know it is, honey, but we'll be here prayin' everythang will go well for you," Susie said calmly, trying to keep her voice from breaking.

This was much harder than she had anticipated. Both her daughters would be gone. She could already feel the empty spot forming a place in her heart next to the one Blanche had left.

The cab honked, and they embraced for the last time. Then Lola hugged the children while the cab driver placed her suitcases in the trunk. She followed him and got into the back seat and sat waving, tears streaming down her face, around her chin and onto her pretty two-piece suit.

Susie and the children stood on the porch watching and waving until the taxi disappeared. She thought she saw something or someone down the street. She took the children into the house, then returned to the porch.

She didn't see Koffee's car down the block, but she knew he was watching, having heard the news about Lola leaving town.

44

"Hello, Hello. Who's this?" Susie asked, squinting at the clock on the table.

"Mama. Mama! It's me, Sistah. I know it's early and all, but I had to call you. I been awake all night, since my interview with Miss 'D'."

"Who? Slow down, chile. You makin' my head swim."

"I said I got the job, Mama. The lady, Miss Dubonski, liked me, even aftah I tole her 'bout the chil'ren, she jest smiled and said, "Yo' mother sho did a fine job of raisin' you,' in her funny accent. Then she ax'd me what salary I want'd to start at.

"Well, I start'd high, so I didn't have to go down too much. I'm gettin' paid fifty dollars a week, Mama. And on top of that, free room and board. In no time, I'll have so much money, my head will spin! Mama, the lady is rich and real nice."

"She sho is. Maybe I shoulda took that job," Susie teased.

Lola laughed. "I'm glad you didn't. Mama, I tell you, this is the biggest place I ever saw. Thaih's pretty trees and paved streets and big houses everywhere I look. And pretty flowers and fancy dress'd people are all over the place." She lowered her voice, "But thaih ain't too many of us here. You know, we 'bout

250 miles from the big city and all. But everybody I met at the bus depot and the people here treats me nice, like I'm jest as good as them."

"You are, Sistah. I always taught y'all that the color of yo' skin don't make you no less then anybody else. Gawd made all of us and to Him, we all equal. You jest be you and you'll do fine with yo' personality. I'm proud of you."

"Thank you, Mama. Thank you for everythang. As soon as I git my first paycheck, I'll send half of it home. Tell the chil'ren I love them."

Susie smiled, then yawned. "I sho will. And don't worry 'bout sendin' money 'til you git yo'self situated. You gon' need clothes for the cold weather they have up thaih."

"Yes, Mam. Mama, will you tell all my friends I'm not comin' back to stay no moe? Nevah."

"That's fine with me if it pleases you, baby. I jest want you to be happy. And I'll let yo' friends know that and tell them you'll write them. Now we best be gettin' off this phone. You take care and write me soon. Bye."

Susie replaced the receiver and covered her mouth in a second yawn, stretched, and pulled herself from the warm bed.

"Well, Susie, ole girl. Now, if you can git rid of the devil followin' you 'round like he wants to take you to hell with him, maybe you can start gettin' yo'self ready for a new life, too."

Susie was sitting at the kitchen table sipping her coffee when she saw Koffee's black Cadillac ease down the street.

"Well, I'll be. If it ain't the damn devil himself," she muttered to herself. She pulled her shade down, went into the bedroom, and sat facing the window.

"I'm gettin' so sick of that man. Sometimes I wish..."

Watch your wishes, Susie. Don't wish anything on anyone you'll be sorry for later.

"Maybe I do wish him harm."

This won't last forever. Just keep your guard up.

"For how long? I'm gettin' weary."

I can't answer that for you.

"Or you won't, you mean. This man's been a nuisance to me for years. How much moe am I 'spose to take? "

The voice didn't answer.

"Well, go away then." Susie said angrily, and lit a cigarette.

The sensations were hot, burning her skin. She could smell clothes scorching, flesh burning and see red flames roaring all around her. The dry wood crackled like bacon frying, throwing hot sparks onto the furniture, books, walls, catching everything in its destructive path. She heard voices screaming for help. A woman and two small children were trapped in the house.

The woman ran towards Susie, her eyes, a mirror of horrifying anguish, her arms outstretched like dead tree limbs, gown bellowing behind her, the burning flames following her, lapping at her legs.

Behind the woman the children screamed, attempting to trail their mother, begging her to wait for them as the flames chased them, leaping onto the oldest one's hair, setting it aflame, causing the child to grab her head and fall to the floor in torture as the flames enveloped her.

The petrified mother screamed, but no sound escaped her as she fought desperately to put the fire out with her hands. Failing, she scrambled toward the door, the other child at her heels.

But her path was suddenly blocked by thousands of reddish, orange flames, seemingly with hands, welcoming them into its fiery inferno.

The horrified woman gasped, and the heat singed her throat. She grabbed her neck and ran back to her fallen daughter and pulled at the burning gown, but it was too late. The woman fell to the floor and gathered her younger child in her arms, closed her eyes and waited for the flames to consume them.

Susie jumped, sat up in bed, fully awake. Her gown drenched in perspiration, she shook her head, then slipped from the bed and pulled the wet gown from her, shivering as she changed into a dry one.

Precisely at 9:00 a.m., Susie knocked on the door.

"Who's thaih?" A warm voice answered.

"My name's Susie Norwood, Miss Johnnie. I need to speak to you."

"Hold on a minute." The woman peeked through her Venetian blinds, summing Susie up, then she opened the door enough to speak to Susie.

"You Miss Norwood?"

She looks jest like the woman in my vision, 'xcept, she ain't scared half to death, Susie thought.

"I sho am. If you would be so kind and let me in, I have to tell you somethin' very importan' 'bout you and yo' two girls."

Miss Johnnie, finally recognizing her name, opened the door. "Come on in, Miss Norwood. You sho welcome." She showed Susie to the living room.

"I done heard 'bout you. Some peoples I knows been talkin' 'bout you and some of the thangs you been doin'. But a lot been kept on the Q T." She tried to smile, but failed. "Have a seat, please."

She sho looks tir'd, Susie thought. After sitting she said, "I don't know what you talkin' 'bout, Miss Johnnie."

"Oh, you know. Some of the free readin's you been doin' for a few friends and all, and them comin' true."

Susie smiled. "They came back and tole me 'bout them." Her voice became very somber. But I'm here to tell you 'bout the vision I had last night," Susie said, hoping she wouldn't have a bad scene on her hands.

When Susie finished speaking, the woman sat still as a pole. Only her eyes moved. Then she focused them on Susie and said, "I'm scared as all git out, but if you say we gots to leave here or me and my two chil'ren will perish, then that's what we'll do. Thank you, Miss Norwood. Thank the Lawd."

"You welcome, Miss Johnnie. Do you need me to do some-thin' for you befoe I leave?"

She gazed at Susie with frightened eyes and smiled. "No, Mam. I thank I can manage. Come on and let me walk you to the door. And thank you again, Miss Norwood, for savin' our life."

"I'm glad I could be of service to you. Jest be out by nightfall. Bye now."

"I sho will, Miss Norwood."

The following morning while hanging out clothes, an acquaintance of Susie's passed by. "Good mornin', Miss Susie."

"How you doin', Mister Joe?" Susie asked after removing the clothes pin from the corner of her mouth. "Fine mornin', ain't it?"

"Would be if Miss Johnnie and her chil'ren hadn't burn'd up last night."

"What!" Susie said, dropping the clothing into the tin wash tub. "You want to say that again, Mister Joe."

"I said..."

"He's got it all wrong, Miss Susie," Miss Cissy, the lady who lived three houses down, said. "It's true; Miss Johnnie done lost her house, but she and her chil'ren is jest fine. They had moved out 'bout a half hour befoe the fire start'd. Boy, was they lucky! I gots to go over to her in-laws and see 'bout them."

Susie felt her chest relax and her heart beating again. She picked up a shirt to hang up. "That's real good to hear. The Lawd is so good to us," she praised, then smiled as her mind wandered briefly.

Like a tornado, word quickly spread throughout the colored community about Susie and how she had saved Miss Johnnie and her children, bringing many people to visit her, some out of curiosity, others because they believed in her Gift.

The next weeks were so busy Susie sought Mrs. Turner's help with the children and some of the chores, allowing her more time with her customers. But even then Susie knew she would soon have to decide if she would quit her job to serve her customers. And if she did, how would she pay her bills?

Mrs. Turner was just walking up the steps when one of

Susie's clients was leaving. "I sho do thank you, Miss Susie. And I'm sho gon' send all the people I know to you. Gawd Bless you."

"Well, Miss Susie Norwood, don't it make you feel good to be doin' somethin' to help othahs?"

"Yeah, Miss Turner, it sho do," Susie nodded as she picked up a dress to mend for work. "Have a sit, Miss Turner. I must say, it took me a long time to git here, a mighty long time."

"Some of us take longer than othahs, but the Lawd gon' make sho we do the work we's put here for."

"Amen to that. It's been a long time since we was able to sit and talk. And I need to talk to you. I jest wish Girt was here so I can tell both y'all 'bout my problem."

"Knock. Knock. Susie, it's me, Girt." She half sang, half spoke, as she banged on the locked screen door.

Susie excused herself to let her friend in. "I jest mention'd you to Miss Turner. I'm glad y'all here. I need some advice."

"We the one that's 'spose to git it from you. But if you need it we sho can lis-sen and try to help," Girt said as she held onto Susie's arm while they walked into the living room.

"Miss Turner, how you doin'?"

"Gettin' long fine for a ole lady, Girt."

"'Ole ain't the word we likes to hear; is it, Susie?" Girt sat down and pulled her shoes off and tucked her feet under her.

"You mean you don't like to hear, Girt." Susie's eyes twinkled in mischief.

"Got any coffee or some ice tea, Susie?"

"Yeah. Go and git it so we can talk befoe the chil'ren wake up from their naps. And brang Miss Turner some too."

When Girt returned with the refreshments and had settled down again, Susie looked at each of them, her face clouding over like a storm about to brew.

"Both of y'all know I put Koffee down a while back, but what y'all don't know is he's been followin' me and havin' me follow'd. He used voodoo to git me, and all the while we was together, he used voodoo on me."

"Naw, chile!" Girt said, grabbing her chest and leaning

towards Susie, a horrified look on her smooth black face. "Not him. Not the preacher man? He was crazy 'bout you."

"I'm 'fraid so, Girt."

"I must say I had my suspicious, but I knock'd them down, that is 'til you start'd havin' all that troubl' and didn't want the Rev'end comin' to yo' aid. But I kept my mouth shut tighter then this color on my hand," Mrs. Turner said.

"I must confess, I always wonder'd what you saw in him and all. You know, y'all bein' so differen' from each othah, like a queen and the tad pole. And I heard tell some of these preachers in Selma use the stuff all the time. But what a terribl' thang to do to you," Girt said as she moved to sit next to Susie.

"He ought to be shot for doin' that," Mrs. Turner suggested, carrying the glass to her dry mouth and taking a deep swallow.

"I sho wish y'all woulda tole me 'bout all this stuff y'all bein' hearin'."

"You know how it is, Susie. Not too many of us good Baptist people offers that kind of information, but if it comes up, we always knows 'bout it," Girt said, patting Susie's hand.

"Well, y'all bettah be able to help me then. I need to git rid of Koffee once and for all. I keep promisin' myself I will, but when it comes down to it, I don't even git one foot in front of the othah."

Mrs. Turner and Girt looked at each other for a long minute, then turned to Susie.

Girt bit her nails. "I know of a man who can git him off you jest like that," she held her hand near her mouth and blew on it. "But it'll cost you plenty."

"And I heard tell of Mr. Windmore. He's a spiritual man and real good. The devil will tuck his tail when that man gits through with him."

"I been to see Mr. Windmore. But I don't want to go back thaih again. What 'bout Miss Para Lee?"

"I hear she's good too. But you already been to her," Girt reminded Susie.

"Then maybe I should go back to her again."

"If you thank so," Girt said, pausing.

"Why you hesitatin', Girt?"

"I... I was jest thankin'. If you can tell fortunes and see visions, cain't you help yo'self, too?"

"I don't seem to work quite that way. Thaih's some thangs I can do, but in this case I cain't help me. Maybe Gawd meant it to be this way; I don't know."

"Amen to that, Girt whispered, "Then yo' best bet is to go see the lady in Montgomery and do it fast, Susie. Now I know why I been' hearin' the Rev'end ain't his self no moe. The man is so crazy 'bout you he will do anythang he can to git you back. You bettah keep a pair of eyes behind you, Susie."

"She got a point, Susie," Mrs. Turner agreed. "You knowed he was crazy 'bout you even when you was mad at him. He would leave and always came back grinnin', now that I thank on it, like some fool." She shook her head. "I don't like this at all. From now on, when you go somewhere, you oughta have somebody with you."

"I ain't runnin' from the man. I ain't gon' run and hide from the red head'd devil his self," Susie vowed.

45

Susie pulled the mail from her mailbox on the front of the house, slipped inside and locked both doors behind her, and placed the mail on her table in the bedroom. After changing into her house shoes, she checked on the children. Seeing they were still sound asleep, she made coffee then found a comfortable spot on the sofa.

She was exhausted, having had a horrible vision earlier that morning which had left her strained, restless and wide awake. She had finally pulled herself from bed, made coffee, dressed, and waited for a decent hour to visit the man to warn him.

She recapped her morning. She had walked a mile to his house, wondering with each step, how she was going to tell him, but before she reached his home, she knew she would have to tell him straight out.

"Good mornin', Mister Jerome. The name's Susie Norwood. I don't mean to disturb you so early in the mornin', but I had to see you befoe you left for work. It's a mattah of life and death."

The man stood, chewing on his cigar, looking as if he was trying to decide whether to slam the door in her face or curse her out. Then he said in a strong bass voice, "Come on in, Miss Susie." He took her hand, assisted her to the sofa, and he sat across from her, waiting.

"Thaih's gon' be a terribl' accident on the railroad this mornin', and if you go, you will be kill'd. The train comin' from Montgomery is goin' to jump the track once it reach Selma and if you out thaih workin' on them tracks, you'll die. Don't go today." She had warned in a rush of words.

He looked at her for a long time, his face showing no emotion, but within, his heart fluttered, raced, and almost stopped. She knew he was trying to decide if to believe her, if she were crazy or if he should tell her to leave with her nonsense. She had been relieved when finally, after a very long silence, he said nervously, "Lawdy, Lawdy. I sho musta done somethin' awful good in my life for the Good Lawd to send you to me."

He scratched his bald head, then rubbed it. "I don't know how to thank you. Is thaih anything... He hesitated then asked," How much do I owe you, Miss Susie?"

"Nothin'. Nothin' at all. Jest heed my words." Then she stood and walked to the door, leaving the baffled, but grateful man still scratching his shiny scalp.

Susie yawned and stretched, erasing Mr. Jerome and the last hours from her mind. She yawned again, and fought the urge to lie down on the welcoming bed.

After breakfast, she changed clothes and glanced at the mail as she sat on the bed to put on her shoes. Familiar handwriting caught her eye. She turned the letter over several times, wondering who else she knew that lived in New York besides Lola. Then the clock caught her eye. She had to hurry or she would be late for work.

Fourteen hours later, Susie climbed into bed and reached to turn the light off when she realized she hadn't opened the letter. She sat on the side of the bed and slipped it from the envelope.

My dearest Susie,

As I write this letter to you, I can almost feel yo' presence here with me. I know I promised I would nevah bother you again, but I have thought of you so often over the last years, I couldn' stop myself from finally writin' to you. I sincerely hope this letter finds you in good health and good spirits.

Susie, do you realize that it's been moe than eight years since I've seen you? Are you happy, Susie? I know I'm not without you in my life. But you deserve to be happy moe than anyone I've ever met. Susie. I still love you, even though I've tried forgettin' you. Believe me, but you are a person that has absorbed my heart and soul; no mattah what or how hard I've tried, you remain and will always will be a part of me.

You are a very special person and woman. No one I've met can ever measure up to you. If you just give me the word, I'll be thaih so quick, you would thank I was right next door.

I love you now and always. Please don't ignore me.

My number is enclosed.

Yo's Always,

Miles JaRett

His letter slipped from her trembling fingers to the floor. Susie reached for and lit a cigarette with hands that shook so badly she had to put the unlit cigarette in the ashtray. Suddenly, she was sweating and grabbing a church fan, but she was so jittery she laid it down as well. She walked on shaky legs to the bathroom and splattered cool water on her burning face, neck, and wrists. Then she leaned against the sink with her eyes closed.

Ten minutes later, she returned to bed, slightly calmer. She lay in bed, unmoving for fifteen minutes. Finally, her pounding heart became almost normal again, and she allowed herself to think about the letter and Miles.

I shoulda held on to him. But that was years ago. I didn't know then what I know now. I didn't know that Koffee was playin' his hand in our quittin', almost as much as Uleena. If only I had the wisdom I got now.

Unnoticed scalding tears trickled down her flushed face as

she remembered his face and beautiful smile, the feel and smell of him. She placed her hands over her face and openly wept until her tears were dried and her eyes burned.

She placed the letter in the drawer and returned to the bathroom. Her eyes were swollen and red, but she ignored that as she looked closely in the mirror at the woman with the mysterious eyes, keen nose, high cheek bones, and thin but shapely mouth. She stood back and examined her heavy, high breasts, her narrow waist, and rounded hips. She smiled slightly, thankful that she showed no signs of aging or the pain of her past. She appeared to be in her late twenties but she was forty years old and a grandmother.

She had no doubt Miles would still like the person he saw, but would he be able to accept the spiritual person she had become. Would they match each other, or had he changed so much they would only be strangers trying to relive their past?

She didn't know.

Later, after washing her face and turning away from the mirror, she whispered, "Oh, Miles. If only you was here with me, everythang would prob'ly be alright, but I'm not ready for you, not yet."

She dreamt.

She ran from a man whose face she couldn't see, blindly throwing her hands in front of her, tripping over stumps, rocks, running into trees, and finally stepping into a brown liquid that was thick as molasses. When she tried to step from it, her ankles were grabbed so tightly she couldn't move.

She struggled to pull herself from the sticky mass, but each time she sank further until she had no strength left.

Suddenly, the hold on her ankles tightened, pulling her farther into the bottomless pit.

Her mind cried out, "Lawd, Jesus, please." Instantly the destroyer disappeared into the gooey floor beneath her, freeing her legs.

Susie's eyes flew open, blinking rapidly; her mind was blank.

It took her several minutes to realize she was sitting in a chair by the window in her bedroom, a full moon staring into her room, winking at her. Trying to figure out how she got in the chair, she glanced at her bed, then the moon, *I bettah git to Miss Para Lee and quick.*

Book IV

HOPE IS THE KEY...
FAITH IS THE ANSWER

Earth is the beautiful beginning....
Yet it is filled with evil people
who forget they are
mere beings....
Yet there is a Supreme
Being that makes
the final decisions of our
destiny....
His power, through others,
always puts the evil away.

Carolyn V. Parnell

46

Susie was very conscious of the potion next to her bare skin as she skirted down the aisle, throwing food into the shopping basket. Even though it was flat and well wrapped, she hoped the darn thing didn't slip beneath her belt and onto the floor. She hated getting caught up in this voodoo world and having to do this... fight evil with evil, but it was something that had to be done to help save her life.

After speaking with Mrs. Turner and Girt, she had planned to see Miss Para Lee, soon, but it was only after the strange dream that sent her running. She had been horrified to learn from Miss Para Lee that Koffee had reached the point where if he couldn't have her, then he would kill her.

She had been distraught for hours before she allowed Miss Para Lee to tell her how to protect herself.

After settling down, Susie had received instructions on how to prepare the potion. On the way home, she had been a nervous wreck. She was relieved that the bus returned to Selma quicker than usual. Upon her arrival, she frantically hailed a taxi home.

Once inside the house, she had secured all the windows and doors, even though it was extremely humid and hot. After putting the children to bed, she prepared the potion as directed: painstakingly writing Koffee's name seven times upside down on a piece of square paper and placing saltpeter, red pepper, turpentine, an orange-brown dirt, and roots in the middle of the paper Miss Para Lee had given her.

A chill passed through her as she rushed down the aisle toward the check-out stand, wishing there were some other way of getting rid of Koffee. Actually she knew there was, but she wasn't willing to stoop as low as he by using his kind of voodoo. It was all voodoo to her: Good and Evil. She didn't like it at all, this potion mess.

Susie paid for the groceries and pushed the filled cart from the store and toward her waiting cab. She felt a sudden chill and knew he was close by.

Just then, her arm was gripped by a cold-vise of iron, almost causing her to scream out in unbearable pain. She tried to pull away, but his hold on her was tighter than the layer of her skin.

"Jest what do you thank you doin?" she snarled, her mysterious eyes turning almost black with hot anger, temporarily forgetting the pain ripping up and down her arm.

"You been iggin' me for moe then a year, and I want to know what the hell you thank you doin'? Didn't you hear me when I tole you nobody leaves me?" he threatened, as he twisted her arm more, raw hatred protruding from his beady eyes.

Susie closed her eyes to suppress the pain, then said, Well, you made a terribl' mistake, 'cause I done quit you. Mattah of fact, I thought you had left Selma by now, you low down scoundrel," she hissed through clenched teeth.

"You bitch. Who do you thank you talkin' too? I'll..."

"I'm talkin' to you," she interrupted, "And I don't aim to stand here and lis-sen to you and yo' sick threats. Now if you don't want me to holler for help, you'll let go of my arm."

His hold slackened, giving her slight relief.

"I said let go of me. I ain't yo' bitch, and if I was one, I would rather be someone else's. You must have me mix'd up with the ones you got, the ones you don't need to use voodoo on."

He tried tugging her toward him, but she prevented him by raising her free hand as if to call for help.

"I ain't through with you, yet...I'm goin' to git you back and teach you a damn good les-son, bitch," he sneered then shoved her arm away as if she had hit him, and rushed down the street.

Forgetting her pain, Susie squared her shoulders, regained her cart, and pushed it toward the waiting taxi.

While the cab driver put her groceries in the trunk, she patted the potion and wondered what would have happened if she hadn't been wearing it. When the taxi driver hopped in the car, she demanded, "Why in the Sam Hill did you jest sit thaih watchin' when that man coulda done anythang to me, Mister Joe?"

"I'm sorry, Miss Susie, but he's my pastor and a Mason. I couldn' do nothin'."

"Y'all men and y'all damn clubs. I guess if he had kill'd me, you would be still sayin' you sorry."

"Naw. I wouldn' let him do that, 'specially to somebody nice as you, Miss Susie," he turned and threw her a missing tooth smile.

She threw him a you-full-of-bullshit look and turned toward the dusty window.

It was Saturday evening. The sun was setting, and the lightning bugs were displaying their glowing bodies while some distant frogs seemed to be mating or having a fight. Children's gay laughter floated like music into Susie's bedroom window.

She stood twisting her hair and pinning it up while watching the children skip rope on the unpaved sidewalk. Their mothers, having worked all week at the white folks' homes, cleaning and cooking their meals, sat on the porch, swinging back and forth, watching them.

Susie knew some of them longed to go to the clubs, cafes or the juke houses with their husbands and hang around the bar, and watch them drink beer and talk trash, while others danced to their favorite blues songs, tears in their hearts as they relived the singers sorrow and claimed part of it as their own.

Some wives knew their husbands were at the juke houses playing cards or dominos, throwing in their last hard earned pennies on a good bet, surrounded by mostly mistresses who rubbed their backs and encouraged them. While the wives wished they could be with their husbands, they knew that decent women wouldn't be caught in one of those places, so they suffered in silence.

Not a weekend went passed that some poor woman wouldn't be awakened in the deep hours of the early morning by a friend with the terrible news that one of their men had been stabbed, shot, or killed by his mistress. Their life would become torture from within, but they would go on. They had to for their children's sake.

Susie backed away from the window. Selma and its wicked secrets. She never thought she would be living in such a place as this. She wondered for a moment how it was in Detroit, then dismissed the thought. She knew she was thinking of everything to avoid thinking about her run-in with Koffee.

She twisted the last strands of hair and patted her head before pulling a scarf from the vanity draw and tying her hair up.

"How y'all doin'?" she asked the children as she walked into Carolyn's room. "Y'all ain't gittin' into no troubl', is y'all?" Susie patted each of their heads and made a funny face, causing them to giggle as her loved shone through like the sun via the blue sky.

"We was jest lookin' at these pretty pictures in this book, Mama," Carolyn said, holding the Sears and Roebuck catalog up to Susie, pointing to the little blond-haired white dolls, fire trucks, cowboy hats and cap guns.

"They sho is pretty; ain't they?" Susie asked as she sat on the bed with the three children.

"They pretty, Mama," Pat's young voice said, peeping at Susie with mischief in her slightly slanted eyes.

Susie hugged her close and looked at Ronney who tumbled on the bed and landed in her lap. "I wan-na be a cowboy, Ma-ma," he said in his baby voice and hugged her neck.

Shaking her head and smiling, she said, "Boy, you too little to know anythang 'bout a cowboy, but if you want to be one, that's fine with me." She let go of Pat to return his hug.

Sometime later, after reading to them, the children were curled up, asleep on Carolyn's bed. They were used to sleeping together from time to time. Sometimes they all slept with Susie, giving her a good rib kicking.

Susie was folding towels and listening to a Platters tune on the radio when someone hit the side of her screen door so hard she jumped. She thought it might have been Rev. Koffee and started to get a knife from the kitchen, then changed her mind. She didn't' want his death on her conscience.

She went to the door and paused. "Who is it?" she demanded.

"Open the door and see," the voice answered mysteriously.

She laid the towel down and peeked through the blinds. She recognized the person and flung the door open.

"Augustus!" she screamed, reaching for him. Then she screamed again. "Mama! Oh Mama," backing into the room as Augustus and Rubye Mae came through the door.

Hugging each of them several more times, she exclaimed, "It's so good to see y'all. My, what a nice surprise," her eyes twinkling as she grinned from ear to ear with pleasure.

"Well, we was in the neighborhood and thought we would jest drop on in and see you and the chil'ren," Rubye Mae explained. "Got any of that good tea or lemonade in the icebox, baby?"

"Yes, Mam. Lemonade. I'll git y'all some." She left the room and was back shortly with two tall glasses of refreshing lemonade and two hunks of chocolate cake.

"Humm, umm. I'm sho gon' have myself some fun eatin' and drankin' this," Augustus praised, "But first let me jest give you anothah hug, it's been so long since I saw you. Look at you, gal, gettin' younger all the time," he complimented and hugged her until she begged to be let go.

Turning to Rubye Mae, she asked, "Mama, what you gon' do with him?" She sat next to her and patted her mother's hand.

"Baby, yo' guess is as good as mine, but it's too late to do anythang for him now. Even the women cain't do nothin' with him," she laughed good naturedly, then her tone became serious. "You do look good chile, real good. I'm so glad to know you finally changed yo' life, honey. You jest don't know how good it feels to know you finally doin' what you was meant to do. The Lawd sho gon' bless you, already blessin' you," she praised and patted Susie's back. Suddenly the silence became so thick it could have cut itself and sat down as another person in the room while Susie looked from her mother to her brother.

"Alright, I know y'all jest didn't happen to be in the neighborhood. Y'all tell me what's goin' on here. And don't say it's nothin', 'cause I can feel it."

Rubye Mae's voice was very hushed as she said, "Bout foe days ago, I got a letter from Selma. Since I cain't read so good, I ax'd Augustus to read it to me. Well, honey, it was the most awful thang I ever heard in my life. The words on that paper is jest too awful for dogs to hear, but you got to read it. I'm scared somebody wants to hurt you real bad, baby," Rubye Mae said as she reached into her pocketbook, pulled out a business envelope, and handed it to Susie.

She recognized the handwriting immediately and walked to the window. As she read the offensive words, her body became like stone. "...I'm gon' take her yellow ass and hang it upside down in a tree by her yellow pussy and leave her for the vultures to eat. When I gits through with her, you and nobody else will know her. Since you her Mama, I thought I'll give you the chance to see her one moe time..."

Not able to finish reading, Susie gagged as the hateful piece of paper slipped from her hand, her heart pummeling.

Seeing Susie's distress, Rubye Mae ran to her, "Come on and sit down, baby," she urged, leading Susie to the sofa.

"Git a cold rag for her face, Augustus," she ordered, holding on to Susie's cold hands.

Rubye Mae held the cloth to Susie's head until it felt warm. "Do you want anothah one, baby?"

Susie nodded no, waving the cloth away. "I'm alright, Mama. Y'all don't need to fret over me."

"We have to. And you have to tell us who sent that piece of mess," Augustus pointed out.

"He did. Koffee." Susie said sadly. "I don't know how he could stoop so low and be so evil. I'm sorry y'all had to read and hear his sick words. I cain't b'lieve he did this."

"It ain't yo' fault, chile. That man is so sick, they jest can go on and put him to rest foe he kill you or his self."

"Mama, don't upset her."

"Don't mind me, Susie." Rubye Mae said.

"Augustus, you 'member when I talk'd to you 'bout him some years back. Well, you was right, and I was a damn fool to git mix'd up in this shit." She stopped, took a deep breath and reached for the pack of cigarettes she had been nursing for a week.

"I'm sorry, Mama. Augustus, I don't mean to be mean or dis-respectful, but this is makin' me so mad I feel like hurtin' him, and that makes me madder, 'cause I'm no bettah then him for thankin' that way."

"You got the right to feel that way, but we know you won't hurt nobody no mattah what they do to you. We just don't want nothin' to happen to you, chile," Rubye Mae said.

"Won't you come back with us, please, Susie?"

"I ain't goin' nowhere, Augustus."

Rubye Mae asked worriedly, "What you gon' do if you stay here with no protection. Cain't you go to the police for help?"

Susie gave a dry laugh. "Mama, y'all musta forgot. The police don't care what we do to each othah. And the ones that do cain't let on that they do. They'll come out and take a report and then to go to the office and file it somewhere it cain't be found."

"The man gots to be outta his mind," Augustus said. "Hey, Sis, you got anything stronger to drank in the house. Nevah mind. I know the answer to that. I'm gon' run to the liquor store..." He felt awful for not being able to protect his sister.

"You know they closed. Oh...on the corners," Susie said, realizing he meant the bootleggers that could be found on almost any block in her neighborhood.

"Now that he's gone, is thaih anythang you want to tell me, Susie?" Rubye Mae urged.

"Naw, Mama. Ain't much to say. 'xcept the man ain't crazy. He's knows what he's doin.' He jest use to havin' his way, and for the first time it didn't work out, and he cain't handle it. I know he's a coward, and he knows I know it, too. I thank that's what make him carry on so."

"Well, I know I'm scared for you, baby. Real scared. Shucks, I feel like I almost need a drank, and I don't touch the stuff. If I knowed he was this bad befoe when I was here, I woulda took you back with me."

"I'm scared too, Mama, but he don't know that. I don't know what he's goin' to try next. All I can do is pray that I be ready when he comes at me and that Gawd is on my side. Othah then that, I done did all that's humanly possibl' and I ain't gon' run and hide. You can bet yo' last dollar on that."

Susie and Rubye Mae had just finished canning chow-chow when she heard Girt's voice. "Susie! Susie! Open the door, quick!"

Susie frowned and rushed to the door and admitted Girt.

"What's the mattah, Girt? You sound like you jest lost yo' best friend."

"Susie, you won't b'lieve this. You know the othah day I tole you that I heard Uleena was still livin' in Selma but ain't nobody seen her for months." Her voice trembled, and her words ran together. "Girt, slow down and come in the living room befoe you pass out."

Seeing Susie's mother, she inquired in flat tones, "Oh, how you doin', Miss Rubye Mae?" before slumping on the sofa.

"Bettah than you seem to be, chile. I'll git her some water, Susie."

After Girt drank half of the water, she took a deep breath. "Oh Susie, it's jest awful. I ain't nevah heard nothin' so bad befoe." she rung her hands and closed her eyes.

"Is it that bad, Girt?"

"Yeah, Susie, real bad."

Susie's mind wandered. Her eyes became large, black lights, shining with yellow specks as she saw Uleena. Or what had been Uleena. "My Father in Heaven, she's dead. Uleena is dead," she whispered and placed her hand over her mouth to keep from gagging.

"Oh, Lawd, Susie, you know, don't you?" Girt said.

"Will y'all please tell me what is goin' on here befoe I lose my mind," Rubye Mae requested.

"I jest saw what happen'd to Uleena, Mama," Susie whispered.

"Then tell me."

"It looks like she left Selma, followin' anothah woman's husband, down to New Or-leans. The man's wife found out that Uleena was aftah her husband, was usin' voodoo on him, and confront'd her. Uleena denied it all, but she kept aftah the man, iggin' his wife.

"The man's wife went to see the seven sistah's, the most powerful voodoo people in New Or-leans, and had a spell cast on Uleena. Three days latah, she got real sick, and the man tole her to go back to Selma.

"But she didn't. She stay'd thaih and tried to git the man and then tried to use voodoo on his wife. But the wife was jest as bad as Uleena and went back to the seven sistahs and had Uleena fix'd so she would die.

"Uleena got so sick, she couldn' stand up most of the time. She lost weight and threw up everythang she ate. Finally, she went to find out what was wrong with her and was tole she couldn't be help'd, that she had mess'd with the wrong people.

"Uleena came back to Selma 'bout two weeks ago to die. And she did. When they found her this morning, she was covered by worms from head to toe." Susie slumped into a chair."Po' thang."

"That's jest the way they found her," Girt whispered.

"Ain't that awful? If only the po' thang had left the evil stuff alone, she coulda been alive. Lawd, I jest don't know why women use that stuff to git a man when men a dime a dozen." Susie whispered, saddened by the horrible death.

"Susie, don't take it so hard, chile. You almost died 'cause of her. And sad as it is, she got back what she was dishin' out."

Susie blew her nose and shook her head. "I know that Mama. But she was so young, and she used to be my friend. No mattah what she was, that kind of death is awful."

47

Several months after having moved to Rome, N. Y., Lola, while shopping with Mrs. Dubonski at the Air Force base commissary, had run into John, Ronney's father. Dumbfounded and speechless, then angry, she ignored his attempts to speak with her and had left him standing with his mouth hanging open.

But John hadn't given up. Some way, he had gotten her phone number and pursued her for a month until she finally agreed to go out with him. Since then, they had been dating every weekend, frequenting mostly clubs because John liked being around his loud friends and their brassy girlfriends.

Lola didn't complain because she wasn't ready for a serious relationship with him, but she did enjoy herself and some of the men's girlfriends.

They had been going out for six months when they walked into the popular club where most soldiers from the base took their dates. They were walking toward John's favorite table when Lola saw him.

Her head snapped so quickly that for a moment it looked as if it were on a spring. She realized she wasn't seeing a ghost.

Christ, what is he doin' here? What am I goin' to do?

She touched John's arm. "Do you thank we can go to the othah club? It's kinda crowd'd in here tonight."

He looked at her with a furrowed brow. "Our table is empty. The othah decent club is closed for remodelin'." Don't you 'member?

She had to get away, but she didn't want to arouse John's suspicions. He was very jealous, even though he claimed not to be. *Man, this cain't be happenin'.* She bit her lower lip.

"Come on, baby. Othah people want to git in here too. Let's grab our table while we can," he urged, taking her hand and pulling her forward.

If only I could disappear. She hid her face behind her hand. After they sat down, she nervously lit a cigarette.

"Is somethin' wrong? You've been actin' kinda strange for the past few minutes. You're not sick or anything; are you, Lola?"

"No. I'll be alright. Would you order a scotch and soda for me? I need to go to the ladies room." She forced a cheerful smile as she left the table on unsteady limbs.

"Hello, Lola," Lawrence said when she walked out of the ladies room.

Her reddish-brown complexion turned gray as she faced Lawrence, the man she had tried so hard to forget.

Before she could speak, he pulled her into his arms and kissed her. She felt herself being swept away by his passion, remembering the past. When he released her, she stumbled.

"Are you alright, Lola?" he asked, smiling that smile that always made women stand up and take a second look. "I won't apologize for that kiss."

She blabbed, "By the time I got yo' letters, I had left Selma. And I was still angry at you, so I nevah opened them..."

"Then you don't know that when I finally wrote to you, I asked you to give us anothah start, in a new town. Here in Rome," he offered, moving closer to her.

"I or...no. No. I didn't," she stumbled, taking in his manly smell, his bedroom eyes she had never noticed before.

"How long you been goin' with John?" He asked, not concerned about the letters he had written, not telling her he had asked her to marry him and that he would raise her children as his own.

"Quite a while now."

"Are you committed to him?"

"No, I'm not. We're just goin' out," she answered truthfully.

"Lola."

She swung around at the sound of John's voice. "I was on my way back when I ran into Lawrence here. John, you know Lawrence."

She waited anxiously, tightly crossing her fingers behind her while the two men greeted each other. They weren't friends, never had been even when they had been stationed at Craig Field Air Force outside of Selma. After the how-do's, both men became stiff. Lola became anxious as the moments slowly ticked away.

She said to John, "I want to tell Lawrence somethin'. I'll be along in a minute."

He didn't move.

"John, I want to speak to Lawrence if you don't mind."

Her eyes became very dark and angry.

"See you 'round, ole man," John said with a stiffed neck and walked away.

"You too, John," Lawrence said to his back.

"A bit rude for a man who has no claims to you. How 'bout ditchin' him?"

Lola smiled, her eyes filled with warmth. "I cain't do that," she said, but she thought it would serve him right.

"Here," she said, quickly scribbling on a piece of paper with her lipstick, "give me a call tomorrow aftah three. See you latah." She rushed back to the table where John was sitting, sulking and gulping on two fingers of scotch over ice.

Several days later, Lola and Lawrence started dating. Lawrence took her places that John never would have thought of. They visited New York City, the amazing art museum which delighted her with all its unique pieces ranging from crazy lines to perfect, pattern-like people. And the sculptures simply intrigued her, causing her to stand before them so long that

Lawrence had to pull her away. They strolled hand in hand in Central Park. Lola reveled in its beauty and inhaled the many fragrances of flowers, shrubs, and trees. They dined on Chinese and Italian food at small hidden restaurants and laughed at a comedy western theater where colored people were welcome.

Each time Lola was with Lawrence, she felt as if she were coming home. She was peaceful and relaxed whenever she was with him. She felt totally desirable and loved by this unselfish man who would do anything for her, it seemed.

Soon John became annoyed that she wasn't dating him and demanded to know why she was seeing Lawrence.

"Cause I want to," she answered.

"You jest a damn tease..." he whispered into the phone.

"Whether you know it or not, I'm not the same person I used to be, John. I have grown up. I have differen' interests now." She had hung up on him, refusing to listen to his jealous accusations. And thereafter, refused all his calls.

Several months later, she and Lawrence ran into John and his date, coming from a restaurant. They had spoken and continued on their way, but John, being the person he was, confronted them, embarrassing everyone as he accused her of using him then turning on Lawrence, calling him all kinds of niggers and a woman stealer.

Lawrence simply steered her away from John as if he had never existed, leaving him looking as if his mother had whipped his butt.

After the incident, they went back to Lawrence's place off base, and it was there that they found each other for the first time, it seemed. Lola realized that she truly loved him when he said, "I love you more than this mere mind of mine could ever express. And I always have loved you."

"And I love you, Lawrence." She had grabbed him and held onto him so fiercely he had flinched.

Then he slowly undressed her. They shared what two people in love must always desire: blissfulness.

48

"Susie, we sho wish you would change yo' mind and move to De-trot. You can do the same thang thaih you doin' here," Rubye Mae advised, referring to her Gift as Susie helped her pack.

"Nome. I cain't do that. My mission is to stay here. That much I know. But I sho hate to see y'all go."

"But Susie..."

"Mama," Susie said firmly, surprising her mother. "It's final. Don't forgit yo' cakes, Mama," she reminded her in softer tones, hoping her mother wasn't offended.

"Yeah. Don't leave them cakes. Give them to me right now, and I'll put them in the trunk," Augustus urged, reaching for the packages.

While he was gone, Rubye Mae turned to Susie and held her hands. "Susie, I'm so scared that man gon' try and do what he said in that letter. I don't want you gettin' kilt. I already done loss one chile and I don't thank I can take losin' anothah one. Do you want me to stay here with you, honey? It ain't no troubl'. I can always make 'rangements for yo' sistah to take care of Boy a while longer. Tears formed in Susie's eyes at the mention of her dead sister. She still missed her dearly after all these years.

"Susie. Is you lis-senin' to me?"

"Yes, Mam. I thank I'll do fine by myself. I'll git one or two of the people I know and trust to keep a eye out for me, but I won't run from him, Mama. As a mattah of fact," she said cheerfully, changing the subject, "I'm thankin' 'bout lookin' for someone to settle down with aftah the chil'ren's mamas take them."

Pleased, Rubye Mae said, "You sound like you finally want to live and enjoy life, and that's good. 'Cause no mattah how much you do for somebody else, if you don't do for you, it ain't worth livin'. I always knowed you was special, chile." Her eyes twinkled with pride, and she went on, "It jest took you a while to know it. You got a fellow in mind yet?" Her eyes filled with mischief.

Susie laughed, a clear mellow sound from her stomach.

"Nome, not yet. But I aim to start lookin' jest as soon as I git this monkey off my back. And you'll be the first to know." Susie's eyes twinkled with playfulness though she was very serious.

"Why y'all carryin' on so?" Augustus asked as he slipped into the room, locking the door behind him.

"Oh, nothin' you want to hear 'bout," Rubye Mae said, patting him on the back and winking at Susie.

"Well, Susie, we best be gettin' on down the road. I wish we could stay longer and help you...I don't want you to let yo' guard down."

"You did help. Moe then y'all know, jest by bein' here. I love y'all," she said with half a smile.

"Always 'member we love you, Susie."

"I will," Susie said lightly, yet her heart trembled with sadness. "I sho hate y'all leavin.'"

"And we hate to leave you, honey, you knows that." Rubye Mae brushed the tears from her eyes and hugged Susie.

"Come on, Mama. We bettah git outta this little town befoe dark comes and the white sheets ride."

Rubye Mae released Susie and followed Augustus.

Susie followed them to the door, waving goodbye until they drove away. Then she locked both the screen and wooden doors and went to her bedroom. Feeling very sad and lonely, she flopped down on the bed and waited, feeling the evil.

The phone rang.

She rolled over and grabbed it. "Hello."

No one spoke, but she could hear faint breathing.

It's him. The voice said.

She sat up in bed and grabbed her forehead. "Where you been?" she inquired of the voice, forgetting him.

The phone. He thinks you are talking to him. Don't speak to me.

"So why are you callin' my house and too chicken to say somethin'? Is you that much of a coward?" She asked and waited, but he didn't speak.

"Suit yo'self then, buster, but don't call my house no moe, wastin' my time."

His breathing became stronger.

Almost feeling his blistering breath coming through the phone, she shuddered and said, "I'm on to yo' tricks, and I don't have to tell you what I'm talkin' 'bout. You know. But nothin' you do will ever make me take you back, and if you follow through with yo' threat, I'll haunt you for the rest of yo' miserable life."

"You lousy bitch, I...."

She hung up the receiver before he could continue and spoke to the voice. "Well, I guess that's what happens when you step in shit. It's hard as hell to git it off yo' shoes."

Yes, Susie. Sometimes it's that way. But you have to keep cleaning them until all the smell is gone, and next time look very carefully before you walk in the same direction. He isn't through, yet.

"Will he ever stop?"

I told you he would.

"When?"

When it's time.

"My time may be runnin' out. And I'm past tir'd of bein' hunt'd by some sick man that I nevah shoulda got involved with in the first place."

All people have burdens to carry. And you can't be an exception. You live in that kind of world. Good and Evil. And everyone gets tired, the good and the bad.

"Do you?"

You know the answer to that.

"Yeah. I know. And I'm bein' awful, but I'm scared. Scared for me and my grandchil'ren."

I know that. But you are a strong and courageous woman, and you are doing what was intended. Things will work out in the end. Just keep your faith strong because you're going to need it.

"My faith is always strong, even when my body is weak."

You will be getting a nice surprise, one that will change your entire life. But I warn you; don't let anything happen to prevent this. Now, I must leave you.

Suddenly excited, she begged, "Not now. You always do this to me."

Always?

"Naw, but I need some answers. Who, what..."

The voice cut her off. *You know as much as you need to know. This person is going to help your whole life change.*

Then it was gone, leaving her tight-lipped.

The following morning Susie received letters from both daughters. She stared at each of them an eternity, it seemed, before finally opening Lola's first.

She read for a moment and smiled.

....Mama, now I don't know what to do
'cause both of them say they love me
and I love them, but in differen' ways.
It's drivin' me crazy 'cause I know soon I'm
goin' to have to make a choice. You
know sometimes life can be so strange.
Not so long ago I was mopin' 'round
wishin' I had someone, now this.
Mama, Lawrence makes me feel like
a queen. Most of the time I float rather
than walk. Well, you know what I mean, so
I'll stop my runnin' off at the mouth.

She finished reading the letter, satisfied that Lola would choose Lawrence and opened Blanche's letter.

As she read, tears of sorrow fell to her lap. Her daughter happily wrote that she had met a wonderful man named John Robert, the man who would ruin her life, Susie believed. She lit a cigarette with nervous hands.

Mama, he's the kindest, most
generous and thoughtful man I've
known, next to Dad. He attends the
same school as me and is studying
to be an engineer.

Susie laid the letter down for a moment to clear her vision and dropped the cigarette in the ashtray before resuming to read. When she finished, she laid the letter down and had a good cry.

Afterwards, she paced the floor for more than an hour, praying that her child would see she had made a dreadful error. She should find Paul and hold on to him with everything that she had in her. If she didn't...

Susie turned and walked from the room and into the study where the children were playing, hoping they would take her mind off Blanche with their sunny dispositions.

49

Who's knockin' at my door this time of night? I know it's not him; he's too much of a coward to knock. Might give me a chance to defend myself. "Who is it?" Susie demanded impatiently, hands on hips.

"I know it's gettin' late, but I couldn' wait 'til tomorrow. May I come in, Susie?" came a strong, deep sounding voice, filled with humor.

Susie's hand flew to her pounding chest. Her eyes became beacons, her mouth a perfect circle as she recognized the voice. *The voice from the past. Lawd, Jesus. It sounds like him. Can it be? Open the door, fool.*

She closed her dry mouth, ran her tongue over quivery lips, unlatched the door enough to peep out, and was astounded to see it really was him.

After admitting him, she stood looking at him, speechless.

"Hello, Susie." he said after securing the doors.

Her thoughts ran rapid. *Oh, Lawd look at him. He's the best lookin' man I ever saw. I had forgot how good he look'd, how good he smell'd. I feel faint. Please don't let me pass out.*

He smiled and said, "Susie, it's me, Miles. I didn't mean to frighten you, jest surprise you. Come, let's sit down." He took her hand and led her to the sofa and sat next to her.

Finally, after holding her breath and gawking at him, she let out a deep sigh. "I'm shock'd. Aftah all these years," she whispered, tears filling her eyes. "Miles JaRett, it's damn good to see you again."

"And it's wonderful to be sittin' here, next to you, Susie. I've miss'd you so much these last eight years. I had to see you again. I can see you've grown in many ways and you're still the most beautiful woman I ever knew. Simply enchantin', Susie," he caressed.

Susie blushed at his endearing words, feeling more alive than she had since she had pushed him out of her life. "You always did know the right words to make me feel good."

"Susie, I came back 'cause I love you. Aftah you didn't answer my letter I had to see you, to find out if I have a chance to be part of yo' life, yo' future."

Susie stood abruptly, suddenly very sad. "Miles, thaih's so much that's happenin' in my life since you left. Some good, but mostly bad. Right now I'm up against somethin'...I cain't thank 'bout nothin' else 'til this is over."

Miles stood behind her. "Susie. If thaih's anythang I can do I surely will. You know I'm yo' friend, and that will nevah change. You jest nevah said you need'd me. I'm here, and I won't let you down. Not this time."

She could feel his hot breath caress her neck. Her mind raced. *I do need you, Miles, but I'm too much of a coward to ask for help. I love you jest as much, but I cain't say it. I cain't be hurt again.*

Miles turned her around and held her chin up. "Susie, you'll still fill'd with too much pride. You've got to start askin' for help when you need it. I love you, woman, and I can help you." He gently pulled her to him, wrapping his strong arms around her, comforting her as a friend and lover.

It took several days before Susie accepted Miles as more than a dream she had conjured up. Then she was able to update him on all that had transpired since she last saw him, except

Koffee. Miles was pleased to learn that she had finally started to use her Gift and offered to help in any way he could.

A week later, feeling she could completely trust him. Susie informed him of her troubles with Koffee.

"I wish'd I had been stronger back then," he said, pacing the floor. "That I had more foresight. I would have been able to keep that evil man from you. This voodoo stuff is awful, but we both know that.

"The thang is, what in the world do we do 'bout that man and his possessiveness with you?"

"Miles, please come and sit down. You're makin' me nervous. I tole you. Thangs will work out, in time. I jest have to wait 'til it comes."

"But Susie, that's awful. You cain't do that. I must help you." He sat next to her, his face shadowed with disgust and determination.

"You are helpin' me, Miles. Jest bein' here," she smiled and patted his hand. "So let's not talk 'bout him for a while. Let's git somethang cold to drank." She pulled him into the kitchen.

He took the glass from her and wrapped his strong arms around her and held her soft, sweet-smelling body next to his.

"Susie, baby, you don't know how many times over the years I've dreamt of this moment. How many times." He leaned over and kissed her tenderly on the mouth.

Susie felt as if she were floating on air as her heart jumped roped, leaving the world behind her as she traveled to a high level of desire and need.

He pulled away from her and looked into her eyes. What he saw made him moan and kiss her again.

This time she held him as if her life depended on it while he kissed her face, neck and mouth, causing her to feel like a school girl again.

Pulling away from him, she said in a small voice, "Come on, let's go back into the livin' room." Then she poured tea, picked up the glasses, and walked out of the kitchen on wooden legs.

Miles sat next to her. He held and kissed the palm of her hands several times before gazing into her eyes. "Susie, Susie. I love you moe than mere words can 'xpress. I'm consumed with desire for you. Please tell me if you feel the same. Tell me you love me."

Tears fell from her eyes as she looked at his endearing face. His words had struck the fiber of her soul, making her feel so good she wanted to cry out his name, jump in his arms and shout the words, but she merely looked at him and murmured, "I love you, Miles JaRett. I truly do."

Shortly after returning to Selma, Miles left for Montgomery on business, promising Susie he would return soon.

Miles owned several homes, three restaurants and several record shops that required his attention. While he was home, he spoke to his father about his relationship with Susie.

"Son, is you sho you want to start this thang again? Don't you 'member how much pain the both of you had?"

"Dad, you know she's the only woman that I have ever loved and I'm not goin' to let her git away from me this time. She's not the same person. She is the same person, but she has grown spiritually and emotionally, and she's usin' her clairvoyance. I thank we gon' do jest fine." He paused as if in thought, then continued, "You know somethin', even if she didn't change, I love that woman so such I thank I would go to hell for her, if I had to."

"Well, I do declare. Son, that is quite a revelation. You got yo'self a fortune teller and a looker to boot. But, I don't thank Gawd wants you in hell. And that fine young lady wouldn' neither. Well, you know y'all got my blessin' as you had befoe." His father patted him on the shoulder as they walked to the door. "My love and prayers be with y'all, son," he said as he hugged and watched him leave.

Miles returned to Selma as quickly as his car would take him.

Susie and Miles spent time with the children, taking them for rides in the car, the movies, and to Larskers for bar-b-que, sweet potato pie, and ice cream cones. Miles enjoyed the children, hating he had missed being the step-father to their parents.

When Susie and Miles had time to themselves, they enjoyed the quiet and peacefulness of sitting on the bank of the Alabama River, their poles in the water, waiting for a bite from the catfish. After their catch, they would clean and fry them in white corn meal and make sandwiches with mustard and hot sauce, and wash the tasty morsels down with a RC Cola.

Susie basked in happiness and sometimes felt guilty. But Miles would remind her that she deserved it and more.

Miles had changed so much, yet he was the same loving, giving, kind man that she had always known. She was pleased that he had been blessed with wisdom and a strong, quiet calmness that made her feel completely happy and loved.

Susie had been surprised to learn that he had traveled in Europe for a year and had been pleased when he had given her gifts from France and Italy. He had also been co-pastor at churches in New York and Detroit.

Though he was well versed and more educated than she, she felt his equal. She knew they complimented each other. He was not looking for an ornament to wear on his sleeve.

When she finally called and informed her mother that Miles had returned, Rubye Mae's voice had been so overwhelming Susie could have sworn she was in the same room with her.

Susie's world couldn't have been any better. But for one exception. Koffee. Even though he hadn't had the opportunity to get to her, she always knew he was close by, even though she hadn't heard from him since his last call several months ago.

Since the return of Miles, she had sometimes seen his black Cadillac trailing them. And lately, she had seen him pass the house several times. She knew he was furious that Miles was back in her life.

She could feel his hatred for her and sensed that he wanted to wring her neck and harm Miles as well. She understood only the buried devil lye was keeping him away from her door. But she didn't know how long it would last before he achieved some way to get to her.

Besides, she had grown tired of the ritual of keeping him at bay. She just wanted him absent from her life.

Susie turned from the kitchen window and put her glass down, a worried expression on her face. "Miles, thaih's somethang I want to tell you. I jest saw Koffee's car pass by here. This is the third time tonight.

"He's been by here befoe, but I didn't want to bother you. Sometimes when you're here and othah times, right aftah you leave. I don't know if he's watchin' the house or someone else is, but it's his car. I'm gettin' this uneasy feelin' that somethin's goin' to happen. I jest don't know what or when."

"Damn," he murmured under his breath. "The man jest won't give up, will he?" He banged his fist on the table. "Thaih's no way I'm goin' to leave you and the chil'ren alone in this house. I'm stayin' 'til we can do somethin' to stop this man."

"Stayin' here? Why, you cain't do that. It ain't proper, and it would make me look bad to my customers. Naw, the chil'ren and me will be alright."

"You can always put a room-for-rent sign in the window, and I can rent it from you," he said lightly.

"That won't help my reputation none."

"Come here, baby," he said huskily. "I want to ask you somethin' importan'." He took her hand and pulled her around to sit on his lap. "What if I ax'd you to marry me? Would that help save yo' reputation?" he asked seriously, glancing into her eyes, waiting for an answer.

"Marry? Me? Marry you?"

He smiled. "You act as if you didn't know I would git 'round to the question. Will it do the trick, do you thank?" he asked again, his voice taking on the husky sound again.

"Well, I guess it will at that. It sho will," she smiled.

He beamed. "Oh my sweet, sweet lady. I do love you. I'll always love you and cherish you. You make me so, so happy."

"And you make me happy, Miles. Happier than I've ever been in all my life. I would love to be yo' wife," she answered, forgetting, their immediate problem.

He reached into his breast pocket, pulled out a blue velvet, square box and handed it to her.

"A little somethin' I pick'd up in Buffalo jest in case I got lucky," he grinned and winked at her.

Shaking her head happily, she lifted the lid and blinked several times before pulling out the bluish-white, diamond ring surrounded by emeralds. She looked at him, her mouth slackened in disbelief. Then she stared at the brilliant ring again."

His eyes crinkled at the corners, smiling at her bafflement.

"Here. Let me put it on for you. I know you love emeralds moe than diamonds. When I saw it I couldn' resist it 'cause it had yo' name stamp'd on it. I hope it fits," he said as he began to slip it on her finger. "I bought the same size as the..." his voice trailed off. He didn't want to bring up the hurtful past.

The ring was a perfect fit. They kissed, sealing their love for each other and their desires soared. But it was quickly dashed as each of them pulled away, knowing they could not quench their sexual thirst for each other, not yet.

Breathing heavily, Susie whispered, "Thank you, Miles.

It's a lovely gift of yo' love. But you got to stop surprisin' me like this."

"Nevah. You love my surprises."

"Well, I guess now that we engaged, you can stay in one of the spare rooms and put a sign outside, jest in case somebody ax me why you stayin' here."

He hugged her to him and whispered, "I wish you could stay with me."

"I can, but only in yo' dreams, buster. Now let me go do what I have to do," she demanded lightly and walked back to the stove to finish dinner.

He followed her, and together they made arrangements for their wedding. Miles's father would marry them. Susie would make all the other plans, and Miles would pay for everything.

The next morning Susie called her mother and her daughters, to spread the news among her few close friends.

She knew they would be her newspaper. Her only letdown

was Blanche. Although Blanche seemed to be happy for her, she sounded hesitant when she informed her that she would have to take Carolyn back with her, after the wedding.

She had until next summer to make arrangements, Susie reasoned. Surely that was enough time. *The one chile I always thought would come out on top. Be stronger than me. Goes to show you, you nevah know yo' chil'ren like you thank you do.*

50

As Susie had anticipated, the news of her engagement spread overnight as fire would in a windstorm. The following morning she received many calls, congratulating her.

On the other hand, the news stressed Koffee so badly he was rushed to the hospital with chest pains. However, he was released when it was discovered he was not having a heart attack.

Then the following morning he was taken back to the hospital with severe pains throughout his body and was detained for testing. He was depressed, despondent, refusing to eat or speak to anyone. Yet the doctors could find nothing wrong. Finally it was suggested that he be transferred to a mental hospital in Birmingham. Suddenly he could suddenly speak and ask for food. Two weeks later, he was released.

Upon his release, Koffee couldn't eat or sleep because his mind was totally occupied with Susie. Susie, Susie, Susie. He thought of her constantly: the way her hips swayed slightly when she walked; the way she held her head proudly; the way she smiled when he could draw a smile from her; the way she sat, straight and regal, her entire substance. He didn't understand why she wanted Miles and not him.

He thought back to the time he had first seen her and knew she would be his. Those years he had waited for the right time, and finally, he went to the voodoo man to ensure that she would be his.

Unfortunately, he had gone to extremes, and having had his way with her, he had tainted their relationship, but she had become his, for a while....

That day in the car, out at the pea-patch, had caused many problems. He had been stunned by the effect of the mojo. He hadn't been warned that the spell would be so powerful. He had broken out in a cold sweat and become nervous, even frightened. His entire plan had backfired because she was supposed to submit to him without any problems afterwards....

He hadn't been able to think of anything else after leaving her house, except that he had to get home and quickly, but he didn't know why. He was feeling remorse after the crime he had committed, but at the time it didn't seem that way.

When he arrived home, he checked on his girlfriend, found her asleep, and then prepared to take a bath. But before doing so, he sat down at the kitchen table and thought about what he had done and why. He realized he was obsessed with having Susie. But there was something else that made him lower himself to such an extreme to get her.

Something else that affected him in such a way that he lost control of himself. It was as if she had a spell on him, but he knew that was far from the truth. He had tried to rationalize his actions but couldn't find an answer, except that he probably needed help.

All he ever wanted was to love her, not hurt her. He had been extremely distraught and went to his study to get a drink, something he never touched, under any circumstances.

He thought of Susie's hysterical crying and laughter, of her crying, moaning, and sobbing; it made him ill, knowing he had gone against every grain of his upbringing and religion.

He didn't remember when or how, but he found himself in his car, sitting in front of her house. When he realized where he was, he became so frightened, he urinated in his pants. But he sat there longer, his mind racing back, recalling the horror....

Now, he was paying for all his wrong deeds. He was miserable, so much so that he often yelled at his wife then apologized to her for being so cruel. She never spoke much, but he had a feeling that she was becoming wise to him. But still he couldn't stop his madness. He had to have Susie, or else.

Feeling restless, Koffee left his house, telling his wife that he was going Christmas shopping, but instead, he sought out the voodoo man in Booth, Alabama, seeking methods to harm Susie.

"I'm sorry, Rev'end Koffee. I cain't help you. I suggest you leave the woman alone. She been touch'd special by the Hand of Gawd. She ain't to be mess'd with."

"That bitch ain't been touch'd by nothin'. When I git through with her, she gon' wish she had. And you can go to hell."

"Rev'end, what in the world is come over you? You sound like you posess'd or somethin'."

"I'm wastin' my time here. Y'all no good liars. Cain't help yo'-self..." Koffee muttered as he fled down the steps, to his car and sped away, leaving the voodoo man shaking his head sadly.

"That's one man who head'd for hell if he keep tryin' to hurt that special lady."

Hot with animalistic anger, Koffee raced down the dusty road, determined to kill her. Then he would kill Miles. He grinned a wild man's grin, his thin hands holding tightly to the steering wheel.

He stopped in a dark desolate area in the country, flinging himself from the car, his entire body seeming on fire, thrashing. All the while he was cursing Susie.

He fell to his knees, becoming physically ill, clawing at the earth until his fingers grew numb. Falling, wallowing like a wild animal, before he passed out.

Hours later, he stirred from the ground, smelling like a dead cow, looking worse. "You yellow lousy, stinkin' bitch, I'll git you and show you how a real man do it, and then I'll kill you," he bellowed as he stumbled toward his car.

51

Susie put the phone down then looked out at the cloudy January day. It fitted her mood after speaking to Blanche. She had called to say she had married John Robert. She could have kept that bad news to herself. "Why, baby?" she had asked her daughter. "You had so much goin' for you. You could do bettah."

"He loves me and promised to make me happy, Mama. And he 'xcepts my chile." Blanche defended.

But Susie knew Blanche had given up on herself and accepted less than what she was worth. Now she would fight to hold on to the empty promises the man had made and have a miserable life.

She wished Miles were here to comfort her. Tears flowed down her face in sadness and disappointment. "Lawd, I sho hope she'll be able to bear what's in store for her.

What 'bout her po' chile?"

Weeks later, Lola phoned with news that two days earlier she had married Lawrence before a Justice of the Peace. They were ecstatic, and she couldn't wait to come home and show him off to her friends.

Susie wasn't surprised because that was more Lola's style. Susie was happy that Lola had made the right choice.

Susie, Susie. You have to stop worrying over your children. They're grown and have to make their own mistakes. There isn't anything more you can do, but be there for them when they need you.

"I know that," she answered the voice. "But I don't see how I can be so happy and have a chile that won't be.

She's a woman, and you have to let go. It's time to start living your life.

She let go of the curtains and sat down near the window. "You want to tell me why this man ain't left me alone. Somebody been leavin' rotten meat in the street in front of my house now for four nights straight. I know it's him."

You'll be able to handle it. Soon things will turn for the better.

"Why is you talkin' ri-ga-ma-row to me? You ain't givin' me no answer."

The voice didn't answer.

Susie became frustrated. "You know I'm plannin' to git marred this summer and this man been on me for years now.

Don't you thank it's time he leaves me alone so I can git on with my life?"

Susie, don't fret so. You will be able to handle whatever comes your way.

"Shit!" she slammed her fist into her palm as she walked from the room.

When Miles returned to Selma, Susie told him about the rotten meat in front of the house.

"Well, I'll jest sit up tonight and see who the coward is and give him what he didn't git from his mama."

And he did. Three nights straight. But nothing else was left again. Several weeks later, they were visiting friends when Susie discovered Koffee and his family had left town. *I hope I nevah see his evil face again,* Susie thought.

Susie soon forgot Koffee as she made plans for her July wedding. The weeks passed, turning into months as she shopped for material to make her wedding dress, the bridesmaid and matron of honor dresses, the groom's attire. All the wonderful things she had always wanted to do. She was also becoming exhausted, and Miles grew concerned, asking her to slow down by not seeing as many customers, but she assured him everything would be fine.

Miles insisted she quit her job since they would be married soon, and he would be paying the bills. She disagreed with him, but he kept after her, telling her she would have more time to do everything and still remain healthy. Finally she relented.

During the days she received customers for four hours, took a break for two, then saw customers for another four.

She spent hours sewing. Sometimes Miles would spend time in the study where she sewed, but she liked being alone and would shoo him out.

Most of his time was spent with the children whom he thought of as his grandchildren, taking care of his business where he was assistant minister at Chapel Hill, or he performed chores around the house. Susie loved his specialty: cooking.

52

July was blistering, and it was worse in the kitchen as Susie and Lola rushed to finish the last bit of cooking to get out of one hundred degree temperature and into the somewhat cooler living room. When Susie had informed her about her upcoming wedding, Lola knew she had to be there for her, no matter what. She owed her mother that much and more. She was so excited for her mother, one would have thought she was the bride-to-be. She really wished that Blanche was here, but Blanche had been evasive and uncertain.

Lola rushed and adjusted the position on the air conditioning, trying to get it cooler in the room, then flopped on the sofa, fanning her perspiring face.

"Whew, it's hot today. I wish I could jump in a cold shower for five minutes."

Susie patted her perspiring face with a damp cloth. "I don't see how you can take a shower. That's like standin' underwater, puttin' soap on you and lettin' it run off; you're still not clean."

"You might like it, if you tried it, Mama."

"I don't aim to try it to know if I like it. I need a good bath to clean me off, then I can rinse the soap off afterwards. But so much for that, I cain't wait for Mama and them to git here."

"Me either. It's been a long time since we were together. Mama, I'm so happy for you I could cry. It's like a fairy tale come true. You, finally happy."

"Baby, b'lieve me. Sometimes I have to pinch myself to make sho this is real. These years of my life have been so up and down, I wonder'd if I would make it, but the Good Lawd didn't stop smilin' down on me." Susie said as she picked up a Cola and sipped at it.

Lola shook her head in deep thought, then said, "If you were to tell yo' life story, nobody would b'lieve it. All the dreadful thangs you went through and you didn't turn wild or go crazy. I sho hope I have jest a little bit of yo' strength and faith. I know I'll go a long ways."

Tears formed in Susie's eyes at her daughter's praise. It made her feel good to know that she hadn't failed her as a mother, that she loved and admired her as a person. "Baby, you give me moe credit then I deserve, but thank you, baby."

"Just thank, Mama. In two weeks you'll be Mrs. Miles JaRett." Then her face clouded. "I jest hope Koffee don't upset thangs. That man is evil. I nevah liked him as a chile, and neither did Blanche."

Susie nodded in understanding and frowned. Koffee and his family had returned to Selma three weeks before. It upset her more than she admitted.

Since returning, he had made several attempts to get to her, none of which she had told Miles. The last had been two days ago. She had been fortunate to have slipped from his grasp when she had walked out of Tepper's Department Store and almost bumped into him. He had reached for her, grabbing her blouse, but she had managed to pull from him, run back into the store where she had received permission to leave by the back door.

Arriving home out of breath, afraid and then angry, she had been relieved to find Miles had stepped out and Lola and the children were off visiting. That had given her time to have a good cry and compose herself.

She shuddered in the warm room, goose bumps appearing

on her arms. She longed to have Koffee vanish from her life, forever, giving her the best wedding gift she could receive.

"Mama. Mama. Did you hear me? Someone's at the door," Lola broke into her thoughts. Susie jumped slightly, then smiled. "Well, let's go and see who it is," she said, standing.

She opened the door to Blanche and her husband. "Blanche," she grinned with pleasure and let them in. "Oh baby, it's good to see you," Susie hugged Blanche close to her.

"It's good to see you too, Mama," Blanche whispered, tears almost flying from her eyes.

Susie gently pushed her away and smiled, "You still cryin' when you happy aftah all these years, ain't you? Well, I guess that's alright."

She held Blanche's hand and looked keenly at the man who stood grinning from ear to ear. He sho do have a big mouth. "And you must be John Robert?" Susie extended her hand in welcome.

"Yes, Mam. It's good to finally meet you, Miss Norwood. I've heard so much about you, I feel I already know you."

Susie let go of his hand and smiled. "Don't fool yo'self, son. I don't even know the real me, yet."

He looked puzzled.

"Don't mind Mama, John Robert. She likes to tease people," Blanche offered.

"So you the man my daughter ran away with and mar-red befoe she could write and tell us about it?" Susie asked, not completely understanding his accent.

"Mama." Blanche intoned.

"Y'all come in and sit down where it's a little cooler...."

Lola, having run from the room to check her makeup, slipped back into the room and ran to her sister. "Blanche!

Wow, it's good to see you again. Don't you look pretty," Lola said, squeezing Blanche to her.

"Hello, Sistah. It's good to see you too." The tears flowed.

"Y'all go in the livin' room while I git some cold dranks. We can git the suitcases latah," Susie said.

While she was gone, Lola sat chatting and throwing sly looks at John Robert. He certainly wasn't the man she thought her sister would have chosen to spend the rest of her life with. He didn't have any special looks, and he dressed sort of old-fashioned, like his name. He was wearing a brown jacket with a white shirt and brown slacks, quite ordinary. But then maybe he had qualities she couldn't see.

Susie returned with the sodas, then sat down to join in on the conversation.

The children ran into the room, and after Susie introduced John Robert to Carolyn, she watched their interaction very carefully.

One couldn't say he didn't try because he did, but no matter how hard, Susie could see that he was by no ways the kind of person that would take a child that wasn't his and love her as if she were his. For a moment she became unnerved and sipped her Coke, deciding she would have a serious talk with Blanche.

Several hours later Susie's mother, her six brothers: Rufus, Taylor Jr., J.D. (James), Augustus, Calvin, (Lorenzo) Boy and her three sisters: Ella Mae, Alice, Willie Mae, arrived, filling the house with more laughter and high spirits.

Lola's husband and other relatives would arrive several days before the wedding which would practically burst the house at its hinges, but being together was very important to Susie. Her family meant the world to her, and she was glad to have them together for this special occasion.

"Where's that good lookin' man of yo's Susie?" Rubye Mae questioned, a smile on her young looking face.

"He'll be here shortly, don't y'all worry. Y'all will git to gawk at him, but be kind to him. He ain't use to fools like y'all."

When Miles arrived Susie introduced him, and they all sat down to eat dinner. While enjoying their meal, they teased, laughed, and carried on so much, Susie couldn't eat her food for fear of choking.

She and Miles often exchanged looks and then would burst out laughing.

52

Susie, Rubye Mae, and Lola, having just left the department store, were walking north on Broad Street when they were approached from behind. Someone rammed a gun in Susie's back. "Keep walkin' to the co'ner," demanded a cracked voice.

"Don't none of y'all turn 'round, or I'll shoot this bitch right here on the street and tell everybody she was tryin' to steal somethin' out the white man's store," he threatened, applying more pressure to the pistol.

Susie flinched, her blood freezing at the sound of Koffee's vile voice and the feel of the deadly pistol in her back. She didn't know what to do. Her mind raced with thoughts of fleeing.

"Keep yo' face to the front and walk to that blue car park'd at the corner," he demanded.

Lola was petrified, trying to think of something that would save her mother's life before reaching the car.

Rubye Mae's chest raced, causing her to feel faint, her body moving on wax-doll legs. She blinked several times, sending up desperate prayers to Heaven, pleading that they be spared from this madness. She prayed that this evil man wouldn't pull the trigger and kill her child.

Lola's eyes searched frantically at the people walking toward them, hoping to see a familiar face. Feeling helpless, she thought of running, but she believed he would shoot her too.

Susie mechanically placed one foot in front of the other, walking toward her death... She thought of her family and Miles waiting for her at home, and of her mother and daughter walking next to her, being threatened by a maniac. She prayed, begging God to save them all from this man, that if it was her time to go, let her go another way, that He intervene, if not on her behalf, then her mother's and daughter's.

Suddenly, like hot liquid bursting from a volcano, her blood boiled. She wasn't going to die without a fight because she had too much to live for and she would be damned if she would let him take it away from her.

Just before they reached the car, she hissed frantically, under her breath, "Sistah, license plate. Don't git in the car. Then, directly before he opened the passenger door, she yelled, "Y'all run."

"Hush yo' damn mouth and git in the car," he demanded, shoving her toward the open door.

Lola and Rubye Mae stood in shock.

"Now, Lola!" Susie said forcefully, just before he pushed the gun in her ribs, forcing her into the death trap. Lola grabbed her grandmother's hand, ran behind the car, got the license plate number. She pulled Rubye Mae and ran back in the direction they had come, hoping she would find someone to help them.

Koffee, satisfied to have Susie, dismissed them as he raced southeast, toward the Alabama River bridge.

"Watch and see which way he goes Mama Rubye Mae while I get help," Lola said desperately, looking rapidly around her, searching for a familiar face.

She saw two old friends of the family, John and his son, Jerome. When she reached them, she quickly explained to them what had happened. Then she gave them hurried instructions. After picking Miles up from the house, Lola said, "Remember. To the ole hideaway. Please hurry," she cried, praying she was guessing correctly.

They rushed toward the river bridge going so fast both cars threatened to roll on the side, but none of them were aware of the danger, concerned only with the safety of Susie as they crossed the bridge, leaving thick dust behind.

Koffee drove through thick, red-clay mud puddles, holes twelve inches wide, and six inches deep, causing the car to bounce badly. Susie's head hit the ceiling several times. He ignored her as he looked for the area used by lovers that didn't want to be found. An old spot that most who lived in Selma knew about, but none would admit.

He stopped the car under a maze of trees that leaned forward, almost covering the roads with its many limbs, brushing against the car, leaving scratch marks on it as he forced the car into the secret hideaway.

He had waited for this moment for years, and though he had not formulated a plan to abduct her, he had quickly made the decision when he saw her enter the department store.

He had parked his car closer to the store, then took his pistol from the glove compartment and waited outside of the store for her.

Now, he had her where he wanted her, and no one was going to save her! She was going to get what she deserved for making his life hell. He threw a glance at her and winced because she had brought all this on herself. If only she had listened to him and done what he wanted her to do, this wouldn't be happening, he reasoned. He turned the motor off, but kept the pistol pointed at her breast.

"I guess you thought I was jokin' when I said I was goin' to git you for what you did to me. No woman of mine tells me to go to hell, make a fool outta me, ruin my life." He paused to wipe his brow with a damp handkerchief he withdrew from his top pocket.

"Susie, I tried to do right by you, but you didn't 'preciate it. Then the first chance you got, you run off and didn't come to yo' senses. Then you go and start up with that JaRett man aftah all these years and throw him in my face like I'm some dog you can throw away, makin' me look like a fool.

"Yeah. I know you givin' him a piece, even if y'all is 'spose to git mar-red." He laughed a blood curdling sound, then frowned. "But then I guess he got his for free, cause y'all ain't gettin' hitch'd aftah all, is you, bitch?"

Susie didn't breathe a word, knowing that if she did, he would kill her. As she tried to move away from him, he yanked her hair and banged her head against the dashboard several times, breaking her skin. Her head felt as if it was being pounded by a hammer, but she wouldn't scream, nor would she faint she reasoned as she became woozy. She wouldn't give him the satisfaction, not even when she felt the blood streaming down her face.

Seeing the blood, he became concerned. "Bitch, you cain't drip this shit on my seats." Frantically, he turned to the back seat to look for something to block the blood, moving the gun away from her.

Run, The voice said.

She opened the door and hit the mud running and sliding in the direction they had come. She started to look back.

Don't look back Susie. Just keep moving. Move as fast as you did when you were a little girl, playing hide-'n'-seek.

She slipped several times, but kept going, feeling the perspiration and blood flowing down her face and into her eyes. She felt like throwing up. She felt faint, but she continued to run.

He called her, and a shot rang out, whiss-ssssing as it passed her left ear. She tried running faster, but the clay prevented her.

The next sound was his car, gaining on her.

Susie, the tree.

She dashed behind the willow tree, just as another bullet whistled within an inch of her head as she lay on the ground. She slipped her muddy shoes off and covered her head as he drove around the tree, firing at Susie as he would fire at a bull's eye in target practice until he ran out of bullets.

When she realized his gun was empty, she wiped the blood from her face with her muddy dress tail, and ran, zigzagging as fast as her feet would let her, but she was getting tired and wondered where help was or if she would get any.

"Oh, Lawd, Jesus. Please help me," she whispered.

Don't give up. They are on their way. Just hold on Susie.

54

"Hurry. She may be dead by now. This has to be the place the bastard took her 'cause we've been everywhere else. My Gawd, I jest hope we're not too late," Lola moaned. Rubye Mae, completely devastated, sat with her head bowed, her mouth moving rapidly, soundlessly.

Miles and John were right behind the car Lola was driving. Their cars bumped and shook over the torn and bruised earth, headed toward lover's lane. She didn't know how they had caught up with them so fast, but she was grateful for running into Robert and John.

Miles, furious as well as afraid for Susie's life, felt helpless, worst than he had when Uleena had done horrible things to Susie. He wondered why this woman's life always seemed to be in danger. If anything happened to her, he would have no reason to go on, and he knew he would surely commit the almost unpardonable sin with his bare hands if harm came to her.

Susie thought she heard cars approaching, but wasn't sure. Her strength was failing, and her head whirled from the loss of blood. Her body felt as if it was on fire. Her vision blurred in and out as she stumbled and went on, only pausing to catch her breath. He was on foot now, and he was not in good physical shape, but she knew he was gaining on her. Suddenly, her knees gave way, and she found herself sitting on the soggy earth, unable to stand. She saw a tree and tried to crawl toward it, but her knees failed her.

Slide on your backside with both your arms as your support. He's getting closer.

Just as she pulled herself behind the tree, Koffee ran into view from the wooded area. He looked like a crazed animal, mud completely covering every part of him, except his face. He gazed wildly around him, the reloaded pistol hanging loosely in his hand.

"Hey, bitch. Thought you got rid of me huh," he growled, his teeth giving an appearance of a wolf's as he gaited toward her, the gun aiming at her head.

"Well, you ca-nivin' witch, I'm gon' sho you who the boss is. When I git through with you, you gon' be glad to go to h..."

The horrible words froze on his lips, and his mouth stretched so wide Susie thought he would explode. Then an earth-shattering sound escaped his huge mouth.

"Owwwwwwwwww!"

Susie watched in awe as he fell to the ground, and a rattlesnake slithered off into the wooded area after leaving his venom in Koffee's leg. He dropped the gun, his eyes bulging. He continued to howl so loudly, she thought he would die.

She knew that if she didn't do something quick he would die. But wasn't that what he deserved for trying to kill her?

He has exactly two minutes before the venom reaches his blood. Do what you must do, Susie.

Shit. She dragged herself over to him and searched his jerking body for a pocket knife. Finding one, she quickly opened it, yanked his tie from his bulging neck. Slit his expensive, muddy pants to the knee, tied the tie around his lower leg, slowing down the circulation, cut into the wounded area, causing him to scream like thunder. "Help! Somebody, please help me. Lawd, help me!"

"Hush yo' mouth, man, befoe I leave you here to die like you deserve," Susie threatened.

He stopped immediately, then fainted. She paused before forcing herself to touch him, willing her mind blank. Then she sucked on his leg several times, extracting as much poison as possible. When she finished she spit, rubbing her mouth on her dress, wishing she could purge his filth from her mouth. Suddenly, all her breakfast pitched forth. When finally over the heaves, she thanked God. She heard cars coming in her direction and tried to stand, but failed.

Miles was the first out of the car, racing toward Susie like the wind. "Oh, Lawd, Susie. What has he done to you?" he demanded, taking her in his arms, more than relieved to see her alive.

He looked closely at her, seeing so much blood on her dress, he thought she might die.

"Susie. It's Miles. We're goin' to git you to a hospital. Hang on, please." He stood with her in his arms, holding her like an infant and carried her back to the car.

"It's not bad as it looks," she whispered before swooning. Rubye Mae and Lola rushed to her. "Look at her. She's hurt bad," Rubye Mae cried. "She needs to go to the hospital Miles."

"That's where we're takin' her, now. Come on."

Susie remained in the hospital for four days with a mild concussion. After returning home, she assured Miles and her family that she would be fine. As if to prove her point, she set out to finish her wedding plans.

Rev. Koffee was taken to the hospital where he had almost died from the snake bite. He remained there for two weeks. When he was released, there was a warrant for his arrest, and he was immediately taken to jail.

Susie and Miles' wedding was one of the largest in Selma. Over four hundred guests attended, including some prominent white people. She was a beautiful bride, radiating so much love, Blanche, Lola and Girt, her matrons and maid of honors blushed.

When Susie finally said the words, "I do," she could feel her heart smile. At the reception, Girt caught the bouquet and thanked Susie. Later, her family and guests gathered around her, wishing her much happiness. An hour later she and Miles slipped away.

55

They stopped in a circular drive close to an immensely beautiful home. She lazily lifted her head from his shoulder, turning her head slowly, taking in her surroundings, amazed at the land and its multitude of trees, flowers, and shrubs.

Her eyes stopped and beheld the grand brick mansion.

"This must belong to rich white people. Why are we here, Miles?" she asked almost breathless.

"This is where we're goin' to spend our honeymoon," he offered with a twinkle in his eyes. "It belongs to the family, and we use it on special occasions," he grinned down at her then brushed her face with his loving mouth.

"You nevah mention'd that yo' family had a fine house like this." She wrinkled her nose.

"You have roses?" She sat straighter.

"Yes, thousands, in the back. We'll see them latah. Come, let's go inside," he urged and moved away to open his door.

"I cain't b'lieve y'all own this. You sho you ain't pullin' my leg with this one, Miles?" she said as he walked around to the passenger side of the car.

"I wouldn' do that to you, Mrs. JaRett." He grabbed her in his strong arms and moved up the steps. He held her tightly while he unlocked one side of the heavy doors, then jumped over the threshold with her and kissed her softly on the mouth before putting her down.

She turned to sniff the beautiful roses resting in a crystal bowl on a gleaming rosewood table. "Umm," she sighed with closed eyes, enjoying the sweet smell, then walked down the foyer before stopping to look around her again.

Everything was so beautiful, so big, larger than life to her. Her imagination couldn't have stretched this far she reasoned as she gazed through the wide doors: picture windows adorned with lace and drapes that seemed to be made of silk; strong, but beautiful rosewood furniture; thick carpets; and high ceilings. She turned after a few minutes and looked at Miles, questioning.

"I want'd to surprise you, and I see that I have."

"Well, you sho did it this time, buster. I cain't b'lieve it. You sho this belongs to yo' family?" she asked, but not expecting an answer as she turned to look at the portraits on the walls.

Susie studied them carefully, finding that some of the people did indeed favor Miles. Then her eyes paused on a lady who was his double. She stared at the painting, then she turned to him.

"Yes. That was my mother," he smiled then turned away, dismissing any further conversation.

Susie thought she saw tears appear in his eyes. She understood and continued to look at other members, finding that they ranged in various shades, from dark bronze to high yellow, some resembling white people, yet all favoring each other. *We colored people sho come in every shade of the rainbow, don't we? From smut black to damn near whiter than them. Gawd sho mix'd us up.*

"Come, let's go see the othah part of the house," Miles urged, taking her hand as they ran up the steps. Susie discovered Spanish, Chinese, French, Italian, Modern and East Indian rooms.

They chose the Chinese room with its low bed and beautiful designs. When Susie walked from the powder room, Miles was waiting with champagne and a fruit and cheese tray that had been placed at the foot of the bed.

He had changed into a thin, blue, silk dressing robe. Susie noticed the revealing hair on his strong chest, and her heart raced. She blushed, suddenly feeling like a young girl as she pulled the matching peach dressing robe closer to her body.

"Come, Susie. Let's drink a toast to our marriage and life together," he whispered seductively, holding out his arms as she approached him.

She stopped and backed away from him, nervously and asked, "Why do you have thirty rooms?"

He hesitated, and she realized he didn't want to talk about the number of rooms in the mansion. "You can tell me latah, Miles."

He cleared his throat. "My parents had the opportunity to travel befoe...befoe my mother pass'd. She loved the countries they visit'd so much she want'd to brang a taste of each back with her, and my father loved her so much he indulged her, so hence the rooms you see," he explained quickly.

"Let's have that toast," she said in a husky voice, and ran her hand across his brow.

He smiled, and she felt better. She wouldn't talk about his mother unless he wanted to because it hurt him too much, and she didn't desire that.

"Here's to two people who have loved and lost and found each othah and share a wonderful love again. May we always be as happy as we are today."

She walked into his arms. He embraced her with one arm and held the champagne glass to her mouth with the other; then he took a sip before putting the glass down.

He kissed her moist, sweet mouth and slowly caressed her lovely body, feeling all his suppressed desires for her surface, rise and simmer over. Susie was feeling as if her body was on fire, but she knew that he would be able to wet and quench her passion such as she had never known.

She held him tightly as he kissed her face, caressed her throat with his hot tongue, slowly moving it down to her breast, sending chills of desire through her tense body. Then she relaxed and moaned slightly.

"I love you, Susie JaRett, with all my heart, body, soul and mind, with all the life that I have in me," he groaned and kissed her again.

When she caught her breath she uttered "And I love you, Miles JaRett, with all I can offer. You make me happy to wake up and start the day." She moaned, surrendering her body to him.

"Oh, Susie, baby. I need you," he groaned as he undressed her then held her close to him, drawing in her love.

"Yea, Miles, I know..." she whispered as he picked her up and lowered her onto the low bed that was surrounded by red and yellow rose petals emanating a seductive fragrance.

He kissed her from head to toe, causing her to whimper and cry with unabashed need and passion.

"I need you, Susie, now please."

"Now," she agreed.

Susie was awake and had breakfast on the low table when Miles returned from the dressing room.

"Aaah, Susie JaRett, you sweet woman of mine, good mornin'," he said, kissing her and holding her tightly to him.

"Good mornin'. I thought I would git you somethin' to eat."

"It's not yo' job on our honeymoon to git us food. What will the people in Selma say?"

"Prob'ly' that we got hungry, or that we already had a honeymoon and didn't need one anyhow," she smiled and winked at him as he reluctantly released her.

Hours later, they emerged from the room and rambled in the icebox, finding food that had been prepared for them by the maid. They only nibbled at it then raced up the stairs to one of the other rooms in the house.

They surfaced from the French room, laughing as Susie ran through the mansion pulling Miles with her, going from room to room laughing as she never had before, feeling as she never had – complete joy.

The next several days, she and Miles forgot the outside

world; they made love in all the bedrooms, made an attempt to eat the food the maid had cooked for them and ran through the house like two kids in a fantasy park.

The fourth day they walked the huge grounds while Susie took in its beauty, smelling the many roses and choosing the ones she wanted Miles to snip for her. They carved their initials on their favorite oak tree. Miles swam in the large pool while Susie put her feet in, paddling the water.

Miles pulled himself from the pool, reached for a towel to dry himself, and sat next to Susie. "How you doin', Susie? Not too hot, are you? Want to jump in? I'll hold you up."

"Naw, thank you. But I want to ax you somethin'," she said in serious tones. "You been holdin' somethin' back from me. Somebody in yo' family must have rob'd a bank or inherit'd all this? Only rich white folks have this, and not many in Alabama."

"You're very astute, Susie," he answered, becoming somber. "This property has been in the family for moe than eighty years. My father's father managed to hold onto his land when all the othah colored people were losin' thaihs.

Maybe it's 'cause he was educated in law from Morehouse and knew what to do, or maybe it was 'cause he could pass for white, and they didn't bother him. In any case, money has been in our family since befoe the Civil War.

And durin' the war it was buried by the white master who died, and my great-great, grand-daddy came back and dug up the master's and ours, or I should say pull'd it out of the bottom of the well.

"I don't judge him for it. I figure our side got the mule and the forty acres and refused to give it back. When my great-great grand-daddy pass'd, my great grand-daddy made sho the land was rightfully ours and nobody could take it away.

Now that we living in the 50's and know a lot moe, my father's made sho it's clan-tight and no one will ever get it unless it's family. When he passes, it belongs solely to me and my family which, of course, is you and yo' children."

She didn't say anything, couldn't say anything. She couldn't even fathom the amount of money he was speaking of.

"You don't mind, do you, Susie?"

"Mind you bein' rich? Naw, I guess not, as long as you stay the way you are."

He smiled. "I plan to."

She leaned over and splashed the water. She didn't know just how to react to such wonderful news. She didn't know how to feel or really what to say. So she said nothing.

Miles caressed her shoulder. "Do you want to hear moe?"

"Let me git use to this first," she said as she waved her hand toward the grounds and the house.

"Take yo' time, baby." he said, kissing her before diving back in the pool. He would tell her about the other property they owned in Birmingham and New York later.

56

She saw it all. The horrible nightmare. The horrible vision. *He had made bail and taken off, driving to Montgomery in search of her. When he couldn't find her, he had returned home, taking his anger and insanity out on his poor wife.*

When she refused to have sex with him, he had beat her, leaving her hovering in a corner while he went out to one of his women's houses.

Returning home again, to his dismay, he found a note from his wife. She had left him, promising she would never return again, and threatening him if he tried to follow her. Storming from his house like a hurricane, he had gone by an old girlfriend's house and found her with another man. He made an excuse of looking for someone else and left.

He drove back to Montgomery, blaming Susie for all his problems. He didn't realize he was going ninety miles an hour. His car screeching from one side of the road to the other, he was a man totally out of control. He and the person that wasn't driving on the road that night, were very lucky.

He leaned forward, pulling a flask from his glove compartment, taking several long gulps, totally deranged.

His life no longer had meaning, not since that day, several years ago when Susie had scorned and dropped him. He had lost his wife, pride in his brick-laying business, his ministry, and finally respect for himself.

He had become more obsessed with her, blinded by his own jealousy of a woman who never wanted him from the beginning. One that never loved him and wouldn't in his lifetime. The rejection had eaten away at him until he was rotten with hatred inside.

The vow he had made to himself to kill her would be carried out as soon as he found her. He had been glad his attorney had kept him out of jail, but his reputation was running down a rusty drain and had no way of cleansing itself. Soon he would have no one that would come to his rescue.

His lawyer had paid his bail and warned him to leave Susie alone or he wouldn't be able to help him anymore. He had grimaced and promised he would, but that had been to get the man off his back. He was worse than a rabid animal; he would attack anyone who stood in his way. He would have his revenge, no matter what.

Suddenly he decided he was tired, and he slammed on the brakes, almost throwing himself through the windshield. He turned the car around and headed back to Selma.

When he arrived, he decided he wasn't that tired after all and ended up at a rat-in-the-hole night spot on Jeff Davis Avenue.

No one with any sense of self-preservation would be caught there. More people had gotten stabbed or shot in that club than in the city of Detroit if it were to be told by those that hung out there.

He wasn't there long before he met a man who was looking for trouble. They started an argument over some woman that smelled of cheap cologne and a dress cut lower than her bosom and tighter than her skin. The man pulled a knife on him, ordering him to leave. He refused to budge and told the man where he could go.

Susie thrashed in her sleep trying to break through to get to him. She felt the danger, smelled death. She moaned, twisted and turned, but couldn't bring herself awake.

The first cut was on his hand, the next his face. Quick and sharp as a razor. Then his chest and stomach took several deep cuts before the blood started running from him in small rivulets.

When the drunken stranger finished with Koffee, he had twelve stab wounds.

Koffee looked at his blood as it spurted from his body, his frightened eyes wanting it to stop. He grabbed his handkerchief and put it to his mid-section, but it became bloody in a matter of seconds. He cried out for help, but no one paid him any mind.

He managed to push himself out of the door and stumble down the street, pleading to anyone who saw him to help him, but they moved away from him and stumbled on their drunken way.

He stumbled and finally fell into an alley and bled to death. All his clothes had been stripped from him, even his shoes.

57

"Naw, Naw!" She screamed out in her sleep, thrashing and throwing her arms in the heady air.

"Susie, Susie. Wake up," Miles said, slightly shaking her until she stopped writhing and opened her eyes.

Her gown was soaked to her skin. She sat up and looked at her husband. "Miles, I have to go home to save his life...Koffee.... He's goin' to git kill'd, stab'd to death. I saw it all," she groaned as he pulled her to him, trying to comfort her trembling body.

"Baby, you cain't go near the man, or he'll kill you. And he's 'spose to be in jail, how can he be killed?"

"But I always go to my customers when I have visions of..."

"Not this time. We'll find a way to git someone to him and also git him some help befoe he self destructs, but you cain't help him. B'sides, I'm tir'd of him in our lives."

"B'lieve me, I am too, but I still have to help him. It's part of who I am. And he's a human being..."

He moaned and took a deep breath. "Come, let's make some phone calls. Maybe we can find one of his deacons that's still close to him."

Susie made the call. When the deacon answered the phone,

she quickly told him about the slaying. Then her face dropped as the man spoke to her. The phone slipped from her hand, and she slumped in a nearby chair.

Miles quickly grabbed the phone, putting it to his ear, but the line was dead. He hung up and dropped to his knees and cradled Susie's shaking body in his arms.

"He's dead. Miles. Dead. They found him in the alley, this mornin', jest the way I saw it. This is awful. So awful. I couldn' do nothin' to save him. This is the first time...I couldn't do nothin'...." She broke down and cried until she was heaving.

Miles took her and carried her to the bed and made her take a Stanback, then got in bed with her held her until she fell into a fitful sleep.

Two weeks later, Susie and Miles returned from their honeymoon. Though she didn't fully understand the vision she had experienced about Koffee, she had come to grips that he was not meant to be. That God was only showing her his death and possibly what Koffee could have done to her if he had been able to get to her.

After much prayer and meditation, she knew she needed to continue her practice because it was her given right and responsibility to her God and herself.

When she saw Carolyn, she smiled, her love showing through for her first grandchild, who had stayed with Mrs. Turner while they were on their honeymoon.

After having had her talk with Blanche, before she married Miles, she had decided, and Blanche had agreed, that it was probably best, for the time being, that Carolyn remain with her.

And she had been right. There was a letter waiting for her from Blanche explaining that she was expecting in March of the coming year.

That night she told Miles about Blanche's news, and he pulled her to him. "It's alright, baby. Between you and me, that little girl is goin' to git all the love she needs."

EPILOGUE

58

During the following months, as word spread from town to town, city to city. Susie became the most sought after clairvoyant in the Deep South, by colored and whites.

Those who saw her on the street immediately recognized her and wanted to shake her hand or talk to her. She was always friendly to them, but asked them to come see her during business hours if they wanted a reading. If asked why her clientele had become so staggering, Susie would simply answer, "It ain't up to me to say. I'm jest doin' what the Lawd intend'd me to do."

Soon her house became too small to hold her waiting customers. More than half were standing outside, flowing into the street, blocking traffic. She wanted to ask them to call for an appointment, but she knew that many of them didn't have a phone. She felt her only solution would be to find a larger house in Selma or move to Montgomery where she knew her husband's heart was.

She never told anyone she refused to charge her clients, but it leaked out, and others who were charging demanded she do the same because she was taking away from them, which, of course, wasn't true.

She knew it was indeed her Gift that kept her clients coming, and others returning, but to satisfy others like herself, she started to charge her customers five dollars.

However, before they left, she found some way to return their money, telling them to buy something for themselves or their family.

Miles was her rock, her comfort, her heart, always there to support her and give her comfort if she needed it, even though she had neglected him badly since they had returned from their honeymoon. Her customers had demanded her attention, and so had Carolyn.

By the time she fell into bed each night, she was exhausted and many times had fallen asleep in Miles loving arms. But she had promised him that she would take time off and spend it with him on their first anniversary.

That time was here. She closed the door, locked it behind her, and placed a closed sign on the outside window even though her customers had been made aware that she was leaving.

She took Carolyn to Mrs. Turner's while Miles waited in the car. Carolyn had grown fond of Miles, calling him daddy. It made him feel "like a daddy," he said proudly.

Miles was much more a daddy than Blanche's husband would have been, Susie was sure.

Susie returned and got behind the driver's seat, proud of her accomplishment and Miles for teaching her to drive. She had been pleased when she received her driver's license.

She looked at him and whispered, "Are you ready? 'Cause now I can take you places you nevah been."

He grinned knowingly at his beautiful, sexy wife. "I'm ready, and I'm goin' to hold you to that promise..." his voice trailed off as he winked at her.

Sometimes it was hard to believe she was that way, spiritual, when she spoke like this. But then he reasoned, he should understand because he was a minister, and his desire for his wife had nothing to do with his spirituality. But in her case it was different, especially when she was working.

Then she was another person, almost lost to him. But he knew she was doing God's work and that was very important to each of them. His wife was fulfilling her destiny, and he was glad to be a part of it.

He smiled and patted her leg, pulling her thoughts from the road. She returned the pat on the leg. "We're almost thaih, Susie, and I can hardly wait."

"I know that," she teased. "If I had known I was marryin' a preacher man that loved to go to bed so much, I 'prob'ly' woulda changed my mine."

"That's why I didn't tell you."

She shook her head, rolled her eyes, and focused once more on the road.

They ran from the Montgomery house into the warm July night, stopping to gaze at the twinkling stars smiling down at them from the heavens. Miles spread a beach towel on the lawn. "Come to me. Make love to me under the stars," he pleaded.

"I cain't do that, Miles. I feel kinda funny."

"Not even if I love you and tole you this place is yo's as much as it is mine, and that you can do anythang you want with it, and on it."

Her eyes widened in the light that shone from the patio.

"What?"

"Yep. It's ours. As of last week the deeds are in yo's, mine, and Carolyn's name.

She grabbed him and kissed him until he was breathless.

"Oh, you silly man. You make me *too* happy. If I had known all this was in store for me... I love you Miles JaRett. I truly do."

"And I you, Susie. Now can we make love on *our* property?"

"Hum," she said, pulling him toward her.